OW

THO

EIR BODIES

RAMANUJAN?

$$c_q(n) = \sum_{\substack{1 \le a \le q \\ (a,q)=1}} e^{2\pi i \frac{a}{q} n}$$

# KATABASIS

ALSO BY R. F. KUANG

*Babel, Or the Necessity of Violence:
An Arcane History of the Oxford Translators' Revolution*

*Yellowface*

The Poppy War Trilogy

*The Poppy War*

*The Dragon Republic*

*The Burning God*

# KATABASIS

A NOVEL

R. F. Kuang

HARPER Voyager
*An Imprint of* HarperCollins*Publishers*

This is a work of fiction. Names, characters, places, and incidents are products of the author's imagination or are used fictitiously and are not to be construed as real. Any resemblance to actual events, locales, organizations, or persons, living or dead, is entirely coincidental.

KATABASIS. Copyright © 2025 by R. F. Kuang. All rights reserved. Printed in Malaysia. No part of this book may be used or reproduced in any manner whatsoever without written permission except in the case of brief quotations embodied in critical articles and reviews. For information, address HarperCollins Publishers, 195 Broadway, New York, NY 10007.

HarperCollins books may be purchased for educational, business, or sales promotional use. For information, please email the Special Markets Department at SPsales@harpercollins.com.

Harper Voyager and design are trademarks of HarperCollins Publishers LLC.

FIRST EDITION

*Cover art, illustrations, maps, and endpaper illustrations © Patrick Arrasmith*
*Cover design by Richard Aquan*
*Designed by Renata De Oliveira*

Library of Congress Cataloging-in-Publication Data has been applied for.

ISBN 978-0-06-344624-3

ISBN 978-0-06-302147-1 (hardcover deluxe limited edition)

25 26 27 28 29   IMG   10 9 8 7 6 5 4 3 2 1

*To Bennett, brilliant, beloved*

# KATABASIS

## AUTHOR'S NOTE

Some of the scholars mentioned in this text are real people, and with several exceptions—which I hope are self-evident—I have tried to accurately represent their views. Derek Parfit's *Reasons and Persons* was indeed published in 1984, which is convenient for my timeline. Aristotle does not use the term "celestial space worm," but it is a nice way to visualize his physics. Michael Huemer's "Existence Is Evidence of Immortality" is from 2019, but here I claim it came out in the 1960s. That is fantasy, as is most of this book.

## CHAPTER ONE

*For I deem that the true votary of philosophy is likely to be misunderstood by other men; they do not perceive that he is always pursuing death and dying; and if this be so, and he has had the desire of death all his life long, why when his time comes should he repine at that which he has been always pursuing and desiring?*

PLATO, PHAEDO

Cambridge, Michaelmas Term, October. The wind bit, the sun hid, and on the first day of class, when she ought to have been lecturing undergraduates about the dangers of using the Cartesian severance spell to revise without pee breaks, Alice Law set out to rescue her advisor's soul from the Eight Courts of Hell.

It was a terrible gruesome accident that killed Professor Jacob Grimes, and from a certain point of view it was her fault, and so for reasons of both moral obligation and self-interest—for without Professor Grimes she had no committee chair, and without a committee chair she could not defend her dissertation, graduate, or apply successfully for a tenure-track job in analytic magick—Alice found it necessary to beg for his life back from King Yama the Merciful, Ruler of the Underworld.

This was no small undertaking. Over the past month she had become a self-taught expert in Tartarology, which was not one of her subfields. These days it was not *anyone's* subfield, as Tartarologists rarely survived to publish their work. Since Professor Grimes's demise she had spent her every waking moment reading every monograph, paper, and shred of correspondence she could find on the journey to Hell and back. At least a dozen scholars had made the trip and lived to credibly tell the tale, but very few in the past century. All existing sources were unreliable to different degrees and devilishly tricky to translate besides. Dante's account was so distracted with spiteful potshots that the reportage got lost within. T. S. Eliot had supplied some of the more recent and detailed landscape descriptions on record, but *The Waste Land* was so self-referential that its status as a sojourner's account was under serious dispute. Orpheus's notes, already in archaic Greek, were largely in shreds like the rest of him. And Aeneas—well, that was all Roman propaganda. Possibly there were more accounts in lesser-known languages—Alice could have spent decades poring through the archives—but her funding clock could not wait. Her progress review loomed at the end of the term, and without a living and breathing advisor, the best Alice could hope for was an extension of funding sufficient to last until she transferred elsewhere and found a new advisor.

But she didn't want to transfer elsewhere, she wanted a Cambridge degree. And she didn't want any advisor, she wanted Professor Jacob Grimes, department chair, Nobel Prize laureate, and twice-elected president of the Royal Academy of Magick. She wanted the golden recommendation letter that opened every door. She wanted to be at the top of every pile. This meant Alice had to go to Hell, and she had to go today.

She checked and double-checked her chalk inscriptions. She always left the closing of the circle to the end, when she was absolutely sure that uttering, and thereby activating, the pentagram wouldn't kill her. One always had to be sure. Magick demanded precision. She glared at the neat white lines until they swam before her eyes. It was, she concluded, as good as it ever was going to be. Human minds were fallible, but hers less than most, and hers was now the only mind she could trust.

She gripped her chalk. One smooth stroke and the pentagram was finished.

She took a deep breath and stepped inside.

There was of course a price. No one traveled to Hell unscathed. But she'd resolved at the outset to pay it, for it seemed so trivial in the grand scheme of things. She only hoped it wouldn't hurt.

"What are you doing?"

She knew that voice. She knew, before she turned around, whom she would find at the door.

Peter Murdoch: coat unbuttoned; shirt untucked; papers flapping from his satchel, threatening to tear away in the wind. Alice had always resented how Peter, who every day presented like he'd barely scooped himself out of bed, had still managed to become the darling of the department. Though this was no surprise: academia respected discipline, rewarded effort, but even more, it adored genius that didn't have to try. Peter Murdoch and his bird's-nest hair, scarecrow limbs balanced atop a rickety bicycle, looked like he'd never tried at anything in his life. He was simply born brilliant, all that knowledge poured by gods without spillage into his brain.

Alice couldn't stand him.

"Leave me alone," she said.

Peter trudged into her circle, which was very rude. One should always ask before entering another magician's pentagram. "I know what you're planning."

"No, you don't."

"Tsu's Basic Transportative Pentagram, with Setiya's Modifications," he said, which impressed Alice, since he'd only glanced briefly at the ground, and from across the room besides. "Ramanujan's Summation with implications for the Casimir Effect to establish a psychic link to the target. Eight bars for eight courts." A grin split his face. "Alice Law, you naughty girl. You're trying to go to Hell."

"Well, if you know that much," Alice sniped, "you know there's only room for one of us."

Peter knelt, pushed his glasses up his nose, and with his own stick of chalk quickly etched some alterations into the pentagram. This was also very rude—one should always ask before altering another scholar's work. But standards of etiquette did not apply to Peter Murdoch. Peter moved through life with an obliviousness that, again, was excused only by his genius. Alice had witnessed Peter spill chocolate syrup all over the master of the college's robes at high table with no more rebuke than a shoulder clap and a laugh. When Peter erred it was cute. She had herself once spent all of dinner in the bathroom hyperventilating through her fingers because she'd knocked a bread basket onto the floor.

"One becomes two." Peter waggled his fingers. "Abracadabra. Now there's room."

Alice double-checked his inscriptions and realized to her dismay that his work was perfect. She would have preferred he'd made an error that left him limbless. And she would have truly preferred that he did not then declare, "I'm coming with you."

"No, you aren't."

Of all the people in Cambridge's Department of Analytic Magick, Peter Murdoch was the last person with whom she wanted to sojourn in the underworld. Perfect, brilliant, infuriating Peter, who won the department's top prizes at every milestone—

Best First-Year Paper, Best Second-Year Paper, Dean's Medals in logic and mathematics (which were Alice's worst subfields, to be fair, but until she came to Cambridge she was not used to losing). Peter was one of those academics descended from a family of academics, a magician born to a physicist and a biologist, which meant he'd been steeped in the ivory tower's unspoken rules since before he could walk. Peter already had every good thing in the world. He did not need Professor Grimes's letter to get a job.

Worst of all was how Peter was so unfailingly nice. Always stumbling around with that blithe smile on his face, always offering to help his colleagues puzzle through hiccups in their research, always asking everyone else in seminar how their weekend had been when he knew very well they'd spent it sobbing over proofs that he could have done in his sleep. Peter never crowed or condescended, he was just guilelessly *better than*, and that made everyone feel so much worse.

No, Alice wanted to solve this problem herself. She did not want Peter Murdoch yapping over her shoulder the entire time, nitpicking her pentagrams because he was just trying to be helpful. And, should she return with Professor Grimes's soul safely in tow, she especially did not want Peter sharing the credit.

"Hell's lonely," said Peter. "You'll want company."

"Hell is other people, I've heard."

"Very funny. Come on. You'll need help carrying supplies, at least."

Alice had stashed in her bag a brand-new Perpetual Flask (an enchanted water bottle that wouldn't run out for weeks) and Lembas Bread (stale, cardboard-y nutrition strips popular among graduate students because they took seconds to eat and kept one sated for hours. There was nothing enchanted about Lembas Bread; it was just the extracted protein of tons of peanuts and an ungodly percentage of sugar). She had flashlights, iodine, matches, rope, bandages, and a hypothermia blanket. She had a new, sparkling pack of Barkles' Chalk and every reliable map of Hell she could find in the university library carefully reproduced in a laminated binder. (Alas, they all claimed different topographies—she figured she would get somewhere high up and choose a map when she arrived.) She had a switchblade and two sharp hunting knives. And she had a volume of Proust, in case at night she ever got bored. (To be honest she had never gotten round to trying Proust, but Cambridge had made her the kind of person who wanted to have read Proust, and she figured Hell was a good place to start.) "I'm all set."

"You'll still need help puzzling through the courts," Peter said. "Hell's very metaphysically tricky, you know. Anscombe claims the constant spatial reorientations alone—"

Alice rolled her eyes. "Please don't insinuate I'm not clever enough to go to Hell."

"Do you have a copy of *Cleary's*?"

"Of course." Alice wouldn't forget *Cleary's Templates*. She didn't forget anything.

"Have you cross-checked all twelve authoritative versions of Orpheus's journey?"

"Of course I did Orpheus, it's the obvious place to start—"

"Do you know how to cross the Lethe?"

"Please, Murdoch."

"Do you know how to tame Cerberus?"

Alice hesitated. She knew this was a possible obstruction—she'd seen the threat of Cerberus mentioned in a letter from Dante to Bernardo Canaccio, only she hadn't seen it referenced in any other materials she found, and the one book that might have contained a clue—Vandick's *Dante and the Literal Inferno*—was already missing from the stacks.

In fact, quite a few books she needed had kept disappearing from the library these past few months, often checked out on the very morning she'd gone in. Every translation of the *Aeneid*. All the medieval scholarship on Lazarus. It was like some poltergeist haunted the stacks, anticipating her project's every turn.

Realization dawned. "You've—"

"Been researching the same thing," said Peter. "We're too far into these degrees, Alice. No one else could supervise our dissertations. No one else is clever enough. And there's still so much he hasn't taught us. We have to bring him back. And two minds are better than one here."

Alice had to laugh. All this time. Every empty slot on the shelves, every missing puzzle piece. It was Peter all along.

"Tell me how to tame Cerberus, then."

"Nice try, Law." Lightly, Peter punched her shoulder. "Come on. You know we're always better together."

Now this, Alice thought, was really laying it on thick.

He didn't mean it. She knew he didn't mean it because it was not true. It had not been true in well over a year, and that had been entirely Peter's choice. She recalled it well. So how could he act so chummy, toss those words out so casually, as if they were still first-years giggling in the lab, as if time had never passed?

But then, this was Peter's modus operandi. He was like this with everyone. All warmth and cheer—but the moment you tried to step closer, solid ground gave way to empty space.

Two bad options, then. Imperfect knowledge, or Peter. She supposed she could demand the relevant books—Peter was annoying, but he didn't hoard resources—and figure it all out on her own. But her funding clock was ticking, and certain body parts were rotting in a basement. There simply wasn't time.

"Fine," she said. "I hope you brought your own chalk."

"Two new packs of Shropley's," he said happily.

Yes, she knew he preferred Shropley's. Evidence of bad character. At least she wouldn't have to share.

She arranged her rucksack next to her feet, checking that

none of the straps lay outside the pentagram. "Then all that's left is the incantation. Are you ready?"

"Hold on," said Peter. "You do know the price?"

Of course Alice knew. This was why scholars rarely ever went to Hell. It wasn't that getting there was so very *hard*. You only had to dig up all the right proofs and master them. It was that a trip down below rarely justified the price.

"Half my remaining lifespan," she said. Entering Hell meant crashing through borders between worlds, and this demanded a kind of organic energy that mere chalk could not contain. "Thirty years or so, gone. I know."

But she had hardly struggled with the choice. Would she rather graduate, produce brilliant research, and go out in a blaze of glory? Or would she rather live out her natural lifespan, gray haired and drooling, fading into irrelevance, consumed by regret? Had not Achilles chosen to die in battle? She had met professors emeriti at department receptions, those poor aphasic props, and she did not think old age an attractive prospect. She knew this choice would horrify anyone outside the academy. But no one outside the academy could possibly understand. She would sacrifice her firstborn for a professorial post. She would sever a limb. She would give anything, so long as she still had her mind, so long as she could still think.

"I want to be a magician," she said. "It's all I've ever wanted."

"I know," said Peter. "Me too. And I—I need to do this. I must."

A taut silence. Alice considered asking, but she knew Peter would not tell her. Peter, when it came to the personal, was a stone wall. How easily he vanished behind a placid smile.

"That's settled, then." Peter cleared his throat. "So maybe I'll do the Latin, and you'll do the Greek and Chinese." He peered down at a segment near his right toe. "Say, why isn't this in Sanskrit?"

"I'm not comfortable with Sanskrit," Alice said, peeved. This was just like Peter. Condescending, even when ostensibly just asking for clarification. "I've done all the Buddhist sutra references in Classical Chinese instead."

"Oh." Peter hummed. "Well, that probably works. If you're sure."

She rolled her eyes. "In three, on go."

"Right on."

She counted down. "Go."

And they began their chant.

THE DREADFUL, TRAGIC DEATH OF PROFESSOR Jacob Grimes had been both foreseeable and avoidable. It was also, unknown to most, entirely Alice's fault.

That day's exercise was nothing more risky nor radical than the thousands of routine experiments Professor Grimes had conducted in that laboratory space for decades. He was only retracing some basic principles of set theory cited in a new article he had coming out in *Arcana*, the top journal in their field. It was all utterly routine, and no more dangerous than riding a bike, so long as one double-checked their pentagrams. Undergraduate-level stuff.

Professor Grimes did not double-check his pentagrams. He'd long reached the stage of his career where one left that sort of grunt work to graduate students. Professor Grimes's days were devoted to profound, deep *thinking*. He saw above the mountains and clouds to discern the truth, and then he descended to utter pronouncements like Moses coming down Mount Sinai, and then his underlings hammered out the details. He never did his own arithmetic or translations anymore. And he was far above kneeling over tracing lines of chalk, straining his eyes, straining his back.

One might find it reckless, foolish even, for a magician to leave his life in the hands of underpaid and overworked graduate students. But for one thing, Professor Grimes's graduate students were the best in the world. For another, even graduate students at bottom-rate American institutions could identify the most dangerous mistakes in a pentagram. And this was Cambridge. After so many years of practice they stood out to any competent scholar like glaring red flags: gaps in the outer circles, misspelled words, false equivalencies, parentheses left unclosed. Anyone in a sound state of mind could have done it.

But Alice was not in a sound state of mind that day.

She was of course underpaid and overworked, but this condition was common among graduate students and no one cared much about it. But she had also not slept properly in three months. She'd drunk so much caffeine that the world shimmered, and her chalk trembled in her grip. She felt, as she often did, that her body had no defined boundaries from the material world; that if she stopped holding herself together as a subject, she would dissolve like a sugar cube in tea. She was in no state to work, and she had not been for a very long time. What Alice needed most then was a nice long holiday, and then perhaps institutionalization at some remote facility near the sea.

But missing lab was not an option. Professor Grimes had not asked her to assist on a paper since last year, and though the work was beneath her, and though coauthorship was out of the question, Alice was desperate to get back in his good graces.

Anyhow, tired to the point of collapse was a default state. The expectation was simply that, through some combination of strong coffee and Lembas Bread, one pushed through until all deadlines were met and one could collapse into an indefinite coma without consequence. Alice had spent most of graduate school in this state, and it was not so bad.

But she was also angry that afternoon, and resentful, and

confused, and such a turbid mess of frustration and fury that the very sound of Professor Grimes's voice made her flinch. Perceiving his sheer physical proximity—sensing him move, kneeling in his shadow—made it hard to breathe. In the brief moments that their eyes met, her breath stopped, and she thought she might like to die.

It was very difficult to concentrate in such an environment.

So, when she drew the pentagrams, she did not close the requisite loops. With pentagrams, it was very important to close the requisite loops. Uttering incantations invoked the living-dead energy of chalk dust, and all that energy had an explosive effect unless contained properly within a defined space. Even the smallest hole could cause disaster. In fact, smaller holes were *worse*, as they concentrated all the energy to terrible effect. Therefore anyone who drew a pentagram performed what was known as the Ant Test: tracing a pencil tip from one point of the inscription all the way around to make sure any ant following the line would complete the journey.

Alice did not perform the Ant Test.

She did not, in effect, bother to ensure Professor Grimes's body remained intact.

It was the kind of mistake that could end careers. It would have, if anyone had seen Alice's name on the lab logs or known in any official capacity that she was assisting at all. There would have been an investigation. She would have been questioned before a board, forced to recount in painstaking detail her every last error while they deliberated over whether it was grounds for manslaughter or merely reckless endangerment. She would have lost her stipend, been booted from the program, been interrogated by the Royal Academy, and been barred from studying or practicing magick at any institution in the world, even the sketchy, nonaccredited ones overseas. All this if she did not go to prison.

But Professor Grimes did not generally credit his graduate students in his experiments. Assisting with his research, at the expense of their own, was simply an unspoken requirement of the program. No one knew, in any official capacity, that anyone was in that room on the day of the accident except for Professor Grimes. No one else saw when howling winds torn from infinite dimensions rushed into the pentagram. No one saw Professor Grimes's eyeballs stretch out of his face before popping like grapes; his intestines spooling out and around his body like a jump rope, crisscross applesauce; his mouth twisting in a soundless scream. No one saw Professor Grimes's body turn upside-down and spin for seven horrible cycles, exposed organs rippling, before flying apart in all directions, splattering every surface with blood and bone and guts. No one saw his brains on the chalkboard; the toothy jaw fragment landing plop into his afternoon cup of Darjeeling.

And no one saw Alice strip naked in the lab shower, scrub herself clean, throw her clothes in the incinerator, and hurry out the back door, dressed in clothes from the overnight bag she always kept at the lab. No one saw her flee in the early hours across campus back to her room in the college, where she stripped down for a second shower and alternated vomiting and crying until she fell asleep.

For all anyone knew, the first anyone heard of Professor Grimes's death was the janitor's screaming the next morning.

By then the blood and bits had ruined the pentagram, and all the chalk was smudged with gore, so that no one could discern precisely what had gone wrong. A piece of Professor Grimes later identified as his liver had, happily, landed square on that segment of the outer circle Alice had fudged. They could only conclude it was a terrible accident, one only waiting to befall the most brazen thinker of his time, and stop the investigations there.

Somehow, University Cleaning Services scooped together enough remains to fill a bucket, which were then transferred into a coffin. The college held a service. The department maintained a state of mourning for a week, during which all the students and faculty were forced to attend mandatory safety workshops run by colleagues bused in from Oxford, who with every sneering comment made it clear that *they* never would have been so foolish as to let a researcher explode himself all over a lab. Professor Grimes's nameplate was removed from his office door. His graduate seminar was reassigned to a poor postdoc who understood less of the material than the students did. The city papers printed some stuff about what a great loss this was—to Cambridge, to the discipline, to the world. And then the summer ended and everyone moved on. Except Alice.

She could have kept her mouth shut and gotten on with it. The university would have supported her to the end of her studies. Cambridge's Department of Analytic Magick was very proud of its high graduation rate, and the faculty would have dragged Alice across the finish line, one way or another, even if this meant lending her out for several years to their rivals at Oxford.

But Professor Grimes was the most influential analytic magician in England, and probably the world. Half the department chairs in the field were his close friends, and the other half were so frightened of him they would do anything he said. All of Professor Grimes's previous advisees had gone on to tenured jobs at top-tier programs—the ones who graduated, anyhow. One recommendation letter from Professor Grimes as good as secured a post anywhere his students applied.

Good jobs were vanishingly rare in academia. Alice very much wanted one. She wouldn't know what to do with herself otherwise. She had trained her entire life to do this one thing, and if she could not do it, then she had no reason to live.

So the next morning after Professor Grimes's death, once his body was discovered and all the dust had settled, it seemed the most natural thing in the world to begin researching ways to go to Hell.

PETER HAD A VERY NICE SPELL-BINDING voice. Alice had always resented this about him, how his voice made hers seem reedy in comparison. She found it particularly disgruntling given how incongruous it was with his stick-thin frame. It seemed unfair such a rich sound could come from that stubbly goose throat. Every now and then a research paper surfaced on why male voices were better suited for magick, citing reasons of pitch, depth, or steadiness, and they always sparked a big hubbub involving outraged statements from women-in-magick societies and apologetic statements from journal editorial boards. Alas, no one had managed to conclusively prove these studies false. Unfortunately, Alice suspected the papers were right, and at this moment she was grateful. Peter's confidence made her confident in turn, and she found herself lulled along by his smooth, reassuring rumble.

"The target defined as Professor Jacob Grimes," they intoned in unison. "The destination defined as Hell, or the afterlife, or the Eight Courts, or the domain of Lord Yama the Merciful."

They finished. Nothing happened. A second passed, then several. Then a freeze suffused the room, a creeping chill from nowhere that cut straight into their bones. Alice shuddered.

"Hand?" Peter offered his palm.

She slapped it away. "Shush."

"Sorry." Peter's hand hung in the air for a moment before he pulled it back, and Alice realized belatedly he might have been asking her to hold *his*.

But it was too late. White light flared up from the lines of chalk, forming a silo around them. The lab room vanished. A great rumbling filled the air. Alice reached for Peter's arm—only for balance, mind—but the ground lurched violently, and she toppled over onto her bum. For a moment she could see nothing, hear nothing over the roaring column. She felt a hooking sensation in her chest—not painful, only *sharp*, like some ghostly hand had reached in and yanked her heart out from between her ribs. The pressure was overwhelming. She could not breathe. She curled in on herself, hoping desperately she hadn't fallen out of the pentagram. The rumble grew and the light brightened to a blinding white, burning through her eyelids. Visions of apocalypse exploded in her mind's eye, oceans of blood beneath tongues of fire, planets collapsing into black holes, and for a brief, terrifying moment she was lost in the eruption, she forgot who she was—

She scrambled for her catechisms.

*I am Alice Law I am a postgraduate at Cambridge I study analytic magick—*

The light faded. The rumbling ceased.

Blinking, Alice turned her hands over before her eyes. She felt fine. Her skin was coated with a thin layer of ash, so that she looked dyed in gray, but it brushed away easily enough. She patted her chest. Her heart was in place. Her limbs were intact. Her entrails still stacked neatly inside her. If the price was paid, she couldn't feel it. All she felt then was a wild, burning elation. It had worked, she had done it, it worked. Chalk, dirt, hours of research—and then one world slipped into another. She had wrought this. A miracle.

Peter stood up, coughing. He brushed an ash-covered clump of hair out of his eyes. "So this is Hell."

Alice peered about in wonder. All around them were gray fields, endless plains under a dark red sky. A sun—*their* sun? a shadow, a twin?—hung low and ponderous, its light maddeningly dim. She breathed in deep. She had brought a cloth mask, in case the air reeked. In Virgil's *Aeneid*, the Greeks had named Hell *Aornos*, "the place that is birdless," for none could fly over its foul breath. But the air smelled of nothing but dust, and the temperature was just this side of chilly. She'd expected more tortured screaming, sulfur, and brimstone, but it turned out that perhaps the American theologians had been exaggerating. Meteorologically, Hell didn't seem much worse than an English spring.

She slung her rucksack over her shoulders. A faint dark mass loomed in the distance and there, she assumed, lay the Fields of Asphodel.

"You all right?" Peter asked.

"Never better." Alice stepped out of the pentagram. "Shall we?"

# On Magick

*Magick, the most mysterious and capricious of disciplines, admired for its power, derided for its frivolity, is in brief the act of telling lies about the world.*

*What magicians of ancient civilizations discovered through accident and ingenuity, and what the English philosopher-magicians of the eighteenth century onward codified into the Euro-American received canon, was that the natural laws of the world were set but fragile. You could cleverly reinterpret them. For brief periods of time one could even bewilder and suspend them, so long as you spun the right web of untruths. Linguistic trickery, logical conundrums, it all worked. All you had to do was find a set of premises that, even if just for a split second, made the world seem other than what it really was. The chalk, and whatever remnants of living-dead magical energy lay in the pulverized shells of those sea creatures that perished millions of years ago, did the rest.*

*Now, magick had progressed a lot since, say, the primitive rituals suggested by the Uffington chalk inscriptions, and there had since been a proliferation of flashy subfields that in fact had nothing to do with chalk, but rather all sorts of arcane objects, enchanted music, and visual illusions. One could now study the archaeology of magick, the history of magick, the music of magick, and on and on. Over in America, visual illusions and flashy showmanship were all the rage. In Europe they were going on about things called postmodernist and poststructuralist magick, which seemed to involve lots of spells doing the opposite of what their inventors wanted, and spells that did nothing at all, which everyone claimed was very profound. But all the best magick was still done at Cambridge, and good, traditionalist Cambridge was dedicated to the bare bones of the art. Analytic magick. Chalk, surface, paradox.*

*The paradox—the crucial element. The word* paradox *comes from two Greek roots:* para, *meaning "against," and* doxa, *meaning "belief." The trick of magick is to defy, trouble, or, at the very least, dislodge belief. Magick succeeds by casting confusion and doubt. Magick taunts physics and makes her cry.*

*Take, for instance, the Sorites Paradox. Imagine a heap of sand. Very simple. To remove one grain of sand from the heap does not make it any less a heap. Neither does removing two. You could sit there with tweezers for hours, but you would not have diminished the heap. What if you remove a thousand grains? A million? Precisely how many grains of sand must you remove before it is no longer a heap? If you sit cross-legged with a pair of tweezers, plucking out the sand one grain at a time, what is the precise moment when you will succeed in your demolition of the heap? No one can name this moment. But if the difference between the heap and the heap-minus-one is minuscule, how can you ever transform a heap into a not-heap?*

*Come on. You know very well what a heap is. You know it when you see it. It is like porn. And you know that if you shovel giant piles of sand out of the heap, there will come a moment when you can definitely call it not-a-heap.*

*But just for that moment, when the paradox is laid out to you in that precise wording, you don't know. For a moment, you think it is true—that it is impossible, indeed, to turn a heap into a not-heap. In fact you are probably so exhausted from hearing the word* heap *that the very concept is a blank to you.*

*Confusion, doubt. And with that, for just a moment, the world blinks. The heap does not run out.*

*It was this blink that had seduced Alice to her field. In her freshman year of college she took an Introduction to Logic class. In their second week, they were treated to a magick demonstration. A visiting postdoc stood before the lecture hall and drew a chalk circle around a small pile of sand on a table. "Watch," he said, and reached in to scoop a handful away. He did this again, and again, and again. He invited the class to line up and, one by one, try to empty the pile with their hands. They tried; they couldn't. Each time their hands left the circle, the space around the pile blurred, and the sand did not diminish.*

*Alice watched the sand spill from her fingers, and something knocked over in her chest.*

*She could not breathe. Now, here was a miracle. Here was Jesus, turning five loaves and two fish into an endless supply. All the fields she had considered for her major—maths, physics, medicine, history—they all fell away, they seemed so irrelevant, for why would you study static truths when truth had just exited left? She felt it then. She felt it every time. The stomach-dropping awe, the wondrous delight of a child at a circus who'd just seen a rabbit disappear. Through all her years of study, this feeling never went away. You thought the world was one way and then it wasn't. One could become zero. One could become two. A blink of an eye, and the fact of the matter was not. If the world could be fluid for you once, how many more times could you make it dance according to your whims?*

*Everyone else lived in such an ossified world. They simply took the rules given to them. They were interested only in articulating their own limits; they moved about as if in stone. But magicians lived in air, dancing on a tentative staircase of ideas, and it was a source of endless delirium, to know that the instant the world began to bore you, you could snap your fingers, and you'd be in free fall once again.*

*All it took was to tell a lie—and to believe, despite all the evidence to the contrary, that all the rules could be suspended. You held a conclusion in your head and believed, through sheer force of will, that everything else was wrong. You had to see the world as it was not.*

*Now Alice, as she proceeded through her coursework, got very good at this. All skilled magicians were. Success in this field demanded a forceful, single-minded capacity for self-delusion. Alice could tip over her world and construct planks of belief from nothing. She believed that finite quantities would never run out, that time could loop back on itself, and that any damage could be repaired. She believed that academia was a meritocracy, that hard work was its own reward. She believed that department pettiness could not touch you, so long as you kept your head down and did not complain. She believed that when professors snapped at you, when they belittled and misused you, it was because they cared. And she believed, despite mounting evidence to the contrary, that she was all right, that everything was all right, that she did not need help, that she could just stiffen her upper lip and keep on going.*

*She believed these things with all her might, with the same delirium it took to keep a heap of sand from ever running out. She had no choice. It was essential practice for everything that came after.*

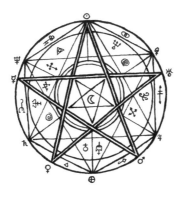

## CHAPTER TWO

Hell stretched. Alice and Peter walked side by side over sand so silky-fine their footprints left hardly any marks. Indeed, the sand seemed to actively erase them as they walked on. She glanced over her shoulder and saw her footprints left first indiscernible outlines, then, three steps on and another glance back, nothing at all. It appeared that Hell's landscape resisted alteration. No matter where Alice looked, she could detect no landmarks—no hills, no shores, no foreboding clouds. She tried not to let this bother her. Hell, she had read, was an inconstant and shifting plane. Its landmarks were conceptual, not fixed. She did not know quite what this meant, but following scholarly convention she interpreted this as, *Hell reveals itself to you in whatever order it so chooses.*

Hell, for now, chose rolling dunes.

Alice longed for sunlight. Her eyes had adjusted now to the dim, though they ached from squinting. She rubbed her temples and hoped she'd grow used to this eternal dusk.

Around twenty minutes later, they crossed under a bridge. At first they heard it rather than saw it: chatter overhead, voices

Alice almost recognized. She looked up and saw in the sky a mirror image of Cambridge, the campus turned upside-down and shudderingly translucent, as if projected across a staticky cable connection. She saw Jesus Green, Sidney Street, and the little winding alleys between St. John's and Trinity. She saw postgrads on their bicycles, weaving around cars. She saw little black masses moving quickly in clusters from one building to the next. Undergraduates, precious things, new and still-creased black robes flapping around their heels.

So this was the Viewing Pavilion. Alice had read about this: first in Penhaligon's *Primer on the Unitarian Hell*, and then corroborated by most ancient Chinese sources. Here was the bridge that all souls crossed before they passed into the Underworld for good; the liminal point between the worlds of the living and dead where each side could just barely glimpse the other.

A thought crossed Alice's mind. She squinted. Yes—if she cast her thoughts outward, she could zoom in to that mirror Cambridge and tunnel into the Graduate Lab Seven, where her and Peter's pentagram remained, their writing smudged and in parts eviscerated by winds blown from the boundaries between worlds. She saw two of her colleagues—Belinda and Michele—standing reverently at the door, peering around, slowly piecing together what had just happened.

She hadn't erased her tracks. No, rather the contrary: she'd left a note in her office announcing that she was off to retrieve Professor Grimes's soul from Hell, that no one should dare follow for the danger was so great, and that if she hadn't returned in fourteen days then they could go ahead and reassign her corner office to one of the first-years. She'd left the lab door unlocked. She wanted everyone to know where she had gone, if only so that when she returned in triumph, Professor Grimes in hand, there would be no doubts about her success.

Belinda and Michele were now kneeling by the outside of the

pentagram, stooping low to read the inscriptions. Alice wished she could hear what they were saying. Belinda kept pressing her hand against her mouth. Michele responded with some gestures that were either very agitated or simply very Italian; with Michele, Alice had never been able to tell which. Suddenly Belinda paused—she stood right over the inscription that designated their destination as Hell—and craned her neck to read.

Alice reached up as far as she could with one hand. The bridge was very close—a low ceiling she could *just* touch, if she strained her arm and teetered on her tiptoes. Could she cross it? She wanted to try.

"*Boo.*"

Belinda shuddered; her hand flew to her neck. Alice was delighted. She wondered at the limits of ghostly mischief—whether, if she wanted to, she might simply haunt the halls of Cambridge forever.

Scholars concurred that most hauntings on record were facilitated through the Viewing Pavilion. It was the only place from which the dead could make their voices heard, from which they might exert some pressure on the living. But it was a dual kind of haunting. Ghosts lingered around the Viewing Pavilion because they were too enraptured with scenes from their lifetime; because they, in turn, were entranced and obsessed with the rituals of the living. They wanted to know what everyone was up to. They wanted to see whether they'd been remembered. All the ghost stories were wrong; hauntings were so rarely malicious. The dead only wanted to feel included.

Belinda stumbled into Michele's arms. Alice snorted. What an English rose Belinda was—everything was always too much for her. Michele wrapped his arms around Belinda, speaking into her ear. Alice guessed at his words—*It's all right, they haven't died—they're not going to die.* Belinda kept shaking her head. *No,* she seemed to say. *No, they're dead, they're gone.*

"Having regrets?" Peter stood beside her, neck craned up. Though his eyes were not on Belinda and Michele, but the flocks of undergraduates bustling happily down the alley. Oblivious, excited for the start of term—or was their first day of classes over, were they now filtering into the college bar for a pint? "Want to head back?"

"Don't joke, Murdoch."

There was no simple path out of Hell. They both knew this coming in. Entering Hell was easy; leaving was hard. If only they could just jump up into their pentagram, say their spells in reverse, and plop right back where they had begun. But if that were possible, the living could visit their dead all the time. No; to ascend from Hell required the permission of Lord Yama—that was, Thanatos, Anubis, Hades, the Darkness of Many Names, Ruler of the Underworld.

Often he granted it. Lord Yama did not like to suffer the living in his realm; they disturbed the dead, they upset the balance. He was more than happy to shoo them back off to whence they'd come. At least, all the stories promised so. Orpheus had made his way back, for better or worse. Dante ascended with no trouble at all. In all the stories, sojourners in Hell rarely perished there. It was in the world of the living where they met their tragic ends.

In any case, they could sort out the problem of living when they crossed that bridge. For now, the trouble was determining how much deeper in to go.

**AN HOUR LATER THE GROUND BEGAN** sloping upward. They were climbing something, though it wasn't immediately clear what. Alice's lungs grew tight, though she tried not to pant. Peter loped on beside her, completely unfazed, and she was too embarrassed to admit she was tired.

Then it was all revealed beneath them: a flat valley filled with Shades upon Shades, some grouped in clusters, some wandering the fields alone. Those were dead souls—translucent gray things, mere echoes of living bodies. Some went round and round in circles; some paced along the same tight trip. Some meandered, drifting more than walking. From high above it was like watching a colony of sluggish, dazed ants, moving with no purpose. Only an endless milling. Limbo, by one name. By another, the Fields of Asphodel.

The fields were not a court of Hell, only a holding area. Here lingered the shocked, disoriented souls of the recently deceased. Here they had infinite space and time to find their bearings before they decided to move on. Talamo's monograph described the Fields of Asphodel as a waiting zone. Not so different from the lobby at Cambridge South, only there was no coffee kiosk, and everyone was still deciding whether they wanted to get on the train.

Alice had good reason to think Professor Grimes might still be here. On the whole, the dead were not typically eager to move on. They needed time to process their memories, their regrets, their wishes. Some stayed in hopes of reuniting with loved ones before they sought reincarnation together. Some didn't believe in reincarnation at all. Some waited in the fields forever out of conviction that the great resurrection was coming, and that they need only sink into a stupor and wait for the end times. Others remained out of sheer terror of what the rest of Hell might hold, for an eternity of boredom was better than the punishments they deserved.

Professor Grimes, in Alice's view, had quite a lot to atone for. If she were him, she would stay put.

But how would they ever find him in such a crowd? The fields stretched on as far as the eye could see, and not a single one of these souls was recognizable to Alice's eyes. Even after they descended down into the valley, into the crowds, the Shades appeared as vague and indistinct as they had looked from a distance. Alice scrutinized every soul she passed but saw only blurry silhouettes, most of them faceless, expressions uniformly dour if not. She could never get close enough to get a better look. The dead flitted away every time they came close, like gnats swarming off from waving hands.

"Remind me what you used for an anchor?" Peter asked after a while.

One of the more vexing problems with a sojourn to Hell was figuring out where to go and where to find the soul you hoped to rescue. Many souls had died since the dawn of time, and Hell was unfortunately a very large place. The solution was a Dowsing Anchor: a clause in the pentagram that used a physical token or object to root one spatiotemporally in the underworld. But Alice's anchor, it seemed, had led them only into indistinct space.

"I used a token from his desk." Alice glanced around helplessly. "The plaque they gave him in Paris last year. He tosses most of his awards but he kept that one face out, so I thought it meant something to him."

"I know that plaque. It's just made of wood, right? No gold lettering?"

"Yes, only a carving."

Peter nodded, pondered a moment, and then asked, "Could I make a suggestion?"

"Yes, of course."

"Only I don't mean to be overcritical." He said this so courteously that Alice wanted to smack him.

He never used to mince words with her. He used to shout, *You daft cow, Alice, you've missed a line, you've fucked it all up.* And she would give as good as she got, and point out it was *his* line he'd skipped, and they would argue furiously, and laugh, and sort out the problem. It used to be they could quarrel, and that quarrelling was fun. It used to be they could speak frankly with each other. But that was a very long time ago.

"We're lost in Hell," she said. "Suggest anything you want."

"So Macedonio's *Apocrypha* states that most objects from the world of the living lose their directional force in Hell," said Peter. "Sorry—I took it out before you had a chance, you couldn't have known. But the idea is that the emotional attachments we invest in objects that have been around for a very long time are indeed quite shallow compared to their histories. Particularly something like a plaque, which is just wood whittled down. It's changed by its polishing, sure, but it still inherently just is that wood. Our particular encounters with that wood are fleeting in the long span of its existence."

It all seemed very obvious to Alice when Peter explained it. "I should have thought of that."

"So your plaque might have put us in the proximity of every carpenter who's ever lived."

"I see."

"Or hiking enthusiast."

"Fair enough."

"Or even tree enthusiast."

"What's your point, Murdoch?"

"Actually, it's a very interesting dilemma," said Peter. "The way Hell is oriented spatially. Suppose Macedonio is right, and that the landscape of Hell reframes itself to form a mirror against the living world. What happens when those worlds overlap? When souls from different times and spaces interact? What Hell do they experience? I wonder—"

Alice cut him off. This was classic Murdoch; if you let him go on he rambled until he forgot what had gotten him started. Peter was always more interested in the problem than the answer. It made him a great scholar but so exhausting to work with. "Does Macedonio offer a solution?"

"Hm? Oh, yes! He says we should make the dead come to us." Peter slung off his rucksack and knelt to the ground. "He suggests a sacrifice."

He took out three objects from his rucksack: a packet of cigarettes, a slice of Lembas Bread, and a tiny sample bottle of tawny port. "A meal," he explained. "Something very temporally rooted. You have to get the precise decade right, you see. Objects have long histories, but foods—the particular ingredients that go into them in those exact ratios, and the routes they have to pass to get there—those are extremely temporally specific."

He assembled the cigarettes in a little pile, crumbled the Lembas Bread above them, and splashed the port on top. Then he struck a match and lit the whole thing on fire.

It all smelled disturbingly good to Alice, tobacco and all. It made her think of the department lounge—of Lembas Bread wrappers, of used mugs, of port-stained couches, of damp coffee filters sitting atop the rubbish bin. It smelled like home.

Thick black tendrils unfurled above the pile and dissipated into the grey. The fields blurred, then began thinning out around them. Whole clusters of Shades disappeared, one by one, until they stood alone against the fields.

A single blur appeared over the horizon, growing larger and larger as it approached.

Peter said, "That can't be right."

It was not Professor Grimes. It was the department cat.

Most departments at Cambridge owned a cat, which was to say, the cats owned them. For the cats wore no collars, nor did they sleep in any professors' homes, nor did they seem loyal to or even particularly friendly with any student or faculty member. All anyone knew was that one day a cat would show up mewling with hunger, and since no one could resist setting out food and water, the cat would stick around, growing increasingly pampered until eventually history was rewritten, and the cat had in fact always been a part of the institution.

Analytic Magick's department cat was a sleek, green-eyed, dark-gray thing with a magnificent feather-duster tail named Archimedes, and to the best of Alice's knowledge he was unquestionably alive. She had seen him just that morning, batting idiotically at butterflies in the front garden.

She knelt down. Archimedes did not like much to be pet, but he did prefer you make eye contact when speaking to him. Something to do with respect. "What are you doing here?"

Archimedes blinked, his tail swishing back and forth around his legs. He circled round the fire and gave it a sniff. If he was bothered to be in Hell, he did not show it.

"Cats *can* cross boundaries," Alice said in a hushed tone. "I read about this! They know the courts, they can see the dead."

"Can you help us, then?" Peter approached the cat. "Can you bring us to Grimes?"

For a moment Archimedes seemed to consider this. His eyes lingered on the fire for a long time, such a long time that Alice felt a swell of hope—he did look so wise, his gaze so significant. *I have crossed oceans of time*, said those eyes. *I have seen the hidden world.* Then he mewed in a very scornful way and streaked back over the dunes.

Alice stood up. "Useless."

"Look," said Peter.

Where Archimedes had disappeared, four figures now appeared on the horizon. Slight, tentative shapes. None with the tall, imposing grace of Professor Grimes. They drew closer, and the soft light of their faces became clear under the low, burning sun. Innocent things. Children still. Mottled patches of black spread across their skin like ink stains.

"Peter." Alice had a sinking feeling. "That isn't . . ."

"Oh, dear," said Peter. "I thought they'd have passed on by now."

"Apparently not," said Alice, and braced herself to meet Professor Grimes's first victims.

THIRTY YEARS AGO AT CAMBRIDGE, A spell went awry and four undergraduates died. The postdoc on duty was stripped of his degrees and banished back home to Bristol in disgrace. All involved parties were students of the then-young Professor Jacob Grimes.

Officially, the university blamed the deaths on a building fire—which was not technically false, because the resulting explosion had burned down the entire left wing—and sent the students' ashes home to their parents, along with a letter assuring them that Cambridge was not in any way responsible, and that litigation would be a very bad idea. Conveniently an investigation revealed some faulty construction in the gas pipes, which allowed the university to place the blame on building codes and contractor malfeasance, not on what types of magical experiments could burn down half a building in the first place. All this meant the department was never blamed for what happened. It was a freak accident, nothing more.

But no one ever asked why Professor Grimes let a fire rip through the lab to begin with. No one ever considered that, as a supervisor responsible for both the intellectual development and the safety of his students, Professor Grimes should have been paying attention to the progress of the experiment instead of being burrowed away in his third-floor office, a formidable "DO NOT ENTER" sign hung over his door. (He was so proud of that sign; a graduating cohort had presented it to him as a joke, and he had accepted it without irony.) No one ever suggested that perhaps, in addition to doing his research, Professor Grimes should have been fulfilling his duties as a teacher. He wasn't the only neglectful professor, after all—all the faculty in the department cut corners when it came to teaching duties. Why waste time babysitting undergraduates when one could work on literally anything else?

So none of this had any effect on Professor Grimes's career. No one could prove it was his fault. You couldn't draw a line between his actions and the fire. He hadn't even been present. And anyhow, accidents were very common in magick. Just two weeks later an enchanted harp recovered from Assyria put half of Harvard's department into a paralyzed slumber, and this greatly overshadowed the Cambridge fire on the conference gossip circuit. (No counter-spells were effective; the cure at last involved enormous amounts of amphetamine, which a surprising number of grad students had in ready supply.) It was generally agreed that magick required taking risks—especially the visionary, field-defining magick for which Professor Grimes was known. In any case, it was the undergraduates' own fault, and they were dead already. That was punishment enough.

AS THE SHADES APPROACHED, ALICE OBSERVED with horror that their appearances seemed locked onto their bodies in the moment of death. One of them seemed mostly intact—she had just a few scratches on her face and arms. One student died of smoke inhalation, said the report. The flames never touched her. She'd crawled into a corner and hidden under a fireproof tarp, and according to the firefighters this was why no one had found her until nearly an hour after the fire was put out. She might have been alive a long time—no one knew for sure, and no one pressed the issue. Her parents held an open-casket funeral in Ely and invited the entire department. This was before Alice's time, but she was fairly sure Professor Grimes wouldn't have gone.

The others were burned beyond recognition. It turned Alice's stomach to look at them. It was one thing to read theories of the dead; witnessing them was quite another. Charred limbs, petrified faces; jawbones stripped clean of flesh, teeth stretched, rictus-like, in unwilling smiles. Only the eyes were uniformly unscarred; staring, pleading, plaintive, curious eyes. Did they spend all eternity like that? Or had they only chosen to present themselves as such for now? The literature on Shades and corporeality was scant and undecided. Some scholars thought Shades were preserved unwillingly as they were in the moment of their death. Others argued Shades had the agency to manifest however they liked. Either way Alice felt it rude to ask.

"Hello," she said cautiously. "We're from Cambridge."

The Shades shuffled closer. They seemed quite excited. Alice could not read the faces of the burnt three—they could never stop smiling—but the more intact girl's expression was open, delighted.

"We're looking for a soul who's only recently passed over," said Peter. "Professor Jacob Grimes."

The more intact girl gasped, and the sound spread across the Shades like wind across rocks.

*"Professor Grimes?"*

"Professor Grimes is here?"

"Grimes!"

So they could speak. Their voices were each an echo of the others'; one statement repeated four times in slightly different registers. Alice could not tell if Shades could speak no other way, or if, after decades clustered together and facing down infinity, their personalities had blended and congealed so that they no longer knew themselves as distinct from the others. They descended into excited chatter, communing among themselves in unintelligible clacks and whistles. All Alice could make out was, "Grimes," "No way," and "Mother of God!"

"Do you have any idea where he might be?" Peter cut in.

"Should still be a Shade," said a girl with braids.

"Yes, a Shade, unless—"

"Unless!"

"But we wouldn't know."

"Doesn't talk to us."

"Too important," huffed a boy with glasses. "Would have just sailed by."

"Sailed."

"Without speaking."

"He did come by," said the more intact girl. "So quickly I thought it was a dream. But now you say it—I did see. I saw. I waved. He said hello."

The other three floated up and down in agitation.

"You saw him?"

"He said *hello*?"

"Why didn't you tell us?"

"Oh, my God!" The more intact Shade flared for a moment; ever so briefly, her form took a more solid, distinct shape, and Alice glimpsed a flash of red in her hair. "Do you know how annoying it is to spend eternity with you lot? It was a memory all my own, something that *happened*, and I didn't want to share."

The other Shades looked miffed. Alice could actually see the shape of their irritation, spiky wisps of gray miasma drifting about their shoulders.

"Could have told us."

"Could have."

"No point keeping secrets."

"There's an eternity for secrets."

"Hold on," Alice said desperately, before she lost them to their chatter. "When did this happen?"

"Don't know," said the boy with glasses. "There is no time here."

This was demonstrably metaphysically false, but Alice chose to ignore this. "What did he say to you?"

"Wanted directions," sniffed the more intact girl. "Couldn't stand the fields. Couldn't wait to get out of here."

"And where would we go?" asked Peter. "If we also wanted to get out of here?"

The undergraduates pointed. Alice and Peter turned, and there it was, a line of white in the distance—a wall or building, she could not tell for sure, but it was at least some structure that promised an end to the silt monotony. Alice did not think it had been there before. She squinted, and saw what from this distance reminded her of teeming ants around their anthill. Shades, thousands of them, lining up for whatever release lay behind the white.

The undergraduates sighed, deflating, all at once.

"The lines—"

"So long!"

"Never make it to the end—"

"Worse than concert tickets—"

"I only ever got to see one," declared the boy with glasses. "I got to see the Chordettes. I stood in line for four hours to see the Chordettes."

This set off another excited shuffle. "You saw *the Chordettes*?"

"Focus," said Peter. "Please. Is that the only way into the next court?"

"Oh, yes."

"Everyone has to stand in line."

"Even Professor Grimes."

"Wait their turn."

"No exceptions."

The more intact girl cocked her head. "Will you save him?"

At this question, all the undergraduates surged forth and flocked eagerly around Alice and Peter.

"Will you scoop him out of here?"

"Is this for your *research*?"

"Is it for a *paper*?"

Alice felt a pang of sympathy. She'd always been fond of undergraduates, no matter how much she enjoyed complaining about them. In truth, Cambridge students were a pleasure to teach. Naïve, eager things. With few exceptions they were never lazy, never insolent. Quite the opposite. They were generally cheerful, unformed minds who still asked for permission to use the restroom during section, who regularly forgot the order of operations when switching from maths to logic, who stuttered from nerves during office hours and opened their papers with inane declarations like "THE OXFORD ENGLISH DICTIONARY DEFINES VALIDITY AS . . ." and "SINCE THE DAWN OF TIME, MANKIND HAS BEEN TROUBLED BY THE PROBLEM OF RATIONALITY." She used to see them bundling into the Pick together after lecture, pink cheeked from the cold, chattering happily over cheap beer and soggy chips. She liked to watch them chatting animatedly about their classes, hands waving about in the air, their vowels just a bit forced, their jargon heavy-handed. They made her wonder, envious, if ignorance was truly the secret to bliss.

"Shall we go in together, then?" Peter asked gently. "Isn't it about time you lot moved on, anyways?"

This was apparently the wrong question to ask. The undergraduates shrank back into a tight, glutinous mass of psychic distress. The air suddenly sharpened with cold. Alice's arms prickled. She made a mental note of this. *Shades can affect atmosphere, if upset.*

"Scared," said the more intact girl at last.

The others nodded.

"Of what, though?" Peter asked. "You're all such—I mean, I'm sure you have nothing much to atone for."

Violently they shook their heads. "That's not it."

"No, no . . ."

"We are scared to *pass*."

"Scared to not be—"

"Scared of the Lethe—"

"Scared to forget—"

"To become—"

"Scared to be other."

"It's only reincarnation," Peter said. "You won't remember a thing."

"Precisely. We were magicians," said the boy with glasses. "If we go . . ."

"We won't be magicians."

"You're joking," said Peter, with his classic lack of tact.

Alice thought he was being a bit daft. Of course these Shades were scared. Souls often lingered in Asphodel for years—decades—before trying for reincarnation. Loss of identity was a terrifying prospect. Who were you without your memories, your background, your relationships, your station? What if your lot in the next life was far worse than the life you'd just lived? It didn't matter that in theory souls enjoyed infinite lives, and infinite chances to experience things good and bad. From the subjective perspective of the soul, reincarnation was no different from death.

What's more, reincarnation was always a lottery. Alice could understand not wanting to try their chances.

"You've barely lived," said Peter. "There's so much more to life—wouldn't you like to try again?"

The undergraduates quivered.

"But magick—"

"But Cambridge—"

"The throne of the intellectual world," said the more intact girl. "Privileged beyond belief."

"It is the only rational choice," declared the boy with glasses. He spoke with such authority, the other undergraduates seemed momentarily to shrink behind him, as if giving him permission to speak for the group. His voice deepened. He gestured as he spoke, in imitation of a professor. "You see, given the population on Earth it is overwhelmingly likely we will be reincarnated into lives under the poverty level. Most of the world population never go to school, let alone come to Cambridge. An unexamined life is not worth living, as Socrates tells us. Therefore to seek reincarnation is to gamble with overwhelmingly bad odds on a life not worth living. For instance, once reincarnated, we could end up doing something like—I don't know, working rice paddies in China."

"Milking cows in Arkansas," agreed the more intact girl.

"Mining diamonds in Africa."

"Now, look here," said Alice. "That's rather prejudiced—"

"Being an idiot."

"Being an idiot!" All four Shades shuddered; a quivering mass of jelly. "Oh, the horror! Oh, to not be clever!" And one of them wailed, "What if you never learn to *read*!"

"But you're dead." This had gone too far; Alice had to intervene. Undergraduates did this often—they worked each other up over the wrong ideas, compared problem sets and confused themselves so much that untangling their thoughts took twice the work. Undergraduates were five blind men and an elephant; were three blind mice leading one another in a circle. "You're in Hell. That seems the worst state to be in."

"We're dead *magicians*," said the boy with glasses. "That's different."

"It's not different at all," said Peter. "You're still stuck here."

"But why are you here?" asked the more intact girl. "Why'd you come?"

They seized on this line of interrogation with glee.

"Why?"

"Why indeed?"

"Half a lifetime—"

"The price—"

"The price!"

"That's different," said Alice. "We could still be magicians. *That's* worth it."

"Oh," said the more intact girl. And then she employed that most annoying of argumentative tactics, which was to agree, while making it clear they thought her reasoning was stupid. "*All right* then."

The other undergraduates said nothing. What rejoinder need they make? They only watched her, bearing identical expressions of silent reproach; until their forms began to fade, until their burns became glimmers, until they disappeared into still air.

"Wow," said Peter. "I think we've been told to fuck off."

"Oh, leave them to it," Alice muttered. She felt a spasm of irritation, a lurking unease, and she did not want to think about these undergraduates anymore. Hell was full of minor tragedies. There was no point fretting over this one. "They have eternity to figure it out."

## CHAPTER THREE

The line of white was indeed a wall: a great, flat surface that disappeared into the sky and stretched infinitely into either direction. Below, a great mass of Shades shuffled impatiently about, their voices like wind rustling through dried leaves.

"Been here for *ages*—"

"Nothing's moving—"

"Birth rate's gone down, they said."

"Has it?"

"Postwar boom's over, everywhere's developed, and all the girls are taking pills—"

"Oh, is *that* it?"

"My word." Peter stood on the tips of his toes, trying to see over the crowd. "It's worse than Fifth on a Friday."

"You've been to Fifth?" Alice asked.

"I tried. Never got in."

Alice did feel as if she were stuck outside a nightclub, only the doors were out of sight, and no one was enforcing the queue. "Do you think he's still here?"

Perspective was not reliable here. It was impossible to tell how quickly the queue was moving, or how much distance separated them from the wall. Professor Grimes might have passed through days ago. He might have been stuck in line, several yards away. Alice wished she had consulted some material about birth and death rates. How many people in the world had died over the past two months? How many had reincarnated since? She did not recall any archival information about queuing to depart Asphodel—Orpheus and all the rest seemed to just walk right into the courts—but then all the sojourner accounts were from a period when the world was smaller, when a more manageable number of souls came and went. Possibly this wall was a recent development. A sort of postwar chthonic immigration control.

"We could shout for him," said Peter.

"Oh, let's not do that." Alice had seen no sign of guardian deities yet, but she knew as a general rule it was best when sojourners did not draw attention to themselves. She sized up the queue, then squared her shoulders. "We might just try and go *through*."

The lines looked dense, but weren't Shades immaterial? Setiya and Penhaligon certainly thought so—Shades had only memories of their bodies, they were spirit stuff alone, and so they could not interact with the physical in any meaningful way. Alice and Peter were flesh and bone, and matter trumped empty space. So suppose she just *pushed*—but she wasn't three steps in before she was swarmed by Shades. Irritation exploded around her.

"Cutting—"

"No cutting—"

"Get out—"

*"Rude!"*

Icy chill spread throughout her limbs. She felt a slimy pressure against her skin. So she was wrong—it seemed Shades could indeed become something resembling the material when it suited them. She recalled the more intact girl from before, how for an instant she had seemed more solid. The crowd formed a frothy irascible mass, pushing and squeezing from all sides until she could hardly breathe. The pressure sharpened. She yelped and jumped back out of line. "All right," she said. "Jesus—no cutting, all right."

The pressure vanished; the chill eased. The mass subsided back into the queue.

"So that's out." Alice rubbed her arms. "Seems like they—*ow!*"

A Shade had bumped past her, elbowing her so hard she nearly fell to the ground. He seemed to have invested all his corporeal memory into that elbow. It *hurt*.

"Blasted magicians," hissed the Shade. "No respect."

The pain to her ribs was terrible, but Alice was too excited to mind. "How do you know we're magicians?"

"Chalk all over your hands," said the Shade. "Chalk on your kneecaps. What else are you, cokeheads?"

Here Alice began to suspect this Shade was a mathematician. Mathematicians hated magicians.

"Have you seen another magician?" Peter asked eagerly. "Here? Recently?"

"*Have I seen a magician*," muttered the Shade. "Have I seen a magician, a snotty arrogant magician, striding about like he owned the place, like the rest of us don't exist—"

That sounded just like Professor Grimes. "When?" Alice demanded.

"A day," said the Shade. "A week. A month. Who's counting?"

"And he's definitely crossed over?" Peter pressed. "He's not queuing still?"

"The rate he was going?" The Shade snorted. "Marching on like he had somewhere to be. Would be surprised if he hasn't reached the Eighth Court by now. They would have admitted him just to get him out of here. And good riddance."

Alice wanted to sprint up to the gates right then. But the

Shades were all casting her dirty looks now, and she doubted they would part politely if she asked. What to do, then? Wait their turn? But even if they got through, Alice didn't know what deities guarded the end of the queue, or whether they were disposed to help the living. And Professor Grimes was moving fast, with purpose. If he didn't want to delay, then he was bent on reincarnation. They couldn't simply stand here. It was a race against time now, and Alice didn't know how long the courts could hold a persona like Grimes.

"Say, Law." Peter was eyeing the wall. From a distance it had seemed a smooth marble edifice, flawless and flat, but up close Alice saw now that the wall was constructed instead of thousands of little bones, stacked up on each other in a dense, ancient mass. Accumulated detritus of millions of years of life. A mountain of preserved time. Though horizontally it was endless, vertically it was not—it appeared to stretch forty, fifty meters before it topped out to a smooth straight line. No taller than the university library.

Peter asked, "How hard do you think that is to climb?"

**THEY MARCHED PERPENDICULAR TO THE QUEUE** until the crowds thinned away. Now they could approach the base of the wall undisturbed. The Shades, for whatever reason, seemed uninterested in climbing up—possibly because they had no incentive to rush, and possibly because their tenuous materiality could offer them no purchase against that surface.

A shame, thought Alice, because the wall really was ideal for climbing. Large bits of bone stuck out all over the place—lovely handholds, easily grasped—and the wall was littered too with grooves, perfect for digging one's toes in. Alice was grateful that the wall was made of bone only—it seemed all the hair, fur, blood, and gristly bits had eroded long ago. There was no smell nor gore. Texture-wise, they were grand. Alice looked upon the wall and saw the Flatirons and Peak District; saw plentiful bottlenecks, chimneys, and cracks. The only problem, she surmised, would be endurance. But perhaps they could rest at the top.

She took a deep breath, stretched out her shoulders, then dug into her bag.

"What are you doing?" Peter asked.

Alice was crumbling a stick of chalk between her fingers. "For the grip," she explained. "It keeps you from slipping when your hands get sweaty."

"How do you know that?"

She dusted the chalk across her palms. "I used to climb in Colorado. I climb sometimes still—there's a mountaineering club on campus."

"How very American."

"Hush." She reached for the nearest bits of protruding bone, found her footholds, and hoisted herself up. "Follow my lead. Don't look down."

Up they went. To her delight, Alice found the climb deliciously easy. The grips were good, the wall full of friction. She yanked at every hold out of caution before she placed her weight against it, but every inch of bone held firm. Eons of accumulation had packed these materials so densely there was not a single loose bit.

For a while she climbed and climbed, relishing the sureness of her grip; how effortlessly she could swing herself from hold to hold. The strain and repetition felt good. It was meditative; it took up all her concentration, so that the anxious radio in her head quieted down. It also felt good to realize she could still do this. She hadn't taken care of herself these last few months; she had been afraid all her muscles had atrophied. On the other hand, she was so much thinner now. Less weight to pull—which did make a difference, though she wasn't sure whether this lovely lightness came from actual agility or from starvation fuzzing up her head.

After a while she stopped to glance about. She had loved doing this whenever she climbed in Colorado. She loved to appreciate the sheer distance to the ground. It never fazed her. At this height she was too far up to do anything about it but keep going, and this immovable fact helped to block out useless feelings like fear.

Hell stretched endless beneath her, plains of silt and rolling dunes. To her tired eyes, this side of Hell abstracted to two rippling blocks of color: silky gray below and an orange burning darkly above, punctuated by a sun that seemed perpetually on the verge of setting. It was quite beautiful.

"This is insane," she said. "Lovely view, though. Are you doing all right?"

Peter did not answer.

"Murdoch?"

She glanced down. Peter was much further below her than she'd thought; he must have stopped moving some time ago. All four of his limbs trembled. His forehead shone slick with sweat. He blinked furiously at the wall, and he looked like he was trying not to vomit.

"Murdoch?"

For a moment Peter seemed not to register her voice. Then at last he replied, "I believe I am having a panic attack."

It was wildly inappropriate, but Alice laughed. "Murdoch, are you afraid of heights?"

"I didn't want to tell you," he gasped. "Thought I could just—suck it up—"

"It was your idea to climb!"

"Yes, but I only meant it in *theory*," he whined. "Oh, God, Law—"

"You're fine, you're fine," she said quickly. "Look, you made it this far—"

"But now my brain's caught up, and I can't move." He squeezed his eyes shut. "Oh God oh God—"

"Stop talking. Just breathe." The gravity of the situation had caught up with her. Alice remained calm. She had talked undergraduates down from quitting Professor Grimes's seminars before. She had, for better or worse, plenty of practice at talking away fear. "There's a solid protruding block a few feet up. You can brace your feet against that and lean forward, which will give your arms a rest. Do you think you can make it just a few more holds?"

"I can't let go." Peter whined again. "My wrists . . ."

"Do it or you'll die," Alice snapped. "*Move*, Murdoch. Don't think, just do it."

Miraculously, Peter obeyed. His feet found purchase, and he leaned forward against the wall, hands splayed for balance. His chest heaved with exhaustion.

"Very good," said Alice. "Now, let's—let's just take stock, have a reset . . ."

"My forearms are burning," Peter gasped.

"You're using your thumbs too much. Look." She demonstrated with one hand. "Try hanging from your top four fingers instead. They'll give you all the traction you need. Hook, don't pinch."

Peter spent a long moment breathing against the wall. Alice wondered if he'd heard her at all. But then he reached out with one tentative hand, the other bracing against the wall for balance, and flexed his fingers.

"Okay," he said. "I think . . . that makes sense."

"And if you ever need to rest, get your feet on a good hold, stand up straight, and lean against the wall like you are now. That'll take some of the pressure off your arms. Do you understand?"

He nodded vigorously, eyes wide.

"Hesitation is your worst enemy. If you see a hold, just *swing* for it. The longer you dither back and forth, the more you exhaust yourself. Do you understand?"

"Yes, ma'am."

"Shush, Murdoch, I'm saving your life." She dusted her hands with a fresh piece of chalk, then passed it down. "Chalk up, you're sweating."

Peter obeyed. Up again they went. From this angle Alice could not tell how far they'd come, whether they'd reached the halfway point or not. All distance and texture were reduced to abstractions, lines on canvas, and all she could see on either side was an endless stretch of jagged white, then sky, or ground. There was no pacing herself to the finish. All she could do was ignore the passage of time, and the rapidly approaching limits of her own endurance, and keep throwing one arm up over the next. A watched distance never shrank. Hands, hands, toes, toes. Hands, hands, toes, toes.

Finally her right hand met a flat, wide surface. She dared to tilt her head up. That was it—there was no more wall, only sky, she'd made it. Topping out, they called it at the gym. She took a deep breath and pushed herself over the edge in one massive go. Then she scampered onto her knees and looked down.

Peter gazed up at her, eyes huge with fright. He was shaking quite badly. She was afraid he might let go, and he was still several feet below her, too far for her to pull him up.

"You're so close," she called. "You're almost there. And it's flat up here—almost three feet wide—we can rest up here, you've just got to finish out."

He might have said something in response, but she couldn't tell what. All she heard was a pained wheezing.

"Just look at me," she said. He raised his head. "There you go."

He reached with trembling hands for the next hold. Then the next.

"Now move your toes," she whispered. "Steady now—good, good—now one more."

He got one hand up to the top. She seized his wrist. He got another hand up, just far enough for her to pull him up and over. One great heave, and then Peter collapsed on top of her with a shout.

They lay still for a long moment, breathing hard. Alice felt something wet against her skin. She tilted her head down and saw Peter's face crumpled against her neck. He was crying.

"You're all right," she murmured. "It's okay."

She would have wriggled away, but Peter was still shaking—a bit, Alice thought inappropriately, like a man after sex—and she thought it better to let him have this moment. She laid her head back and closed her eyes, relishing the sweet fatigue that pulsed through her limbs.

Good God. She hadn't felt this sort of pain in a long time. She'd been exhausted, yes, but this throbbing soreness—this screaming reminder that she'd pushed her body to the limit, and hadn't broken; indeed, that she *had* a body that could do what it did—felt good.

She tried to focus on that pleasant burn. Not Peter's warmth against her chest. Not the absurdity of Peter lying on top of her, which was somehow, compared to rock climbing in Hell, the most ridiculous thing about this situation. Not the very weird stir in her gut she felt at his being vulnerable, *depending* on her, and how very unsatisfying this was despite the fact that she'd wished for so long that Peter might reveal to her any weakness at all. But all this did was make him seem human, and the more human Peter seemed, the more he baffled her.

At last his sobs subsided. "I'm sorry." He pulled himself off of her and sat up. "I feel very embarrassed."

"Don't be," Alice murmured, eyes still closed.

"I'm just so afraid. I think I've never been so afraid in my entire life."

"That's natural."

"I think with every move I'm going to fall. Every time I let go I think it's about to be the end."

"It takes a lot to fall." Alice hauled herself up to sitting, then reached out to pat his knee. "Trust your body. You're not going to fall."

What she didn't tell him was how common it was to slip, or how good it felt when you did. The shock of the release. That split-second moment when you lost all touch with the wall, when all your supports gave. The subsequent weightlessness. The thump. Back in Colorado, people were always flinging themselves off the rock wall in various embarrassing positions, just to make their friends laugh.

Sometimes she did it on purpose. She let go when she was nearly at the top of a problem, or let her fingers slide off holds that were designed for beginners. These pleased her the most. They were so firm; convex so as to catch the curve of your fingers. It took real effort to slip off those. You had to want to fall.

She was pleased by the tenuousness of it all. How quick the ground would rise if for one moment you stopped paying attention. If you loosed a breath, made your peace, and just. Let. Go. It felt good, knowing how to fall. Feeling out the worst. Knowing that was an option.

She realized this knowledge was not very helpful at the moment, so she kept it to herself.

"Think you can go again?" She glanced over her shoulder, and just then caught Peter looking at her with the oddest expression on his face.

She couldn't make sense of it. Not wonder, no. Certainly not desire. But a kind of wide-eyed, open-mouthed vulnerability—a childish openness, really, was the best way she could describe it. She didn't like it. It was too familiar. It recalled a version of her, of *them*, that no longer was. It made her feel *things*—and this was unacceptable, because over the last year Alice and Peter had determined the best way to behave around one another was to pretend they were both invulnerable as stone.

The moment stretched—so long, indeed, Alice had opened her mouth, casting about for anything with which to break the silence. But then it passed. Peter blinked down, rubbed his hands across his thighs, then pivoted on his knees to peer down the other side of the wall. "My God."

Alice joined him.

She thought at first that she was gazing upon a sea, for her first impression was of roiling, nauseating movement; a steady churn of mass. *I am dreaming*, she thought. And then, *Oh no, not again.* For this happened sometimes, all the time in fact; when she let her gaze go slack, then all sorts of things started creeping in at the edges, fantastic things: serpents with many heads; wolves devouring the sun. A friend studying neuroscience had told her once that eyesight was largely memory, that your brain saw a pattern and filled in the rest. Alas, Alice's memory bank was bursting at the seams. The mix-and-match mechanism was broken, and her brain filled in patterns with the most inappropriate things. Chalkboards became parking lots. Apple trees became Jesus on the cross. Often she stood in the checkout line at Sainsbury's and saw corpses instead of cabbages on the belt.

But this only happened if she did not concentrate. She was concentrating very hard now, and every time her gaze fell upon a single point, the plane stabilized, and she could make out the contours of a recognizable terrain—mountains and deserts, winding paths, demarcated territories that she hoped numbered eight. Once she blinked, and she saw what seemed like Cambridge from a bird's-eye view; bell towers, college courts, old stone department buildings along cobbled roads. But try as she might she could not sustain her gaze for long. This was not her fault; the landscape was playing with her. It was like standing before an autostereogram illusion. If her eyes shifted focus ever so slightly, then the image transformed. She saw straight paths morph into winding labyrinths. She saw a sprawling terrain morph into a radial pattern. She saw reefs of coral. She saw a shimmering black line that at times seemed to bind the entire plane; but at others, it vanished into a pinprick at the center of a circle, a black hole that pulled everything within it.

Alice tried to focus, to forcefully wrestle Hell into a mappable image. But then she felt an acute pain behind her eyes, and she had to look away.

Peter's palms were pressed against his temples. *Thank God*, thought Alice; *he sees it too.*

"We're going in there." His voice was strained.

"Yes."

He looked wan. "It will swallow us up."

"No, it won't." Alice had no idea what gave her this confidence, except that none of the other sojourner accounts mentioned a carnivalesque fun house terrain. Everyone else had enjoyed a pleasant ramble of the standard Euclidean sort, and it just seemed fair that they should as well.

It was only a problem of perspective, she decided. The mountains she'd grown up climbing had the same effect. The scale could be dizzying. You reached the mountain base and craned your neck to find the peaks, and the ground seemed to fall away behind you. But then you trained your gaze back on the dirt you stood on, and focused on putting one foot in front of another, and before you knew it, you were at the top.

"We only need to get down," she told Peter. For one of them had to keep the cheer; one of them had to be delusional. This was the key to flourishing in graduate school. You could do anything if you were delusional. "I'm sure it's very nice below."

## CHAPTER FOUR

Down-climbing was harder than going up.

For one thing you couldn't see your next foothold and just had to assume that if you shimmied down, then your toes would find something to latch on to. And climbing down was no easier on tired arms, for one expended just as much energy making sure that the downward momentum didn't take you too far.

But Peter fared better this time around. It helped, psychologically, that they were shrinking rather than growing the distance from the ground. It helped also that, halfway to the bottom, he shrugged off his rucksack and let it thump to the ground. "Just books," he panted. "They'll survive."

He tumbled the last meter but landed all in one piece. Alice jumped down beside him and landed sprightly on her feet. This hurt her heels, but she had a silly urge to impress Peter. People in the climbing club were always impressing each other by landing like cats. Sadly, he did not notice.

Hell, on this side of the wall, appeared as a flat, empty field—no Shades, no paths, no shape on the horizon that indicated any place or thing. Gone was that rolling plain. They were stuck again in endless desert, with no clear destination. Alice felt a dull panic at this sight, for they had nothing to show for a whole day's effort, and she hated to ever pause her work without an idea of where to pick up next. But their limbs were jelly, and their brains complete fuzz, and they agreed between them to leave this puzzle for tomorrow.

They made camp in the shadow of the wall. The literature had been split on whether day and night existed in Hell—the more dramatic accounts claimed endless night—but it turned out that the too-dim sun did eventually set, and the air did chill, and about half past six Cambridge time (Alice's watch still worked) everything turned pitch-black. It seemed Hell had no moon, or if it did, she was hiding. They sat alone in the solid dark, and their only comfort was the silence—for if anything lurked beyond, at least they didn't know.

Alice made a small fire with matches and starter kindling. Peter parceled out two sticks of Lembas Bread each. Technically one should have been enough for every eight hours, but they both felt they deserved to chew on something for more than several seconds.

"Thank you." Peter broke the silence. "For earlier. That was—that helped a lot."

"It's nothing."

"You know, I really thought I was going to die." He shook his head. "Dear God. I've never felt so sure I was going to die."

"I wouldn't have let you die," Alice said blithely. The words just rolled off her tongue, since they seemed so obviously the right things to say. Though the moment she heard them out loud, they felt off. Those were easy utterances between loved ones, even between friends—between any two people friendlier than whatever Alice and Peter were right now. There was an implicature of trust. But the problem was, bluntly, that she didn't know if it was true. She suspected Peter didn't know either. "Professor Grimes would be very disappointed, for one thing."

"Well. Can't disappoint Professor Grimes."

For a moment they chewed and swallowed in silence. Lembas Bread had a terrible way of sticking in your mouth. It got up in your gums and under your tongue and made you feel for hours like you'd dragged your open mouth through a sand bank. The only way to get it all out was to swish with liquor, for Lembas Bread dissolved in alcohol, but they had none. Alice wished she could dig a pinkie around her molars—but alas, not in front of Peter. To some fool part of her brain it still mattered that she didn't look childish in front of Peter.

"It's strange, you know." Peter tilted his head back, eyes half-lidded. "Hearing you talk about him."

"Who, the professor?"

It was always Professor Grimes with them. The full word and surname. Not "Grimes," not even "Prof Grimes." Most faculty encouraged their graduate students to address them by their first names—they were colleagues now, their relationship was different, more equal—but Professor Grimes would have recoiled in disgust if they were ever to try calling him Jacob.

"Yeah," said Peter. "I thought you didn't like him all that much."

Alice prickled. "What's that supposed to mean?"

"I—well, nothing in particular. I just thought—I don't know, you always seemed a bit on edge around him. Recently, I mean."

"He's the greatest magician alive. You'd be stupid not to be on edge."

Peter considered this, then nodded. "I didn't mean to imply that your—your relationship was bad. I just thought you weren't too fond of each other. I mean—just in the last term—I suppose it wasn't hard to notice . . ." He trailed off.

Alice blinked down at her hands.

Yes, things had been decidedly chilly between her and Professor Grimes in the weeks leading up to his death. Yes, he had yelled at her once or twice and she had yelled back and the rest of the department had probably noticed. Had probably talked about it when she wasn't there. The thought of their whispers made her insides curdle with shame—and so too did Peter's inquisitive, purportedly concerned face.

"Any private issues aside," she said flatly, "Professor Grimes is my best shot at getting a job."

"No, of course," Peter said quickly. "I mean, same here."

"Oh, please."

"What's that mean?"

"You're Peter Murdoch! Aren't they falling over themselves to hire you?"

Peter hesitated. His mouth opened slightly. Something, clearly, was on the tip of his tongue—but he wouldn't say it, at least not to her.

Alice almost asked him what he'd meant earlier, when he said Professor Grimes was his last chance at this profession. She wished she knew what had happened. Every department in the field had a raging boner for Peter Murdoch. It was open knowledge that second-rate departments had been sniffing around trying to extend an early hire offer ever since he passed his qualifying exams. But she couldn't think of a way to ask this that wasn't nosy, or downright rude.

Perhaps once she might have. But that intimacy had long disappeared. And if she pressed, she knew, he would only vanish.

"Well," he said at last, "I suppose I would have found a new advisor after the Cooke."

Alice's heart stuttered. "You won the Cooke?"

"I only found out last week," he said. "They were delayed in their admissions cycle this year on account of—well, you know. The accident."

Alice found it a bit difficult to breathe just then. Her cheeks burned, and her head felt uncomfortably light. She'd hoped, as an undergraduate, that this intense physiological reaction to jealousy might eventually go away, but as she progressed through graduate school it only grew worse. Every published paper, every conference invitation, elicited a panicked, fight-or-flight response, one that she'd never gotten good at concealing.

So it wasn't her after all; so she'd been wrong to hope.

"Congratulations," she said, ever so lightly, so her voice wouldn't break. "That's marvelous."

"Thank you," said Peter. "I really wasn't sure I'd get it, but I suppose they liked my proposal after all."

"Of course they liked it," she said flatly.

"Sorry, I wasn't trying to brag."

"Of course not."

"I just—it all happened very quickly, so I'm still wrapping my head around it." Peter cleared his throat. "Sorry, that was tactless. I suppose—I guess, if you didn't get it—I mean, I guess they just didn't want a linguist this year. Er—I mean, not as a slight against linguists. But you know what I mean."

*Oh, fuck you*, thought Alice.

The previous year she had applied for, and expected to win, the prestigious Cooke Fellowship for dissertation research. The Cooke Fellowships, founded a century ago by a widow of one of the founding theoreticians of English magick, were incredibly prestigious. They offered not only ample funding for summer travel to anywhere in the world, but also a procession of dinners and cocktail parties before and after with the Cooke family descendants. The descendants were invariably insufferable, but the parties were well attended because no one liked to say no to free food, and so this let you rub elbows with the academic elite for weeks on end. Cooke Fellows could only be nominated by senior members of the Royal Academy of Magick, whose ranks included Professor Grimes.

"You'll get the Cooke," he had assured her, all those months ago. "Oh, they'll love you. You'll be the best candidate they've seen in years. They've been dying to nominate a woman—you're a shoo-in." And since back then Alice still believed every word out of his mouth, she spent days after that conversation delirious with glee.

But then some months passed, and Professor Grimes had started changing the subject every time she brought it up. She tried to do it with subtlety. She would mention another research opportunity and follow it up with, "Though I suppose it'll conflict with the Cooke." But all he ever gave her was evasive nods and murmurs. "We'll see," he said. "It's always a coin toss." And then, later on, "You know, the Cooke's very competitive." And later than that, "I heard they're not overfond of linguists."

Around the time the Cooke short list was supposed to be announced, she began checking her pidge three times a day. Funny how when something enormous was at stake you refused to believe the evidence of your own eyes. Every day she stared into that empty cubbyhole and tried to convince herself that all her perceptions were wrong; that if she only stared hard enough, a thick purple envelope would materialize amidst the dust. She jumped whenever the phone rang. She eavesdropped on faculty meetings. She was triggered by the very mention of the word "Cooke," which made conversations about food very difficult.

She felt so stupid now. Of course it hadn't gone to her.

She wanted something to hurt him with then. Peter knew what he'd done, throwing that in her face. He ought to know how it felt.

"I thought about a new advisor too." She tried to sound very casual. "I mean, Grimes did introduce me to some colleagues while we were in Italy. I thought about reaching out after the accident, but Europe really isn't my first choice for a degree. They're all so—postmodernist over there, don't you think?"

It worked. Peter went rigid—only subtly, but she could sense the shift. He took the bait. "When were you in Italy?"

"Last summer," said Alice. "It was a very last-minute thing. I'm not sure what happened. But Professor Grimes called me to his office one morning and told me to have all my things packed by Friday."

She knew full well what had happened. Everyone knew Peter was supposed to accompany Professor Grimes to Rome for the biannual *Arcana* conference. But Peter, Professor Grimes grumbled, had not been feeling well as of late. "Unreliable," he'd muttered; which Alice delighted to hear, since she had been waiting for everyone else to catch on to this for years. "Something's going on with that kid. He's out. It's yours, Alice, if you want it."

"I'll pack tonight," Alice had breathed. She'd felt so lucky then that she didn't even bother to wonder why he hadn't picked her for the trip in the first place, or what was going on with Peter, or indeed whether perhaps someone should check up on Peter. Professor Grimes had that effect. If he got you alone, if he said even a slightly flattering word, everything else melted away.

It was, indeed, a glorious summer in Italy. Alice and Professor Grimes made not one crucial breakthrough in the field, but three. She came home tanned, well-fed, and beaming with attention and praise. It was the peak of her career at Cambridge, and she wanted Peter to know precisely what he'd missed.

She couldn't tell if it worked. Peter's expression was decidedly—calculatedly?—neutral.

"It sounds like it was a very nice trip."

"Thank you," Alice said primly. "It really was."

"I just thought . . ." Peter coughed. "Never mind. I'm glad you got to go."

Silence hung between them. Alice should have been satisfied, but she felt sillier and sillier as the seconds trickled past. It was very clear now what they'd both done, and she felt supremely childish about it.

They both broke the silence at once.

"Honestly, let's just—"

"Look, Law, maybe we should—"

They stared at each other.

"I don't want to make things awkward," said Peter.

"Oh, were things awkward?"

He brushed this off. "Suppose we bracket all problems for the living. We can't fight down here, Law, we've got to trust each other. We're all we have."

She sniffed. "Fair enough."

"Look, I *am* sorry I brought up the Cooke."

"And I'm sorry I brought up Italy." Alice felt so tired then. To be alone, with Peter Murdoch, in Hell—she didn't know how much more of this she could take. She unzipped her rucksack and dug around the bottom until she found her camping blanket. "Suppose we just shut up and go to sleep."

"What's that?" Peter asked.

"A hypothermia blanket." Alice unfolded the aluminum squares and arranged it over her legs. "It insulates body heat. I borrowed it from one of the residents."

One advantage Alice had in Hell was that she knew how to pack for long journeys; knew exactly which shoes and rucksacks she needed to last for days on her feet. Cooking gear—no, she had Lembas Bread. Warm layers—yes. Chalk and knives—absolutely, yes. She'd been quite outdoorsy before she came to England. At Cornell, she'd spent most weekends doing gorge trails. She'd grown up in the Rockies. She had hiked Yosemite and the Appalachian Trail without help. This was what had convinced her she could make the trip. She'd done the White Mountains. How much worse could Hell be?

Though in truth, it all felt like reaching into a previous life. Alice had not been hiking in such a long time. Nor climbing, to be honest. She'd had so many hobbies before she started at Cambridge. She used to know what fresh air felt like. All this time in Grimes's lab had turned her into a ghoul that lived on canned soups and crackers. And she'd been stunned, after digging through to the very bottom of her closet, that she still had the hiking bag at all.

"Very cool." Peter settled back, resting his head on his rucksack. He folded his hands over his chest.

She stared at him. "You didn't bring a blanket?"

"I guess I forgot."

"Didn't you consider sleeping?"

"Well, I've slept in the lab plenty before, remember? We didn't need blankets then."

"Murdoch, it's freezing." Alice sat up. A part of her already regretted this, but she felt she had to offer. He was too pathetic otherwise. "Do you want to share?"

"Ah—well, it looks rather small."

"It folds out further." She lifted up an edge. "See?"

He blinked, considering. "I'll just slide my legs under."

"You sure?"

"That'll keep me warm enough."

"Whatever suits you."

Peter scooted toward her. There was the requisite awkward fumbling of limbs, of shuffling into a determination of boundaries both physical and emotional, but at last they settled into an arrangement that minimally covered Peter's lower half but did not bring their bodies unbearably close.

"Well, good night," said Peter.

"Good night," Alice mumbled.

Alice had always struggled to sleep when camping. She didn't like being out in the open at night, without at least five solid walls separating her and the things that wanted to eat her. And she should have been even more anxious out here; under Hell's moonless, starless sky; with who-knows-what lurking in the dunes. But exhaustion trumped all—and to be honest, so too did the even, steady rhythm of Peter's breath, familiar as a lullaby. Very soon she was fast asleep, and miraculously, for the first time in many months, she did not dream.

EVERYONE TOLD MAGICIANS IN TRAINING TO at least consider careers in other fields before they went on the job market. "Alt academia," they called it, like it was some punk and rebellious lifestyle, like failing at the single thing you'd been trained to do made you cool. But halfway into her degree, Alice felt that anything but magick was simply not an option. She became a tenured magician, or she died. She could envision no life worth living otherwise.

Besides, no one really meant it when they said alt academia was *just as prestigious* (or, more commonly, that there was *no shame in it, really*). They meant it even less when they emphasized that alt academia paid better, had kinder hours, was less stressful, gave you better job security, made you happier. *Oh, magicians do really well in consulting*, they said. *Employers like critical thinking and problem-solving skills*, they said. *Fewer people die in industry*, they said.

These aphorisms were uttered by tenured professors who had already caught the golden goose, who could comfortably know they would never face the terrors their students now did. "Oh, he took a job in industry," they would say, as if "industry" here was a euphemism like a farm for old sick dogs. And they said it with a kind, patronizing lilt that betrayed what they truly meant: alt academia meant failure. The life of the mind, unfettered from commerce, was the only kind worth living.

Of course one could demand why anyone would put themselves through such nonsense in the first place. But here most academics' thought processes mirrored the logic of Pascal's Wager, whether they realized it or not. Pascal's Wager said that you could choose to believe in God or not, but if you bet wrong on God and didn't live as though he existed, you were missing out on the infinite wonder of Heaven. Similarly, you could choose to believe the job market would work out for you or not, but if you bet wrong and opted out of the cycle, you were missing out on the infinite miracles of the Life of the Mind. Now, like in the case of Heaven, no one in Alice's generation had yet experienced this Miraculous Life of the Mind, but all their professors assured them it was possible and so they plodded along.

Alice had also known, before she matriculated to do a PhD in analytic magick at Cambridge, that Professor Jacob Grimes was perhaps not everyone's first choice for an advisor. Her undergraduate advisor at Cornell, a kindly junior scholar named Dr. Mills, had been doubtful when she first presented him her list.

"You seem very set on going abroad," he had said.

"Well, here they've fired all the Communists."

"Fair enough," said Dr. Mills. "Still, I'd go to England over France. Everything seems a good fit except for Grimes."

"He's the best in the world at linguistic magick," said Alice.

"Oh, his work is excellent," said Dr. Mills. "No one's questioning that. Only it's rumored his graduate students aren't very, ah, happy."

"What does that mean?"

"Well—he's quite hard on them, for the first thing. They tend to burn out quite fast. He doesn't have a very good completion rate."

"How bad is it?"

"I'd say about half don't finish."

Alice, who up until then had been blessed with kind and helpful professors, didn't know how bad an advisor really could be. She thought, then, that if you didn't get along with a professor, that was your fault. She thought, simply, that she would make sure she was in the half that *did* finish.

"But I want to work with the best in the field," she said. "I want to get a job."

This, Dr. Mills could understand. Good jobs in magick were increasingly hard to find. Every starry-eyed undergraduate wanted to become a magician, but the market was simply not good. On both sides of the Atlantic the conservatives were several years in power, and this meant funding cuts for universities, shrinking departments, vanishing opportunities. Most schools had stopped offering magicians tenure when it became apparent that their researchers were more interested in the trivial and esoteric than producing anything useful or profitable or at least somewhat resembling the next nuclear weapon. It was the age of technological revolutions, of quantum physics and cable television with more than three channels and personal computers. Magick had been left behind. Magick was good only for dinner parties. Magick did not get you hired.

And there was no magick without the academy. Universities supplied the chalk, the syllabaries, the pentagram repositories. Universities published the journals, which determined which spells were valid and which ones weren't. Of course there was such a thing as hedge witches—typically PhD students who'd failed out, terminal masters, or college graduates who had never gotten into a graduate program at all. And they weren't entirely bereft of resources—many hedge witches scrounged up their own chalk, and organized amateur conferences, and published in poorly rated journals about their wonderful discoveries. In fact, some of these discoveries were quite interesting. The open secret, really, was that sometimes the hedge witches found stuff that even tenured professors couldn't imagine. But none of it was going to be published in *Arcana*, and so none of it had credibility.

"I'll write you the best recommendation I can," Dr. Mills had said. "You have a good shot everywhere you apply—I'd feel good in your shoes. But do be careful, Alice. At this stage it seems like all that could possibly matter is getting in. Remember there is more at stake than your advisor's approval, however. And there's more to life than magick."

Rich advice, Alice thought, from a man who was well on his way to tenure. She filed these words under "platitudes from adults who think they know better than you," and then she promptly forgot them.

At Cambridge, the warnings redoubled. Graduate students, even those who weren't studying magick, cast her sympathetic looks when she explained she was here to work with Grimes. Other faculty members went out of their way to ask if she was coping all right. And then there was Professor Grimes's only other woman advisee, Olivia Kincaid, a puffy girl who seemed always to be crying during the first year Alice was at Cambridge and then was curiously absent during her second. By Alice's third, when Olivia should have graduated, she was bizarrely still in coursework.

"He is a monster," Olivia told her in no uncertain terms over many pints of ale the first night they met. "He is simply a sociopath."

"How so?" asked Alice.

"You'll find out soon enough," Olivia said, vaguely and dramatically, which impelled Alice to write her off as a drama queen.

Olivia took medical leave her fourth year, returned for three weeks of coursework, and then promptly disappeared. No one in the department had ever heard from her again.

Other students recoiled when Alice revealed who her advisor was, and she observed their fear with an immodest thrill. Though she would never admit it, the idea of working with someone dangerous excited her. Alice had dazzled her way through years of higher education by being a teacher's pet; by miraculously succeeding where others had failed. She relished the thought that her advisor might be harsh, impatient, even cruel to others—for that made his attentions to her worth all the more. She liked being the exception to the rule. Favoritism was well and fine if she was the favorite.

Anyhow, Professor Grimes's cruelty was not random. You only had to try hard enough, to grind through sleepless nights, to meet his every impossible standard so that he considered you worthy of respect. This was fair. Wasn't that just how academia worked? How any competitive industry worked? The best students got the best jobs.

Alice, for much of her graduate career, considered Professor Grimes a necessary trial. What didn't kill you made you stronger—or at least gave you a thicker skin. For most of her life she had been first in her class, and she saw no reason why the PhD should be different. She only had three more years to go—and then two, then one—she only had to rub the sleep from her eyes and take a deep breath and survive every day and ignore every inconvenient truth until she had her diploma, until she was free.

And she'd nearly made it, too. That's what made this whole mess that much more frustrating. The staircase had nearly held. She'd almost survived what no one believed she could, had almost tasted the rewards. If only she'd lasted just a little bit longer. She'd been so, so close.

## CHAPTER FIVE

Alice awoke to Peter's arm slung over her chest.

She registered this and, before throwing it off, lay there for a moment, considering. It did not feel terrible. Hell got very cold at night, and the warmth Peter emanated—she'd forgotten how hot he could get; really, he was a proper furnace—was rather nice. She shifted slightly, just to work out a kink in her neck, and decided she may as well lie there a bit longer. She was really quite comfortable. The sun wasn't up yet. A sleeping, silent Peter was less annoying than a waking, talking Peter. And it was the first morning in a long while that she hadn't woken up to dry-heave from stress. The enormity of the problem, the mess of conflicting reports, the piles of scrolls left to decipher, the sense of a clock ticking down. That was done. The research bore fruit, it had all *worked*, she'd made it to Hell. Now all she had to do was survive it.

Something hard dug against her thigh.

"Jesus!"

She scrambled away, yanking the blanket off them both.

Peter awoke with a panicked, "What? What?" Then he glanced down at his lap and yelped. "Fuck—I am so sorry—"

"It's fine." Alice's cheeks burned. She wanted to fan herself, but that would only make her look like a panicked Victorian lady, so instead she pressed her palms against her cheeks. A dizzying wave passed through her temples. Peter sat with both hands covering his crotch, and this only made things worse, because it drew attention to the thing and now they couldn't not talk about it. "It's fine, just please—"

"We don't have control over it," said Peter. "I mean—men. It just happens sometimes, when we're asleep—I didn't meant to—I mean, I'm so sorry, I really—"

Alice dragged her palms down her face. If only she could melt the flesh off her skull. "Don't *worry* about it."

"It's not you," said Peter. "Really—it's not even sexual—I mean, it's just an instinct—"

*Instincts are often sexual*, whispered the part of Alice's brain that had sat through all those seminars on Freud, but she shut this down. "Yes, I'm aware."

"I don't think about you like that, truly. I haven't ever—"

"I'm sure." She had a terrible urge to punch him, accompanied by an even more terrible urge to wail as loud as she could. Neither seemed appropriate, so she settled for a muted, keening sound into her palms. "I know how male anatomy works, Murdoch. Please. It's fine."

"I would never disrespect you on purpose." Peter seemed about to cry. "Never, *ever*—"

"Stop," she gasped. "Please, can we just—can we eat some breakfast."

"Yes. Breakfast." Peter reached for his foil of Lembas Bread, grabbed it by the wrong end, and spilled food all over the gray sand. He stared at it in dismay.

"It's fine," Alice choked. "Have some of mine."

They sat opposite one another and chewed, blinking very much and saying nothing. There was nothing to look at on the monotonous desert plane, so Alice could only stare into space if she wanted to avoid Peter's eye, which she could not do without being very obvious about it. Instead she concentrated on her Lembas Bread. Cardboard. Mm.

It was an excruciating morning.

Somehow Alice had not given much thought to the daily indignities of the journey, and she had not accounted for daily hygiene, let alone daily functions in the presence of another. They packed their things and freshened up in silence. Peter had to pee, and Alice had to do the other thing, which she piled sand over like an embarrassed cat. She reflected on the horrors of embodiment. In many ways, she thought, the Shades had it much better.

Finally Peter broke the silence. "Maybe—maybe we should think about charting the rest of our way."

"Hm?"

"Through Hell, that is."

"Oh—yes, all right."

He pulled a notebook out of his rucksack and began fumbling through the pages. "Honestly, I didn't expect to get this far. I really hoped he'd be in the fields."

"I did too." Alice brushed the crumbs off her lap and then reached into her rucksack for her own notes. "But I've got some maps drawn up . . ."

"Me too." Peter turned his notebook around to show her. "Suppose we head for the Court of Desire first?"

"Desire's the Second Court."

"Yes, but I think we can skip over the first, don't you?"

"I've no idea how we would do that." Alice peered down at his notes, frowning. Peter's map of Hell looked bizarrely like a pizza. An anus, really. He'd circled in red a dot at the center, with courts branching off all around and arrows pointing in all directions. "What map is that based on?"

"The Orpheus map," said Peter. "Penhaligon's reprint. Find the center, where all the courts converge . . . which means we're looking for something like a mountain, something elevated. The Sumeru Throne, as it were. And then we can simply make for the court we need, instead of wasting our time going in order."

"Oh, Murdoch, that map is trash."

"How do you mean? Everyone cites Orpheus."

"Orpheus was mad with loss," said Alice. "He was driven solely by longing for Eurydice."

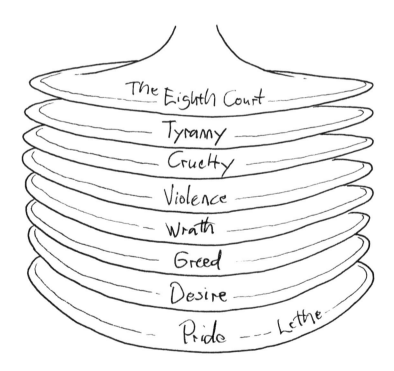

"So?"

"So he didn't care about anything around him. From his perspective of course it was a straight line to wherever Eurydice ended up because that's how it went in his mind's eye. That map is worthless. It's a fantasy of grief."

Peter lowered his notebook, deflated. But this was a virtue of Peter's—he wasn't an asshole when proven wrong. "How do you figure, then?"

"I subscribe to the accumulative theory." Alice flipped to her own maps to demonstrate. "That is, the courts proceed in order of karmic severity. First Pride, then Desire, then Greed, et cetera and onward. Now, there's some disagreement over whether one sin really entails all the lesser ones. For instance, if you're guilty of wrath, do you necessarily need to be punished for pride? Does greed entail desire? Is it all a nesting doll of wrongdoing, or can you skip over some courts? It's not clear to me how the judges handle that. But it does seem that you've at least got to travel in order. And when you've passed, you get to cross the Lethe over to Lord Yama's throne."

Alice tapped a black line running round the edge of the courts. "The river Lethe runs perpendicular to all eight courts and marks the boundary of reincarnation. So Hell looks less like a pizza anus—"

"Excuse me?"

"And more like," she continued without clarification, "I don't know, a Möbius strip. The Lethe bounds all. You're trapped on this plane until you're done. And then you go somewhere beyond. Makes sense?"

Peter rubbed his chin. "May I see?"

"Go on."

He hummed as he flipped through her notes. "Where did you find all this?"

"The Dunhuang cave texts."

```
                        THE EIGHTH COURT
                        ─────────────────
                           TYRANNY
                        ─────────────────
                           CRUELTY
                        ─────────────────
  KING    ⋛            VIOLENCE
  YAMA'S  LETHE         ─────────────────
  DOMAIN                  WRATH
          ⋛            ─────────────────
                           GREED
                        ─────────────────
                           DESIRE
                        ─────────────────
                           PRIDE
```

"I couldn't find any translations of the Dunhuang cave texts."

"There aren't any. You just don't have any Asian languages."

"Fair enough." Peter read a while longer, tracing his finger over each page. It made Alice oddly nostalgic to see him bobbing his head as he went along, making sense of her furious scrawls. They used to do this in the lab—show each other their wildest ideas, and offer each other proof they weren't insane. She had missed Peter's mind. It was like wearing a parachute—she could trust that he'd catch any mistakes she'd made.

At last he said, "I think this checks out."

"Thank you."

"But that's consistent with my map," Peter continued. "That is—it's just an oversimplified version of my map, if we take Hell as non-Euclidean."

Alice had only been to one lecture about non-Euclidean geometries, and what she remembered was a lot of diagrams of potato chips and coral reefs. "I don't know what you mean."

"Suppose it's less like a . . . what'd you say, a pizza anus? Less like that, and more of—well, a spiral." He drew a diagram below hers to demonstrate.

"Suppose we're in hyperbolic space," he said. "Take the parallel postulate out of Euclidean geometry, and assume we are dealing with negative curvature. Then we might visualize the courts as a twisted pseudosphere, bounded on the outside, but infinite on the inside—"

"But we're not *in* hyperbolic space," said Alice. She did not know much about hyperbolic space, but this at least seemed obvious. "We'd *know*, we'd see all sorts of—of freaky coral patterns around us, we wouldn't be walking on this flat plane—"

"Actually no," said Peter. "That's the point. When you're inside it, of course it's going to look like a flat plane. We see the freaky coral because we're three-dimensional beings visu-

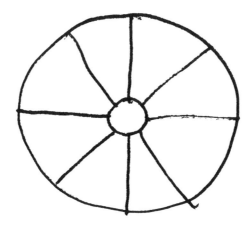

alizing two-dimensional hyperbolic space. But we're not four-dimensional beings, so we can't actually *see* the wonkiness of three-dimensional hyperbolic space. Curved lines appear straight to us."

"Oh, stop it." As always, mathematics induced in Alice the acute urge to weep. "What's the *point*?"

"The point is that we could just head to this peak here." Peter tapped the top of the spiral. "The center of Hell, the point that oversees the rest of the Eight Courts.

"Sure," said Alice. "*If* that point exists. *If* this is hyperbolic space. Which we don't know."

"I think we probably do, though," said Peter. "I mean, how else to make sense of that weird view from above?"

"But that wasn't a pseudosphere, that was just chthonic flux."

"I don't think so, Law. I interpret that as Hell signaling its geometry."

Alice was unconvinced. "I interpret that as Hell screwing with us. It's just as likely."

They stared at the notebooks. This was an impasse. Two maps, and no good reason to prefer one over the other.

"I wish I could measure the speed of light here," Peter said unhappily. "And also the size of the known chthonic universe."

"Very helpful," said Alice. It was clear to her now they would have to decide on pragmatics. If she let Peter go on, then he'd while away the day speculating about geometry. "I think we should go in order."

Peter groaned. "But that's such a waste of time."

"So is hiking to a mythical peak whose existence is uncertain!"

"The peak is a shortcut. The peak keeps us from turning up every stone in the lower rocks—it lets us see everything at once, and then just—I don't know, jump there—"

"Fine," said Alice. "Say your peak exists. Where would you

jump to? What sins do you think he's committed?"

A silence. For once Peter had no easy rejoinder. They were both thinking, then, of undergraduates burned to a crisp, and whether that counted as murder, or just as lying. They were thinking of Olivia Kincaid and Elspeth Bayes and all the students who never graduated. They were thinking of everything Professor Grimes had done over his storied career and everything they didn't know about. And Alice, for one, was thinking of cold laughter, fingers digging into her shoulder, hot breath on her face, a burning in her skin.

"Well," Peter said lightly. "That's just the question."

For a moment neither of them spoke. They did not want to answer that question. They did not even want to crack it open. To do so would involve a great number of admissions. And Alice, at least, was not ready to make those admissions.

"I think we should search them all." Alice hugged her arms against her chest. "Let's—let's just be thorough."

Peter looked as though he wanted to say something else. But a moment passed, and he deflated. "Fine." He closed the notebooks. "We'll have to move fast, then. We only have seven days. That's fewer than one for each court."

"How do you figure seven days? I have twice that."

"Well, Hecate's scrolls—"

"Hecate's scrolls imply that mortals can only last in Hell for seven days before they expire due to bodily needs," said Alice. "I interpret that as concerns about food and water, and not a strict limit."

"Interesting." Peter frowned. "I translated it as the limitation of the soul."

"If she meant the limitation of the soul, she would have said so," said Alice. "It's a distinct term in the Greek. There's textual evidence from books eight, ten, and twelve—"

"Okay, okay." Peter held up his hands. "You're right."

"Anyhow, since Hecate could not have predicted the innovations of Lembas Bread or Perpetual Flasks, we know we can survive for far longer than she supposed," said Alice. "You shouldn't take seriously anyone who's expressed an opinion on food before the twentieth century."

"No, you're right." Peter nodded thoughtfully. "I've never thought about texts like this before."

"What, in terms of close reading?"

"I just mean—I don't know, taking into account when they were written, and the author's social context, and such."

"Historicization, Murdoch. That's what we call it. What, do you just take everything you read at face value?"

"I mean, if the math checks out."

"Unbelievable," said Alice. "This is why everyone hates logicians."

"It's a *compliment*, Law. I am showing you some disciplinary respect."

"Well, don't bother," she said, though she did feel a stupid flutter in her chest. Lab work used to be like this, she thought. Peter's jabs, her rebuttals; two different methodologies clashing until, always, they settled on some compromise that was closer to the truth. Oh, but this hurt—she had not realized how much she had missed this. "It's condescending."

In short order they packed up camp and shoved everything into their rucksacks. Alice stretched and winced as she stood. She'd forgotten how much climbing could ravage one's muscles. She hurt all over, and her knees buckled when she stepped. She'd really mistreated her body these last few months; she'd hardly slept, she'd barely eaten, she certainly hadn't exercised. She hoped the remaining trials of Hell would be more metaphysical than physical. She ought to have done a push-up at least.

Peter cleared his throat. "By the way, Law?"

She noticed with alarm that his face had turned the shade of moss. He looked like he was trying to swallow his own tongue.

"I just . . . want you to know that I respect you very much."

Alice wished the ground would swallow them both up. "Oh, don't do this."

"As well as your bodily integrity. And I am very sorry to do anything that makes you feel uncomfortable."

"My God, Murdoch, please—"

"Therefore, I feel—I mean, I think it is best that we do not share the blanket anymore. I will simply bear the cold. I shall not mind the chill, if I am asleep. I think anything is tolerable when one is asleep. And if there is anything I can do to make you feel safer—I mean, that is, more comfortable around me—"

"Murdoch." She pressed her hands against her face. How unfair this was, she thought. As if she had never seen him asleep. As if she had not curled in next to him many times, their breathing deep in matching rhythm, both of them murmuring about stars and numbers until their conjectures bled over into dreams. It used to be so easy. Yet here they were, negotiating space like strangers. "Shut. Up."

He did not. "We can even sleep in shifts, if you like. Take turns. Whatever makes you—oh, God." His eyes went wide. He pointed. "The wall."

Alice turned. The mass of bones was growing translucent before her eyes. She reached out, panicked, and her fingers went right through bone, as if the wall were nothing more than a shimmering mirage. It lingered several seconds more and then faded away completely, so that they were once again surrounded on all sides by endless, gray silt.

"There is no way out," Alice murmured. This was the opening epigraph to Penhaligon's treatise. She had skimmed over it during her first read-through, figuring this was just another one of Penhaligon's attempts at poetry. But it turned out this was literally just how Hell worked. "No way out but through."

This made sense, in theory. Souls that had passed bureaucratic clearance should not get to wander willy-nilly back into the Fields of Asphodel. It would throw the accounting all out of joint. You couldn't just decide you didn't like being punished and nope back out into Limbo. Alice should have anticipated this, but still it frightened her, the fact that their paths were erasing themselves behind them. It made the stakes permanent. Either they succeeded, or they died.

Yet even as the wall disappeared, gray tendrils of mist poured out of the ground and swirled inquisitively around them—darting around their forms as if sentient, as if listening to their thoughts and feelings to get a sense of who they were and what they had come for. Then the tendrils swirled back into the fold, where they coalesced and spiraled, shuddering as if to a magician's drumbeat before his great reveal, before dispersing to the sides like curtains swinging open. Here, said Hell. Have a look at this.

"Is that . . . ?" Peter tilted his head up, following a bell tower into the orange sky. "That's impossible."

"But Hell adapts to us," Alice murmured. Penhaligon's scattered appendix on Hell and temporality had not been clear to her until now. "Hell is a mirror."

The Eight Courts of Hell reflected the world of the living. Nearly all the ancient mythologies converged on this principle. So many ancient rituals were conducted as if in Hell, all the patterns of life continued on. Mourners put coins under the tongues of their dead so as to pay their passage; they buried them with favorite pets and treasures. The recently deceased soul was disoriented by his tearing from life. Hell had to resemble the familiar, otherwise he could never move on.

This theory, though not universally accepted, did explain

why Dante's Hell involved all the poets and artists and politicians he was personally familiar with over his lifetime. And why paintings of the Buddhist hells displayed all the ritual trappings of Chinese palaces: gardens and pools and harems of concubines. And why both Greek and Mesopotamian visions of the afterlife involved neat, orderly systems of justices, gatekeepers, and accountants armed with records and scales, processing lines of the dead the same way passport offices process citizens. At the end of the day, human beings preferred the predictable order of their known bureaucracies. One's sins took on meaning in the context of their moral universe, comprised of their loved ones, their idols, their rivals, their victims. Dante saw philosophers and politicians. Aeneas saw ghosts of warriors past. One was hurt most by what one knew. If Alice had to guess, Professor Grimes's moral universe—the full accounting of things that delighted him, the things that brought him pain, and the people by whom he could do wrong—did not stretch beyond the Cambridge station.

So perhaps they should have expected, then, for Hell to take on a most familiar landscape: Gothic towers, courtyard walls, and winding between them, a single paved path—just wide enough for pedestrians and cyclists, not wide enough for cars. You always knew, stepping into such places, what they were for. You knew precisely where you were from the uniformity of design; the same shades of brick and stone across buildings. You knew from the lack of wide streets and shop signs; from the quiet absence of children. You knew from the arched gates that marked the boundary. Fairy gates, signaling departure. The mundane world ended here. These were not places of leisure or business. These were places to be still, to think, and to step out of time.

"Christ," said Peter. "Hell is a campus."

# On Reincarnation

*The one thing on which all Tartarologists can agree is that Hell prepares souls for reincarnation.*

*The Eight Courts of Hell are not arenas of eternal punishment. For one thing, this would be wildly unjust. No sins, no matter how heinous, deserve an eternity of punishment. That would be disproportionate; the math does not check out. For another, the universe needs balance. As Socrates put it, "If the living were to be born from the other world, and the living were dying all the time, what would there be to prevent everything being used up in death?" When it comes to death, the Christians are right about the immortality of the soul but wrong about everything else. Here the Pythagoreans, the Platonists, the Buddhists and Daoists, the Manichaeans, the Jains and Sikhs and Hindus, have a better grasp of things. Living and dying are two sides of the same coin. It makes more sense to conceptualize souls as continuously flowing from one world to another than to think everything that ever lived is forever accruing in an underworld tomb.*

*In the 1960s, the philosopher Michael Huemer argued for the plausibility of reincarnation on probabilistic grounds that most scholars have now come to accept. According to Huemer, we have reason to believe that time stretches infinitely into the past and into the future. If time is infinite, the probability that our singular lifetime happens at this very moment, at this very speck on the line, vanishes toward zero. So either time is finite, or we live more lives than one. Huemer argues it is at least plausible that the past is not finite, so we have decent evidence to believe in eternal recurrence. Theologists and religious studies folks do not like this argument for the same reasons they don't like Pascal's Wager, which is that it seems to mathematically cheat to conclusions that religions have taken thousands of years to articulate.*

*Magicians love it.*

*Theories of reincarnation overlap nicely with theories of eternal recurrence, an idea championed by both Friedrich Nietzsche and the Pythagoreans. Broadly understood, eternal recurrence argues that the events of the universe are fated—or doomed—to repeat themselves over and over again, for there is a finite amount of energy and material in an infinite universe, over an infinite amount of time, and the combinations with which they can interact are finite as well. The eternal hourglass of existence, so to speak, turns over time and time again. We are reborn to flow with the sand.*

*Unfortunately, scholarly consensus only goes this far. Tartarologists disagree wildly over how reincarnation works. How long must one wait before rebirth? Is rebirth familial—does your dead grandmother become your daughter? Do karmic goodness and badness accrue over time, so that the virtuous live better and better lives? Can one ever escape the cycle of reincarnation, as the Buddhists hope? Can human souls be reborn into animal bodies? For that matter, do animals have souls at all? We know memories are washed clean between lives, for there is no record of anyone credibly remembering a past life. We know very little else for certain.*

*Most baffling of all is the question of punishment. What purpose does it serve? Is it rehabilitative—must we only suffer until we've learned our lessons? Is it retributive—must we balance the karmic scales, lose an eye for an eye, and suffer as much as the suffering we wrought? How many hours in pits of boiling water balance out a murder? Is punishment a form of contrapasso, as Dante describes, wherein punishments arise from the nature of the sin itself and represent wrongdoing's poetic opposite? Does punishment entail the universalization of broken maxims, as Kant theorized? Is Hell one great metaphysical manifestation of the Golden Rule?*

*The only thing we know for certain is that souls in the Underworld eventually travel, in some shape or form, to the domain of Lord Yama—that is, Hades, Anubis, King of the Dead, Lord of the Underworld, Judge of Life and Death, or however else one wishes to perceive him. As with many concepts in magick, Lord Yama is defined more by absence of proof than proof itself. He is a concept that stands in for what we do not know. He could be a rational agent, fair and just, a philosopher-king of the chthonic realm. He could be a demon, volatile and capricious. He could be imperceivable divinity, which in these circles is code for "no one's published on this."*

*For all our theories and stories and myths, Lord Yama's design remains an utter mystery. No one knows for certain what precisely happens in those courts, or why; least of all the Shades within them. If it is a test, no one knows how to pass. If it is mere torture, no one knows how long it will go on for. One cannot anticipate, cheat, or find a shortcut through redemption. We cross the Lethe and reincarnate whenever Hell deems us ready. It happens when it happens. Until then, we get what's coming.*

## CHAPTER SIX

Alice felt a little thrill passing under that gate.

She had always delighted in starting a new term at a new institution—elementary, middle, high school, college, and at last Cambridge. She liked learning her way around the buildings, getting library access, nestling into tucked-away study nooks, finding her favorite shortcuts between her department and the dormitories. She liked becoming a person that befit the institution. With each new matriculation you had the chance to reinvent yourself, to deserve your place there. And now Alice felt, though she knew this was dangerous, an instinctive want to fit into this place.

If Hell was just another institution, then it couldn't be so bad. It wasn't even a city university, which would have involved horrifying things like shopping malls and subway stations. No brutalist eyesores here. Hell was ancient in the comforting way, an Old World campus, neoclassical pales over American reds. There were no trees or grassy lawns, for nothing grew down here, but that was all right; the silt was arranged in its own elegant manner. All told, this current Hell was rather pleasant. And she would have thought she was right back above, save for the quiet.

It was the absence of undergraduates, she decided. It was undergraduates who made a university come alive, with their clumsy hustle, their self-importance and newfound freedom. Undergraduates were fresh blood. They asked questions. They brought ideas, and when they couldn't come up with ideas they at least brought problems. Without their chatter, campus was frightfully still. But even this failed to frighten Alice as it should have. It had been so loud in her mind for so long. She liked the quiet.

"You might be right," said Peter.

"What?"

"It might be progressive," he conceded. "It might be there's only one way forward."

Alice saw what he was seeing. Unlike other campuses, there was no crisscrossing of roads and shortcuts. There was only the one path, and when Alice tried to trace where it led, she found that most of the campus blurred in her vision, undeniably present, but pushed to the background. All she could see in detail was a round building directly before them, several stories tall, its sides ringed with columns, and its top curving into a dome. There were no windows, only plinths, and atop each stood robed statues of scholarly affect.

You cannot go back and forth, Hell informed them. You cannot jump this queue. You can only proceed in order. The First Court, and then the others.

"The map's decided, then," said Alice. "We'll go one by one."

So they strode up to the building and pulled open the heavy doors of the First Court, Superbia, the Court of Pride.

PRIDE WAS A LIBRARY.

In fact, Pride had everything Alice liked in a library. Pride had pale marble tiles and polished wooden shelves; high ceilings and sloping walls; lovely stained-glass patterns of vaguely religious imagery; leather reading chairs with generous backs. Pride had leather spines arranged not on flimsy plastic shelves nor Erector set metal, but heavy wooden cases. The best libraries were like the best churches: old and musty, preindustrial.

Everyone knew that the nicer a library was, the better the work you did within it. Nice libraries meant donors, meant support, meant the time and resources to accumulate the best collections. More important, nice libraries put you in a certain frame of mind. You could unpack the precise same set of archives in the Rad Cam or a nondescript warehouse, and still you'd do better work in the Rad Cam. The atmosphere mattered. You became the thinker the library expected you to be. Nice libraries whispered: Everyone who has passed through here is very important, and so are you.

How bad could Hell be, if it housed a place like this? Alice wondered. The doors opened to stacks upon stacks, shelves stretching in every direction, and researchers bustling about with arms piled over with manuscripts. There was no screaming, no hissing or flaying of skin. The books looked normal, smelled normal; even had normal titles, written in English, on subjects that had nothing obviously to do with death. The air was just a bit too chilly, like in all university libraries, but otherwise it was quite comfortable. There were even green, softly lit banker's lamps of the sort that always induced contentment in Alice's brain. For a moment she had a terrible fear that Hell had been a hallucination, that she'd fallen asleep in the stacks and was now right back where she'd started. But then she saw the Shades passing straight through shelves, their bodies solidifying only when they reached to take down a book and flip through its pages.

"It's nicer than expected." Peter peered around. "I fear death a bit less now."

"Ouch!"

Something hard dug into Alice's hip. She flinched back. The Shade who had bumped her stormed past, a great stack of books teetering in his arms.

Alice rubbed her hip. "Excuse you."

The Shade tossed her an impatient grunt and marched off.

Now Alice noticed the Shades here were not quite so content as she had thought. They were, in fact, rather hostile. As they wandered deeper in, she began picking up a tense, busy energy about the place, akin to the college libraries during exam time. The simmering frustration of exhausted, exasperated souls. This sort of mood was contagious. Alice's skin prickled with unease. Around the stacks she heard a symphony of angry mutters and books slamming onto tables. Someone sneezed, and half a dozen voices went, "*Shush!*"

Several rows over a Shade stood hunched over a big, yellowing manuscript with a magnifying glass. He looked harmless enough, which was to say, he looked like an archivist. Alice got up the courage to ask him, "What's going on?"

He blinked up at her. "What do you mean?"

"What's everyone researching?"

"Oh." Annoyance crossed his face. "Freshly dead, then?"

"Actually, we're—" Alice began, but Peter cut her off.

"Yes," he said. "Just got here, and very confused. What're you reading for?"

The Shade pointed to a brass plaque on a wall behind him. It read, in big serif font, *DEFINE THE GOOD*.

"I don't understand," said Peter.

"Just what it says." The Shade waved his hand impatiently. "Figure it out, give an oral defense, and they pass you through."

"Figure *what* out, though?"

"Law, look." Peter picked a printed sheet off the table. Alice glanced over his shoulder. It was titled "Recommended Reading," followed by a list of authors. *Immanuel Kant. Jeremy Bentham. Herbert Spencer.* "Oh, look. Nietzsche."

Alice ignored him. "What do you mean, pass through?" she asked the Shade. "Who passes you? How long does that take?"

"Christ," said the Shade. "Do I look like your tutor?"

"But can't you just tell me—"

The Shade turned his back to her, pressing his face determinedly against his magnifying glass.

"Let's walk a bit," Peter suggested, gently tugging Alice away. "See if there's a floor plan, or a librarian deity, maybe."

They wove round and round the maze of shelves, dodging irritable Shades, until they came upon an area that seemed like a main lobby. The stacks stretched radially from a circular study zone, and the ceiling opened to reveal a great central staircase. They looked up. The staircase went on and on, adorned at every floor by great bronze statues in various postures of deep thinking. The library had seemed finite from the outside—Alice was sure she'd seen the roof of the tower—but from within it stretched onward as far as the eye could see, floors spiraling toward an ever-tinier center, and Shades moving busily all throughout.

Like all good scholars Alice sometimes had fantasies of an infinite library, a Borgian Library of Babel in which one could be forever lost. But this sight now gave her stabs of panic. It was so vast. And they had no *time*. Professor Grimes was moving with purpose, the Shade at the wall had said. He was bent on getting through, and when Grimes was bent on something it was like walls did not exist. They had to reach him before he reincarnated; they could not dally.

"Gosh." Peter looked similarly helpless. "Should we just split up and search one by one?"

"That could take forever."

"But maybe there's some order," said Peter. "Could be it's chronological, could be more recent arrivals are near the bottom."

"Hold on." Alice rubbed her temples. "Let's just—give me a second to think."

Pride, *superbia*, arrogance. *Hubris*, the defiance of gods; *māna*, the puffed-up mind. None of the sojourners' accounts said anything about a university library, and so she had to return to first principles, philosophical basics. She riffled through texts, images, treatises, that resided in her mind. Icarus, hurtling from the sky; Arachne, limbs splitting into eight. What was pride? For Augustine, the original sin; for Pope Gregory, the root of all evil. For Plato, the First Court punished those possessed of a timocratic soul—the soul who purported to love justice and honor and beauty, but who cared more about preserving the appearance of such things rather than making the sacrifices necessary to fulfill those things themselves. For Confucius, the Court of Pride housed the *xiaoren*, the petty men, who chased the names of things but not their nature. A mismatch between the name and the thing—yes, that was it, the common thread running through all these theories. But what did all this have to do with defining the good? And how did one go about defining the good? If she just could figure this out, then she could retrace Professor Grimes's path, for he surely would have cracked this in an instant.

But she found it so hard to think. Her thoughts kept flying away from her even as she tried her best to sort through what she knew. The library no longer seemed quite so hallowed. Noises kept crowding her mind—bickering, whispering, scratching, coughing, breathing, pens scratching, pens clicking—none of it above an atypical volume, but it was all so blindingly *present*, harsh to distraction. And someone the next shelf over kept moaning, an insufferable sound that grew louder and louder.

She whirled round the shelf. "For heaven's sake!"

It was the Shade of a young man, skinny and long limbed, hunched on the floor with his knees drawn to his chest as he rocked back and forth. He had the look of a law student, though Alice couldn't say why; she just felt this was the case. Something about his chin. Books lay scattered all around him, and streaks of spilled ink marred the carpet. At the sight of Alice and Peter, he wailed even louder. "They won't pass me. Seventeen times, seventeen times and they still won't pass me, I'm such an idiot . . ."

"Oh, no, no." Alice was sorry she had snapped. She was familiar with sights like this, and normally when people had mental breakdowns in the college library you spoke to them in a soft, calming voice and confiscated all the sharp items on the table and sent them off for a biscuit and a nap. "You're not an idiot."

"But I've done everything," hiccupped the Shade. "Read all the recommended texts. Read *Russell*, for Christ's sake." He smacked his palm against the side of his head. "I even followed the regimen in *The Republic*. I studied *mathematics*—oh!"

He slumped sideways and knocked against the table leg, which sent a stack of notes cascading across the floor. At this, he made a keening noise and rolled forward onto his hands and knees. "And now my notes are out of order."

Peter knelt down to help him collect them. "Here—"

The young Shade clutched them to his chest. "They're color-coded," he wailed. "Not that *they* care."

"Werner, please." A second Shade, a shorter and older-looking fellow, hurried down the aisle toward them. He placed his hands under Werner's armpits and, grunting, hauled him upright. "We have talked about this. You may not have mental breakdowns in the stacks."

"They failed me again," sobbed Werner. "They hate me."

"Yes, I know." The older Shade patted him on the cheeks. "But pull yourself together, please. There've been noise complaints."

"I'll never get out . . ."

"Crying fits are to be conducted in private, that's library rules." The older Shade clapped him on the back. "I've booked you a place. Study room C-56. Third floor. Go on."

Werner, still weeping into his hands, stumbled obediently off toward the staircase.

"Good man." The older Shade dusted off his palms, then turned to Alice and Peter. "So very sorry, won't happen again—why, you look new! Just arrived?"

"Yes indeed," said Alice.

"Double suicide," Peter added, which Alice found rather dramatic but did not challenge.

"You're remarkably well-presenting!" The Shade brushed the back of his hand across Peter's shoulder. "The stitching on your collar. Incredible. How do you manage?"

"Er," said Peter. "I really try?"

"It's quite magnificent! You wouldn't believe the laziness that passes here. Most new arrivals don't even bother with a face." The Shade bowed low before them, hands clasped as if in prayer. "George Edward Moore. At your service."

He was the most human-looking Shade Alice had seen thus far, which was to say that every part of him was richly detailed and solid, from the gray wisps atop his head to the scuffed tips of his leather shoes. He had the slightly lopsided smile of lifelong pipe smokers—and yes, there it was, a pipe hanging from his left hand. This he waved in their direction. "And you are . . . ?"

"Peter Murdoch." They answered both at once. "Alice Law."

"And where did you study, Peter Murdoch?"

"Oh, I'm—we're at Cambridge," said Peter. "Department of—"

"Ah, Cambridge!" Moore grasped Peter's hand and shook vigorously. Alice he ignored. "A Cambridge man! What wonderful news. I was at Trinity myself. Come, come. Let me give you the tour."

He set off for the staircase. Alice glanced to Peter, who shrugged as if to say, *Why not?*

No better options presented themselves, and Moore did not look obviously dangerous—in any case Alice did not know of any demonic entity calling itself George Edward Moore—so they fell into step. Moore, turning, gestured magnanimously toward the first floor.

"Now, the floors alternate between workspaces and stacks. Stacks are organized in ascending order chronologically by century, and then alphabetically within discipline. It is a bit complicated, but I do recommend starting at the sixth century BC and working your way up." Moore paused, overlooking the first floor, which was indeed composed of busy study tables and endless hallways of study rooms. "You'll find it a shock at first, being newly deceased and all, but there are no bathroom facilities or kitchens. No one needs to sleep or eat. They are freed to engage full-time in their work."

"Defining the good," supplied Peter.

"Quite right. So the plaques tell us. That's the only rule of this place: figure out the meaning of the good. When someone comes up with a definition they like, they go out to the shore for an oral defense. If they pass, they cross on. If they fail—well, you saw poor Werner." Moore nodded over the dozens of toiling Shades. "Most have been at it for years. Look at them go."

Alice felt the twitch of an impulse to join them. Not because the project sounded so interesting—in fact it sounded overly vague and a little annoying—but because there was pleasure in being handed a simple, defined task and pursuing it with vigor. All those Shades looked so diligent and purposeful, which seemed somehow virtuous. It was always good to be engaged in research. As Aristotle put it, complete happiness was some form of study.

"But that doesn't seem so difficult," said Peter.

"That's what you think."

"But isn't it just like—you know, good things?"

"Ah," said Moore. "But that's a tautology."

"Happiness, then," said Peter. "And justice. And kindness, and . . ."

"You're just saying synonyms now."

"But surely they're all parts of the good—"

"Oh, so there is a complete list? And what else qualifies for your list? What is the common quality of all virtues on your list? Can you give me a comprehensive, tightly defined version of your list?"

Peter paused. "I see."

"It's harder than you think." Moore smiled. "Everyone comes in believing they already know the answer, and they fail many times before they turn to the literature. And now the really severe cases, they never make any progress at all and then they end up bronzing—"

"Bronzing?" Peter repeated.

"A terrible affliction. Starts in your feet, and then you can't move, and then you're stuck where you are. We move them to the pedestals when that happens. Look, there's Newton."

Alice had been leaning on a plinth; she flinched back. "These statues are *people*?"

"Yes indeed, every one." Moore knocked his knuckles against a plinth that read, *Galileo*. He continued up toward the second floor. "They do wake up, though who knows after how long. Between you and me I think they like it in there—they get a break from the work, and everyone has to marvel at them."

"So what puts in you in this court?" asked Alice. "I mean, what's everyone in for?"

"Don't ask! You're not supposed to ask, that's the first rule you've got to learn. It is considered very rude." Moore lowered his voice to a conspiratorial whisper. "Though rumors travel, of course. People get distracted and leave their transcripts where anyone can see." He pointed. "For instance, that fellow there—he told everyone he taught at Oxford, where really he taught at Oxford *Brookes*."

"That's enough to put you in Pride?"

"Oh, yes. You wouldn't believe the sort we get in here." Moore kept pointing as they walked. "That one there, he rejected submissions if they hadn't cited his own work.

"That one gave eighty-two presentations on Goethe.

"That one likes to remind folks that Dartmouth is in the Ivy League.

"And over there—creative writing students." This was said in reference to a study room of eight Shades, all glowering at one another in silence. "Somehow they always come in groups. Can't understand why."

They passed another study room, where one Shade was droning on to another in a very loud voice, ". . . of course, it's all very *Derridean*, which I am uncomfortable with because of Derrida's obsession with *feces*. Did you know I saw Derrida speak at a conference once? All anyone could talk about was how he got high on LSD and smeared *feces* all over the walls."

"Continental philosophers." Moore shuddered. "Here we have dozens."

The procession of petty sins continued as they circled up the floors. Moore seemed to delight very much in explicating the moral failure of his fellow residents, for his hushed whispers nevertheless carried over the floors, eliciting the occasional peeved glare. "Now, *that* one self-published self-help productivity books.

"Calls himself a Communist, but hasn't read *Das Kapital*.

"Recites pi to show off.

"Had more of a comment, not a question.

"Wouldn't accept papers written in the first person.

"Turned his exam papers over very loudly.

"Still asks people what they got on their A-levels.

"Still tells people what he got on *his* A-levels.

"Made his wife call him *Doctor*. He's a medievalist, mind you.

"Now, *that* one keeps saying he went to school in Boston and expecting everyone to know what he means. Every few years the other Shades gang up on him and brick him up behind the stacks."

They passed a series of rooms overflowing with texts. "Book hoarders," Moore explained.

"Why would you hoard books in a library?"

"To prove that you've found them," said Moore. "To prove you know *of* them. To prove you have proximity to them. But reading them, that's too much."

At this point Alice had made up her mind Professor Grimes could not have been sentenced to Pride. She felt indignant, actually, at the thought of this gossipy little man lumping Grimes in with these posers and imposters. Yes, Professor Grimes was occasionally very rude; yes, the whole Royal Academy called him arrogant behind his back; yes, he habitually reduced undergraduates to tears. But weren't all great thinkers of their generation a little prickly? And hadn't he earned his prickle? She recalled that Aristotle distinguished between proper and improper pride. The worthy man could justly boast of his accomplishments, so long as he had actually done them. Professor Grimes could only be charged with behaving as befit his station, which was lofty, and Alice really did not think this was as morally egregious as calling oneself a Marxist.

Anyhow, Professor Grimes hated peacocking. She knew this because once she had been caught up with the thrill of competition herself. At her first conference—after a dizzying night of cocktails with students from Oxford and London, all comparing the sizes of their stipends, their research budgets, who had recently published where—she had gone up to Professor Grimes in the hotel lobby and blustered, drunk on superiority, "Can you believe they don't have a *proseminar* at Imperial?" She had thought he might laugh, that they could share this condescension. But he had looked down at her with such blistering disdain. "Don't play stupid games, Law."

Peter was there; he snickered. And Alice spent the night in red-faced shame.

It was a lesson worth learning. She had not repeated this mistake. Those who had nothing substantial to brag about bragged the loudest. Stay silent and ignore the chattering crowd—this was proof you had something real to be proud of.

She fell back so she could speak to Peter. Moore did not notice. He had worked himself up into a rant about psychoanalysts, and his arms flapped so vehemently that should Alice and Peter have kept pace, he might have whacked them in the face.

"He's not here," she murmured. "Let's go."

"What are you talking about?"

"It's a waste of time." Her irritation had sharpened to urgency. Every minute spent here was a minute in which Professor Grimes pushed further into Hell. "And Moore said we were the first from Cambridge in years, so he would have met him—"

"Well, maybe they didn't cross paths."

"Then let's ditch him and search on our own. He's a clown—"

"He's not so bad."

"He's a petty gossip!"

"He's the first Shade we've met who will explain anything to us," said Peter. "We've no idea how Hell works, Law. We've got no other leads."

"Aha!" Up ahead, Moore turned and waved enthusiastically. He gestured to a door. "Here we are. My office. Do come in."

ALICE HAD SEEN OFFICES LIKE MOORE'S many times before. They were offices of decadent accretion, offices of men who had earned tenure back when earning tenure just involved being friends with the department head and who treated their space like a clubhouse until they grew old enough the university could boot them out. A massive, cluttered desk; plump armchairs; porcelain tea sets; memorabilia from trips to Asia and Africa—where Moore had found a Turkish carpet in the Underworld, Alice had no idea. Books overflowed from the shelves, lay scattered in piles on the floor and the desk. These included, she noticed, the aforementioned copy of *Meditations*. Framed diplomas hung on every wall—from where, Alice had no idea, because she was not aware of any degree-granting accredited institutions in Hell.

"Please, please." Moore ushered them in. "My little sanctuary. Be comfortable."

Alice and Peter sat gingerly on the couch, while Moore bustled around his desk, muttering things like "If I'd known I'd have company . . ." and "Pardon the mess."

"There we go!" He turned round and offered them a tobacco tin. "Smoke?"

They both shook their heads. Shrugging, Moore packed his own pipe, lit it, and sucked in with great relish. He exhaled. Thick smoke wafted into their faces. Peter suffered the mist with blinking, eye-watering fortuity. Alice coughed.

"So!" Moore plopped himself down across them and kicked his feet up on the ottoman. "A Cambridge man. What college, may I ask?"

Alice glared at Peter, who said, "St. John's."

"A John's boy!" Moore clapped his hands together. "*Good* man! We're going to have such fun."

"Excuse me," said Alice.

Moore ignored her. "Last fellow of any standing to come through was a Durham man," he informed Peter. "And now, I do have standards, yes, but years of solitude and I thought, *Durham, all right, we can work with that*. But he was so frightfully dull. Paleontologist. Wouldn't stop dusting at the floors trying to find ammonites. He's on the fifth floor now, somewhere, working out a naturalistic theory of the good."

"Excuse me," Alice said again, more forcefully.

This time Moore paused, though he glared as if she were a persistent mosquito. "Yes?"

"Please help me understand," said Alice. If Peter didn't want to leave, then she'd pry for all the answers she could. "What precisely is keeping us here?"

"How do you mean?"

"Suppose we walk right out the door and leave," said Alice. "On to the Second Court, that is. Desire. What's going to stop us?"

"Well, nothing." He blinked at her as if she were stupid. "You can wander wherever you like, but why would you? You've got to stay until you've passed. They won't pass you in Desire if you didn't pass Pride first."

"Right," said Alice. "And who's *they*?"

"The deities, of course. Niutou and Mamian. The Oxhead and the Horseface, balancers of karma, the right and left hand to Lord Yama the Just." All this Moore rattled off like a schoolboy reciting scripture. "They don't talk much, but they can understand your heart in an instant. You can beg all you like, but if you've incomplete marks on your transcript, then they'll always know. If your transcript says pride, then you must pass Pride."

"Sorry—transcript?"

"Haven't you got your transcripts?"

Alice hesitated.

"Er—" Peter made a show of patting his pockets. "Must have misplaced . . ."

"Oh, don't worry about that." Moore waved a hand. "They'll reappear, give them time. Impossible to lose." He nodded to a slip of paper lying facedown on his desk. "Anyhow, you get marks on your transcript as you go along, you see. The transcript lists your major sins, and then you've got to go in order. Pass Pride and you enter Desire, pass Desire and you enter Greed . . ."

"And then what if we finish at Pride?" Alice pressed on. "If we're not guilty at Desire, or Greed? Suppose we define the good, whatever that means. What would Niutou and Mamian do then?"

"Ah. Yes." Moore leaned back. "Well, supposedly they come for you in a ship. Those big doors in the lobby lead to the sands, you know. And past the sands, the river. Supposedly you see a great golden ship on the horizon. Supposedly it glides across dark waters and extends a plank to shore. They'll be waiting for you there. They'll help you board."

"And then?"

"And then they offer you the draft of the Lethe, brewed by the Lady Meng Po herself." Moore's eyes grew distant. The lopsided smile sagged off his face. "They say it tastes of dandelions, of dewdrops at dawn. You drink. Your memories are wiped from your soul, like dust from a mantel. You are mere starstuff, like once you were before. Fresh. Clean. And you are then ferried to Lord Yama's court, to pass through the Gate of Reincarnation to wander back down into that red mortal chamber, to billow among the dust. So they say."

Silence fell between them.

Moore sucked at his pipe, blinking at nothing. He looked a bit translucent then. Alice could see his diplomas through his neck.

"So you've never seen this happen?" Alice was not quite sure she should take Moore's word for anything.

"What? Oh, no." Moore stirred. "It's frightful dense stuff, ethics. Quite impossible to master. No, not a soul's been invited to cross the Lethe in all my years here. Not even I—" Moore paused, winced. He took another puff of his cigar. "It's very hard, anyhow."

"Have you tried many times, then?" Peter asked sympathetically.

"Oh, no, I don't bother."

"Why not?"

"Why, the classic dilemma." Moore spread his hands. "Administration interferes with research. I'm a bit like a dean around here, if you haven't noticed. The Shades here behave *very* poorly. Hoarding texts. Stealing each other's notes. Wailing in the stacks—I mean, the number of daily breakdowns in here, it's unbelievable. Someone's got to keep them all in line."

"And you took this job yourself?"

"Happily."

"But then you never get to leave."

"Noblesse oblige," said Moore. "We're Cambridge men. We must set the example."

"I see." Peter's brows furrowed, but he clearly thought better of arguing the point. "Well, that's very generous of you."

Moore beamed. "So you'll help."

"Sorry?"

"It has been so long. So long since a real scholar came through. A Cambridge man. You and I, we could really whip this place into shape."

"Oh dear," said Peter. "I don't think—"

"There's an empty office just down the hall, we'll have you set up in no time at all, I have rugs and furniture to spare. We can alternate floors. I'll do odds, the study rooms are where all the riots happen—"

"Look." Alice had had quite enough of this; indeed, if Moore said *Cambridge man* one more time, she might explode. "Professor Moore. We hadn't actually planned to stay."

"But you can't go." Moore stood. He exhaled slowly, and the smoke unfurling out his mouth formed a thick, purple cloud that condensed and hung rather pointedly in front of the door. "There's nowhere for you to go."

"Well, we might just step outside," said Peter. "If you don't mind—"

"But you haven't defined the good." Moore's voice took on

a singsong lilt. "You haven't passed, you can't go on, it's the rules."

"We'll take a chance on that," said Peter.

"I really don't think you should."

Smoke continued unfurling from Moore's pipe.

They all three stood, regarding one another. Alice recalled then that very few of the affable pipe-smoking fellows in college were that genial through and through. The manners and smiles were always a veneer for something a bit rotten. Good old-fashioned misogyny, usually. Racism on a good day. Snobbery in most cases. Sometimes dementia. So many old men in the Senior Common Room who demanded you help find their glasses, and also explain what all those colored folk were on about. In this case, what lay beneath was a hollowed-out and wide-eyed look that seemed quite lonely, and quite mad.

The smoke thickened.

"About that office," said Moore. "I think a maroon design, perhaps."

Alice had a wild thought then. It was a page stolen from Peter's book—a logician's page, and a pedantic one at that—but if ever there was a time for pedantry it was now.

"How's this," she said. "If you can prove to me we ought to stay here, then we will stay. If you can't, then you let us leave. But it must be a proper proof. You must compel us with pure reason."

"Easy enough," huffed Moore. "I am indeed a man of reason."

"Aren't we all," said Alice. "Break the argument into two premises and a conclusion. A, you can only leave the Court of Pride once you pass. B, we have not passed. Therefore, C, we cannot depart."

"Right as rain!" Moore lifted his pipe in triumph. "You see?"

"But I refuse to accept the conclusion," said Alice. "I don't see why one and two lead to three."

"Because it is the rules of Hell," Moore snorted. "That's all there is to it!"

"Okay," said Alice. "Let me see if I can get it all straight. A, you can only leave Pride once you pass. B, we have not passed. C, we must follow the rules of Hell. Therefore, Z, we cannot depart. Is that right?"

"It's obvious, dearie," Moore scoffed. "Logic compels you."

"But I refuse again to accept the conclusion," said Alice. "Why do A, B, and C lead to Z?"

"Then add another premise," Moore scoffed. "If you accept A and B and C, then you must accept Z."

"Okay." Alice took a deep breath and recited it all back. "A, we can only leave Pride once we pass. B, we have not passed. C, we must follow the rules of Hell. D, if we accept A and B and C, then we must accept Z, that we cannot pass."

"Precisely!" Moore cried. "You've said it perfectly!"

"Still I refuse to accept that," said Alice. "I simply don't get it."

"Are you dim, girl?"

"I am not dim. I am simply uncompelled by this syllogism."

"But it's so simple!" Moore bent over his desk, dipped a pen in ink, and began scrawling furiously. "I shall spell it out for you. A, you can only leave Pride once you pass. B, you have not passed. C, you must follow the rules of Hell. And then you simply add *another* premise, D—" He stopped himself, and muttered something that sounded like, "No, then we must add an E . . . but to get those fools to accept the conclusion of E, very simple, we must add an F . . ."

Alice tugged at Peter's arm. "Let's go."

Moore hardly glanced up as they tiptoed their way past his desk. By the time they were at the door, he was on premise J: "And *this* will do it, *this* little extra premise is all you need . . ."

"Nicely done," said Peter as they hurried down the hall.

"Oh, it's nonsense," said Alice. "I'm shocked he hasn't read Carroll."

"It's a big problem for logic, actually!" Peter flapped his hands in the air. "Why *should* any two premises compel the conclusion, valid though they might be? No one has a good solution. You actually can't prove *modus ponens*. But if we don't have *modus ponens*, then we might as well be in the Stone Age, because *modus ponens* is the foundation for everything else . . ."

"Not you, too." She smacked him in the arm. "Come on."

They hurried down the stairs and back out into the lobby, past the squeaking and squelching bookshelves, the flickering study lamps, the squabbling study groups, and Shades sobbing within the stacks, until they saw a set of double doors. These were not the doors they came in, but at this point it did not matter. Above, a howling came from Moore's office. Below in the lobby, all the Shades suddenly pointed their way, whispering excitedly. *Passed*, they whispered, *someone thinks they've passed*. The curious crowd surged forth. There was no time. Alice gambled and pushed. The doors swung open, and they stumbled out of that frightful, chilly space into blissful quiet, the dead outside.

This time, they faced the river.

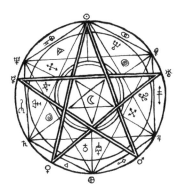

## CHAPTER SEVEN

The Lethe. A great expanse, fathomless and immeasurably wide. From the shore all one could see was endless darkness stretching toward the dim horizon. Whatever waited across—King Yama's throne, the gates back to the living—lay out of sight. The Lethe was a visual paradox, two things at once. At first glance, eyes unfocused, the waters were still and silent, a glassy obsidian surface reflecting glimmers of the ever-dying sun. But then one looked closer, and the Lethe became an agitated churn, all whorls and eddies in currents without direction, and the longer one gazed the louder those waters sounded in one's ears, bone-deep rumbles from waves roiling beneath the surface.

Alice stepped closer, entranced. As a child she had learned that white was all the colors wrapped in one, and she found this profoundly unfair; that one could have seen rainbows everywhere but instead, with weak mortal eyes, saw only plain light. The Lethe seemed an inverse of this principle. It was all darkness. But the moment you fixed your eyes on any one point it began to disambiguate, until you saw that what seemed like sheets of obsidian were in fact waves of color, and those waves of color formed memories. You could just catch fragments if you squinted. Here a faded teddy bear; there a pouring stream of red wine; and there a ringed, wrinkled, reaching hand . . . all fragments teasing richer memories, specific details, all the detritus of human experience swirling, condensed into one unending wash.

Oh, great Lethe. Hell was *always* bound by a river. All the sources confirmed this, regardless of period, geography, or religion. You didn't have to call it the Lethe. You could call it the Apanohuaya, or the Vaitanya. You could call it the river of Meng Po. The domain of Neti. But you could not deny there was the river, delineating boundaries between worlds, severing the cord between this life and whatever came after. On this side, the courts of punishment. On the other, Lord Yama's domain—and the promised golden circle where souls returned to the world of the living. There were many rivers of power in this world—there were rivers of death, and rivers of love; rivers that could grant immortality, and rivers that could take it away. Some washed away sin; some merely washed away the guilt. But only the Lethe washed memory.

Western Tartarologists preferred the name *Lethe* for its etymology. *Lethe* comes from the Greek *lēthē* (λήθη), meaning "forgetfulness," "oblivion." *Lethe* also has connections to the Greek *alētheia* (ἀλήθεια), meaning "truth." Though what connection truth had to forgetfulness, Alice was not sure. By some accounts, stripping all memories was a way to reveal the most fundamental truth—some ineffable element of the soul that was eternal. By other accounts, the causation was flipped. Truth was the necessary condition to deserving forgetfulness, and therefore reincarnation. Only when one acknowledged the truth about themselves could they wash away the burden of past lives to begin anew.

Dominant theories linked the memory powers of the Lethe to Heraclitus's theory of flux. In most respects Heraclitus was a complete ass, and he was famous for bizarre proclamations like "Everything is its own opposite" and "All things in the universe are manifestations of an ever-living fire." Despite this, Heraclitus had made the profound observation that one could never step in the same river twice, because it wouldn't be the same river, and one wouldn't be the same person. The Lethe, then, equated forgetting with rebirth. The continuity of one's soul was tied inextricably to the persistence of one's memories. When memories were gone, a new soul was born. The Lethe was forgetting was death was change.

"Suppose this is another way to go." Peter was rifling through his notebook, thinking out loud. "Around the courts, I mean. Jesse Hagen had these theories—well, I don't know if you read Hagen, I did take out the only copy. But we might move a lot faster if we traveled over water. The Lethe must pass by every court, so theoretically . . . hm." Peter tapped his fingers against his chin. "But we've nothing to build a raft with."

Alice had considered the same problem. Get on a boat. Sail across; either to successive courts or even to King Yama's Land across the way. Yes, Alice had found a footnote citing Hagen's theory. But where would they get a boat? It was hard enough to take one's mortal soul to Hell. Pentagrams only stretched so large. No one had ever managed more than a bit of luggage, much less a vehicle. And the boat would have to be airtight, waterproof; they could not risk even one drop spilling onto their skin. On this subject, the literature was very clear. The waters of the Lethe ate memory. Even trailing your fingers across the surface could strip you of truths you'd known your whole life.

Alice had concocted some half-baked ideas about forming a raft with the supplies in her sack. She might inflate the blanket, perhaps, and try enchanting it so it held the weight of two, and formed a protective barrier besides. But those waters looked impossible to fool with magick. Those eddies looked *hungry*. They exuded a vicious gravity. They were negative space, irresistible magnets, black holes of thought. *Try me*, the river seemed to say. *I'll eat your chalk.*

Her arm twitched suddenly. She tugged her sleeve down. An old injury.

Peter was saying something else, but her mind drifted, lost in the river. She simply could not stop staring at that shifting, swirling surface. She had the absurd urge to take a swim, and it was the same kind of thought that invaded her mind when she stood any place high up. What if she climbed out that window? Tumbled off the edge? The waters seemed so cool, so soothing, and she imagined herself dropping down through that glassy surface without so much as a ripple.

A blur marked her vision. Alice blinked, and when she opened her eyes she saw a woman standing by the shore, old and hunched, terra-cotta jugs arranged neatly on a table beside her. "Murdoch!"

"What?"

"Don't you see her?"

"Who?"

"The woman." Alice pointed. "The woman by the shore."

Peter's voice wavered. "I don't . . ."

Why couldn't he see? This was no hallucination. Alice was certain. She knew this deity. She'd seen her crop up over centuries of texts. Old Lady Meng Po, guardian of the river, mother of memory. Her task was to distill those violent waters into a fragrant herbal liquor. When souls crossed over it was the lady's wine they drank; sweet and cooling, eternal relief. The forgetting of rebirth, not of obliteration. The lady met Alice's eyes, and her mouth stretched into a slow, wrinkled smile. There was no malice in that smile; only a simple, guileless kindness. *Drink*, she said; and though no sound carried over the waves Alice understood perfectly what she meant. *Drink, and be at peace, and be gone.*

Oh, how wonderful that would be! Alice had thought rescuing Professor Grimes from Hell was the solution to her problems—but why go to all that effort? She almost laughed. Here was the real answer: to wash away the dregs upon her mind and come out the other side dewy clean; a mewling babe ready to start afresh. Memories rushed to the fore of her skull, hot and choking foul, and all she could think then was how nice it would be to offload them to the depths; to swirl away and then disseminate forever. She was so tired of the contents of her mind. Her thoughts were so loud; they *pounded* her skull, it never stopped, it was all too much. For a long time now it had been all too much. Everyone was so afraid of the Lethe—keep away, they said; stay dry—but why didn't they understand it was mercy? All the stories were wrong—no siren's call was as alluring as the sea itself, and the quiet dark beyond the shore.

Peter said sharply, "Law."

She looked down, and saw she'd crossed halfway to the river. Peter stood yards away at the bank above. That was odd. She didn't remember moving her feet. "How . . . ?"

Peter waved, the way one might at a misbehaving dog. "Why don't you come back up here."

Alice blinked at the river. "How very strange." But she couldn't move.

Peter waved again, more urgently this time. "Come on, Law. Please."

"No." Someone else's voice came out of her; a musical tone, indifferent. Alice liked it; she liked to be spoken for. The river decided for her. "I think I shall go for a swim."

The river roared louder, drowning out whatever Peter said next.

Alice did not care. She could actually feel her mind deflating, like a pricked balloon, all that terrible pressure removed at last. The image of forceful waters rushing through every crevice, flushing out the debris, smoothing the contours of her mind, until the whole worm-eaten rot had vanished and left only smooth bone, baby clear. She felt that unanchoring again, which ought to have terrified her—she reached for her staircase but it was not there, the rush was too loud. But this time she had no fear. The tumble was a good thing; the fall was not further in, but toward the empty. The baptism was upon her. *Yes*, she thought—*yes, yes, we are almost there—*

Suddenly Peter was beside her. He gripped her arm, so hard it hurt.

"Ouch," she said.

"Law, look at me."

"Let me go."

Hands clapped against her temples, forced her gaze from the river and upon Peter's face. She had not looked into those eyes up close in so long. *What long lashes he has*, she thought, *miraculously long for a boy; what a lovely face, too, pity it makes me think of cruel laughter, slamming doors—*

"Breathe," said Peter. "Just breathe."

Don't patronize, Alice wanted to say, but by instinct she obeyed, and the whooshing in her lungs dimmed the river's roar, just a little bit. She felt again the edges of her mind. Tired grooves of being.

"What's your name?" asked Peter.

She knew the answer! Yes, her catechism—she had practiced this, this was easy. It all came out in one breath. The staircase reappeared, and up she climbed. "I am Alice Law I am a postgraduate at Cambridge I study analytic magick—"

"Very good," said Peter. "Now can you follow me?"

Alice wasn't sure; she had forgotten how to make her limbs respond to her command.

"Just look at me," said Peter. "Hold on to me. There you go."

Step by step they started back up the bank. Alice's legs

moved like lead. It seemed inordinately difficult to put one foot in front of the other.

"Almost there," said Peter. "You're so close. You've just got to finish out."

She spoke as if in a dream, half-unaware of the words coming out her own mouth. "I feel sometimes it is so difficult to be conscious."

"I know," said Peter.

Such heavy feet. Like dragging rocks. "And I think anything would be easier. Anything at all."

"There's time for that." Peter grasped her by the elbow; firm, but gentle. His voice was soft. "It'll always be waiting, Law. But we've got things to do."

ON THEY TRUDGED, FOLLOWING THE PATH along the river. Peter strode ahead and Alice kept pace in silence, feeling embarrassed. The allure of the Lethe had diminished now that they were further off the bank, and Alice wished she had not made such a fuss. She was not sure now whether she'd seen the Lady Meng Po after all. Really, it was such a brief glimpse. She might have just been remembering a painting, or even a firm description become imagination. Her memory did that sometimes; she confused memories and reality, her imagination was too vivid, she couldn't help it. But Peter politely made no comment, and Alice made no defense, and gradually they sank into a thoughtless, plodding trance. Alice probed about her skull and found to her relief that the sloshing had settled, the rush faded. The catechism had worked, and she had a grip on her thoughts once again.

"Hey." Peter paused. "Haven't we been walking awhile?"

Alice had not been paying attention to the time. "Have we?"

"They didn't look so far apart," said Peter. "The library and the next building. But look—does that building look any closer to you?"

Alice summoned the picture from her memory. He was right. Before the gates, the campus had seemed as closely clustered as any typical campus, all its buildings no more than a five-minute walk apart. But the Second Court, Desire, remained just as far away as it had when they had started walking. Alice thought she could make it out in better detail now—it was a two-story building with ornate tiling all around the front and sides, and two bronze lions sitting guard at the front. But it had not grown any larger.

"I knew it," said Peter. "We're in hyperbolic space."

"But that's backward." Alice did not remember much from geometry, but she did remember this. "With negative curvature, objects should be closer than they appear. Like with a convex mirror. Light spreads outward. So we should *be* there—"

"No, no. What we saw from the wall was a clustering at infinity. Haven't you ever seen the Poincaré disk model? It's like we're walking on coral. Down here on this plane, things could be miles apart, and they would still look like a regular campus from a different plane."

Alice did not know what the Poincaré disk model was, and did not wish to know. "So what's the implication?"

"The implication is that we ought to go to the peak," said Peter.

"Not your mythical peak again."

"Now we have some idea of where it is, because we've seen the outer bounds." Peter pointed to the Lethe. "So we know to track *away* from the river, and that will take us toward it—"

"If even that point exists! If it doesn't, we just wander into infinity."

"But just suppose it does. It would save us so much time!"

"The point isn't to save time, Murdoch. The point is to *find* him. We can't just randomly assume about his sins—"

"Why not?" Peter threw up his hands. "You think he's too good for petty sins. You also won't believe he's done something really bad. So what, then, Law? What's the Goldilocks mean of acceptable badness for dear Grimes? Where do you think he's landed?"

Alice felt she was under attack, and for no good reason. "I don't know," she said, and hated how small her voice was. The question frightened her. She did not want to open those floodgates. Behind lay a confused and guilty tangle she knew she could not sort out. Memories strained, always threatening to burst—but she had done so well at keeping those gates closed, at redirecting her thoughts, finding her planks. Better to keep it all locked away. Better to treat the whole matter purely as an experiment, and proceed methodically. All outcomes were possible. No biases. "There's no way we can know. And that's why we have to search in order."

Peter must have noticed her shrinking, for his expression softened. "I understand that, I'm just—I'm just afraid we'll be walking forever."

"The Shades must get around," Alice reasoned.

"Yes, but they have an eternity to get around, so that doesn't matter."

"But we haven't seen any on the path."

"So?"

"If it's a long distance to the next court, we should see them," Alice reasoned. "If it's a shorter distance, then they're already inside. We haven't seen anyone, so it's more likely that they are already inside."

Peter considered this. "That is valid."

"Thank you."

"Then we just keep walking?"

"I don't see a better option," said Alice. "Do you?"

So they fell back into line, trudging toward a building that was probably—but not certainly—getting larger.

Somehow it was not unpleasant, this endless stroll. Alice was rather grateful for the reprieve. They could have been a Victorian couple, sojourning to the seaside for fresh air. The wash and lull of the Lethe was far preferable to the whining buzz of Pride, and if she closed her eyes Alice could imagine that wash sweeping over memories, sweeping them away, leaving a pure, clean slate behind. She knew that wasn't how it worked. Still she felt much calmer than she had over a long time; her head emptied of thought; her mind blissfully quiet. She felt that she could breathe.

Sometime around half past noon she heard the clicking.

Later she would come to dread the noise. This warning that began always as a faint whisper, so faint you thought or hoped you'd imagined it, but intensified until it could not be ignored. Later she would learn the whisper always turned into a clicking, until the sounds were disparate enough that the ear discerned it was not a single sound but a dozen constant clicks at once, echoing so you could not tell from which direction they came, and that by the time you could make out each one—vertebrae clacking, tibias and fibulas rubbing against their joints—it was too late.

"Do you hear that?" Alice stopped walking.

"Hear what?"

"It's like—a snapping. Or clicking. Listen."

"Might just be the river," said Peter. "All sorts of stuff churning in there."

"Right, maybe . . ."

Alice could not shake the sensation that something was wrong. Every now and then she thought she heard something behind her. A footstep, a brush of sand. Every time she turned around, however, she saw nothing. Only her neck kept prickling, now, with the conviction that something stalked behind her.

"Do you see something?" Peter asked after the third time she did this.

"I should like to," said Alice. "Otherwise I'd *really* feel mad—oh!" She pointed upward of the bank. "There—*look*—"

Over the hill came a procession of three little animals. Malformed, twisted-looking things, empty sockets somehow more expressive than the eyes that should have lain inside them. Clicking and clacking they prodded around the sand, tails wagging, sniffing. They could have been dogs or foxes or wolves; it was impossible to tell.

Alice thought, at first, they were just malnourished things—poor creatures wandered down the wrong tunnel and now trapped in Hell. This happened sometimes, said the literature. All boundaries were porous. Cats crossed them on purpose, other creatures by accident, and then they got lost, and then they died. But as the things drew closer she saw there was no muscle on those creatures, no stretched sheet of skin. No eyes, only hollow sockets. No flesh, only clean white bone, alabaster bright, held together by some force unseen.

"Remarkable," Peter whispered. "Do you know what they are?"

"No, do you?"

"I've read about Cerberus." Peter did not look nearly as frightened as she felt. "And the Buddhist guards, sometimes, can take the shape of dogs. But *bones* . . . I don't know. They're kind of cute, don't you think?"

"It's chalk," Alice exclaimed. "Look at their joints."

Those bones were, indeed, bonded together by gleaming, powdery chalk. Something or someone had stitched these bone creatures together by magick techniques too difficult to fathom—

first because inscribing pentagrams on living things rather than a flat surface was still deemed impossible, and second because the inscriber, whoever they were, was not even present. No Magician alive could induce such effects outside a pentagram.

The creatures were very close now. The largest one crept forth past its peers, head tilted to the side as if curious. There was no flesh of nose over that skeletal maw, but the front of its skull twitched right and left in a manner that resembled snuffling. Peter was right. It was strangely cute.

Peter stepped forward. "Do you think they're friendly?"

"Don't—" Alice began, but Peter was already kneeling, stretching out one hand at the leader.

"Hey there. Good boy—"

The bone-thing's head snapped out. Peter yelped and jumped back, just as the bone-thing leapt for his face. Peter's arm swung up to ward it off, and the bone-thing's jaws clamped around his wrist. No, only his sleeve, thank God—Peter waved his arm twice through the air and at last flung the bone-thing away. It landed on its back, inches from the water. For a second its limbs waved like cockroach legs, then it rolled over, skittered to its feet, and raced back up the slope to join its comrades.

A theory clicked together in Alice's head. "They don't like the water." She shuffled to the shore, moving sideways so as not to turn her back on the creatures. "Murdoch—come on—"

He backtracked to her side. The bone-things did not follow. Her hunch was right—the Lethe water ate memory, and chalk worked by recalling memory, the echoes of millions of years of life. Indeed the closer they got to the water, the further back the bone-things fell. They crouched, shoulders hunched in agitation, like coyotes debating whether to pounce. But they drew not an inch closer.

"Back." Alice made a shooing motion with both hands, the kind one used on persistent gulls. "Back, *back*—"

The bone-things ignored her. Still an invisible boundary seemed to separate them from the water. They could not come closer than ten or so yards from the Lethe, and indeed the more Alice inched toward the bank, the more agitated they grew. They kneaded their paws against the sand, shaking their heads in distress. Alice half-expected them to start yipping.

"Careful," Peter warned.

Alice glanced over her shoulder. Her left heel had crept up to the water's edge. She felt a wave of vertigo. Peter flung out his arm and she clutched it, bearing down against him for balance.

At last the bone-things had had enough. With a final clack of their jaws, they turned tail and scrambled back over the dunes.

"Are you all right?" Peter asked her.

"Fine. You?"

"Yeah, just a tiny scrape—Jesus." He examined his sleeve. It was torn clean away, up to the elbow. Several angry red streaks ran up the length of his forearm. The bone-thing's teeth had been sharp. Alice winced to imagine what would have happened had its teeth sunk two inches further. "*Not* a good boy."

Alice squinted, following the creatures down the dune as far as she could. In seconds they were over the horizon, hidden from sight.

Not a single sojourner's account made mention of creatures of bone and chalk. Nothing on the record came close.

Her tranquility cratered. The beach was no longer a fantastical and lulling retreat but an anxious and overexposed plane. The sight of chalk meant the presence of another magician. A frightfully talented one at that, one capable of techniques not even Professor Grimes had ever dared attempt. Chalk meant a creator, another keen rational mind whose motives were unknown, save for one thing.

He was watching.

## On Chalk

*In all the myths and lore it is assumed that magicians use a variety of special implements: scepters, staffs, cauldrons, wands. But those in the learned sciences know that a proper magician needs only one tool, and that is a humble stick of chalk.*

*Chalk is the foundation of all analytic magick. Easy to write with, easy to fix mistakes. Chalk is made of limestone in turn made by compressed, tiny fragments of ancient sea creatures that died millions of years ago, and therefore possesses the curious, still-mysterious quality of manifesting magical statements. Chalk is, as wrote the magician-philosopher Aldous Huxley, a link to the abyss of the remote past, the natural product of the forces originally possessed by the substance of the universe. Some evidence indicates that the Cerne Abbas Giant, a massive chalk drawing of a naked man holding a club, is prehistoric evidence of a vast and terrifying work of magick. (Though in the absence of a recognizable paradox, any evidence of its intent is lost to history, and probably for the best.)*

*The efficacy of chalk depends on where you dug it up. In England, the trusted standard for magick chalk is the Barkles brand, mined from closely guarded deneholes along the Thames. The most expensive chalk, used only in very important public demonstrations and dissertation defenses and the like, is Shropley's Premium—produced by the Shropley's company from deposits at Grime's Graves in Norfolk. Shropley's also issues a more affordable line of chalk mined in Hangman's Wood—Shropley's Standard—which carries a signature yellowish tint. Most English magicians bear allegiance either to Barkles or to Shropley's Standard, and debates over which is superior have ruined friendships.*

*Whatever your preference, what distinguishes everyday chalk and magical chalk is that magical chalk writes on almost every surface. Magicians do not always enjoy the ideal conditions of blackboards in lab rooms. For practical effects, they must be able to draw pentagrams in all sorts of conditions—on concrete, grassy hills, plastic boards, wooden floors, and cobblestones. Magician's chalk glides beautifully on every texture, no matter how wet or dry, crumbly or slick. The highest-quality Shropley's can even activate successfully on sand.*

*This is perhaps why, in all their research, Alice and Peter had overlooked one crucial detail: nowhere in any records, mythical or scholarly, has there ever been evidence of chalk working in Hell.*

# CHAPTER EIGHT

They made camp when they were too tired to keep walking. Alice checked the time—one in the morning, much later than they ought to have slept, but they had both kept pushing through that last stretch of their hike, forcing numb feet onward along the banks. They were both rattled by the bone-things. Alice was unable to shake the creeping, sticky fear from her throat, the certainty they were being watched, and the only solution seemed to be putting as much distance between them and the bone-things as they could. This, despite Hell's purported infinitude and unreliable topology. Despite the fact that for all their efforts, whoever or whatever it was might still appear before them in a blink of an eye.

Alice sat, chewed through a stick of Lembas Bread, and tried not to let her despair creep. Fortunately graduate school had prepared her for this, the constant managing of despair. Everything was always falling apart; nothing in lab went right; you couldn't afford groceries, your cottage had a rat problem, all your instructors hated you, you were always one step away from flushing all your life's work down the toilet. You shoved it to the side of your mind and went to sleep and deferred it all to tomorrow when your brain again functioned well enough to pretend.

Peter hissed as he pulled a strip of gauze from his arm.

"How's it look?" she asked.

"Not infected, I don't think." He held his wrist over the fire, examining the wound. "You'd be able to tell at this point, wouldn't you?"

"Want some more antiseptic? Just in case?"

"Yeah, all right." She passed him her travel bottle of merbromin. He dabbed a droplet onto his arm, then held out his wrist so she could rewrap it in gauze. "Thank you."

She settled back against her pack and closed her eyes. "Of course."

"Hey—let's try something." Peter pulled a box of chalk from his bag. "I wonder if we might speed things up."

Reluctantly Alice lifted her head. "How do you mean?"

"Well, what's the worst thing you've ever seen Professor Grimes do?"

"We've already had this conversation."

"I'm not saying we should find the end point," said Peter. "I'm just saying, maybe there's another shortcut across the courts. Let's just assume we have a good guess where he is. Suppose this—he's done worse than greed, surely?" Peter drew an enviously perfect little circle by his feet. These were called test circles: pentagrams drawn in miniature for safety checks before you stepped inside the real thing. These were best practice for spells that involved any movement or bodily alteration. You put your hand in the test circle, and if you didn't lose your fingers, then you could chance putting your whole self in. "Worse than wrath?"

Alice thought of flying spittle, of mugs smashed across tiled floors. Rare instances—but clear in her memory nonetheless. Professor Grimes never had patience for stupidity. "Probably, yes."

"Then we ought to just skip ahead to cruelty, shouldn't we?" Rapidly Peter scribbled a series of algorithms around the circle. It seemed to involve a lot of maths. Alice saw more geometry than she did Greek, and this made her head hurt. Peter set down his chalk. "What do you think, Law?"

"Hold on," she said. "Backtrack. How does your shortcut work?"

He pulled his notebook out of his rucksack, opened it to a page in the middle, and tossed it at her. She took one glance and instantly her thinking mind shut down, as it always did when confronted with a lot of numbers. "You need to explain that to me like I'm five."

"Gabriel's Horn," he said happily. "Also called Torricelli's Trumpet. It's a mathematical paradox that bounds a finite volume within an infinite surface area. The plane of Hell is that infinite area, and in configuring us as the volume inside the horn, we could make a finite shortcut . . ."

"Sorry, what?"

"It's a bit complicated," he admitted. "You have calculus?"

She'd taken it in college; she hardly remembered it. That was one of the joys of specializing in linguistics: the escape from pure maths. "Only the basics."

"So then you remember curves, right?"

"Let's pretend I do."

"Basically, you rotate one branch of a hyperbola around its asymptote. That gives you a shape that looks a bit like a trumpet. Hence the name! Very apt, eh?" Alice was too confused to laugh. Peter looked disappointed but continued. "Now you can calculate the surface area with these equations here"—he tapped pertinent equations in the pentagram—"and also the volume here"—he tapped it again. "The surface area is infinitely big, just like Hell! But the volume, miraculously, is bounded. Some people call this the Painter's Paradox, because you can theoretically fill up this whole bounded area with an unbounded amount of paint."

She blinked at the page. "That's just your twisted pseudosphere again."

"It *looks* like the twisted pseudosphere," said Peter. "Mathematically it is very different. You're right that they both rely on some assumptions about hyperbolic space. But this spell doesn't assume Hell is hyperbolic. Rather it produces a hyperbolic solid within the circle."

Alice could never make up her mind on how she felt when Peter explained things. On the one hand, it was so condescending, the way he postured as if he were her tutor. On the other hand, he *was* very good at maths, and she really didn't know this stuff, and competence was always attractive.

"Murdoch, this makes no sense."

"It's a paradox, Law! It's all a bit abstract, I know. But I think if I can draw the right equivalencies, we might bound the infinite space of Hell into something like—a shortcut. A wormhole, sort of. Here: I'm going to make a shortcut ten yards to your left, just to demonstrate. You'll see my hand stick out of the sand. Don't be alarmed." He chanted out his incantation—two steady minutes of incomprehensible geometry and calculus, and then waggled his fingers over the circle. "Voilà."

Nothing happened.

Alice peered at the ground. All the silt inside the pentagram looked the same to her. "Well?"

"Huh." Peter frowned at his inscriptions. "That's funny."

"What's wrong?"

"It's not sticking." He poked at the dirt. "The ground, it's—it's swallowing it, almost."

Alice slid her fingers through the sand. It was true that chalk held better on firmer surfaces, but the good brands left smooth, solid lines no matter what the surface. And these dirt particles didn't seem particularly special in any way. Perhaps they were darker, more glassy, more fine and siltlike than the sand particles you might find at a beach. In grade school, she'd done science fair experiments with cornstarch where it held solid in your hand if you squeezed it, but melted if you let it go. The silt felt like that. Solid to the touch, until you weren't looking. Discomfiting, certainly. Still, it was just sand: solid, stationary, dry.

"What grade are you using?" she asked. "You've got to go softer with sand."

"I'm using 5H." Peter clawed at the pentagram. An obsidian stream poured from his fingers; no white particles in sight. "Look! It's not that it doesn't draw. It just—it faded away. Like the silt absorbed it all."

"Have you ever tried this spell yourself?"

"No, it's new . . ."

"Well, could be you've missed something." Alice pulled her own chalk out and arced out a circle beside her feet. "Small errors in the margins can make the pentagram erase itself. It's rare, but it happens sometimes, especially in linguistics." She began tracing the premises of the Sorites Paradox. Just a basic spell, something they all learned in their first year. Sorites spells did not achieve great effects, but still no one had ever come up with a satisfactory debunking, and so they always worked at least for a little.

"A heap remains a heap," she recited in Greek. "Remove a grain, and the heap remains . . ." Her voice faltered.

Her pentagram, like Peter's, sank away into the silt.

No Barkles'-over-Shropley's superiority, then. "I don't understand." She pawed at the sand. She could not see even a hint of white. All trace of the chalk was gone. "That shouldn't—it's never not worked before."

Peter scooped a handful of silt into his palm and poked at it with his fingers. "I wonder if it's a problem with Hell itself."

"How do you mean?"

"I mean we have no understanding of Hell's metabolism. Or

Hell's entropy." He let the silt stream through his fingers. "Possibly its energy flows are all out of whack and it's eating the chalk, eating its living-dead energy, instead of glitching against it—"

"But the sojourner's accounts," she said. "They were using magick the whole way through, and they were fine. Dante, Orpheus—"

"They weren't drawing pentagrams, though. The magician's accounts are all pre–Carne Abbas. They had enchanted objects, that's not the same."

Alice rifled through her mental catalog, trying to find a counterexample, and came up with none. "But that means . . ."

"That means we have no magick."

Alice considered the implications of this, and dread congealed in her chest.

It was not that she was so reliant on magick to live. She was not like some older magicians, who habitually used magick so often for little things like brewing a pot of tea that they could not function without it. Wartime chalk rations had ended that culture. The magicians of her generation were minimalists; their work was about pushing the boundaries of known laws of the natural world, not about avoiding hardship. She had packed to hike through Hell without magical assistance. She had water and food and supplies to last two weeks. So long as they were prudent about their Lembas Bread, and did not lose their Perpetual Flasks, they would retrieve Professor Grimes and get back upstairs before they came close to starving.

Still. Alice was not particularly strong, fast, or skilled in any martial arts. She was quite sure Peter wasn't, either. She had packed knives, sure, but what did she know about using them? They had nothing to wield against Hell's deities and guardians, or the infinite demons that haunted its dunes. Nothing against those bone-things. Nothing against their creator. The one proper defense they had against Hell was their magick, and without that, they were just two ordinary people—two idiot hikers, really—who'd ventured down here on a whim. And the archives were hardly crammed with stories of idiot hikers who'd made it to Hell and back alive.

Oh, dear—now her thoughts were racing. Visions swam before her eyes. Stories she'd read, videos she'd seen. Lions stalking. Vultures circling. Crumpled bodies at the bottoms of ravines. Chthonic beasts—were they worse than bears? She had become so practiced at keeping herself contained, but she'd forgotten that this was in the safe and contained circuits of Cambridge, where she had a thousand landmarks to reorient her racing thoughts. She had not accounted for new stimuli, for the stress. *They go for your stomach first*, she heard David Attenborough say. *Not the artery, they don't kill you right away; they want you fresh, unspoiled; they'll eat you slow, you'll feel every bite—*

Her chest felt tight. She looked at Peter, and saw bones.

"I feel so silly." Peter kicked at his rucksack. "Shropley's chalk makes up like twenty percent of my pack weight."

*There is no bear*, Alice told herself. *This has not happened. Peter is not dead. You are still here.* She forced a lightness into her voice. "Ah, Shropley's is useless anyways."

He waved a hand in mock horror. "Shropley's slander!"

"Shropley's crumbles upon touch." Chalk—chalk was an easy subject. She consolidated her thoughts around chalk. "Barkles has integrity."

"Barkles writes like fingernails on a blackboard."

"At least it writes!"

Peter snorted. "Did Gareth ever show you his Japanese chalk?" Gareth was a fifth-year logician. "He got it imported from Yokohama twice a month. He said it was the nicest chalk he'd ever written with. He let me try once, but I was only allowed one little circle, because he'd calculated how long he could make each stick last."

"And how was it?"

"Just felt like normal chalk."

Alice laughed. This story was not that funny, but the laughter gripped her all over her body; her shoulders shook, her ribs hurt, and she found it hard to breathe. Air escaped her in odd, syncopated bursts. Oh, she *really* could not breathe. And then the laughter turned to sobbing and to her horror she could not stop; the moans came out of her without end, and then hot tears spilled out over her cheeks.

"Oh," said Peter. "Oh, no, no . . ." One hand reached for her face as if to brush away her tears, then stopped abruptly in midair and hung there, confused. He drew it back. "Don't cry."

"Sorry." Alice wiped her eyes. Oh, this was terrible. To break down in front of Peter Murdoch, of all people. Now he would certainly think she'd gone mad. "Sorry, I don't know why—"

"It's fine." Peter gave her shoulder an awkward pat. "It's going to be fine."

It was so manifestly not fine. Here they were trapped in Hell, still with no idea where to find Professor Grimes and packs upon packs of chalk that didn't even work. Hell felt terribly real all of a sudden, no longer a dreamscape of rolling dunes and buildings emerging from mist. It was a place that could kill them. The magnitude of their plight hit her all at once. It was the first time since they came to Hell that she'd perceived any real danger. And honestly, when she thought about it—when she really considered the bloody mechanics of it, and not just its romantic abstraction—death frightened her.

"Would you like a tissue?" Peter offered.

She took it. "How can you be so calm right now?"

"I don't know. Why are you so freaked out?"

"Because we're going to die."

"We're not going to die." Peter pulled his legs up to his chest, rested his chin on his arms. "We'll figure it out."

"But how do you *know*?"

This she had never understood about him: his optimism, his sheer unflappability. Everyone Alice knew at Cambridge was constantly on the verge of a breakdown. Everyone but Peter, for whom life was only a lark through the meadow. Peter took the worst news with a blink and a shrug. Professor Grimes would impose the most insane deadlines, and Peter would only laugh. She wondered if this was the consequence of winning every lottery of birth. You refused to think things could go wrong, because they had only ever gone right.

"Here—try seeing it like this." Peter twirled a stick of chalk round and round in his fingers. He always did this when he was thinking, Alice recalled, and the familiar gesture was oddly comforting. "When I was deciding whether to come to Hell I asked myself which set of problems I'd rather deal with. And the problem of Hell seemed so much easier. It wasn't even a debate. I suppose you made that choice too."

"I—I guess." Alice was rather shocked, actually, to hear Peter's logic so closely mirrored her own. Though he articulated it so much more nicely. For her, it had rather been a question of *fuck it, nothing matters, everything's gone to shit, so let's go to Hell*. But what, she couldn't ask, had gone so wrong for Peter?

"Cambridge was a closed loop. No way out." The chalk twirled faster. "But Hell—Hell's infinite possibilities. Isn't it fun?"

"*Fun?*"

"Yes! We're off the edge of the map, literally. Where theory meets its limits. Where the closed loop runs out." He spread his hands. "Here there be dragons!"

She wiped her eyes against her sleeve. "That's a pretty way to say we have no idea what we're doing."

"Wouldn't be a contribution to the field otherwise, would it?" He nudged her with his elbow. "Trust your brain, Law. Trust the process. We're *Grimes's* students. Best in the world. We'll be all right."

*Yes*, thought Alice; *yes, I can do that, I can believe that.*

This was after all the trick of magick. There was a camp of analytic magicians called the Intuitionists, who argued the following: When it came down to it, magick was not really about how much complicated maths or logic or linguistics you had. Rather, the final push to make a spell work was just the power of belief. It wasn't about the algorithms at all, it was about self-deception. You had to assemble enough proof to convince yourself the world could be another way, and as long as you could trick yourself, then you could trick the world. Even the non-Intuitionists practiced what the Intuitionists thought, because why not? You did the work, you drew your spell, and still at the end, you closed your eyes and hoped. When it came down to it magick was a wish, a prayer, and a little, anchoring fiction.

So was personhood, for that matter.

So was a coherent subjectivity.

And so was the courage to get up every morning and not plan to die.

It wasn't so difficult. Alice was very practiced at this. She knew the mental gymnastics involved: you assembled the smallest staircase you needed to get through the day and as long as you held the steps in your head you would make it to the next. So she took a deep breath, shut her eyes, and climbed her staircase.

*I am Alice Law. I am a postgraduate at Cambridge. I study analytic magick. I am in Hell. And everything is going just fine, just fine, just fine . . .*

A blur shot across the flame. Peter jumped, Alice shrieked—but it was only Archimedes, reappeared from wherever he'd fucked off to. He looked properly spooked—fur frizzed, eyes wide, his pupils dilated to pinpricks. Alice lifted her elbow. He needed no further invitation; he hurled himself against her ribs.

"Now, what happened to you?" Alice murmured, scratching his head.

Archimedes pushed his face into her side and stayed there, quivering. Something had gotten him in the side, Alice saw. Dried blood streaked across his fur.

"Bone-things, was it?" Peter asked.

Archimedes swished his tail, which seemed like a yes.

Had any of the sojourner's accounts mentioned this lurking threat? Alice racked her mind as she stroked Archimedes's trembling flank but could think of no mention of the bone-things. Orpheus, Dante, Aeneas, Lucian, Seneca, Saint Brendan—their accounts were doom and gloom, no doubt, but the dangers they described were divine and obvious. They ran from Satan. They quarreled with gods. But no one mentioned the skittering creep, the terror of being watched by something not of Hell's own making.

No one except Eliot.

*The Waste Land* came to mind, the most recent sojourner's account on record. *Your shadow at morning striding behind you*, wrote Eliot. *Your shadow at evening rising to meet you*. Alice shuddered as she stared out over the dunes.

*I will show you fear in a handful of dust.*

## CHAPTER NINE

To Alice's great surprise, Archimedes was still with them by morning. She suspected he only liked them as human shields, but she could not complain. Cats had many talents, and one of them was finding paths. Once they'd finished breakfast (Archimedes demanded, and ate, an alarming amount of Lembas Bread mixed in with tea), he marched several steps forward, tail pointing straight up, and glanced back expectantly at them.

"The second court?" Alice asked.

Archimedes blinked as if to say, *Where else?*

"Is it very far off?"

Archimedes turned to show her his bum.

"Are you excited?" Peter asked as they packed up camp.

"What on earth for?"

"Why, the Court of Desire." He waggled his fingers. "Filthy lust. Don't you want to meet Jezebel? Bathsheba?"

She snorted. "You think Desire is all brothels?"

"I think it's a treat compared to the dunes, at least." He

zipped up his rucksack and stood. "What do you think's waiting for you?"

Alice slung on her own rucksack, caught a whiff of her armpits, and winced. "I'd be happy with a hot shower."

Desire posed an interesting puzzle for Tartarologists, who widely believed that this second court was strangely more lenient than the rest. It was Dante who posited that lust, the sin of "carnal malefactors," was a lesser sin; a sin of incontinence, weakness of the will, rather than active malice toward others. Those guilty of lust had made reason slave to appetite. Dante's circle was full of lovers; mutually indulgent sops whose succumbing to their passions hurt no one but themselves. For this reason, many Tartarologists argued that the punishment of Desire, which by most accounts encompassed both lust and gluttony, was the source of addiction itself—both motivation of appetite and cause of harm. It trapped you with enticements; it made you the cause of your own suffering. Every other court kept you trapped with locked doors and difficult challenges and vengeful deities, but Desire trapped you all on its own.

The sojourner's accounts supported this theory. The Christian explorer John Bancroft described Desire as a false imitation of paradise wherein punishment lay in temptation. You succumbed, you indulged, and you were never able to leave. *For three days I pillowed against breasts and thighs, smoking and drinking among the Lotus Eaters*, he wrote. *Only through sheer force of will did I leave their sweet company. O they cried for me, those poor women, and I as well at our parting. But they understood I was sworn to my divine mission, and were persuaded to let me go.* And then he went on about the breasts and thighs upon which he had pillowed for another several pages.

"He won't be in there," said Alice. Professor Grimes had many flaws. Overindulgence in appetite was not one of them;

she had never met a more disciplined man. "We'll be wasting our time."

"Well, we've still got to check."

"But suppose we get trapped."

"We won't," Peter said cheerfully, trudging off after the impatient Archimedes. "We have extreme moral fortitude."

**ALL THE SCHOLARS ALICE KNEW AT** Cambridge were so proud of rejecting their desires. It was the other departments that had sex addicts, drug addicts, alcoholics, foodies. But in the Department of Analytic Magick, gross sensual pleasures were looked down upon as a distraction from the life of the mind. Everyone liked to pretend they did not exist outside of their research, that their earthly bodies had no wants at all. No one admitted to watching television. No one kept up with pop culture. No one admitted to their professors that they were going on dates (to admit to being a sexual creature at all was so humiliating!). Those few who were married mentioned their wives and children with great embarrassment, and only to assure skeptics that the wives were managing the children. No one even admitted to liking the taste of food, which perhaps explained why the department only ever catered Yorkshire puddings that tasted of sand.

The only acceptable hobbies were those that honed the mind and body for sustained study in some way. Chess was mandatory. A light rambling was tolerable. Marathons were especially lauded because they demonstrated the discipline and focus of one's mind. It was rumored that Professor Helen Murray could run for hours at a time listening to nothing but operas she replayed in her head. Yes, leisure for self-improvement was allowed. But pleasure for pleasure's sake—how useless, how embarrassing.

Professor Grimes was the most fanatic about his asceticism. "To learn is the most godlike thing we can do," he told them. He had given them this lecture in their first years, back when they were foolish enough to think they could make time for things like sleeping or seeing movies. "Humans, unlike animals, are born with the faculty of reason. This places us above beasts, and near to God. And so as Aristotle says, we ought to be pro-immortal, and go to all lengths to live a life in accord with our supreme element. The life of the mind is all there is. Anything else is degeneracy, is bodily, is filth."

Alice had tried, really tried, to obey his command. To whittle herself down to just the burning core of a mind. She stopped going to the cinema. She stopped reading novels—goodbye, Henry James! She even stopped cooking for herself, since the campus butteries both cost less and took all pleasure out of eating. She could not reach the freakish discipline of Aleco, the postdoc who ran two miles every morning to the department; or of Chloe, the junior hire, who bragged she ate only one meal a day at five in the morning, and otherwise meditated if she felt dizzy. Alice did manage to imitate Harris the fifth-year's habit of taking icy-cold showers every morning, in hopes that it energized one for the day, though she could not tell if her rush of excitement after the shower was merely due to her relief upon stepping out. There was the question of whether all this was character-building asceticism or simply the demands of poverty, since none of the graduate students made close to a living wage. But nobody liked to talk about that.

There was a period when she did succeed in curing herself of most mundane needs. Some days she would eat only a piece of Lembas bread with coffee for breakfast, and then become so absorbed in her studies that she did not think to eat again until midnight. Sometimes she managed to put off even the Lembas Bread until well after noon. She liked the light, absent feeling she got when her stomach was completely empty and she was running only on air. When she felt a pale and ethereal shade, a mind that existed without a body.

But the crash always came. Alice always broke; always ended up lying in a stupor on the couch watching without processing whatever came on the television in the cottage lounge. Never could she quite achieve that blissful intellectual Zen; that runner's high of peaceful contemplation. More often she felt bereft; unsatisfied and unsatisfying, trapped in a body that needed. And hungry, so hungry, for a kind of nourishment she could no longer name.

**IT TURNED OUT HELL HAD INCLEMENT** weather. The storm came on all at once. The sky darkened, the air chilled and thickened. There was a crack of thunder, and then the sky poured down thick sheets of rain. This was bad news for Alice and Peter, who had not thought to pack raincoats.

"No way around?" Peter shouted to Archimedes over the winds.

The cat mewed.

The storm intensified quickly. In minutes they were soaked. The squalls of wind and rain whipped so fiercely around them they had to clamp their hands around their faces just to breathe. Archimedes stopped and refused to go on until Peter scooped him up in his arms and tucked him into his coat. A miserable little huddle, they inched forth. Somewhere in the howling winds Alice thought she heard a weeping, a human voice, or many of them, but that could easily have been the winds themselves, which had risen to a deafening shriek. She could not tell how long they went on like this. She lost all sense of time. The storm stripped her of any thought, any sense. She was just a core, quivering against the squall, inching along.

Yet this, too, was familiar. Alice had survived several English winters now, winters of faulty radiators and broken umbrellas and surprise storms cracking above you just when you thought the skies had no more to give. She had run all over Cambridge in those storms, and she knew that sometimes the struggle was not over indefinitely stretched space, but the simple agony of getting from one building to the next when the rain bashed like a hammer. So she knew to shrink into herself and press along, inch by inch, until at last they passed under Desire's roof, between the bronze statues that guarded its entry. Not lions, Alice saw. Pigs. The doors swung open. Dripping and shivering, they tumbled inside.

Desire was a student center.

This greatly disappointed Alice, who despite herself *had* hoped for something out of those terrible Orientalist paintings—gilded sofas, hanging grapes, roast boars with apples in their mouths, and lute players in loincloths. Or even a deranged sight out of a Bosch painting—naked revelers, flowers growing out of buttholes, bodies copulating in giant mussel shells. Giant strawberries, crowns of cherries. Most of all she wanted to see some food. Of course it would be imprudent to eat anything—one was never to touch the food of Hell—but after those endless dunes even a facsimile of a feast would have been welcome.

Instead the lobby was all too-bright lights, high-top tables, and randomly arranged couches with suspicious yellow stains. At the center stood a fountain, from which burbled something thick and purplish brown. From the ceiling, a musical number played over a faint, staticky crackle—some almost recognizable Dusty Springfield number, something you might close your eyes to and sway to before last call at the pub, a bit too soft to make out clearly either the melody or the lyrics. In the far corner sat a foosball table, abandoned, though when Alice glanced over the top she saw the little white ball still pinging about, knocking against wooden feet with a will of its own. Her hand twitched instinctively to try it, to see if she could knock that ball into the goal.

"Oh, hello," said Peter.

A Shade came shuffling from the corner, bearing a golden goblet in its hands. It seemed to move straight for them. Alice tensed then, suddenly frightened. But it was headed for the fountain.

"Excuse me," said Alice.

"Hello there," said Peter. "I wonder if—er, if you've seen anyone new pass by? Tall man in black?"

The Shade ignored them both. In silence it filled a goblet from the stream, took a long draft of that thick dark liquid, then shuffled on back to the hallway where it had come. It entered the first room on the right, and the door swung shut behind it.

Alice and Peter followed tentatively. Around the corner loomed an endless hallway resembling a student dormitory, rooms lining either side, uniform and windowless. Some of the doors were shut. Many were not. They hung ajar, and Alice and Peter peeked inside them one by one as they strode through. A single Shade occupied each room. One lay flat on its back, hands wedged inside its pants. Another smoked a pipe in a room wafting over with tobacco so pungent it sent Alice into a coughing fit as they hurried past. A third sat cross-legged on the floor, eyes closed, sipping slowly from that same kind of golden goblet they'd just seen. No one glanced up when Alice and Peter peeked in. No one seemed aware of their surroundings at all.

A few doors down, they heard a loud snuffling noise. A Shade sat hunched over a table in the corner. He held books up close to his nose, and every time he turned the page he sniffed up and down the spine, eyes rolling to the back of his head with pleasure.

"Carry on." Peter gripped Alice's wrist and tugged her along the hall.

"What was that?" she hissed. "What was he *doing*?"

"You've never sniffed a book before?"

"Not like that!"

"Well, it's very nice," said Peter. "Something about the binding. It's like—glue, I don't know. Wood shavings. I get it."

Alice muttered, "I would simply have kept that to myself."

Down the hall was more of the same: Shades upon Shades sitting freely in their cells, repeating singular, rote activities. Alice looked at every face as they wandered by, scanning for Professor Grimes's scowl, but all she saw were blank, vaguely satisfied stares. It became hard to look at, after a while. All those uniform expressions of complacency. Some of the Shades seemed to be losing their outlines, their faces smudged and blurry at the edges. Some Shades seemed not to have eyes. Others had no definition to their mouths, ears, or hands—all senses extraneous to the drive, satisfaction at hand. They were caught in an endless compulsive loop with themselves, repeating a motion that apparently never gave full satisfaction, or was otherwise so delightful that they just kept doing it, again and again.

The whole place was suffused with an aura of decay. The hallway smelled of something foul and antiseptic both at once, like rubbing alcohol sprayed on rot, and the lights were too dim, crackling with fluorescent hum. Cracks and patches of mold littered the walls, lines of ants ran along the stains, and it was all so foul that Alice was agonized that these Shades could not simply stop, take a look around, and flee the place. *Stop it*, she wanted to shriek, *put it down, get out*—but half these Shades did not even have ears. If she screamed to them, would they hear?

She and Peter had both long lapsed into silence. It grew progressively more uncomfortable, looking voyeuristically into these addictions, trying to pretend they were completely unstimulated by anything they saw. Alice felt exposed and naked. She felt she was being tested, monitored to see if any of these enticements aroused similar interests in herself. *Do you like feet? Do you like dolls? Do you like hard wooden objects?*

What did Peter desire? Alice wondered. Probably nothing. Peter came into this world with a silver spoon in his mouth; Peter had never wanted for anything. But that was the wrong sense of *want*. Desire and need were very different, and she wished she knew what Peter craved, what made him weak in the knees, because then at least she would know that Peter had any vulnerabilities at all. Here, though, Peter's expression never changed. He kept such a straight face; he only peered around with clinical, faintly condescending curiosity. Saint Peter could not be tempted.

The objects of lust kept growing to ridiculous proportions. They saw Shades fellating dogs, licking chalkboards, writhing upon beds of panties; Shades pouring wine in a stupor, Shades shuddering over furls of smoke. One Shade paced back and forth murmuring *Thank you, thank you* as staticky machines played tapes of canned applause. It wasn't remotely funny anymore—far from the sensational temptations of Bosch's paintings, the sights in these cells were only sad and sickening. So much of the *body* was on display—breathy moans and slapping and licking and squelching; bodies pierced by needles, bodies choking on food, on wine; just bodies all around, not even full bodies really but reaching organs; working mouths and darting eyes and grasping hands, abandoned by reason, lost to appetite.

Why couldn't they just walk away? Alice couldn't understand it. She had never been able to understand this gross, physical desire. She was familiar with the basic pleasures, yes, but she had never felt such bodily longing that it overwhelmed her mind. It baffled her that in all the stories, heroes were constantly letting cities collapse so they could rub their bits on someone else. David lost his kingdom for Bathsheba, the Greeks gave it all up over Helen, and the great Dr. Faust, when he had Mephistopheles at his disposal, only wanted to use his newfound powers to seduce Gretchen. Sex was not a noble desire, it was such an embarrassing capitulation. There was a kind of genuine longing, Alice knew, but in her view it had so little to do with clumsy machinations of the body, with mashing teeth and sandpaper stubble, rough hands and foul breath. To her they seemed worlds apart, but she had never figured out how to sublimate it, this confused, burning want; this full-body desire she felt most acutely when she looked at—

"Gosh," said Peter. "It just keeps going on."

It was getting harder to keep walking, to keep peeking in; and harder to breathe; and the fluorescent hum and mold and damp were so much that finally Alice could not take it anymore.

"He's not in here." She halted. "Let's go back out, let's walk around."

"I thought you wanted to check every court," said Peter.

"Well, we've checked."

"We've only been here an hour—"

"That's enough to know. He's not in here."

"You said that about Pride, too."

"Well, it's true." Alice sniffed. "He's not here—he's *better* than this—"

"How do you know that?"

"Because it's all so pathetic!" Her head felt oddly light. She couldn't understand why her chest was constricting, why it felt so hard to breathe. "It's base, disgusting—he won't be here, whatever he's done, it's above that—"

"I don't think so." Peter's voice was oddly cold then. "I think there's every chance he's here."

"That's ridiculous."

"You think so highly of him."

"It's not a *compliment*." Alice folded her arms. "Lust is a sin of incontinence. It's a weakness of will—I mean, just look around us—and whatever Grimes was, he was not weak of will."

"Jesus." There again, that cold tone. It baffled her; she had never seen him like this, and she couldn't understand why he was so angry. "Sing his praises some more, why don't you?"

"I'm just scared of wasting time," she said. "That's all I'm saying. We've seen enough, this isn't like him, and I'm tired of walking through this stupid—"

Peter threw up a hand. *Shut up*, it said, the universal gesture—and Alice was about to voice her indignation when Peter pointed to a door down the hall. Faint, muffled noises came from within—shouting? Screaming? Peter cocked his head, eyebrows raised in a bizarrely suggestive manner. He lifted a finger to his lips and crept closer, motioning for Alice to follow.

"Don't." Alice felt an instinctive dread. "Please, Peter, don't—"

"But there's something," he exclaimed. His steps quickened. "There's *someone*."

The muffled voices grew louder. Peter ran up to the door and threw it open.

Behind the door was an office. And in the office two shades were locked in torrid embrace, their faces blurred and unclear—all facets to their existence unclear and forgotten, in fact, except for bright, red genitals. Neither took notice of Alice or Peter. One had the other bent over the desk in what looked like a terribly uncomfortable position, but both were going at it with frantic desperation, howling so loud that the sound shook the walls: "*Oh! Oh! Oh!*"

Was all sex so vulgar? Alice stood frozen, staring as the

rhythmic exchange seared into her memory—the sloppy, wet squelching, the pulsing and throbbing of organs enlarged, exaggerated, the only defined feature of Shades who remembered nothing else—and then was superimposed on every other memory she'd ever had, every touch, every moment she had ever come close to another wanting body. All need, compulsion, satisfaction; and it was just bodies in the end, mounds of female flesh served up like pork, Marilyn Monroe's splayed fingers, Jessica Rabbit, breasts bouncing. Jezebel dressed to the nines, leaning out a window, and dogs gnawing at her flesh. DJs laughed and the headlines whizzed. Fucking bunnies, fucking like bunnies, a jackhammer, a sledgehammer, iron into flesh, the needle the chalk and the ink, in and out and in and out, and it all culminated in a grip, a squeeze, a sigh. Alice tried her catechism, tried to reel it all back, but it did not work, the visions kept spiraling out, it was happening again. She felt so far away. Her body was not hers and she was drifting back, spilling out. She grasped for the staircase, but it was not there—

Peter stepped back so quickly he stumbled against Alice.

"Wasn't him." He let out a hysterical giggle. "I guess—I thought—"

She reeled back.

"Are you all right?" He reached out to touch her arm, but she smacked him away. Just then she couldn't stand his presence, any presence. If anyone came near her she would scream.

He reached out again. "You're breathing all funny."

She dashed past him back down the corridor. A terrible wrenching roiled her gut. He followed her down the hall. She pressed both hands against the first door to the outside she could find and pushed, spilling back out into the storm. Then the world tilted, and the ground came near, and Peter caught her just as she keeled over and vomited.

"WHAT DO YOU DESIRE MOST?" PROFESSOR Grimes had once asked her.

They were sitting at a seaside café in Venice, drunk on victory and Aperol spritzes and baking in the afternoon sun. It was their first afternoon in the city; they'd just arrived from a weeklong hiking expedition through the chalk deposits of the Vena del Gesso with representatives from the Italian Academy of Magick, and now they were tanned and pleasantly exhausted.

Professor Grimes was lapsing into riddles and sophistry, and Alice, buzzed, responded lightly in kind, saying just enough to keep Professor Grimes talking. She loved when he just rambled, effortlessly profound, without an ounce of self-consciousness. She loved seeing how he processed the world; hearing his messiest, unformed thoughts. It gave her clues for how to imitate him, to model her life and career after his. She knew she was silly, thinking she could take up space in the world like he did when they presented so differently. But could she not at least remind people who her mentor was? Academic lineage mattered so much in the right circles. And back then all she wanted, with every fiber of her being, was for people to remember she was his echo.

"Nothing," said Alice, trying to be droll. "I live the life of an aesthete."

"Very funny. But what do you *want*, Law?"

"Success." She fiddled with her glass. "I want a job, and a lab of my own, and several books to my name. I want your office and my name on the door," she added, hoping to make him laugh.

But his face was dead serious. "Those are by-products of desire. What do you *want*?"

"That *is* what I want."

"No, it's not." He reached out and seized her wrist; squeezed it with surprising force. She winced but did not cry out. She was shocked more than hurt; frozen in place like a deer in headlights, all senses trained on whatever he did next. With Professor Grimes, she never knew.

"You've got to think about what keeps you up at night," he said. "What burns inside you? What fuels your every action? What gives you a reason to get up in the morning?"

She was delirious from the force of his attention, and she so badly wanted to say the right thing. But she hadn't a clue what that was.

"It's got to be the work itself," he said. His eyes were shiny with drink, and uncomfortably intense. She couldn't keep holding his gaze; she had to blink and look askance. "The pleasure of analysis. You've got to love cracking things open to see what they're made of. These trips and parties are nice, Law, but you can't enjoy them too much or they'll distract you. You've got to float above it all. You must be fueled by the truth, and the truth alone. It must devour you."

"Yes," she wanted to say. "That's it, that's how I feel."

But it wasn't true, and she couldn't articulate it as such. She couldn't come up with a single research question that motivated her as much as he expected it to. In that moment she couldn't remember why her research, tedious little projects into linguistic puzzles, mattered at all. And even if she weren't buzzed on prosecco she would never have had the vocabulary to sort through the complex rush of fear and desire that got her up before dawn and kept her late at the lab.

Earlier that week he had given a lecture in front of the Italian Academy of Magick in Rome—a prestigious invitation, a named lecture that happened only every three years, which many scholars from around the world flew out to attend. Alice had watched from the first row, trembling with pride as he held in rapt attention the most discerning audience in the world, as words came out of his mouth in such perfect, articulate paragraphs, ideas hanging in the air like shining beacons. It didn't matter that she had heard them all before, that she was in fact the one who'd typed them up, organized them into a structure that made any sense. It seemed like she was learning them for the first time, beholding their significance. A world of possibility hung before them, and he was its prophet come down from the mountains, illuminating it all.

*I want that*, she remembered thinking. *I want that so badly*—but what was *that*?

It wasn't the old need for good grades, or a craving for validation. She was not a child anymore; she had left this pathology behind in college. But it wasn't just the search for answers, either, or the simple satisfaction of a puzzle solved. It was a primitive thrill, a heady realization of what she could become, what worlds she could unlock, and it was all inextricably bound up in him.

"WE DON'T HAVE TO GO BACK in," said Peter while Alice rinsed the bile from her mouth.

She screwed the lid back onto her Perpetual Flask. "Thank you."

"You're right, anyhow. I don't think he's in there."

"I know." She leaned back against the concrete wall, letting the rain wash over her face. Lembas Bread was disgusting the second time around. She felt like she'd swallowed a handful of wood dust. It sat in her throat like acrid, concrete sludge, and no amount of swallowing could resolve the lump.

Archimedes twirled figure eights around her legs, which was just then the most comforting feeling in the world. She bent down and scratched him behind the ears. She wished she could lie down quietly and dissolve in the storm.

Peter did not ask what had happened, which was a mercy. "Let's just walk around, like you said."

"Yes, okay."

"I think it'll pass soon, anyways." Peter squinted against the storm. "We've just got to get out of the range of the building. Do you think you can make it?"

Alice was already striding on.

The storm felt a mercy this time. It all felt cleansing, the screaming winds, the sheets of rain, and even if it couldn't wash out her memory, then it could for the moment drown it out, overwhelm her senses so she could think of nothing but struggling forward. And because they walked with heads bent, eyes squeezed shut against the rain, they did not see the pack until it was far too close.

Movement across the dunes; a rippling sheen of white. A moment longer, and the white disambiguated into all different shapes. A whole pack of bone-things, nearly a dozen.

Peter saw it too. "Oh, Christ."

Archimedes leapt out of Peter's arms and took off at a full sprint for the dunes. This seemed a decent idea, so Alice turned round toward Desire. If they could just get inside, they might bolt the doors shut, or lean against them—but they'd already come so far. The bone-things moved horrifically fast. In seconds they'd halved the distance between them. They were about a hundred meters away now.

"The water," Peter shouted. "Get to—"

Alice followed him, rifling frantically through her rucksack as they ran. She felt she had to do *something*, that she could not just stand there while their doom impended. She pushed past piles of chalk—*useless*—her blanket—*useless*—iodine, books, all useless. All she had was her hunting knives.

"Do you even know how to use those?" Peter asked.

"No." Alice handed him the longer one, hilt-first. She'd bought them last-minute at the charity shop; she'd only unsheathed them once. "Would you like to figure it out?"

He hefted it in his hands, frowned, and held the blade awkwardly before him in a way that did not inspire confidence.

The bone-things halted in a line. They seemed much less afraid of the Lethe than their predecessors, for they had come right up to the shore, sandwiching Alice and Peter between them and the waters. They were of a greater variety this time—some as tiny as kittens, a few the size of wolves, and their skulls cobbled from every kind of animal. A few tilted their heads in a way that could have been cute; if only there were more than nothing in their eye sockets, if only their limbs were not magically enhanced with claws and fangs from other species stitched into every joint.

Alice crouched, since she'd read once in a martial arts novel that this helped in a fight. Bend your knees, lower your center of gravity, that sort of thing. She felt stupid.

"Hold on," said Peter. "We might still—he might want to talk."

Indeed the creatures had not moved. Their neck joints kept clicking as their gaze roved over Peter and Alice, as if processing every detail about them. Alice wondered where their creator was now. Whether he was waiting beyond for their dispatch, or controlling these things through some magical connection, seeing through their empty sockets.

"Hello," Alice called tentatively. "Do—do you understand what we're saying?"

The bone-things made no indication that they did.

"We're just passing through," said Peter. "We're—we're alive, as you can see. But we don't mean you any harm."

The bone-things crouched, preparing to pounce.

"Maybe we can talk," Peter said. "See if we might help each other."

Alice said, "We're magicians too."

The creatures sprang forth.

Alice slashed about, but it was hard to get purchase with her blade when the things came from so many angles. Blindly she waved the knife, and it seemed a good thing that metal clanged against bone—she thought maybe she was succeeding in fending them off. But there were so many of them, she didn't know where to look, could only try to keep them from her neck, her face, her chest. Something landed on her shoulder. Pain exploded, white-hot, blinding. Alice cried out and slashed wildly at the bone-thing. Her blade hit something by sheer luck—something critical, even, because the bone-thing flopped through the air and landed beside the water.

"Get the spines." Peter was hacking at two creatures clinging to his legs. A pile of bones lay at his feet. "Weak spots, try—"

Alice adjusted her grip on her knife and took a breath, bracing herself for the next flurry. But she noticed something then. The creature she'd flung away was not getting up. Instead it lay belly-up by the water, tail flailing, back legs skittering like some horrible overgrown cockroach.

She had a wild idea then.

A trio of bone-things crouched in formation before her, as if gearing up to take her head and shoulders both at once. It felt suicidal to turn her back on them, but instead of standing her ground she dashed up to the water. She tried not to overstep, but the Lethe's waves surged unpredictably. Icy water brushed her ankles. She felt a pang in the back of her skull. A sharper pain in her upper arm. Memories fleeing? She could not tell what she'd lost, nor did she have time to probe. She unscrewed her Perpetual Flask, bent down, and scooped as much water as she could. Then she spun about and sprayed it around her in an arc.

Droplets hit the bone-things with a loud sizzle. Instantly they backed away. The water kept on sizzling where it had landed. At this sound even the creatures attacking Peter left off and shrank back, yipping and whimpering in unison.

"Yes," she panted. "Don't like that, do you?"

The remaining pack clustered in a huddle. The Lethe water was effective beyond her wildest hopes. She saw whole limbs dropping off, joints disintegrating. The water *did* something to chalk, melted and corroded it so that the entire algorithm turned black, withered, impotent. Could it be this easy?

"Back." She brandished the flask. "Back where you came from."

All at once the pack coalesced and flung itself at Alice.

She had only time to throw her arms above her face. They landed everywhere else; teeth sinking into her clothes, her shoulder, her side, her legs. Peter shouted her name. Through the mess of bone she glimpsed him back on the shore, hand stretched for hers, but it was too late. Something sharp nipped her hip. She jerked round, and her ankle twisted. Her balance gave, and she and the whole teetering mass splashed backward into the water.

## CHAPTER TEN

"Are you all right?" Peter patted frantically at her cheeks. "Alice?"

Alice blinked her eyes open. Peter had pulled her onto the shore. The bone-things were scattered across the shallows, and water fizzed as it sloshed round the chalk. Some bone-things were still moving, trying to get out, but their legs came loose at the joints, and their spines disintegrated vertebra by vertebra. She watched as disembodied fragments kicked, twitched, and then sank below the surface.

Peter grasped her shoulders and shook. "*Alice?*"

She startled. "Oh. Yes?"

"What's my name? What's the date? What is your favorite Beatles song?"

"I'm fine." Alice frowned. She supposed if she'd lost her memories, she wouldn't know in the first place. But she at least felt no confusion about who she was, or what she was doing here. She reached for her staircase and found it. She was Alice Law, postgraduate at Cambridge; she studied analytic magick. And Peter was Peter. "Murdoch. Peter Murdoch. Aboveground, it's—October second. Third, maybe, I've lost track. 'Mister Postman.'" She shook her head. "How do you know my favorite Beatles song?"

Peter slumped back with relief. "You listen to it all the time at the lab."

"But I use headphones."

"Your headphones are very loud."

"You should have said something!"

"It's all right." Peter put his hands under Alice's back and helped her sit up. "You have very repetitive tastes, however. I wish you'd put on *Abbey Road* sometime."

"Oh, for heaven's sake."

He stood; she took his hand and hauled herself up. She felt a dizzying rush of blood to her head, but nothing else, nothing to suggest she might have lost some crucial part of who she was. Her temples throbbed, but even worse was the sharp pain in her upper arm. She glanced down, saw the blood tracks and bite marks all down her front, and reeled. "Lord. Oh."

"Come on." Peter slung her arm over his shoulder and wrapped one hand around her waist. "Let's get out of this rain."

LEAVING DESIRE WAS VERY HARD GOING. The storm did not seem to want to let them out. The winds whipped at enormous strengths, and the rain hammered so fiercely that breathing felt like drowning. It took great effort even to stand still, for unless they dug their heels hard into the ground, the gusts kept buffeting them toward the doors of the court. Alice could hardly see where they were going; everything was a howling, wet wall. All she could do was dip her head against the rain and press forward one little step at a time, clutching Peter's arm for guidance. But then it passed, just as quickly as it had come on. The winds died, the rain lightened; a few more steps, and the sky cleared completely. Alice could still see those thunderous clouds above, divided from dusky light by a neat, straight line.

There they made camp, safely in sight of the Lethe, on the border of Desire and Greed. Peter got a fire going. Alice sat shivering madly, drying herself until she felt like a person again.

She coughed. "Could I have some of your water?"

"Oh—sure." Peter passed over his Perpetual Flask. "I don't have rabies, or anything."

"I don't think you get rabies from water bottles." She unscrewed the lid. "We'll have to share from now on."

Her own flask had been submerged in the river. Lethe water had gotten into the Pentagrams in its cap, and it wouldn't replenish any longer.

"That's all right, so long as we keep together." Peter cleared his throat. "So. Now that you've had a breather, could I just ask some—"

"No, thank you."

"But we've got to make sure. I mean . . ." He leaned forward, his eyes huge with concern. "Don't you want to be sure?"

Alice *was* sure. She'd been probing her thoughts ever since they sat down, looking for gaps. But the pain in her skull had faded now, and nothing had gone with it. Her memory was like a badly locked trunk, straining at the clinch, always full to bursting. She would know if something had leaked, she thought. She would have felt the release. "Nothing's gone, I promise."

"But how do you *know*?"

She hesitated.

*Don't you tell anyone.* This memory was very vivid. Professor Grimes had only said it once, but once was enough. But how else to explain? She did not want Peter splashing about the Lethe, for *he* was certainly not immune.

It would get her in terrible trouble. But she thought of Peter's outburst in the Court of Desire, that inexplicable anger—and thought perhaps, out of anyone, Peter might understand.

"I think I'm immune," she said. "To the Lethe."

"Immune *how*?"

She trailed her fingers against the sand. It was so hard to say this out loud. She had been so practiced at saying nothing out loud; it was hard, actually, to find and then speak the right words. Her first impulse was to dance around the truth. "Well, I don't forget things."

"We've all got good memories, Law, but the *Lethe*—"

"No, I mean that I *can't* forget things."

"What does that even—"

"Look." She rolled up her left sleeve and shifted so that he could see the skin around her upper arm. "This won't let me."

He looked. Then breathed in, so sharply that Alice blinked and turned away.

Etched in her flesh, in neat white script in a perfect circle, was a permanent pentagram.

Magick never lasted forever. You drew a sphere of influence, you put an object inside, and when you were finished with the spell, you took the object back out. The most talented magicians could create enchantments that lasted hours, even weeks in the case of Perpetual Flasks, but you always needed to bring objects back to the pentagram once they'd lost their charge. What's more, pentagrams were written in chalk, not ink; by nature, they could not last long. They were under constant threat from vacuum cleaners, brooms, a gust of wind, a sneeze. Every stroke of every letter in a pentagram mattered, and the slightest smudge negated all the hard work of inscribing it in the first place. The best magicians erased their work at the end of every day to prevent accidents the next morning. It was a massive waste of chalk, but there was no way around it. Magick was ephemeral. You fooled the world for a breath, and then everything went back to the way it was before.

Professor Grimes had made it his career's work to defy this one basic rule of magick. He wanted to keep the lie going. And he had proven, with Alice, that pentagrams etched in living human skin might keep their charge for a lifetime. Or at least a year and counting—which was all they knew so far.

Peter stared at the tattoo for a long time. He lifted his hands, and when she nodded permission, he poked and prodded, kneading her skin with his fingers. At last he said, "That's not your handwriting."

"No. Guess whose."

Something unreadable passed over his face. "He made you?"

"I wanted to," she said, and felt a hot vicious thrum in her chest. Yes, this was right, she knew this was true. "I let him."

THIS WAS HOW ALICE AND PROFESSOR Grimes spent that summer in Italy.

He had started with animals. First rats and guinea pigs, and then cats and dogs shaved down to trembling skin. Animal research rules were laxer in Europe; the streets were littered with strays. Alice spent hours holding cats in place while he worked the tattoo needle over their shaved, bare skin. She'd been in charge of disposing of the corpses, too; she became familiar with every *spazzino* collection point in Venice.

But the problem with animal experimentation was that there was only so much that lesser creatures could *do*. You could make them run in circles, or withstand tests of hunger or pain, but in the end you didn't really know how much of an impact you'd made. Who cared if a cat remembered which cup a treat was in? Something more expressive would be better. Something that, at least, could talk—that could tell you what the injection of living-dead energy *did* to a body. Whether it felt like nothing, whether it burned you up from the inside.

Alice always knew it'd be her turn under the needle down the line. Professor Grimes had made no pretensions otherwise. She had freely given her fully informed consent from the beginning, and in her opinion, that made it all fine. It put her in control. And she trusted Professor Grimes to do it safely, to do it well.

She was so good, both during the procedure and the night before. She didn't let on how scared she was; how she was having second thoughts. She knew this would only annoy him. When she sobbed from fear she did it in the privacy of her hotel room. Oh, but she did not want to die. She did not want to lose her mind. But she kept this to herself. In the morning she was calm, placid, docile. A perfect blank tablet.

She kept reminding herself: *It's been two whole weeks since we killed a cat.*

He offered her anesthetic before they began, but she refused even a local injection. She knew it was important that she keep talking, responding, throughout the procedure. She had to stay alert, to catalog every part of the experience. She needed to feel every dip of the needle into her skin, every burn of living-dead chalk.

He'd been so kind, so encouraging, as he worked across her skin. He stroked her shoulder every time she flinched, murmuring low, soothing assurances. "You're grand. You're doing so well. Sit still for me, darling. That's it. We're almost done." He stopped when the pain became too much; he let her take as many breaks as she needed. And when he closed the circle and she dropped to her knees, moaning as the living-dead energy rushed through her body, he bent down with her and rubbed circles into her back and gathered her hair behind her head as she vomited blood across the floor.

The experiment was a great success.

When Alice's fever subsided and she regained consciousness, Professor Grimes held before her a series of slates inscribed with languages she didn't know, each for three seconds at a time, then requested she reproduce the script on the blackboard. She copied them all without mistake. Two weeks later he asked her to do it again, this time without showing her the slates, and once again she copied them out perfectly.

The week was a thrill of discovery. If her memory had limits, she had yet to find them. She could sit down with six books in an evening and, as long as she read every line carefully, commit them all to memory. Her mind now functioned as an on-call encyclopedia. She couldn't suddenly read fluently in French or Arabic, but she could, if she sat long enough, flip through mental dictionaries to compile passably good translations. Entire worlds opened before her. She learned Cyrillic, Hungarian, Nastaliq. She learned Linear B.

Of course it hurt. It never stopped hurting; the pain only migrated from her arm and manifested instead as a constant throbbing at her temples. Her mind felt stretched thin, crammed with things she could never dispense with. She had not realized, until that day, how humans needed to forget to function. Now she could not erase from her mind the million awkward encounters of any given day. Misreading the menu. Spilling her wine. Dropping her wallet, holding up the post office queue. She was already such an anxious personality, and her mind now forced her to relive in excruciating detail every mistake she made with every human being she'd ever met.

But the benefits so clearly outweighed the costs, for what scholar wouldn't have killed for her perfect recall? It was the age when everyone was getting excited about computing machines, and here Alice had become one. She would adapt; she had no choice.

"Now, you can't tell anyone about this," Professor Grimes instructed. "At least not for a long while. This is very important, Alice. It's not like the war anymore. The Royal Academy are all so conservative now, and if anyone knew, I would lose my certification. I have a great deal of enemies in this department. Any one of them would use this information to destroy me. There cannot even be a rumor. You must be discreet."

Which was a blow, actually, because deep down Alice had been hoping to flaunt it all over the world. In her deepest and silliest fantasies, Professor Grimes touted her around the conference circuit like a vaudeville performer. He would be Grimes the Great; she would be his Dazzling Living Pentagram.

But they were talking serious magick here, and she wasn't a little girl. "Of course," she said, and pulled her sleeve over her arm.

"Very good." He patted her shoulder. "It'll be our little secret."

When they returned from Venice he moved on to other projects. He'd grown bored with testing Alice's memory after a week. He had confirmed his pentagram worked, and now he could turn his attention to jumping all the little hoops, the years-long process of publishing intermediary proofs before he could do anything useful with this result. Alice was secondary. He stopped checking on the state of her tattoo; by the start of term, he'd stopped mentioning it. Their little secret. And so Alice had to content herself with the mere knowledge that, among all his students, Professor Grimes liked her best. The evidence was written in her skin.

"DID IT HURT?" ASKED PETER.

"Only a little. I did all right."

She didn't tell him about the burning. The effect of her tattoo was not unlike how Gothic novels described vampires reborn: all their senses sharper, the world gleaming bright. She remembered waking up to a surge of detail, all etched permanently into her brain at the same time she registered it. Professor Grimes's face hanging over hers, eager, anxious, a hunger in those sharp, dark eyes she would never forget.

And she didn't tell him about the flood: the vicious procession of memories, the constant random associations, the immense strain it took to sort out what was relevant and what was not. She did not tell him that her vision had become a roller coaster ride through infinite screens, every television show playing at once. She did not tell him that she had to focus, hard, on a simple tomato before her brain recognized it as tomato, and not apple, not dodgeball, not bloody, beating human heart. She did not tell him how easy it was to lose herself in the wash, how it happened every time she let her attention slip. She did not tell him, *I have to rebuild a staircase by the hour to keep in mind who I am, where I am, and what I am doing.* He couldn't help her, after all; he could only pity her, and so she just didn't see the point.

"I see why you never told anyone." Peter spoke very slowly. He seemed to be mincing words in his head, carefully choosing euphemisms so as to not offend her. "That—that's a lot to sort through."

"It's really not as bad as it sounds." Alice's voice took on a defensive edge. She hadn't meant to share what happened as if it were some great tragedy. She hated when women in her department complained, as if they hadn't asked to be there. She hated the way Peter looked at her now; his pity made her squeamish. "I mean—he knew what he was doing. He always knows what he's doing, he never would have taken the risks otherwise." This was what she'd told herself in the days leading up to the inscription, as she tried to keep the piled-up bodies of shaved cats frozen in rictus from invading her nightmares. "He was very careful."

"Did he tell you it was more for your good than his?"

"Of course not." Alice hated this too, the way people so often assumed that Professor Grimes's students were infantile cultists who didn't know any better. "I told you, *I* wanted to do it."

Her vehemence seemed to startle Peter, for he held his hands up in apology. "I was just asking."

"It's not like he forced me," she reiterated.

"Yes, you mentioned . . ." Peter was blinking quite a lot. "I'm sorry, I'm just wrapping my head around it all. It just seems so—I mean, I can't believe he put you in that position."

*Good lord*, thought Alice. *Not* that *line*.

One time at a conference in New York, a young postdoc from Princeton had engaged Alice in vibrant conversation for nearly thirty minutes about a panel they'd just attended—something that felt validating and comradely, for they were the only two women in the room—before Alice mentioned she worked in Professor Grimes's lab. The postdoc's entire demeanor changed then. She shrank back as she looked Alice up and down, eyes crinkled with pity. "Oh dear," she said. "So you know about the—well, you know."

Alice knew very well, because this wasn't her first conference, and she'd heard it all by now. Grimes was evil, Grimes was toxic, *blah blah blah*. Some contrarian part of her soul was indeed proud to be associated with such a notorious advisor. Everyone else was so boring. Professor Grimes at least had some personality.

Alice had put on her blandest, most innocent smile. "How do you mean?"

The postdoc had chuckled awkwardly. "Surely you know what I'm talking about."

"I don't, actually—is there something I need to know?"

The postdoc had blinked around the room, as if checking for eavesdroppers. "Uh—I mean—I'm sorry, I just assumed everyone talked. If you don't—" She stammered over her words then, and this gave Alice some fierce satisfaction. "I'm sorry. I shouldn't have said anything. That was silly of me."

"I'd suggest doing less gossiping about people behind their backs, if you haven't got anything substantial to say." Alice had felt as if she'd scored some rhetorical victory, though really all she'd done was torpedo a budding friendship. She knew when she flew home she would never hear from this postdoc again, which was a shame, because women in her field were supposed to form alliances whenever they encountered each other. She did not care. Her delight over this burned bridge was probably the wrong response, though all she could perceive in that moment was that the rush of blood to her head felt good. "But thank you."

It was this same contrarian attitude that made her say coolly to Peter, "I didn't get *put in positions*."

"Fine, fine, I believe you." Peter, to his credit, quickly moved on. "So do you think it makes you a better scholar? The pentagram, I mean."

"There's benefits, of course." She hesitated, wondering how to untangle the mass of contradictions that was her memory; how to explain that keeping too much in your mind wasn't necessarily a good thing, that more often it made her jumbled and confused and weighed down with things she wished had never happened. "I feel a bit—less mortal. Less fallible. Most of the time."

"Sounds nice."

"But I think more than anything it makes me—well, afraid. Like I've cheated my way into being an expert, and by *not* doing the hours of hard rote memorization, I've lost something important. I've got this bank of knowledge, but I don't know how to sort through it. And the payoff's not as good without the process, somehow. If I didn't have to sweat for it, it doesn't count."

"Law, that's deranged."

She shrugged. "I'm a Grimes student."

"Certainly that." He blinked at the fire. His mouth worked several times as he apparently reconsidered what he wished to say, and Alice braced herself for another moralistic recrimination. "Did Professor Grimes—um, did Grimes ever ask you to do anything else that you thought wasn't right?"

"This is my only tattoo. He never—"

"No, that's not what I meant. Um." He began tugging at the frayed edges of his sleeves. He always did that when anxious, she recalled. But that meant he was anxious. This wasn't about her, it was about him. "Not just illegal. But something—I don't know. Things that felt unscrupulous."

Alice thought of the mice in Venice, their miserable, twitching bodies. The way they shrieked and scurried when she reached to pluck another one out of the cage. As if they knew precisely what was happening on that lab table, as if they knew what that chalk would do. She'd become so good at displacing their spines to give them the quickest, easiest death while chalk burned into their skin; at severing their neural cords before they could fully process the pain. If she'd ever felt ethical compunctions about it, she'd stopped caring by the end. You got used to just about anything in a lab. Anyhow, they were only mice.

"No," she said. "Why? Did he ever ask you?"

Peter kept fretting at his sleeve. He'd worked several threads undone. Alice was about to smack his hand to make him stop when finally he uttered, "He asked me to get him a human colon."

*"What?"*

"Not from, like, a living patient." He flapped his hands in distress. "From a corpse. One of the corpses they use for anatomy lessons."

"They still do that?"

"Of course, how do you think they practice surgery?"

This seemed to Alice far worse than anything she'd ever done. At least her only victim was herself. "Sounds like you violated some rights."

"The dead don't have rights."

"Well, debatable—but how—why—I mean, *what on earth*, Peter?"

"I don't know." Peter shrugged. "In the scheme of things, it just seemed like such a small deal. Maybe that's how you thought about your tattoo. He was—we were working on something—it never went anywhere, but it seemed for a while like it had some potential. But—well, you know, chalk interacts differently with organic material. We needed a human organ to be sure."

"You stole a colon." Alice could not get over this. "A human colon!"

"Well. Three or four."

"Jesus, Murdoch."

"I wasn't going to say *no*."

"You could have reported that," she said. "That's an ethics violation. You could have taken it to the dean."

A silence. They looked at each other, and then burst out laughing.

"Was it very difficult?" Alice asked.

"Actually, no. I thought it might be, but I sort of just walked in and—took what I needed. Three people saw me, so I waved, and they just waved back."

"Sounds about right."

"I know it's insane," said Peter. "I probably shouldn't have done it. It just never crossed my mind to say no."

"You know, he used to make me type up all his lecture notes," said Alice. "He'd dictate, and I'd type. I felt like a secretary. Never crossed my mind to say no, either."

"Oh, that's nothing. One time he made me grade sixty undergrad exams in an afternoon because he forgot to do it himself."

"Well, one time he made me clean up all my chalk dust and weigh it so he could estimate how much money we'd wasted."

Peter snickered. "One time he threw a fully charged capacitor at my head without warning."

"Did it hit you?" Alice asked, alarmed.

"Just my hands. I tried to catch it, I didn't know it was charged. The shock sent me convulsing on the floor, and my hair stood up for hours. I'd never seen him laugh so hard."

"He never hurled anything at my head." Alice couldn't decide if this made her feel superior or jealous.

"It was only just the capacitor," said Peter. "That one time. The rest was mainly, you know, verbal."

"Right. You're not cut out for this. You're a waste of funding. You don't seem like you even want to be here."

"Oh, yeah, he's fond of that one. One time he said offhand that I was worthless until I learned German."

"Did you?"

"I bought a phrasebook that afternoon and stayed up all night." Peter's voice hitched, and she shot him an alarmed look, before she realized he was breaking up not with sobs but with giggles. "Then I greeted him with '*Wie geht's*' the next morning, and he—and he looked at me like I'd gone mad."

"*Lebensmüde*," said Alice.

"*Sitzfleisch*," said Peter.

This sent them into hysterics.

"God." Alice pressed her hands against her face. They came away wet. She was crying from laughter. This had never happened before; she did not know that people actually cried from laughter. "If anyone heard us talking they really *would* report it all to the dean."

"Oh, I know! Inappropriate faculty-student relationships. Abuse of power. That sort of thing."

"I hate that language. It makes it seem like we're children."

"Helpless victims."

"Didn't know what we were getting into."

"Eyes wide shut." Peter glanced sideways at her. "You know, I went to his funeral."

"*No*, really?"

"Not the real one. Not with his family, or anything like that. Just the university memorial service."

Alice remembered seeing the invitation, staring at it for a very long time, and then ripping it into tiny shreds. "I guess I forgot to go."

Which was an obvious lie, as she did not forget things, but Peter did not press. "Right, I didn't see you there."

"So how was it?"

"It was so odd," said Peter. "They were giving these eulogies about how kind and magnificent and generous he was—basic stuff, you know, they could have been describing anyone. The master called him a legendary teacher. Helen Murray got up and uttered all these platitudes about what a great mind he was. You know what he used to say about her behind her back?"

"That she was a spousal hire pretending to be a scholar?"

"Well—that too. But also, Thatcher without an ass."

Alice snickered.

"Anyhow," said Peter, "the whole time I was thinking, we're the only ones who knew him. All of him. The good, the bad, the hilarious, and all the contradictions. The honest part of him. He was only ever his real self in the lab. Even at his very worst. Even when he was frustrated, when he was being a bully, all that. All he cared about was finding the truth. He wept and prostrated himself before the truth. And we got to know that part of him. I feel very lucky for that."

"God." Alice dragged her palms down the sides of her face. "What a tyrant."

"But he was *our* tyrant."

"Yeah."

"I mean, we're in Hell because of him."

"*For* him."

"Right."

They looked at each other with the brotherly fondness of foot soldiers, ones who had been on a very long journey, united by their love for a common general. Alice wondered if the Athenians felt like this, when they stumbled home after the sacking of Troy, when they'd left their wives and children behind for a decade, when they'd only ever done it all for Agamemnon. They couldn't say if the battle had been worth it, or even what it was all for. But surely the trials, the extreme experiences that no one else in the world could understand, had to count for something. There was a kind of virtue in that ability to withstand extremes. Proof of character. Something like that.

And maybe they *were* Grimes's foot soldiers, infantrymen of a dying order. He certainly made them feel that way. Magic was out of favor, he liked to tell them, one of the signs of a decadent civilization. He went on this rant so often they knew it by heart. Men used to be giants, and with every next generation the decline grew. Aristotle invented logic, Euclid geometry, Kant systematic reason. The gains of thought after were marginal. No one invented whole systems anymore; they could only fiddle with what came before, if they could even grasp the ancients well enough to fiddle. Their generation was the most decadent and stupid of all. Grimes's generation were at least war magicians; they had pushed the field forward by leaps and bounds in its practical applications. But Alice and Peter's cohort quibbled over philosophical details. They made flashy gadgets for toy companies. The best among them sought residencies in Vegas; the worst among them became consultants. No doubt, magic was on the decline. And this was merely a symptom of a world where children did not read but sat drooling before a screen; where artists splattered paint at random and thought themselves Michelangelo's equal. Theirs was not a world of learned men; it had no attention for sustained inquiry; the people of their age only wanted tabloids, gossip, entertainment. Civilizational collapse, impending apocalypse—they forgot the greatness of their forefathers, they were trapped in pointless little debates; they could not get out, no one knew how to think anymore. At this point in the rant he was always drunk on wine, and more powerful for it; and they were rapt, guilty as accused, desperate to prove him wrong. How could they become giants? It would take genius, he told them; immense effort; a monastic dedication to rise above the detritus of their addled world and see clearly above the clouds. Could they do it? Could they restore the valor of the old, could they keep the faith?

They promised him that they would.

The point was that Professor Grimes hadn't tormented just anyone. He'd tormented *them*. Because they were strong enough to withstand it. Because they kept the faith. Because they were special, and worth the effort, and because whatever they became when he was done with them would be so dazzling.

Perversely, it made her glad that Professor Grimes had been just as insane with Peter. It made her feel less . . . wrong. This was evidence, at least, that she wasn't the only one Professor Grimes did this to. And she wasn't the only one who found it worth it to say yes.

And really, this was the challenge in anticipating which court of Hell Professor Grimes had been sentenced to. For all his crimes, there was a part of Alice that was deeply convinced he'd never done anything wrong. Only what was good for her, what any student needed from a teacher.

"You should get some sleep." Peter pulled a thick paperback out of his rucksack and shuffled until his back rested against the wall. He drew his knees up, then rested his elbows atop them. "I'll keep watch."

"You sure?"

"Oh, yeah. I brought Tolkien for company."

"Give me two hours, then. Wake me up and we can trade." Alice pulled the blanket over her shoulders and settled down. She felt very loose and empty then; not only from exhaustion, but also from relief. She felt a great weight had been lifted from her shoulders. She felt she no longer had to hide.

*Thank you*, she wanted to tell Peter. *For listening.* But her eyelids were like weights, and she couldn't more than think the words before she fell into the dark.

"ALL QUIET ON THE WESTERN FRONT." Peter shook her awake. "Mind if I take a turn?"

"Go on," she yawned, and smiled as he pulled as much of the blanket over him as he could.

"It's my feet or my chest," he said. "I have to choose. Which do you think?"

"Probably protect your feet. You never know what's going to come up and nibble those toes."

"You wouldn't defend me?"

"Your legs are so long." She smiled. "I wouldn't see them coming."

She pulled out a book of her own—it was Proust's turn at last—and Peter curled onto his side. Moments later his breathing deepened, and his mouth went slack, and he curled in on himself in a way Alice couldn't help but find endearing. He was all angles, Peter. Long floppy limbs knotted together in an absurd, unbalanced mess.

Peter looked so funny when he was asleep: eyebrows furrowed, mouth downturned as if he were clinging to slumber with resentful concentration. His eyelashes were very long. Alice had always marveled at Peter's lashes. She had never seen such long lashes on a boy. They made her want to run her knuckle against their tips, just to feel their brush—so soft, she imagined, like butterfly wings.

What went on in that head of his? She felt a pang in her chest then; the ache of an old, tantalizing, unsolved problem. She had never been able to figure him out. She knew better than to think they'd made some great breakthrough this evening, that they were now the best of friends. Peter had a talent for making you feel like this, like he was the only one in the world who understood you, and you him. Like you two existed on a plane of your own. Then the next morning he would act like a complete stranger. As if you had never spoken at all. She had been through this whiplash many times before. She knew better by now.

Still she felt very close to him at that moment—if not for the secrets they'd disclosed, then at least for the simple fact that she had not spoken like this to him, honest and unguarded, in so very long.

A hot flush rose to her cheeks. It was certainly the effect of Hell, its endless dunes and terrors and all its attendant deprivations, and the fact that Peter Murdoch was the only being in the entire realm who wasn't insubstantial as breath. Still she could not rid herself of the fancy to lean down and put her palm against his cheek.

This horrified her. She blinked and cast her eyes about, searching for literally anything else to do. Anything to stare at other than Peter's face, his splayed and ridiculous form. He had a habit of casting one arm above his head as he slept like Christ in a painting; chin upturned, awaiting salvation. Lord. What an accident of nature. Astonishing that human beings had evolved over millennia, just to end up like Peter Murdoch.

A packet of notes peeked out from his bag. She glanced at the top and snorted. It was just like Peter to keep his notes in an unbound, unorganized bundle of loose papers.

Curious, she tugged them out. She'd always enjoyed reading Peter's work; it was fun to see where his thoughts matched with or diverged from hers.

The first two pages were sketches of pentagrams—four failed ways to get to Hell, and one that succeeded. She recognized those theorems; she'd spent weeks puzzling through them herself. She felt the thrill of the familiar as she traced his work, as she glimpsed at what stage and how he'd solved the same riddles she had. Peter's process was, of course, brilliant. Several of his solutions were far more elegant than hers, and at one stage he'd bypassed a thorny formula she'd struggled with by apparently intuiting the solution. In the end, he'd settled on the same method she had—Ramanujan's Summation, with Setiya's Modifications. No wonder he'd realized immediately what she was up to. All their work was the same.

The last several pages were pure logic. She almost flipped past them—she hated logic and was only passingly fluent because taking Fundamentals of Logic had been a degree requirement—but something about the final page made her stop.

He'd circled and underlined the last formulas several times over. It was so unlike the rest of his handwriting—hurried, scrawled, most of it barely legible—that these conclusions must have been of great importance.

She flipped back up to the previous page and read the derivations again, taking care this time to decipher it all as best she could. The endeavor hurt her head—she'd taken logic before her tattoo, and she barely remembered what half the symbols were—but at last the scribblings solidified into a certain shape.

It was a spell for organic exchange.

Her hands went sticky with a sudden, cold sweat. She rubbed them hastily against her shirt, glancing backward at Peter. He hadn't stirred—which shocked her, for her heart seemed then to beat so loudly it was deafening.

When had he come up with this?

She'd seen these proofs before. She'd herself chased down equations for living exchange into the most obscure corners of the library, from alchemical scribblings of Samarkand to Wittgenstein's lost notebooks (not lost, it turned out, only hidden in a special room in the faculty library and under constant lock and key). She'd given up on exchange after a week of searching because it seemed so clearly like a dead end, and all the references kept turning up lost, destroyed, or misplaced. She should have realized someone else had gotten to them first.

Here, right before her, was the final piece of the puzzle that she'd never been able to solve.

Professor Grimes's name on the left. And at the bottom of the page, under the right side of the equation, the thing that had first caught her eye: her own name, written in clear, bold letters. Then underlined twice. Then punctuated with three question marks.

That was undoubtedly Peter's handwriting. She'd seen him etch her name so many times before. On labels. On stacks of papers meant for her to grade. In the corner of the chalkboard, on little jokes meant for her. *Dear Alice. Ha ha.* Always the same spidery letters, always fully capitalized; always the *c* looping into the *e*.

You could not perform organic exchange on yourself. This was an inviolable axiom of magick. The pentagram required the sustained consciousness of its user to take effect. You needed a human mind present, willing to believe in the logical contradiction. No pentagram that deliberately destroyed the magician would take effect. You could only rend yourself apart by accident.

You could not, in effect, use magick to kill yourself. Alice knew this to be true. She had looked into the matter, as it were. You could use pentagrams to eviscerate a soul, but you had to do it to someone else.

*If Alice.*

She clamped a palm over her mouth, so Peter would not hear her panicked whine.

There was only one possible interpretation for what she was looking at.

Peter intended to trade her soul for Professor Grimes's.

Peter was going to trap her here in Hell.

# CHAPTER ELEVEN

Two principles ground the whole of classical logic. They are the Law of Noncontradiction and the Law of the Excluded Middle. The Law of Noncontradiction holds, quite simply, that two contradictory propositions cannot both be true at once. You cannot have both P and not-P. It cannot be true both that it is snowing and that it is not snowing. It cannot be true that Alice and Peter are friends and not friends. Schrödinger's cat is dead, or it is not.

The Law of the Excluded Middle holds that either a proposition is true, or it is false. There is no hazy middle ground. As Aristotle put it, sentences can be ambiguous in their meaning but not in their truth. So either the statement that Alice and Peter are friends is true, or it is false. This statement cannot be some mysterious third thing.

Many problems threaten to break classical logic. The Sorites Paradox and the Liar Paradox, for instance, are difficult puzzles that force classical logic to reexamine what it means by truth. classical logic also has yet to come up with an answer to Russell's Paradox, which is too complicated to explain here but has to do with a contradiction of set theory. And classical logic especially falls apart as a language applied to human relationships, which are messy and complicated and often situated in that excluded middle; that space where no one is right and no one is wrong and things are neither true nor false. The upshot here is that classical logic does not know what to do with the statement:

S: *Peter and Alice are friends.*

ALICE WOULD ALWAYS REMEMBER THE MOMENT she first laid eyes on Peter Murdoch. Michaelmas Term, two years prior. Cambridge was gorgeous in golden autumn sun. The wind was pleasantly cool, the leaves reddening ever so slightly in a way that had always excited Alice, for the end of summer meant the start of a new semester; new classes, new instructors, and new classmates. A chance to reinvent herself, and become the person she wanted to be.

Six students had been admitted to their cohort but that afternoon only five were present at the tea in the courtyard behind the department, clutching cups and saucers close to their chests as they cautiously made introductions. There was Belinda Wilcox, an English rose whose red-gold hair and pert nose made Alice hopelessly jealous; a Frenchman and an Italian whose names she could not make out over the clamor of voices; and Calvin Bailey, a fellow American transplant from Michigan, who shared Alice's ineptitude with all the little spoons, saucers, and tongs that went into constructing a cup of tea.

The small talk was polite and meaningless. Alice was too focused on keeping her hands from shaking to say much. She felt badly out of place—American colleges were grand, but they didn't have *history*, didn't have *tradition*, and her advisor at Cornell had actually invited her to a sit-down dinner in which he taught her how to use cutlery before she flew out to London—and the easy shine and polish of her new cohort-mates made her feel doubly inadequate. Even the Europeans seemed more fluent in British English than she was; she could barely keep up with what they were saying. She didn't know what a tripos was; she was still saying "math" in the singular; she didn't understand what anyone meant by Mill or Peterhouse. That morning she'd put on her best summer dress, a frilly yellow thing with a lace collar that normally made her feel sharp, but now, among her sleek, darkly dressed colleagues, she felt like a cheap and gaudy daffodil.

She tried to squash her anxieties and focus on Belinda, though up close Belinda was so dazzling it was hard to get any words out. The sun kept catching her eyelashes in a manner that was truly unfair, for how could lashes be so dark and shimmering both at once? Belinda was telling some story about a Chinese undergraduate she'd mentored over the summer—"Her English was fine, and she was very sweet and polite and all that, but my *God*, she never talked. It was only ever *Yes, Belinda*, or *I'm great, Belinda* in these little simpering tones—and I was getting really angry at her for it, that is, the fact that she was so uninteresting, because being boring is a trait I find *unforgivable*. And then halfway through the summer she revealed that her father is one of the richest men in Taiwan, one of those real estate millionaires, and he didn't approve of women in the sciences, and she'd told him she'd come to an art history program and was learning magick on the sly! Can you imagine!"

Something in this story disposed Alice to not like Belinda but she couldn't immediately articulate why, especially as the punch line to this story indicated that Belinda was *not* racist, and everyone else was laughing so hard. Anyhow Belinda had pulled all the attention into her orbit; there was no other conversation to escape to.

"Did you do your undergraduate studies here as well?" Alice managed.

"Oh no, I was at Oxford." Belinda squinted at Alice. "And you're from—somewhere stateside?"

"The hotel school," Alice joked, then regretted it. No one here understood the reference; truly, no one back in America understood the reference. "That is, um, Cornell."

"I've heard good things about that program! Did you work with Zohar?"

"No, he went emeritus a few years ago. His wife had a stroke, and he stays home to take care of her—"

"That's just awful. I was wondering why he'd pulled out of that edited volume. How's she doing?"

"Much better now, I'm told. They got a dog, which helps—um, with the depression—"

"Oh, very good—my own advisor had a bout of cancer a while back, and they got a cat. Supposedly an animal companion *really* helps—"

She and Belinda carried on like this for a little bit. Alice thought she was doing quite well. She recognized all the names Belinda dropped, she'd mentioned the right connections for Belinda to take her seriously, and she hadn't managed to make a mess of her tea or her biscuit. Except Belinda's eyes kept trailing to a spot over Alice's shoulder, as if seeking someone to rescue her from this conversation. The third time she did this, Alice wilted.

"Sorry," said Belinda. "I don't mean to be rude—I'm just wondering where Peter is."

"Who's Peter?"

"He's the sixth," said Belinda. "In the cohort. We were undergraduates together."

"Are you talking about Peter Murdoch?" the Frenchman piped up. Felix? Philip? "That's the Oxford prodigy?"

"I heard he's the only advisee Jacob Grimes's taken on in years," said the Italian, whose name Alice thought was either Paolo or Lorenzo.

"That's right," Belinda said proudly.

"I'm working with Jacob Grimes," Alice said, but no one heard her. The conversation drifted on to Professor Grimes's reputation, Peter's reputation, and the way Peter had supposedly impressed Professor Grimes by inventing a new pentagram, a twist on the Liar Paradox, on the spot during his entrance interview. Did they know that Peter Murdoch was the youngest person ever to publish in *Arcana*? Did they know Harvard had written to Peter Murdoch with a job offer after his *Arcana* paper came out, and that Peter had responded politely that he needed to finish his A-levels first?

"Does he have scholars for parents?" asked the Frenchman. "He must have."

"I think his mother does biology," said the Italian. "And the father—mathematics, isn't that right?"

"I wish I had academic parents," said the Frenchman.

"It's a terrible advantage," said the Italian. "He's a magician made in a bottle."

"*There* you are." Belinda shouted toward the garden gate, where stood a lanky young man who'd either forgotten or decided against wearing the requisite black gown. "Late as usual. Peter Murdoch, everyone."

The famous Peter Murdoch had overlong arms, overlong legs, and a wild bird's nest of light brown hair under which sat a massive pair of wire spectacles. The lenses were very thick, which had the effect of making his brown eyes appear owlishly huge against his face. When he smiled his whole face split apart, revealing slightly uneven teeth. He looked like someone who wore a retainer. The overall effect was not unpleasant. He was decidedly no Greek god, and yet Alice could not stop staring at him. She kept looking him up and down, trying to determine if he was a real person.

They all made their introductions. Peter was a cheerful, easy interlocutor. You got the sense, watching him nod and smile, that everything in the world was interesting to him. He kept asking everyone about their research, then asking follow-up questions about particular methods, but because everybody wanted to impress him and because the Italian (his name was Michele, Alice finally learned) went on and on so long about his work on rational choice theory, it was an eternity before Peter's eyes alighted finally on Alice.

"Hello," said Alice. "We're advisee siblings."

"Oh, we are?" Peter enthusiastically shook her hand. "I didn't know he took on another one."

She chose not to take this as a slight. "Right, well, that's me."

"I suppose we'll be working together a lot. I do logic, by the way."

"Linguistics and wordplay. And, um, some archival work."

"A wordsmith!"

Alice's cheeks felt very hot; she wondered if anyone could see. "Well, you know, Americans are only good for the weird, experimental stuff."

"I love it," he said. "I love Americans. So unconventional."

Emboldened, she took a chance. "Say, do you want to get drinks sometime? Talk about our projects?"

"Yes! Tomorrow, the Pick? I've got a meeting before—so, five?"

Alice made a note to find out where, and what, the Pick was. "I'll be there."

"You're being very rude!" Belinda materialized on Peter's arm. "Come here—Jean's a logician too, he's been waiting to meet you—"

She dragged him off. Peter glanced over his shoulder and beamed at Alice. There, again, that disturbing thump of her heart. A spoon clinked against a glass, and someone announced it was time to for pre-drinks inside with the faculty. Alice squeezed her eyes shut and shook her head to clear it, and then followed them all through the doors.

**AS IT TURNED OUT THE PICK** meant the Pickerel Inn, which was just across the bridge from Magdalene College. The next day Alice arrived at five on the dot. She didn't see Peter, so she took a table near the front where he couldn't miss her. She felt very self-conscious; she kept glancing at her reflection in the mirror above the bar, tucking her hair behind her ears and checking her teeth for lipstick stains. She almost never wore lipstick, and now she regretted it, but it would only make matters worse to wipe it off. She didn't know why she felt so nervous; she'd had drinks with plenty of classmates before. Perhaps because they would be working so closely over the next six years—she badly wanted to start off on the right foot. Perhaps because she'd not stopped thinking about his crooked smile all night. (The problem of Peter's looks was a great puzzle to her. Nothing was symmetrical or classically handsome, so why was his face so *absorbing*? Further investigation was required.)

Five minutes passed, then ten. She peered out the window; first hopefully, expecting every new figure on the bridge to take his reedy form; then with sinking, embarrassed hopes. She ordered a half-pint of Cambridge pale ale just to have something to do, and drank most of it much too fast when she started feeling self-conscious about taking up the table. Over the hour her nerves went from humming to frantic to completely shot. Peter never showed.

**SHE LEARNED, OVER THAT FIRST SEMESTER,** that Peter Murdoch almost never showed up where or when he was supposed to. He was late to almost every lecture, absent for mandatory trainings, rarely at the lab when Professor Grimes expected them both. There was no pattern or explanation to this behavior. He would ignore you for weeks and suddenly show up with a beautifully complete research proposal. He would make enthusiastic plans for dinner over afternoon tea and then, hours later, never show.

That first evening, she had waited from five to seven. She had even ordered an entire dinner of fish and chips, sheerly out of guilt for her occupation of the table—before getting up at last. A cluster of rowdy undergraduates came in and took the booth opposite her, and she could not even enjoy her dinner for fear of what they must have thought of her—who is that stood-up, dour-faced postgrad eating dinner all alone? A sudden downpour cracked open just as she walked outside. She had not thought to bring an umbrella, for she wasn't used to this land of unannounced rains, and she walked home wet and shivering.

She never made that mistake again. From then on, if Peter was even two minutes late, she took that as confirmation he wasn't coming at all. She was usually right.

She ran through all sorts of theories that first year. Peter had some sort of short-term memory-loss problem—but then why did his lapses never extend to his coursework? Peter was living a double life as a government agent and could not keep track of his lies—but what life would that be, and what spy would choose to pose as a graduate student of all things? Peter had some sort of addiction problem. This suggestion was popular among the rest of the cohort—especially Belinda, who began fretting that Peter was on heroin—but the evidence simply didn't exist. There were no track marks, no nosebleeds, no bizarre habits or bad breath. He was looking very thin—but then, he had always been very thin. Peter, when he showed up, was never anything but bright, focused, and alert. And so very nice.

Most likely Peter was just that brilliant, arrogant, and absent-minded all at once; a combination of traits that only talented men like him could be, for the world forgave them any number of transgressions so long as they dazzled. For Peter, probably, making a date was the same thing as making small talk; it smoothed things over, and didn't signify commitment. It wasn't his fault. He wasn't ignoring them on purpose. You couldn't blame a typhoon for its casual destruction; you couldn't fault the sun for disappearing the stars. He simply did not notice the consequences of his actions. None of them were worth his attention, and this fact stung more than anything else.

"Peter's the nicest guy in the world," Belinda observed once, "who always holds you firm at arm's length."

Still, Alice was a professional. She did not let her resentment show, for what was there to resent him for? You couldn't be mad that someone didn't rate you.

Over two years, their working relationship reached a comfortable, friendly equilibrium. Peter, when present, was both helpful and hilarious. He made her life in the lab very easy. He did all the grunt work without being asked, he kept his station clean, and he labeled everything with beautiful clarity. And he never sniped at other graduate students behind their back the way that so many in their department did—perhaps because he was so blissfully secure about his position at the top. At times, she truly enjoyed his company—during late hours in the lab, when they were the only two people at the department, when it seemed the whole world was asleep except for them.

But this was the most baffling thing of all. Alice had these memories—they were from before she was tattooed, and so she could not scrutinize them in detail, but she knew they were *there*. Her head drooping against his shoulder; his jacket draped around her. His tap-dancing across the lab floor, singing out loud a song she had just started humming. Tossing chalk across the room when one of them had run out; reaching, missing, chalk scattered broken on the floor. And their exhausted, deranged laughter, in the late hours when everything seemed funny; the kind of hysterical, rib-aching laughter that left you unable to breathe.

All this had happened. She had not invented it. She had been there, she knew how it felt to make him laugh.

So she might be forgiven if, once upon a time, she had even once deluded herself into thinking she *had* risen to deserve space in Peter's inner world. That she could reach through his shell at last and crack open whatever it was he kept hidden from the rest of them.

This was always the temptation with Peter. He could make you feel so important. His proximity drenched you in the sparkle. The full force of his attention was like a drug. He laughed at a joke you'd made, or he followed you around with questions on your work, and you thought, *I've caught the nature boy.* But he always pulled away, and left you wondering what you had done. Had you offended him? Said the wrong thing? Or had you simply not been enough; not been smart enough, or clever enough? Had he just gotten bored, gotten up, and wandered away?

Alice used to torture herself with the wondering, scrutinizing her still-imperfect memory for how she had driven him away and what it might take to summon him back. But there were no answers. She was not at fault. Peter was a wild thing; he would not be approached by anyone. An abyss yawned between him and everyone else. The rest of them were so plodding, mundane, earthbound; and Peter was always flying off to worlds where they could not follow.

So she had simply stopped wondering. It hurt too much. There were no answers; there was only the gulf. All she knew was this: She could coexist with Peter Murdoch. She could even, when she let her guard down, when she was either sleep-deprived or desperate enough, be very fond of and unfortunately attracted to Peter Murdoch. But she would be a fool to think that she knew him.

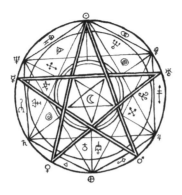

# CHAPTER TWELVE

Alice dreamed.

This was horrible, because in the last year dreaming had become a threat to coherent subjectivity. Dreams were flying-carpet rides through loosely associated memories and Alice simply had too many of them; the routes multiplied infinite, all wish and no repression; in a split second her mind could go from innocent childhood memories to three-headed serpents writhing over crypts, angelic choirs with faces melting away. Freud had argued dreams were the language of the unconscious, and Alice's dreams were written in fine print. She did not float oblivious through vague images; she saw and felt everything, in harsh minute detail; even as those chunks of memory spliced and layered on each other in dreadful combinations. Not only did she remember every dream with exact detail, she remembered all her daydreams and fantasies too, and so the visions compounded, and new dreams built on previous mad fantasies, and each time she entered a dream the pandemonium had expanded, the demons had copulated and multiplied, and each time upon waking it was harder and harder to reconstitute the real.

That night in Hell she imagined that Professor Grimes, with a horse's face, abducted her into a series of underground tunnels that he promised led to the lost archives of the Library of Alexandria. She imagined crawling on her hands and knees, scooping up a silvery-white substance that might have been liquid chalk. She imagined wielding a pair of scissors; stabbing fiercely at a horse's neck until black blood coated her face, and licking at the blood like it was licorice.

She woke to Peter prodding her shoulder. She jolted.

"Shit—sorry." She was supposed to have been keeping watch. "I don't know how—must've—"

"It's okay," he whispered. "I woke up early. We'd better get going. Cat's back, by the way."

"Hmm?"

She blinked around with bleary eyes. Archimedes sat by the fire looking very satisfied with himself, curled chummily against Peter as if he had never abandoned the two of them to probable death.

"Judas," Alice muttered. "Suppose you wanted breakfast."

Archimedes mewed and licked the crumbs off his whiskers.

Peter had already warmed up some Lembas Bread over the fire, and even heated water in two collapsible tin cups for tea. Alice pulled herself to a sitting position and accepted a cup of Darjeeling. "I didn't know you'd brought tea."

"Just a few bags," he said. "It's not so heavy, after all. I was going to save it until the second week, but I thought we deserved a treat."

"Well, thank you." She blew on the surface. "Darjeeling's my favorite."

"I know. You're always snapping at people not to touch your tea bags."

"Well if it's clearly not marked as *department* tea, then it's not communal property."

"No, that's perfectly reasonable. For what it's worth, I always thought it was Michele swiping them. Too many Fortnum bags in his office bin."

She laughed despite herself, and then her mind caught up and she remembered what she'd seen and what she now knew Peter was. A bitter taste seeped through her mouth. She dropped her gaze.

"You all right there?"

"Oh yes," she said, and hastily rearranged her face into a neutral calm. "Just tired."

She kept stealing glances at Peter as they ate. Observing his smile, watching for the cracks.

Part of her wished she'd never seen his notes, for now every interaction with Peter meant filtering through a façade. Was his affable demeanor just a front? Some calculated jester's affect to trick everyone around him into lowering their guard? Deep down, was he just as competitive and insecure as the rest of them? Or worse: was Peter the most dangerous kind of rival, the charming sociopath who never let you suspect for a moment until they slid the blade into your back?

But how did one keep that up for years without slipping? Peter was flaky, yes, but Alice had never once heard rumor of him acting maliciously toward anyone. If anything, he was famously, unnecessarily kind. Everyone adored him, despite having every reason to hate him. Bless Murdoch, everyone said. Annoying as all hell, but his heart's in the right place.

Was it all a grand performance? Had Peter been playing them since the day they'd met?

Alice had spent hours that night staring at his sleeping skull, wondering what thoughts swirled around in that mind. Who *was* he? For all her ambition, Alice could not imagine bringing a friend, or even a colleague, into the pits of Hell like a lamb to the slaughter. She could not fathom Peter's intentions, and this scared her more than anything else: the possibility that, despite years of trying, she did not know who Peter Murdoch was at all.

She felt like an idiot for sharing all that she had last night. She cringed to recall how he'd nodded along, humming in sympathy, his hand on her shoulder. And all the while he must have been cackling inside. *Poor Alice, dear Alice, what an idiot.*

It was no accident he had found her in the lab. She realized this now—he must have known she was going. He *needed* her to go, needed her soul intact for the exchange.

How long had he been awaiting his chance?

Oh, dear God. Now she was trapped in Hell with him.

"Are you doing all right?" Peter asked.

She blinked. "Sorry?"

He nodded to her elbow. "It looks like the swelling's gone down a bit."

She peered at her arm. "Huh. Guess so."

"Fine to keep going?"

She did a quick inventory of her body. Her limbs ached, and her cuts still stung, but it was all superficial. The only thing that really pained her was the anxiety gnawing in her gut, but this she had no choice but to endure. "I think so."

"Let's be on then." He smiled, stood up, and extended his hand. Archimedes stood further ahead, tail swishing impatiently.

"Yes, all right."

*Pretend*, she told herself as she grasped his hand. *Pretend for your life.*

AS DESIRE FADED BEHIND THEM, THE terrain changed rapidly beneath their feet. The campus path became bumpy and riddled with potholes. Then the bricks gave way to unpaved dirt. Soon it became clear they were descending a yawning slope, the ground crumbly and treacherous. They had to pause with each step, carefully testing their purchase before they put their weight on the ground. At least Alice had some practice with this—one summer there had been construction on Mill Road between Magdalene College and the department, and the whole sidewalk was torn up. It was a season of twisted ankles. In time they came upon a rift in the ground, a wide abyss cleaving the space between Desire and beyond. Their path thinned into a perilous strand of stairs that wound down to the bottom and crawled up the other side. Below on their left, level with the base of the abyss, churned the Lethe; no longer still now, but a foaming, vicious rush.

"Oh, dear." Peter halted.

But Archimedes proceeded with confidence. Alice examined the path, and saw footholds. They weren't very good, or visible, but they were there. "Keep your knees bent and your arms out for balance," she said. "It'll be fine." In Ithaca she had hiked the slippery paths near the gorges, and even on rainy days it looked worse than it was. You only fell if you were trying. Alas—in Ithaca, they were so often trying.

She supposed it made sense that such a barrier separated the first two courts from the third. Petty pride, insatiable desire—these were self-centered things, and their harms turned inward. But from covetousness sprang plotting; sprang malice toward others. Here, however, to get what you wanted meant making sure others did not get it. Bhishma said in the *Mahabharata* that from covetousness proceeded sin. Saint Paul warned the church that money was the root of all evil. So here now were the proper schemers; the ones who knew what they were doing, and deserved to pay.

She wished she had thought to bring hiking sticks. She kept tripping against the rocks, and Peter kept catching her, which irked her, because she hated to still find comfort in his presence. It was a horrible paradox; the fact of his intended betrayal on one hand, and the empirical evidence that he was still *Peter*, the Peter she remembered, the Peter she liked.

Worse was the fact that Peter would not stop talking. He had decided riddles would be a fun way to pass the time. So far they had done the burnt ropes (you have two ropes that burn down within an hour; armed with a match, how do you measure forty-five minutes?), the Ping-Pong ball (how do you get a Ping-Pong ball out of a pipe?), and the nine weighted balls (using a balancing scale only twice, how do you identify which one of nine balls is slightly heavier than the rest?). Now he kept going on about some story involving fairy worlds. "What goes through the glass green door, Alice?"

"Um. I don't know. Elves? Children?"

"The moon can pass. The earth cannot. Kittens can pass. Cats cannot. What goes through the glass green door?"

*Shut up*, Alice wanted to screech.

She could handle all sorts of cruelty. But she would not be made an idiot. Professor Grimes had instilled in her a deep horror of ever being made an idiot.

"Fools can pass," Peter went on. "But wise men cannot. Geese can pass, but ducks cannot."

"I don't—oh, hell, is it something about plurals?"

He shook his head. "A stool can pass. But a table cannot."

"Just tell me the answer."

"It's the double letters." He looked put out. "Simple. Thought you did languages."

Alice did not have a diplomatic reply to this, so she trudged on in silence.

**THREE WEEKS INTO ALICE'S FIRST SEMESTER**, Professor Grimes had taken her to the faculty club for tea. Alice was very nervous and excited about this. She had stayed up late the night before preparing talking points about what classes she'd enjoyed and what she'd struggled with so far, and a seven-point proposal for new projects. She had never gone out socially with Professor Grimes and she wanted reassurance that he liked her.

But the first question he asked, after he'd ordered them two sultana scones and a pot of Darjeeling, was, "You see that kid?"

Alice glanced out the window, and with a start glimpsed Peter Murdoch wandering past. He wasn't paying them any attention. He was just doddering around on the sidewalk, blinking at a sheet of paper. Alice's chest tightened. She didn't have any classes with Peter that term, and she hadn't spoken to him since that orientation tea, though her heart always beat oddly when she saw him in passing around campus. He looked lost. He kept glancing up at street signs, then turning round in a circle, like a dog chasing its own tail.

"That's your competition," said Professor Grimes. "Your yardstick. The only thought in your head these next five years should be whether you are keeping pace with him."

Alice glanced back outside at Peter, who now waved apologetically at a honking car as he darted across the street.

*Keeping pace*, he'd said. Not beating him.

"The world will be much easier for him," Professor Grimes continued. "He looks, acts, and speaks like a magician. He does the classical sort of research the Royal Academy favors. His parents are famous. Everyone in our field already knows his name. When he goes in for job interviews, he will know to ask about his colleagues' children, because firstly he might already know them and secondly he will remind his interviewers of them. You, on the other hand. You don't talk like them, you don't look like them, and your research doesn't fit what they're looking for. You will always have to perform twice as well for half the acclaim. You have no room for mistakes."

Alice had suspected all this for a while. She'd just never expected anyone to lay it out so bluntly, and she wasn't prepared for how much it hurt. She stared back into Professor Grimes's impassive face, and wondered why he'd brought her here at all.

"I don't say this to discourage you," said Professor Grimes. "I say this because I've been where you are. You and I—we were not so blessed. We have to climb our way up. You're doing good work, Law. But that's just it. It's merely *good*. I need you to be exceptional."

"I can be exceptional," Alice said, for it seemed the only reply she could make.

"Good girl." Professor Grimes nodded at her untouched cup. "Drink your tea."

He did this often over the next few years. Every failure of hers was cast in direct reference to Peter's success. You've coauthored one paper. Murdoch has coauthored three. You've won a thousand pounds in funding. Murdoch's won twice that. You can't make the same mistakes as Murdoch, he told her. You don't have as much room to fail. And she knew he was only being a good advisor, for a good advisor kept you aware of the reality of your situation. Professor Grimes had come up from humbler origins than she had; he'd come to magick late, he was the first in his family to graduate college, he didn't know which fork to use either. From his perspective, surely, he was showing her the keys to the kingdom.

But she couldn't help but feel a little sting every time he brought it up. As if she'd disappointed him by being born to the wrong sort of parents, with the wrong sort of face, without connections, without a cock. As if he were coaching her to run a race they both knew she'd already lost.

So perhaps she watched Peter more than was good for her. Her eyes lingered on his shadow every time they were in the same room. She studied his habits, his mannerisms, the cadence of his speech. She pondered which traits she could adopt. She couldn't get away with his haplessness; no one would afford her that much grace. And she couldn't study the way he did, or the way he claimed he did; she could not comprehend dense pages in a single glance. But maybe she could try to move with his lightness, or at least smile half as often.

She developed a hyperawareness of Peter. She knew the precise patter of his footsteps. She always knew if he was in the building—she could spot his scuffed shoes, his broken umbrella, the brown wool coat always hung on the third hook from the left. She could always tell when people were talking about him; it was comical, really, the way her ears perked at any mention of his name. She knew his laughter from across the hall. She would have known it from the other end of the world.

She would come to regret this later, the year everything went south, the year she lost the ability to forget things she should not have heard.

She was napping in the lab that day. She napped in the lab often; no one minded, they just walked around her. And Alice always had a habit of disappearing into the bench. She was slight, and she did not snore; if you didn't look carefully, you might think she was a pile of coats. She had just awoken when the door opened and Peter walked in, chattering animatedly to someone she didn't know.

She could have gotten up. It would have been the polite thing to do. But that old impulse, the need to observe Murdoch in every context, made her lie very still.

She tried to make out his interlocutor. It was hard to guess from voice alone; a table blocked her view. She was never sure thereafter of his identity. She could only guess, and the guessing was worse. The guest spoke with an American accent but seemed well-versed in the Cambridge way of magick. A visiting scholar, then. Someone here for a talk, or just passing through, catching up with colleagues. Possibly Princeton. Probably Harvard.

"—not so bad," Peter was saying. "I mean he has his fits,

everyone knows, but you just learn to read his mood. On the whole he's been pretty good. Nothing like the rumors."

"What about the girl?" asked his guest.

Alice would always remember how easily the words slid out of Peter's mouth. There were words you said to create an effect, words constructed to influence your interlocutor. Then there were words you really believed, had believed all along, words just waiting for the right prod to spill.

"Oh, her," said Peter. "No, I wouldn't say she has a problem."

"What do you mean?"

"I mean she's like a bird," said Murdoch. "Hopping where the seed is. Eating right out of his hand."

"Burrowing in for warmth," said his guest.

"Warmth," Peter drawled, the nastiest sound Alice had ever heard Peter make. There was the sound of fists against palms, some unquestionably vulgar gesture. They both laughed.

Peter suggested they go look at the glass suspensions in Helen Murray's lab, and his guest agreed. The door clicked shut behind them. Their footsteps faded down the hall.

They probably did not remember this conversation. This was not cruelty for them. They had not decided, *Now, since we are misogynists, let us make fun of a girl!* These were just words like water; hear them, laugh, and move on. Probably. Peter was not trying to sabotage her then. He just really did not care.

But little impressions spread. Peter never had to think about this, but Alice did; the simmering mass of gossip that underwrote who got positions and power. Academia involved so many hairsplitting decisions between identical candidates, most made ultimately on a whim. The reach of someone's advisor. A fragment of hearsay. She could never state this theory out loud, because it sounded crazy. But she was certain of it now: she could draw a straight line from that laughter in the lab to her failure to win the Cooke.

Harvard had thrown a Cooke reception in July. The selection committee would have gone. No decisions had been made yet. There would have been wine, and then gossip. Impressions would have solidified. It was very plausible. She was not crazy.

Of course she wanted to be wrong. For months and months she held on to the hope that she was wrong, that it was all in her head, and she was making it all up. Surely no one else lived like this—burdened by the tiniest details they assumed had enormous consequences. Surely no one else was so anchored by anxiety. Other people could stumble and shake their heads and move on. How she envied their lightness.

This marked the difference between them. Alice fretted, and Peter danced on air.

If ever she brought it up, he truly would not remember. And if she tried ever to explain how he had hurt her, then he would think her mad. "You sabotaged my career," she would tell him. And to this he would say, quite innocently, "What?"

AS THEY PICKED THEIR WAY DOWN the ridge it became clear they were not alone. A caravan of other journeyers—all Shades, all souls who had passed or bypassed Desire—appeared on the rocks around them. The slope was funneling them all in the same direction. Alice peered round at the Shades' faces, trying to imagine what they had done. It made sense that so many progressed from Lust to Greed, if one trusted Dante's account of things. They were both sins of incontinence and desire; only greed was the sin of desire turned against others, a sin committed when one realized that others, too, would do anything it took to get what they wanted.

Could Professor Grimes be here? It was possible, and she supposed she ought to be looking. But she simply didn't feel Professor Grimes was motivated by riches. No one went into academia if they wanted to get rich. Certainly some were there for the paychecks—and they were bottom-rung, bottom-feeder types who inevitably left for industry. But if what you wanted was money, then you'd just go become a banker or lawyer or something like that. Certainly all of Alice's undergraduate classmates thought she was crazy, to keep studying at Cambridge when she could have gone and worked in minor magickal industries for six figures and a yearly bonus. At least two folks Alice knew who'd majored in magick were now vice presidents at regional banks. But Alice had never wanted money, she had wanted the truth.

She was certain this was true as well for Professor Grimes, who was always turning down lucrative speaking opportunities so as to focus on his research. No—despite his nice town house, his nice clothes, and his nice collection of scotch, Alice knew that Professor Grimes wasn't in this field for money. He'd just gotten rich by accident. Maybe minor academics squabbled with each other over funding, but Professor Grimes never had the need. He was simply too good for it all.

"I bet those are trustees." Peter had made a game of guessing the sins of Shades they encountered, which would have been annoying if his observations weren't quite so funny. "I bet that's a serial plagiarizer. I bet those are assistant deans. There's a special place in Hell for deans, don't you think? Upping their own salaries when the rest of us are scraping by on digestives?"

Alice did not think Peter had ever scraped by on anything but did not have the energy to contest this.

In time they saw they would not have to trek to the bottom of the abyss after all. There was a bridge, hewn of the very same stone of the cliffs, camouflaged so they had not seen it from above. It was generous in span, wide enough they could walk across comfortably side by side, and ornately carved. Each step was made of a half dozen embellished tiles, each column and window lined with figurines. Alice wondered what deity had done this. It seemed bizarre to construct a bridge down here, hidden against the rock. Like plucking out a chunk of Venice and balancing it inside the Grand Canyon.

A Shade dithered at the center, as if unsure whether to cross. He kept taking a few steps forward, then a few steps back. When he saw them approaching he asked, "Stone seventeen?"

"Sorry?" said Peter.

The Shade waved his transcript at them. "There it says stepping stone seventeen, stone seventeen for three years or until I've learned my lesson, whichever comes first."

Peter frowned at the transcript. "I still don't—"

"Oh, here." The Shade darted around them. Alice noticed an empty slot on the bridge, marked with the Roman numeral XVII. The Shade climbed down and assumed a kneeling position. The most extraordinary thing happened then. His features blurred; his extremities faded away; and his grayness deepened. In seconds he had become rock, and the softest sigh emitted from the gap where once had been his mouth; a low note that took several long seconds to fade, and even then, persisted in the wind.

"Gosh," said Alice.

It was apparent now the entire bridge, and all its ornamentation, was formed of petrified Shades. Everywhere she could trace out clues of human forms. Here, an extended leg; there, two arms wrapped over a head. But the footsteps held firm, and there were no other trails that got them across, so it seemed only reasonable to proceed forth. Archimedes darted across without hesitation. A chorus of moans echoed in his wake, and as Alice followed, all she could think of was the particular pitch of each moan on each step; how if you could just jump across five steps at once, you could play the opening to Mozart's Symphony No. 25.

The path was thinner across the bridge, and more treacherous—this time, they had to haul themselves uphill. Further up, two Shades were tussling over a particularly bendy part of the path.

The dispute seemed to be over who should have made way for the other, which struck Alice as rather pointless, since they were all going to the same destination in the end. But the Shades kept jostling one another, until one placed his hands on the other's shoulders and pushed him clean off an overpass.

"Watch out!" Peter yanked Alice back.

Concerned, Alice peeked over the ledge. But the fallen Shade simply picked himself up and proceeded at an undignified crawl up toward the bank, none the worse for the wear. They were already dead, she supposed. Anything that happened now was just an indignity.

The Shade who'd pushed the other peeked over the ledge as well, then huffed as if with satisfaction before continuing on his way. Alice and Peter followed cautiously in his wake.

"What a dick," muttered Alice.

"I wonder what he did." Peter squinted at the Shade, then cried in a too-loud whisper, "Why, that's Bill Cadeaux!"

Fortunately the Shade named Bill Cadeaux did not hear. The name rang only a faint bell for Alice. "Who's that?"

"He and Hollis Galloway were up for the same job back in the sixties," said Peter. "It was a terrible scandal."

"Hollis Galloway the semiotician?"

Peter nodded. "They're both semioticians. *Were*. So Cadeaux and Galloway were up for the same job at Chicago, and after the job talks they decided to make an offer to Galloway. Only Cadeaux got wind of it and started sending anonymous letters to Chicago pretending to be graduate students alleging that she'd—you know—"

"Diddled them?" Alice supplied.

"Basically, yes. Which wouldn't have been such a big deal, except that Cadeaux was pretending to be *female* students, which made Galloway out to be some sort of predatory lesbian. Now, Chicago doesn't mind predators; lesbians, that's another story. So

Chicago launches this whole investigation into Galloway, who might actually *have* been a lesbian, just not the predatory kind, and so she gets so scared off that she rescinds her job application, and Cadeaux gets the job, and no one knew any better until word got out he was bragging about it to graduate students at the pub. He'd made the whole thing up. He'd got his mum and sisters to handwrite anonymous letters and everything. Galloway found out and swore she'd ruin his career, except she died in a car accident before anyone could get to the bottom of things."

"Jesus," Alice muttered. "I'd think he belongs in worse than Greed."

"And then once the word spread, he insisted he was innocent. Swore to his dying day that none of the allegations were made up, that Galloway really *had* harassed all those students." Peter stared after Bill Cadeaux, fascinated. "I just can't understand it. How you could do that to someone else. How you could live with yourself after."

Alice thought Peter was laying it on rather thick, considering. "I think some people are just that selfish."

"I mean, but to sabotage a colleague! That's demonic!"

"Oh, sure." Alice could not restrain herself. "And you're an absolute angel yourself."

Immediately she regretted saying this. Peter slowed his pace. "What does that mean?"

"Sorry—nothing—I only meant, we're all competitive, aren't we? There's department politics everywhere."

He seemed unconvinced. "Are you angry with me?"

"No." She tried to speak calmly, and instead her voice came out a bright chirrup. "Why would I be?"

"You've been short with me all morning."

"Sorry." Alice hugged her arms across her chest. She might have done a better job acting the fool, she knew, but she simply wasn't a very good actor. "I'm only very tired, and very hungry. It's not you."

"Okay." They continued walking in silence for a moment. Then Peter asked, "Is this about the Cooke?"

"What? No!"

"It's just you've been a little weird ever since I mentioned it. And I know it was rude to brag, and I'm sorry . . ."

She was certain now he was fucking with her. How cruel, how unbelievably cruel this was. She felt like a small animal, trapped in a cage.

What if she laid it all out in the open? She had half a mind to do so. Anything to put an end to this torture. I know what you're doing, she could say—your puppy dog act won't work on me, *fuck* you, Murdoch. But then what? Would he confess, apologize? Ludicrous. More likely he, too, would push her over the ledge. He didn't need her whole, he only needed her alive. The only relevant feature in that spell was the presence of a living soul. And Peter could do anything to her before he dragged her over the finish line.

She fought to keep her voice level. "It's not the Cooke."

"Then what is it? Have I done something?"

"It's not you, honestly—"

"Was it about that one morning? Is it my—"

"*God*, Murdoch, no!"

"If you're angry with me, just *tell* me."

"It's just—" She broke off. She could not shake the sudden conviction that someone was laughing at her. She was sure she'd heard a woman giggle. She glanced about but saw no one. Peter's face set in familiar concern, and she felt the panic again that she was going mad. "I'm just—"

There it was again, a definite tinkling laugh.

Alice spun around. "Stop that!"

"Stop what?"

"Can't you hear it?" She marched around the embankment. Someone was hiding, lurking, she knew it—only everywhere she turned she saw only rock. The nearest Shade was Bill Cadeaux, and he was well up the slope by now. Still the laughter intensified. It was so clear now; she couldn't have imagined it. Archimedes, too, had sensed something. The cat froze in its steps, eyes like slits, tail stiff as a board.

"Alice, stop." Peter grasped her arm. "Sit down, have some water—"

She wriggled away. "*Stop*, listen—"

Archimedes yowled.

A flurry of color emerged out of the rock—rippling skeins of reds and pinks and purples, truly, an attack on the senses, after all that endless gray and burning red. At first Alice thought they'd been swarmed by butterflies, or sentient rosy clouds, until the silks stopped ballooning and settled against the form of a tall and slender woman.

"Hello, there." She beckoned to them, waving. "Come closer."

Alice froze, unsure whether that was the kind of "come closer" mermaids uttered before they dragged you underwater.

"I'm sorry I've been rude." The woman lifted a sleeve to her lips and giggled in a way that was not sorry at all. "I get so nosy. Don't run, dears." Her silks rippled, and suddenly she was right in front of them. "I don't bite."

She was terribly beautiful. A dimpled smile against a round, open face. Black hair so shiny it was reflective, drifting weightless around her waist. She floated within robes changing colors as quickly as water dappling under sunlight. She held skeins of thread in both hands; as she spoke, her fingers worked quickly, pulling them through some loom that floated on its own, and the cloth she produced seemed to disappear just as quickly into the rippling folds of her dress.

Alice racked her mind but could not match this woman to any of the descriptions of Hell's deities. The woman lifted a sleeve to her brightly painted mouth and tittered. "Cat got your tongue?"

The silks at her waist arced back and forth in the air. Some bell rang faintly in Alice's mind; some half-forgotten footnote, some arcane mention she hadn't bothered chasing up. Not Arachne, not the Yellow Emperor's wife. A deity of stars, feathers, and longing.

"You're from above." Alice remembered now. She hadn't run across the Weaver Girl in any of her research on Hell, but rather in an undergraduate seminar on translated mythologies. The Weaver Girl, a daughter of the stars, fell in love with the mortal Cowherd, and their love was forbidden by the gods. Only on one day of the year were they permitted to reunite, and when they did, a flock of magpies formed a bridge beneath their feet. "You're the goddess of lovers reuniting. Lovers long separated."

The Weaver Girl beamed. "Very good!"

"But what are you doing here? Your sort don't die."

"Right again," said the Weaver Girl. "But mortals do."

"Your lover," Alice realized.

"My Cowherd." The Weaver Girl's silks flashed blood-red, brown, then listless gray. "My star sisters warned me his hair would whiten, that his bones would crumble, that one day I would look into that face and feel no passion at all. But it all happened so *quickly*. One day, the strapping man I adored. The next, a skeleton. Then one night his heart stopped. I followed him to the next world. But this was not enough!" Her silks turned pitch-black, heavy. "He wanted to reincarnate. I could not. Our souls are not like those of humans; to be washed clean and plopped into new bodies to try again. I begged him to stay here with me. But he grew bored by sands with no ocean and a sky without stars. We thought once we had conversation enough to last through eternity. It turns out we couldn't even last the year." The Weaver Girl's voice shook. "One day, I awoke and found he had abandoned me for the Lethe. Ever since I have roamed these fields alone. At the crossing from Desire to Greed, where desire runs dry, and lovers think only of themselves."

A tear trickled glistening down her cheek. The effect was very tragic, though Alice thought she was rather hamming it up. Perhaps this was how immortal deities passed the time, perfecting their own mythologies.

The Weaver Girl pointed up, and the two ends of her sash did a spiraling dance toward the sky. "The next chance you have, look up at the night sky. It's missing a constellation. A bridge is broken." Her sash collapsed. "Darkness, now."

"Haven't you ever tried to find him?" asked Peter.

"We aren't allowed, dear boy. And in any case, he would not know me. He's washed all memory of me out of his mind."

"Oh," said Peter. "I'm sorry."

"You're so sweet." The Weaver Girl reached out and tweaked his nose. Peter's entire face turned red.

Alice was not sure how she was supposed to react to all this. The Weaver Girl was talking quite a lot. But this at least offered her some respite—it gave her time to assess whether this deity wanted to play with them or kill them.

"But still I am a romantic!" The Weaver Girl spread her sleeves. A magnificent display of color. "It was never wise for a deity to wed a mortal, I see that now. One needs a shared perspective on time. Deities do not love so fleetingly, so hopelessly, with every ounce of their soul. But humans—you live for a breath, you die, and you spend your whole lives wondering how you might stay together in the afterlife, when you don't even know if that's what you truly want."

She drifted closer—uncomfortably close—and her long fingers stretched out to dance over their shoulders. Alice had the absurd fear she might knock their heads together and make them start kissing like dolls.

"I see so many of you. Murder-suicides, that's common. Or accidents. Sometimes both parties die natural deaths, and one party waits years in the Fields of Asphodel until the other dies of old age." The Weaver Girl sighed. "Everyone thinks their love is eternal. I like to let them keep believing."

"So let us through," said Peter. "Love isn't a crime."

"Indeed it isn't," said the Weaver Girl. "I do not inflict punishment, dear boy. I offer a solution." She clasped her hands together. "I offer you a test. No arduous quest; only the answer to a question. I test your loyalty. If you pass, I build a bridge." She brought her hands together. Her fingers moved quick, and threads spilled out between them, conjuring just for a moment a fabric that rippled and glittered; twinkling gold and silver against velvety black. A carpet made of stars. "My bridge will lead to any place you wish. Any boundary, any court. The Rebel Citadel, if you wish. Or straight to Lord Yama's throne. Pass, and I will let you walk this bridge just once, to any place you wish to go."

"What if we fail?" asked Peter.

"Then, into the Lethe you go."

"But we're not dead," said Alice. "We aren't Shades."

"Oh, you're *sojourners*!" The Weaver Girl's hands flew to her mouth. Her eyes shone huge. "But even better. Then you must *really* need safe passage." Her fingers danced; the bridge rippled over the abyss. "These rocks are tricky, my loves. Prove your faith, and I'll send you safely through."

Alice did not like this. The Weaver Girl in her simpering giggles reminded her of the heroines from Chinese dramas her mother liked to play when she was a child—scheming, nefarious creatures who were always trying to shove their rivals down wells. And though she could not fit the Weaver Girl into her schema of Hell, she knew of every tale about bargains and wagers with the divine. Orpheus failed Hades's challenge. Sisyphus tried to cheat Hades as well, and failed. There had to be a catch, there was always a catch.

"Can we consult?" she asked. "In private?"

The Weaver Girl flicked her sleeve. "Be quick."

Alice tugged Peter by the arm until they were out of earshot. "I don't trust her."

"We don't need to trust her," he said. "We just need to play. What's the worst that can happen?"

"Well, amnesia, weren't you listening?" Alice was not certain about the extent of her tattoo's protection, but she did not want to test it against submersion.

"Then we'll just win, it can't be hard—"

"And that's supposing she's telling the truth," said Alice. "Deities above don't wander often in Hell, you know—she could be in disguise—"

"What else would she be?"

"I don't know. Could be the sorcerer—"

"If she's the sorcerer, we're screwed anyways! Look, Law." Peter spread his hands. "This is a godsend. We're struggling enough as is, and she's promising safe passage—"

"I don't want to get dropped into the river," said Alice. "Which is, by the way, exactly what will happen, since we are not in love."

"But can't you pretend?"

She stared into his face. Open, beguiling—how long had it taken him to master that hangdog look? How could he possibly look at her like this, intending what he did?

But maybe she could pretend too. Maybe she could beat him at his own game. She had one great advantage, after all, which was that Peter didn't know that she knew the truth. "You want me to pretend that I love you."

"It's easy," he said. "Just assume our wills are united."

"What does *that* mean?"

"Well, that we want all the same things. That we want what's best for each other. That we take one another's ends as our own, and that our ideal outcome is one in which we're together. Haven't you ever been in love?"

"No. Have you?"

"Well, no. But it can't be all that hard to imagine, can it?"

"I think being in love might be the hardest thing to imagine." She paused, considering. "I mean, the erotic complications alone. I haven't even seen your penis."

"Oh my God," said Peter. "Law. We do not have time to articulate a philosophy of love."

"How else do we decide our dominant strategy, then?"

"Just assume we are one person. Your ends are my ends and vice versa. What hurts you hurts me. Our goals are staying together, and pursuing what is best for ourselves as a joint unit."

Alice did not think this was how real relationships worked, at least not from the ones she'd witnessed, but it did sound nice in theory. "Where did you learn that?"

"Immanuel Kant."

"Wasn't Kant a virgin?"

"He was a great philosopher! He revolutionized metaphysics!"

"I believe it was Kant who thought it immoral to masturbate," said Alice. "Something about treating yourself as a means to an end."

"Do you have a better idea?"

Alice's head hurt. To begin with, she did not in fact have an alternate account of love; but second, even if Peter's account of love made sense, she could not disentangle it from his possible ulterior motives for offering it. Deep down she suspected being in love just was two people lying to each other, concealing their violence, and so Peter's proposal was thus misaligned with her priority to look out for herself.

"Come on." Peter nudged her arm. "Law. Is it so hard to pretend you're in love with me?"

The way he said this—it made her chest hurt. He knew exactly what he was doing, and the worst part was that it was working. She wanted so badly to trust him, to be the object of his love, if only for pretend. *Stop it*, she wanted to scream. *Stop, can't you see what you're doing to me?*

"Well, my lovers," called the Weaver Girl. "What will it be?"

"You're on," Peter announced. "We'll play."

"Wait—"Alice began. But the Weaver Girl seized both their arms and, with startling force, dragged them up a rock until they stood facing each other, atop some hellish parody of a wedding altar. Swathes of silk shot up and made an opaque barrier between them. Peter yelled something, but his voice was muffled by the silk.

"No coordinating." The Weaver Girl shimmered, then split into two translucent doubles. Each stepped to either side of the silk wall, and they spoke in unison.

"My Cowherd met me on the seventh day of the seventh month for eighty years without fail." The silks created silhouettes in the sky: two figures running toward each other and embracing, becoming one. "Years passed when I did not see his face. His entire village begged him to forget me and marry—for I could not give him children, you see, nor fulfill any of the duties a wife should. And if ever he did not come, the bridge would break. If ever we were unfaithful, the bridge would break. We were never unfaithful. Always, we chose each other, until the end of his life. Until he chose differently, and condemned me."

The silks spread to create a fork; one red, one green. "I give you a choice, my lovers. The very same choice. You may choose to go on alone, or to go on together. If both of you choose to go together, I will build you a bridge of stars. If you both choose to go on alone, I will throw you both into the Lethe."

"What if we choose differently?" asked Alice.

"Then the one who chooses to go on alone may walk this bridge as many times as they like. You will have safe passage throughout your sojourn. I will guard you against everything and everyone. Nothing will touch you." The bridge danced, shimmered, split into a dozen forking paths. "And the other—well, we might say merely that they will wish for oblivion."

Alice blinked down. Suddenly before her stood a tray table, atop which sat two shiny, waxy apples. One was blood-red, the other deep green.

"What will it be?" asked the Weaver Girl. "Red to go on together. Green to go on alone."

"He has the same choice?"

"The very same."

Oh, Alice thought; then this was just the prisoner's dilemma.

They'd all done prisoner's dilemmas in their first year. The obvious solution to the prisoner's dilemma, if you trusted each other, was not to screw the other party over. The problem of course was that one's dominant strategy was always to screw the other party over, no matter what they did. But if you cooperated beforehand, then you could both get out of jail free. And they had cooperated. Hadn't they?

"Just to clarify," she said. "What happens to him if I choose to go on alone?"

The Weaver Girl's smile seemed to stretch over her entire face. Any further, Alice feared, and her head would split in two. "Hell gets so lonely. I enjoy companions." Great white skeins of fabric emerged from her back and hung poised behind her. A spider's web. If she squinted, Alice could see human remnants in that web; the detritus of centuries of lovers leeched from and discarded. Some of those victims had been alive once. Sojourners. Shades did not leave bones.

Alice shuddered.

This shouldn't be difficult. Their dominant strategy was obvious. Peter had said to pretend they were in love, and if they were in love, they would both choose the red. If they cooperated, they got through, easy as that. She reached for the red apple—but then why wouldn't her fingers close?

She could not help but wonder. Suppose Peter chose the green?

He couldn't do that. It was not in his interest. Peter would not betray her here, Peter still needed her—at least, he needed her soul—

And what, would she simply give it to him? Serve it up on a platter, trot along like a lamb to the slaughter? What silly logic was this?

Her hand drew back.

What then? Should *she* choose the green?

She would not need him then. She would have free rein of Hell, easy access to every court, and Professor Grimes's soul at her fingertips. She could find him in a day, she could be back home by tomorrow. She would have everything she had ever wanted, and all it would cost was leaving Peter behind.

But that was murder.

But then, to go with him, and speed along her own demise—how was that better? How was that smart?

*You cannot do exchange on yourself. You cannot do exchange on yourself, we know this for a certainty, so where does that leave us? What can we possibly conclude except—*

And all this assuming he needed her at all. He might have another plan, he might not even need exchange; he might decide that safe passage was worth it, he might condemn *her* . . .

She felt a stabbing in her temples; twin forces, pressing in. There was too much information, too many memories, and she didn't know how to sort through it, she didn't know what they *meant*. She had gotten this far on a single-minded narrative etched into her brain—*I am Alice Law I am going to Hell I will find Professor Grimes and everything will be all right*—and now that catechism gave her no guidance, the way forth was not clear. The entirety of the past rose vivid in her mind's eye, a thousand television screens playing all at once, and none of them told her the truth, all they gave were snapshots, a useless deluge of detail.

An empty glass of beer, an empty chair. The Pick, quiet before closing, and a bitter taste in her mouth. Belinda's airy sighs. *Have you met Peter Murdoch?* The shape of him; the length of his lashes; chalk on her fingertips, chalk on his shirt. *Look outside*, said Professor Grimes; *you see that kid?* Darjeeling tea, brewed too long, tasting like acid. Dry scones like cement in her throat. She could not swallow it down. Grimes at a blackboard, Grimes at a chessboard. Fortune favors the bold, magick rewards the decisive. The first mover wins; the losers play catch-up. Are you a born loser? Do you have the guts?

Laughter in the lab. *I would have found a new advisor after the Cooke.* A slapping sound, open palms against buttocks, and laughter reprised, louder and louder, footsteps fading away. *Eating right out of his hand.* Big, bold handwriting—there was no hesitation in this writing, this was the scrawl of a mind made up, a mind moving faster than a hand could keep up with, this was not wondering, this was a declaration. *IF ALICE—???*

She felt a whooshing in her ears. She squeezed her eyes shut, tried to assemble the staircase. What is relevant here? What is strategic? What evidence do I have to build premises, so that I may reason to a conclusion? *What would Grimes do?* But this was so difficult. All information was a scramble, she didn't know where to start, she couldn't even seize on foundational premises—

*My name is Alice Law—*
IF ALICE—?
*I am a postgraduate at Cambridge—*
IF ALICE—?
*I study analytic magick—*
If ALICE—?

The planks scattered. She could not latch on to building blocks, she could only cling to a feeling, a sharp panic, ringing in her ears like a dozen fire alarms. Her arm hurt; the pain was back, pinpricks again, but it spread all over. *Not again*, she thought, though she could not even place what *again* meant; it was only a sensation. A needle flashing down. Chalk beneath her skin. Pigment blooming and pain blinding, so many bursts of white—*Not again, please, I'll give anything, but I don't want to feel like this again*—

Vertigo hit. She swayed. Where was this? Where was *she*? Was Hell the memory, was Hell the dream? She raised her hands to her face and could not see them; where her fingers should have been stood figures in miniature, tiny copies of Peter and Grimes all dancing in a procession. *You see that kid?* Green and red circles pulsed behind them, grew larger, drifted against each other until all she saw was a Venn diagram, and in the center, a needle and chalk, the thin blade bobbing, agony up her arm. An imagined conversation from the future: Peter and Grimes, safely returned, sipping tea in the office—*What happened to Alice? Oh, you don't want to know.* And that handwriting again; massive, dancing letters. *If Alice*—? She watched them laughing, watched them rolling their eyes, and felt such a stifling, shameful rage she almost screamed. Pathetic Alice. Everybody's fool.

Peter glanced up, caught her gaze, and grinned.

*I hate you*, she thought; faintly at first, just testing out the idea. And found, to her surprise, that it latched. It fit. She had not dared to think it before, but it was right, it was just—she was not a dog, she would not be kicked. *I hate you, I HATE YOU*—

"Very good!" The Weaver Girl clapped. Her doubles merged back into one. The curtains shimmered, like a magician drumming up a crowd, and then lifted.

There stood Peter, grasping a red apple.

"Alice?" He glanced down at her hands. His brow furrowed. "What did you do?"

## CHAPTER THIRTEEN

In the winter of their first year, Professor Grimes's head lab assistant—a fourth-year named Joshua—abruptly quit the program and fled to Canada. It was a big scandal at the time. Rumor had it Joshua's pregnant girlfriend, fed up with his long hours, imposed an ultimatum that he needed to pay more attention to her and, when that didn't work, packed everything up and fled to her parents' home in Ottawa. Joshua dropped everything for love and followed her there. This involved spending all his savings on a last-minute flight and racing to Heathrow at midnight. It was not this drama but the fact that anyone would leave Cambridge for *Canada* that got the department in a tizzy. Did Canada even have universities, or did everyone just ski and eat maple syrup and run away from bears all year round? Anyhow, as far as anyone knew Joshua was now happily married and working as a tour guide at the Château Laurier.

The relevant part was that Joshua left without wrapping up his projects, or indeed even informing Professor Grimes that he was leaving. This would have been salvageable, if Professor

Grimes were not on deadline for a conference presentation at the Royal Academy of Magick in London.

Alice and Peter were thus recruited to fill in the gaps. They champed at the bit. Who cared if it was unpaid overtime? Who cared if it meant thirty extra hours a week for which they would not be credited, at the same time that they were still burdened with coursework? Professor Grimes wanted their help with real research! The thing they'd trained their whole lives to do! They would have been such fools to say no.

They were only friendly acquaintances when they began the work. Alice had seen little of Peter since their first encounter in the garden, as their classes kept taking them in separate directions. She approached their first meeting with trepidation. What if Peter condescended to her? Worse off, what if she came off as stupid?

She needn't have worried. Difficulty had a way of forging fast friendships; there was no time for interpersonal awkwardness when there was so much to do. How pleasant was the exhaustion of those first days. Every day at five Alice and Peter met in Professor Grimes's basement laboratory, loaded down with stacks of manuscripts, hands dusty with chalk. Those nights they worked frantically for hours and hours until they couldn't see straight. Those nights they spent on the floor of the lab laughing at their own mistakes, eating chips and curry from halal carts and sometimes, if they felt like treating themselves, chicken tikka masala from the Indian place up north of the bridge. This was the best life had to offer: chalk smears on their faces, turmeric-stained fingerprints on graph paper. Complete happiness was some form of study, said Aristotle. And they were so happy; covering entire blackboards with chalk in an inspired frenzy, then erasing the whole thing to start over again. Suppressing their giggles, putting on a straight face every time they heard Professor Grimes's footsteps coming down the stairs.

It was in the midnight hours, when the mind fractured and things stopped making sense and the boundaries of the possible became fluid, that they did their best work. And in these hours, Alice experienced for the first time what she thought it might be like to fall in love.

She was not new to the language of courtship. There were boyfriends in high school, boyfriends in college; nervous young men in button-downs smelling of aftershave who traipsed one after another in a forgettable procession of silent films, fumbling hands. Dimly she understood this kind of socializing turned into "going steady," into marriage—she just couldn't understand how, when it all felt an exercise in concealing your distaste. Peter did not belong to this genre. This was an entirely different type of feeling, and Alice could not consign what they had to the trash heap of romance. This was love, a love she had never known; *At last*, she thought, *this is the real thing*—this gradual unfolding of another soul, charting one's course into privileged inner territory, making discoveries of which you felt you were the first. Alice loved her work for just this reason, so why wouldn't she fall in love with people, too?

She learned that Peter liked to hum Mendelssohn as he worked, but would blush and stop if she started humming along. She learned that Peter loved lentils, but hated mashed potatoes and bananas because they had a quality he found "deceptively mushy." She learned that at approximately two in the morning Peter transitioned into what they called his "manic state," which was when his hair fluffed up and his eyes went wide and started windmilling and he got so excited about everything they were working on that he was unable to communicate with anything more than a frenzied, "AHHH!"

And if falling in love was discovery, was letting yourself be discovered the equivalent to being loved? For it tickled Alice to hear Peter make observations about her; to announce facts she'd never noticed about herself. Did she know, for instance, that she flopped her hands like a jellyfish whenever she disagreed with an argument? Did she know that she always ended up with the same diagonal streak across her forehead, left by pushing her hair back with the same chalky fingers? Peter determined that when Alice got sleepy, she lied—not in any malicious way, but in absurd ways; words just streamed from her half-conscious mouth in no sensical order. He was so amused by Alice's unconscious lying that for weeks he recorded the sillier things she said, all so he could announce at the end of the month: "I have concluded that your lying, sleeping self has a single motive. And it is to continue sleeping for as long as possible. You will answer in any way that convinces your interlocutor to leave you alone. For instance, see here, my transcript from Wednesday—I ask you if you are an eggplant. And you agree you are an eggplant, but that I shouldn't worry, and that everything is fine. In the past month I have heard you agree that you are the princess of Belgravia, that your toes are really baby hamsters, and that over the holidays, you will join me skiing on the sun. You are incorrigible, Law. Your unconscious id is fiercely protective of being left alone."

There were no thoughts they could not share. They reached that rare state of comfort with another person, in which speaking out loud was just the same as thinking in your head—nothing filtered, nothing hidden. Often, instead of going home to sleep, they would stay up until the latest hours of the morning talking. They argued over the Monty Hall problem. Peter thought it obvious you should switch; Alice refused to be convinced. They argued over whether numbers had colors and personalities. Peter insisted they did: three was blue, five was red, two was yellow, and four was orange; eight was a ponderous bore, and nine was a voluptuous seductress—and what color? Oh, obviously, burgundy. Nine was wine. Alice thought he was making this up for attention. They argued over whether, on the question of language's relationship to reality, Wittgenstein and Lacan were climbing the same mountain from different sides (possibly, they concluded, but neither of them could comprehend Lacan well enough to say for certain).

Peter was the best kind of interlocutor: generous, open-minded, inquisitive. He thought every new discipline was fascinating, and he asked her questions about her own field she'd never considered before.

"What's Jakobson say about language?" he would ask. "What's metonymy? What's metaphor? What does it mean for the unconscious to be structured like a language? What *is* a language?"

When they spoke he would stare, unblinking, at her face in a manner that, every now and then, made her stutter and drop what she was holding. It was hard for her to receive Peter's attention. She had wondered for so long what it would take to get it, and now, although she had it in spades, it paralyzed her.

He taught her that maths could be fun, sometimes, so long as you were solving paradoxes about potatoes. Suppose you have a hundred kilos of potatoes. They are 99 percent water. Suppose overnight they dry, so that they are now only 98 percent water. How many kilos of potatoes do you have? Only fifty! *Fifty?* Yes, fifty, down from one hundred! But you've only lost 1 percent water. But how could this be? "It's simple arithmetic," he said, but Alice did not believe.

Alice, in turn, taught him about Chinese acrostic poems—written so as to be intelligible no matter which direction you read them in. She taught him about the intricacies of Chinese grammar, or really how there was none, and how in Chinese the conceptual metaphors for time and space were the opposite of in English. The Chinese believe you can see the past, but not the future, she explained; therefore you can only walk backward into the future. And Peter, fascinated, declared he was going to learn

Chinese so he could understand her better, until a brief exercise with tones—and tone-deafness—disabused him of the hope it could be so easy.

Back then they even developed their own shorthand language, an idiotic combination of symbolic logic—which was just funny to utter out loud—and French, which only Alice spoke and which Peter thought sounded funny. There was a lot of honking, in lieu of actual French. This language was not at all efficient, but it amused them; it made them feel even more that they existed on a mental plane removed from everyone else, that soon they would disappear into their own symbolic order and never be understood by anyone else again but each other.

Often they descended into incoherent laughter. Oh, how she loved his laugh. At a certain point past midnight when their minds were addled they would start to giggle at everything, but every now and then Alice said something so absurd it made Peter erupt into helpless, full-body laughter. It lurched through him, syncopated his breath, made his arms flail, elbows up before his chest like if he didn't try to hold himself together that laughter would break him into a million pieces. When Peter laughed it felt like the entire warmth of the sun was turned on her, because *she* had done it, she had uttered the words that so surprised and delighted him that he couldn't even breathe.

There was a time when she felt all she ever wanted to do was to make Peter Murdoch laugh.

Just as often, they fell into a happy silence as they worked. They could go for hours without speaking; they'd developed such a comfortable natural rhythm around each other. All Alice needed for company was the confident scribble of Peter's chalk beside her. She was not alone. She was safe. There was at least a single other soul in this universe who vibrated at her same frequency. And really that was the happiest Alice had ever felt—how wonderful, truly, to have a friend whose silence you adored.

Anyhow.

All this happened before the period when Alice remembered everything, so it was a mere fog to her now. And even if she could remember, she suspected it would feel absurdly distant no matter what, like a life lived by two entirely different people—younger, happier, more innocent people. They were not the same people. Distant cousins, maybe. Passing resemblance.

How quickly things could change. The term ended. The project concluded. Professor Grimes gave his presentation in Bruges to a standing ovation, and Alice and Peter no longer had any reason to grind midnights at the lab. And instantly, Peter pulled away.

It took Alice far too long to get the hint. Fool that she was, she thought their friendship extended outside the lab; that whatever had happened across all those midnight hours would endure. She thought he'd felt it too. They had no classes together, but she invented reasons to come across him. She started lingering in the graduate students' lounge, just in case he came in for a coffee. Weeknights she would swing by the halal cart hoping she would find him ordering his usual chips and curry. She had no particular goal in mind. Nothing so concrete as a dinner date. Nothing so bold. She had not thought that far; the question did not even take form. She only wanted to hear him laugh.

But he was never there.

She could not blame him for this. Their teaching schedules did not overlap. They shared no lab assignments, nor were they taking any classes together. There was no reason they ought to spend time together, except that she had enjoyed it, and wanted to do it more. But he had not promised her his time. He did not owe her anything. He was busy, they all were, and increasingly so as their responsibilities doubled. She couldn't begrudge him that.

But even this did not account for the way he behaved when

their paths did cross. When they walked past one another in the hallway—one leaving Grimes's office, one about to enter—he only nodded. When they attended the same department functions, they exchanged nothing but bland pleasantries. Hi, how are you? Fine, yeah, same old, grinding away—great, yeah, good to see you, take care. She cracked jokes, references meant only for him, but he did not laugh, or did not hear. On many occasions she lingered at doorways, hoping to walk out with him, but he walked past without seeing her.

It was so humiliating the way she'd lingered, hoping for his attention—like a dog that didn't know that it had been abandoned, that kept on coming back. He was not rude to her. In fact he was perfectly polite, wearing that classic Murdoch smile. He gave her the same kind attentiveness that he would to any stranger.

But this hurt, for she had thought they were anything but.

And when at last the fact of the matter sank in—that Peter did not wish to see her, and did not hold her in special regard—she still could not wrap her mind around it. She could not understand how you could open your mind to someone so completely, for so long, and then slam it shut again.

She wanted to ask him what had happened but could not formulate the question in a way that wasn't childish. *Why don't you like me anymore? Why don't you want to be my friend?* Questions for the playground; pathetic utterances. She would not say them, she would not confirm for him that she was too dull for his attention.

That following term she cycled through every emotion she might have felt toward Peter—disappointment, anger, resentment, longing—a whole slew of one-sided angst. But above all she was confused. All the walls were up. She had been thrown out in the cold. An abyss lay between them, and she did not know how she had caused this.

Then she went to Venice. Then several things happened in Venice, and Alice began to feel everything slipping away from her. That was the start, she had since realized; the moment she learned that when it came to Professor Grimes, she really had no ability to say no.

And then she came back, and everything went wrong, and for the last year, Alice had been unable to pass Peter in the hallway without dropping her gaze.

There was a time when everything was going sideways that Alice tried to fix things. Let the record display she did not give up so easily on love: that she actually did try to sit down, hammer it all out, and understand what was going on. Peter was still avoiding her, so she slipped a note into his pidge instead. She put it right on top of his stack of correspondence, a place where he could not fail to see. It had been a while, she wrote. She was wondering how he was. She wanted to sit down together. Have a cup of tea. Talk.

He saw the note. She knew he did, because the next morning when she checked, the note was gone. Peter knew she had tried. He simply never responded.

If she'd had her perfect memory back then, then she could pick through their interactions—all those late nights, all those smiles—for clues, if not the sheer comfort of reminiscence. But all she had now was icy nods in the hallway; curt greetings; and the flap of his coat, the back of his head, as he hurried out the door.

And then the gossip; the innuendoes, the laughter. Footsteps disappearing down the hall.

That summer, the philosopher Derek Parfit published the very controversial *Reasons and Persons*, and for a while it was all that anyone at Cambridge or Oxford would talk about. Alice read it with great interest. In fact, it helped her sort through much of her confusion. *Reasons and Persons* argues for a reductionist account of personal identity: that is to say, no special essence of personhood that remains stable across one's lifetime. Using a number of thought experiments involving brain transplants, brain divisions, and tele-transportation, Parfit argued that the qualities which we think define essential personhood—psychological connectedness, for instance—do not actually ground any deeper fact. We might share the same cells, bodily continuity, and memories as previous iterations of ourselves. But that is all. There is no further fact of the matter—no essential *us* hovering like a specter. We bear the same relationship to the version of ourselves from ten years ago as we might to a sibling.

Now, Alice did not understand much about moral philosophy, and she was inclined to be skeptical that some thought experiments about tele-transportation could disprove the idea of an immortal soul, but she did find this perspective liberating. It helped her understand that she had never really known Peter, and he had never really known her. She knew only a version of him, at a brief moment in time. But without those hazy recollections, without the historical fact that she had once giggled helplessly with her head lolling on Peter's shoulder, she had no significant relationship to the Alice Law who was falling in love with Peter Murdoch at all. And if you could constantly reinvent yourself, cut away the parts of you that ashamed or hurt you, then how could you ever come to really know someone else? Were people all just living paradoxes, keeping up an illusion just long enough to survive contact with others? Were people then all a series of lies in the end?

And if *that* was true—then what difference did it make, what history you had, what love you'd shared? That staircase was gone; the planks had reassembled, and the soul you had come to know was a newly crafted fiction. And so perhaps it was entirely possible—common, even—for you to look into the eyes of someone you'd been falling in love with, someone you had spent every waking moment with, whose breathing sounded as familiar as your own—and fail to recognize them at all.

# CHAPTER FOURTEEN

"Alice?"

She stood frozen.

She blinked at her hand. This was not imagined; this configuration was real. She had not meant to act, she was only thinking through her options, she had not finished reasoning, it was only a what-if, it was not what she wanted—

But this was her hand, and it held the green apple.

If she had not grasped it, then who had?

"I didn't mean to—" Alice flung it back, reached for the red. "Hold on—I choose—"

But the Weaver Girl snapped her fingers, and both apples and table vanished before her. "And that's the game."

Peter shouted, "Alice, what the *fuck*?"

Alice shrank back. *Please*, she wanted to cry, *don't blame me; I don't know what I'm doing, I am not even a subject, I am not here.* She heard a roaring in her ears. Her hands felt so far away. She tried to focus, but she couldn't see where they began, where the boundary separated her and the rest of space; where the past ended and the present continued.

"Poor things," said the Weaver Girl. "You were so confident."

Peter started forward. "What is wrong with you?"

The Weaver Girl held him back. Silk billowed out between them. Alice felt a pressure at her back; it grew harder, and she stumbled forward. "You—go on. Walk alone into Hell, and see how freedom feels. And *you* . . ." A tendril flittered around Peter's face. White bands shot out from the Weaver Girl's sleeves and wrapped around his arms, ankles, and waist, spinning him around like a spider spins its prey. "I shall keep you."

"Stop," Alice managed. "Don't—"

"Don't worry, dear. I know what you meant."

"But that's not what I—"

"You made your choice."

More and more silk poured out her sleeves. Peter flailed, shouting, but the silk around his arms and legs tightened until all he could do was wriggle. He strained his neck toward Alice. "Alice, *help*—"

She fumbled for him. Panic made her focus, and Peter's form sharpened, the only clear thing in view. Peter—yes—she had to help Peter—

"No, dear." The Weaver Girl's red silk billowed up between them. "Trust your instinct."

Alice batted the silk away. "Stop . . ."

"You know there's no future." The Weaver Girl spun Peter to face her. She had left everything above his mouth uncovered; all Alice could see of him was his eyes, huge and terrified. "You'd think more often it'd be the man. But it's always the girl. She's always afraid. She wants to believe him, but she can't. He's let her down too many times in the past. She knows he'll do it again. And in the end, she has to look out for herself." The silks hoisted Peter in the air and left him dangling there, twitching like some grotesque overgrown larva. "You're all part of the same story. The same ending, every time. I know your script, and I can rewrite it. I am doing you a favor."

Alice strained. "Stop, please—"

"Don't worry," sang the Weaver Girl. "I'll love him. I'll love him well and long. I do love flimsy twig men. They need such care."

Peter tried to cry out, but a band of cloth tightened over his mouth, another over his eyes; and then the only sign he was struggling was the bulging of his veins.

"Go on, dear. You won't like to watch."

Oh, God, what had she done? She fumbled in her rucksack for the hunting knife. When she found it, the skeins had proliferated; a wall of crisscrossing cloth separated them. She tried to hack her way through, but the silk did not give; it only tautened, caught the blade. She flailed, slicing harder. The wall held firm. Peter was nearly swallowed in cloth. She could hardly see him—only a tuft of brown hair, the rest a mummy, unable to budge. She tried yanking instead at the cloth, to pull open a hole so she could get him, but each time she touched the cloth it thickened. It did not matter, she was powerless, she couldn't stop it, she couldn't take it back.

*This keeps happening*. She redoubled her efforts, sobbing in frustration. It always went like this—it didn't matter what she intended, it all went to shit anyway because she was so stupid, worthless, she could not stop falling apart, she could not hold the thoughts inside, she made all the wrong choices and it hurt everyone around her. She faltered and Grimes died; her mind slipped and Peter was doomed—

"Don't fret," the Weaver Girl cooed; a silken tendril stroked up and down her shoulder. "Don't think about it, dear, it will all be over soon."

*Click-clack.*

Alice's neck prickled.

*Click-clack.*

The Weaver Girl heard it too. Her spinning paused; the skeins dropped Peter to the ground. Her head jerked this way and that, scanning the cliffs, her eyes wide with panic.

*She knows*, Alice thought; *she's seen them before.*

Over the hill they came, a horrible wave of white.

First they set upon the Weaver Girl. She shrieked; a flurry of cloth whipped around her face, a pointless silk shield, but they were undeterred. They nipped and dragged, pulling in all directions until she could hardly stand, wrenched down by the growling mass.

The bone-things were most interested in Peter. Alice they largely ignored; they skirted right past her to get to him. They made short work of his cocoon, flinging shreds of fabric through the air. He wrenched himself free and batted his hands around his head, trying to protect his face and neck. But they would not stop coming.

"Here—" Alice tried to slide him a knife, but they were too many; they swarmed the blade the moment she set it down. With shaking hands she uncapped her flask. But it held such a flimsy quantity of water, barely a splash, enough only to stall the bone-things around her for seconds. And the Lethe lay so far down the ledge, too far for rescue.

Peter cried out in pain. A bone dog had landed on his back, its teeth fixed in his collarbone. Alice made to reach him but felt a dozen sudden stabs of pain. They'd decided to pay attention to her now, and they were at her ankles, at her knees. And they kept coming; an endless stream of white rippling down the rocky hills. It seemed then they might be swallowed by a veritable pile of bone, that when it subsided there would be nothing left but flesh picked clean.

Their mass was so great, there was nothing to do but succumb to the surge. Alice shut her eyes and hoped the end would come quick. She anticipated excruciating pain, a million tiny bites. But perhaps the shock or blood loss would numb her first, perhaps her consciousness would fade. And then the rest, easy, like going to sleep. But the pain never came. A thousand tiny pressures against her side; snouts digging not into but beneath her. Suddenly they lifted her up. Some scurried beneath her to make a bed of bones. Then off they went at a dizzying pace, a horde of ants delivering spoils to their master.

Alice writhed, but it was pointless. Any way she turned another mass of bone was ready to catch her, jolt her back into its center. The dim sun spun overhead, sharp ledges against the orange sky, which disoriented her so she had no idea where they were going except the vague sensation they were traveling down, down, deeper along the cliffs until she could hear the churning Lethe roaring by her ears, the mist against her cheek. The bone things turned sharply. Down the bank, Alice glimpsed a bone-thing larger than the rest; a chimeric amalgamation standing upright on two legs, its head an enormous, fanged skull.

A horn's blow pierced the air.

The bone-things lurched to a halt. The effect was instant; it was like a string was cut. Their tight coordination vanished; their limbs shook listless, confused. The bed disassembled. Alice tumbled to the ground.

For a moment all hung still and silent.

The horn sounded again; a solid, vigorous note. Then, over the churning water, a very human voice: "Away, you!"

A dark shape appeared over the Lethe, growing larger and closer with every passing second. Alice made out the strangest river craft she'd ever seen—an unbalanced barge-type thing composed of scrap and bones, flying a tattered black flag with no symbol she recognized. On deck stood a single boatman, outfitted much the same way; a ragtag pirate from no era or nation, just the detritus of the underworld. A mask of bone covered the top half of his face, leaving visible only an eager, grinning mouth.

"Away! Back!"

The boatman sprang gracefully onto the shore and, in one fluid motion, drew a spear from his back. He spun it round twice above his head—a bit showy, Alice thought—and then jumped out and swung it so quickly toward Alice that it nearly scraped her nose. A crunch, a whine. The bone-thing by Alice's chest shattered to pieces at her feet.

He'd made the opening volley. The bone-things responded in kind. The boatman became a flurry of spins, whacking bone-things left and right. He was wonderful to watch. The bone-things redoubled their attack, but the boatman seemed well practiced at their maneuvers. They lunged from every angle, but he anticipated their blows—smacking their joints, their spines, all those sticking points that held the rest together.

"En garde!"

He jammed the rod through the ribs of the one straddling Alice and yanked. The pressure disappeared. Alice sat up, gasping.

"Avaunt!"

Alice did not think this was standard dueling vocabulary. The helmeted figure seemed rather to be playing a part, reveling in his performance. He seemed indeed to be having fun, whirling among these creatures—as if they were partners in the same old dance, their moves rehearsed, perfected.

The fallen creatures crowded around their two-legged leader—circling, it seemed, for a coordinated attack. For a moment they regarded each other: the lone boatman on one end, the hissing pack on the other. The leader threw its head back and issued what seemed like a series of orders—*clack clack clack*. The pack lowered their jaws all at once, back legs coiling to spring.

The boatman swung his staff around and yanked a lever on

its other end. It was, Alice realized, a very fancy spritzing bottle. Lethe water rained through the air and the bone creatures whined, skittering backward.

"Back!" cried the boatman.

The bone creatures hissed. The boatman spritzed with the bottle once again. "I say, back! Or I'll make you a pile of useless bones, I will."

A series of defiant whines. Then the bone things re-formed a pack and skittered away, rushing past Alice's legs as they did. They rallied behind their two-legged leader, which stood a moment, gazing silent at the boatman, until it too turned back. Within seconds all had disappeared into the hills.

"Good riddance." The boatman extended a hand to Alice. "Come aboard, quick."

Alice saw a clear advantage to trusting a stranger who'd just saved them versus a semi-deity who'd tried to dismember them, so she grasped the boatman's hand and let him pull her onto the barge. He was reassuringly solid.

The boatman turned and helped Peter up just as the Weaver Girl rushed to the shore. "Come back!" Silks stretched from her waist like reaching hands. "I'm not done with you."

"*I'm not done with you*," mimicked the boatman. "Away, you jealous cow."

"Lord Yama will smite you for this!"

"You irritate Lord Yama more than I do. Away, harpy!" The boatman shoved the pole at the shore, and the barge pushed off the bank just as the Weaver Girl reached the edge. The boatman held the spear at her face and spritzed her, too. Alice was not sure what effect this might have but the Weaver Girl sputtered, wiped at her face, and fell back.

Silks exploded from the shore and swarmed the air like a kraken's tentacles, pulsing, reaching. Alice shrank back, batting cloth from her face. But the boatman was faster. The black ship tore into the heart of the Lethe and the tendrils fell away, stung and sizzling from the spray.

On shore the Weaver Girl threw her head back and cackled.

"Good luck," she called, "fickle lovers. You'll need it!"

## CHAPTER FIFTEEN

"Hold tight!" The boatman jammed his staff against the riverbank, and the boat pitched accordingly. Alice stumbled into Peter, who stumbled against the railing. "The breaks are dangerous here. Let me get us out of the shallows..."

The little ship bobbed perilously against the Lethe, but the boatman seemed skilled at keeping them afloat. Alice saw a variety of navigating instruments about the deck—several punting poles of varying lengths, two oars, a steering wheel, and even a battery-powered motor that looked suspiciously modern. The ship seemed a patchwork combination of punting canoe, rowboat, and sailboat all at once. The boatman dashed about arranging the sails, then did something complicated-looking with the rudder, until the ship was chugging at a merry pace parallel to the shore. Then he set down his staff and stepped forth to appraise his guests.

"Hullo!" He pulled the mask off his face, revealing large brown eyes on a thin, friendly face. He was a she. "Welcome aboard the *Neurath*. I'm Elspeth."

Alice knew this face. She knew this name.

She wasn't supposed to know it. All mentions of Elspeth were scrubbed from the department records. A framed photograph of every year's cohort hung along the department walls, excepting the class of 1975. All the faculty liked to pretend Elspeth had never existed. But rumors survived, passed down from cohort to cohort, and when it came Alice's turn to receive the secret she could not help going to the university library, like so many others had before her, and digging up the microfilm to find the same *Cambridge Daily* article with a smudged photograph of that face, stubborn and lovely in profile, dark eyes glaring over sullen cheeks.

Elspeth Bayes. Bachelor's from Radcliffe, master's from Berkeley; Jacob Grimes advisee, specializing in maths and logic. All this Alice recalled from the first paragraph of the *Cambridge Daily* headline. She had died ten years before Alice arrived.

Alice knew well the story. She knew every gruesome detail, etched deeper into popular memory with every retelling, details so chillingly precise that you knew they had to be the truth. They said that one winter's morning the Lady Margaret women's VIII went for a pre-Bumps training session up the Cam. They said when the rowers returned to the boathouse, the cox saw something dark floating in the river—a trash bag? A clump of leaves?—just in time to order, "Hold up"—for the rowers to jam their oars perpendicular against the water and park the boat. *Bump bump bump bump.* Four bow-side oars thwacked the dark thing in succession as the boat drifted past and glided parallel to the shore. They said only the cox realized what had happened at first, since only she sat facing forward; that all the other rowers had left the boat and were straggling up to the boathouse before the cox stumbled out on wobbly legs and fainted dead on the shore.

Emergency services were called, statements were given, and

since the unlucky cox had taken an undergraduate survey course in applications of magick the previous term, the blue and bloated body was quickly identified as that of Elspeth Bayes. The punch line of this terrible story, the line no one failed to repeat in a hushed voice over chips and beer: "And the coach said—well, if they weren't dead before that bludgeoning, they surely are now."

An autopsy found no evidence of foul play. She hadn't been strangled, beaten, or stabbed. She was fully dressed, clothes wet and tight against her skin. No evidence of sexual abuse. All anyone could conclude was that Elspeth had drowned in the river Cam of her own accord, and a note found later in her room, in her own handwriting, confirmed the police conclusion: *Tired—I am so tired—and I can only go now into the dark. Tell them I am sorry. Tell him—*

But that was all they printed.

Professor Grimes never spoke of Elspeth. Alice had met several of his other former students at conferences—invariably tall, deep-voiced young men who laughed comfortably with other faculty the way that only young tenure-track faculty can. They boasted of their time surviving Grimes, and Grimes boasted of their accomplishments in turn. To graduate from under Grimes put you in a rare and exclusive club, self-satisfied veterans with golden futures, to whom the name Elspeth meant nothing.

But Alice had found the records. There was a time—about six months ago—when she became obsessed, and spent a week going through microfilm of city newspapers in the university library, stopping every time she came across mention of *body* and *Cambridge* and *suicide*. She had to know if Elspeth's story was real, and if so, what weakness it was that sent her into the river. Was she predisposed to suicide—or had something happened in the lab? How flimsy, really, was the line between each and survival? The students had their own theories, and every retelling ascribed a different motive. Failed her viva voce. Rejected for publication. Turned down for the Durham job. But the news coverage was so scant and offered such vague platitudes. Tragic story. Fragile girl. Graduate school isn't for everyone.

"*Ahhhh!*" Archimedes made a happy yowling noise and darted forward, skirting between Elspeth's legs like they were slalom poles. She laughed in delight and knelt to scratch his head. "Hello, you!"

Archimedes purred. Elspeth beamed up at them. Alice was startled to discover that she was beautiful. The newspaper photograph made her out to be severe and mousy, but in person, she moved with a blinking, birdlike charm. Elspeth was precisely Professor Grimes's type—slender, underfed, dark hair pulled into a ballerina's bun—and this identification put a sharp twist in Alice's gut.

"You're magicians, then?" Elspeth appraised them. "You've got to be. Chalk stains all over."

"Peter Murdoch," said Peter. "And that's—" He did not look at her. "Alice Law."

"Peter and Alice. My pleasure." Elspeth grasped their hands in succession and shook vigorously. Her palm was warm and clammy, and Alice jumped to feel her solidity. George Edward Moore would have envied that texture.

"You know Archimedes?" Alice asked.

"Who doesn't? Here, sweetie." Elspeth held out her arms. Archimedes jumped up and snuggled against her chest. "So. Ramanujan, was it? Yes. Clever. You're the first pair I've seen who've actually managed it, you know. Everyone always gets stuck on Setiya's Modifications, they don't have the maths for it." The words rushed out Elspeth's mouth without pause or punctuation; she seemed unaware she was speaking in full paragraphs. Perhaps a decade of loneliness did that to you. Perhaps they were the only souls Elspeth had spoken to since her death. Her gaze darted eagerly between them, drinking in their faces. "Journeying to Hell was all the craze during my days. Everyone kept threatening to do it, but no one ever managed it, and the first few years I sat at that bridge watching and waiting for someone to make it over. Five years in I figured they'd just stopped trying. So how much did it cost you?"

She paused so abruptly Alice did not realize they'd been asked a question.

After a beat, Peter said, "Half our natural lifespans."

"You must have really wanted it."

"We're here to—" Peter began.

But Elspeth chattered on. "I wonder about the mechanics. Do you think you'll age prematurely? Do you think death has set in now, like a cancer? Or that some terrible accident will befall you when you're fifty? Do you think the ground will just crack open beneath you and the underworld will swallow you up?" All this she uttered without any semblance of tact. Alice could understand this—after a decade in Hell, probably tact didn't seem so important.

"Er—I really don't know," said Peter. "Hopefully not the latter."

"I suppose it's a bit scary, though," said Elspeth. "Hitting forty and wondering if you'll keel over from a heart attack the next day—"

"What were those things?" Alice cut her off. She felt if Elspeth was going to chatter on like this, she might steer the conversation into productive territory. "You've met them before, clearly—"

"Oh, I call them little rovers." Elspeth made a face. "Apparatuses of bone. Set in motion with power beyond me—but they're scared of the Lethe, as you've noticed. That helps. I've been collecting spray bottles for ages." She waved her staff. "This one's a perfume bottle. Dior. Smell."

They sniffed as commanded.

"Very nice," said Peter.

"But who's controlling them?" asked Alice. "Is it a deity?"

"Oh, worse. A magician." Elspeth lowered the staff. "Have either of you ever heard of the Kripkes?"

"No," said Peter, as Alice said, "Oh, Jesus."

THE KRIPKES HAD NOT BEEN FACULTY at Cambridge. Not in their wildest dreams—they were anathema to English academia. Rather the Kripkes were visual artists and illusionists at Berkeley, where that sort of wild and unconventional magick was encouraged. Magnolia Kripke worked with oils and watercolors. Nicomachus Kripke did sleight-of-hand magick tricks. They were the rare academics who could fill both a Vegas auditorium and a lecture hall at Harvard. They could, with only black and white paint, create mazes inside a closet that made entrants feel as if they were walking around an entire courtyard. They could, with nothing but mirrors and light, convince their audience that they'd traveled back decades through time.

Their commercial appeal led many in the academic establishment to discount their scholarship. It was, after all, a golden rule in academia that the more popular one was among the masses, the less valuable one's research had to be. Alice did not agree—in fact she had been something of a Magnolia Kripke fangirl during her undergraduate years, as were many young magicians of her age, and she felt that beneath the Kripkes' pomp and spectacle lay truly breathtaking theoretical advancements. But to most of their colleagues, the Kripkes were all smoke and mirrors; showmen only, not serious thinkers. The administration at Berkeley seemed to agree. The same year that the Kripkes sold out a headliner tour across North America, their tenure applications were denied. Insufficient contributions to the field. If only they'd spent less time partying in tour vans and more time publishing.

Possibly this slight led the Kripkes to disappear from the public view for five years—it was rumored they took on private funding from millionaire dilettantes after they lost university affiliation—and then reappear for one dramatic exhibit at Royal Albert Hall. Their latest trick, the Kripkes announced, was to return from Hell.

They distributed invitations all over the country in the weeks before this performance—cryptic, all-black papers with the words "TO HELL AND BACK," with the subtitle, "Professors Nicomachus and Magnolia Kripke."

Only a smattering of academics showed up. The way Alice heard it, most people were put off by this ploy for attention. The Kripkes had invited three board members of the Royal Academy of magick, which was the number needed in attendance to verify the efficacy of any new magical technique, but those invitations were declined. Probably the Kripkes would put on some great, Gothic spectacle; lights, hellfire, maybe "summon" a demon or two. A pretty show, but not real magick.

So no one expected it when, in front of a thousand people, Nicomachus and Magnolia Kripke carefully slit one another's carotid arteries, lay down, and bled to death on stage.

Immediately the academic community distanced themselves from what had happened in London. That wasn't magick, that was all vulgar theatrics. The International Conference of Magick had a big role in that. They couldn't have the Kripkes' reputation bring down the rest of the field. They had come so far from the days they were maligned as a pseudoscience, as witchcraft, and all the pagan, Satanic spectacle of the Kripkes' work was very damaging to the field's legitimacy.

Consensus was that the Kripkes had gone mad. The narrative was so convenient. Magick, especially of this variety, made one lose their grip on reality. The first rule every graduate student learned was that at the base of every paradox there existed the truth. That you should never fully believe your own lie, for then you lost power over the pentagram. That magick was an act of tricking the world but not yourself. You had to hold two opposing beliefs in your head at once. You had to know your way back.

But Nicomachus and Magnolia had been living within increasingly complex webs of fantasy. It was inevitable—they had finally lost their grip on reality, had actually fooled themselves into thinking they had power over life and death. They were not magicians anymore. They were mere charlatans now, lost in their own illusions.

So when the Kripkes died, the academic community greeted their disappearance with little ceremony. No one issued a retrospective of their work; no one edited a Festschrift; no one named any endowed chairs after them. The Kripkes' two graduate students dropped out of their respective programs. One found work as a visual effects designer in Hollywood, and the other was living in a commune outside Palo Alto the last anyone heard.

Alice knew of the Kripkes, for she had fanatically researched everyone and everything tangentially related to underworld sojourns. She'd found a torn and bloodstained copy of their Royal Albert Hall pamphlet, crumpled carelessly at the bottom of a records box. She'd found what few research notes by Nicomachus and Magnolia were accessible to the public—the rest were lost when the Kripke family home was sold off. But small wonder Peter didn't recognize their names. After all, there wasn't much point studying someone who went to Hell and failed to come back.

"THEY'VE BEEN ROVING THE EIGHT COURTS ever since." Elspeth was doing something complicated with the ropes and sail. They were quite far from shore now, and the *Neurath* glided smoothly over deeper, calmer waters. "In the beginning, they still looked human. When they still cared about what they used to be. They've adapted since, taken on more and more of . . . the attributes of deities, we might say. I started seeing those little rovers a few years ago." She made a face. "Nasty little things. They've produced a veritable army since."

"What *are* they?" asked Peter. "I mean, what kind of magick—"

"I wish I knew. I've got two theories about it. The first is that they've found Shades and bound them to living matter—which is terrifying, because if they can do that then they're well on their way to doing anything. That's why I think it's unlikely."

"And what's your other theory?"

"That they've split off parts of themselves into the bones. That the constructs are satellites of their own minds."

Peter blanched. "But that—I mean, that's incredibly sophisticated magick."

"Well, the Kripkes have had a lot of time. They always were underestimated as proper magicians, I think. The stuff they've come up with down here would revolutionize the field above, if only they ever got out to publish."

"What about that large construct?" Alice asked. "The one on two legs."

"They've still got that thing with them?"

"It moves differently than the others," said Alice. "It's . . . more deliberate, like it has a will of its own. Have they been innovating?"

"No." Elspeth's face tightened. "No, that's their son."

Alice and Peter spoke at once. "*What?*"

"Theophrastus," said Elspeth. "Cute kid. I saw him at a conference hotel once. He was playing with these plastic dinosaurs. Kept banging them together and shouting they needed to reproduce to save their species."

Alice's chest felt tight. "They didn't . . ."

"They decided they didn't want to leave him behind," said Elspeth. "So they brought him along. Gave him some juice laced with arsenic before the show, and collected his dead little soul shortly after they journeyed down themselves."

"That's horrible," said Peter. "They—I can't believe they *murdered*—"

"Not murdered. Not from their perspective," said Elspeth. "You have to understand: they think they're still finding a way out of this mess. So the way they see it, all they did was bring him along for the trip. No different from joining Mum and Dad for a weekend conference in Birmingham."

"So they're still trying to see things through?" Peter asked.

"The Great Quest." Elspeth nodded. "They've been stuck on it for years. They've traveled all over the eight courts by now. Found some parts that even I haven't explored, I'm sure. And they've been amassing their—research assistants, let's call them. Used to be just one or two rovers I'd see loping around. Now there's dozens patrolling every court. Until now, I've never seen so many assembled in one place. They must be really excited about you."

"What are they looking for?" asked Alice.

"Anything that could be of use," said Elspeth. "All sorts of things find their ways down to Hell, you see. Not always on purpose. Usually it's objects. Childhood toys. Old furniture. Things buried in coffins or discarded at places of death. Bones, lots of bones." Elspeth gestured at herself and Alice noticed, upon closer examination, that her armor was not of fine steel, but an intricate sheet of bones and metal rubbish stitched together. At her waist dangled what Alice hoped was a rabbit skull. Around her neck hung a metal chain that might have once been used to flush a toilet. She looked like she'd dressed for a rock concert wearing only found items from the sewer.

"Sometimes it's animals. Rats, mostly. Your occasional dog.

They don't mess with cats—nobody messes with cats." Elspeth scratched Archimedes behind the ears. "No, we don't—you good boy. Sometimes people come before their time. That doesn't happen often. They have to be very lost, or very close to death. It's dreadful to watch happen. They don't ever find their way back up. They pass, and then their soul . . ." Elspeth fidgeted with her chain. "I saw a child once. Such a skinny thing. Unloved. Didn't care where he was, to be honest. No one ends up in Hell if they have anywhere else to go. I tried to send him back up. The Kripkes got to him first."

"And what did they do?" asked Peter.

Elspeth blinked hard at him. "What do you think?"

Alice stared back out over the shore, the deceptively empty sands. How lucky they'd been. How foolish.

"They are not human anymore," said Elspeth. "They have no sense of compassion or justice. There is no reasoning with them. They have lost all perspective on life and death. There is only knowledge, resources, and the Great Quest."

"Jeez." Peter hugged his chest. "We might as well just reincarnate, then. Get it over with."

"Oh, love." Elspeth shook her head. "Didn't anyone tell you?"

"Tell us what?"

"You don't reincarnate if you die in Hell. Hell already operates on another metaphysical plane. We're all soul stuff here. When you die in Hell, it's not just your mortal body that disintegrates—it's your soul stuff, too." She smacked her chest. "All this, it dissipates. If you die down here, that's it for you. Total annihilation of the self."

"But nobody said," said Alice.

"Because nobody knows. All the sojourners' accounts are by people who made it back, aren't they? Survivorship bias, and all that. But I've seen it. The death of the soul. I've seen the Kripkes murder a soul, in fact. They do it to Shades, too. They've figured out how. It's a horrible process. The screams alone. It's always a small explosion, when a soul destructs."

Peter was silent.

Alice, still gazing over the dunes, thought to the creatures in the Weaver Girl's web. Those contorted figures. She hadn't let any of her lovers move on, either. Just kept stringing them along, wringing them for shreds of entertainment, until. Until.

"Anyway," Elspeth said brightly. "Who's hungry?"

They stared blankly at her.

"Starving, aren't you?" Elspeth was pushing their boat toward the shore. Alice had not paid attention to the direction of their sailing; she knew only that they had skirted round the perilous cliffs and were back on flat, monotonous banks. "You've got to be. I assume you're living on Lembas Bread; nothing else keeps. But that's no way to get your nutrients."

"True," said Alice. "But what—"

"Splendid! Let's have dinner."

"I thought you didn't need to eat," said Peter.

"Course not." Elspeth scratched the back of Archimedes's head. "But I do need to feed this one. How do you feel about rats?"

Neither Peter nor Alice knew how to respond to this.

Elspeth laughed. "The traps are just across the bank. I won't be five. Don't unmoor the boat and don't wander off." She slung her perfume-spritzer staff over her back, then clambered up onto the railing. "More spray bottles under the deck if you need them. Stay dry!"

In one graceful movement she sprang off the side of the boat and landed clean on the shore. She turned, tossed them a wave, and then vanished at a sprint over the dunes.

**FOR A MOMENT ALICE AND PETER** stood side by side, watching the empty shore. The silence was excruciating.

"Well." She glanced over at him. "Gosh. What a day."

He said nothing.

He was furious; that was clear.

Alice had never known Peter's anger before. For most of their career she hadn't known it was possible for Peter Murdoch to get angry. Always he wore that affable smile in lab; when undergraduates made a mess of his pentagrams, he only cheered them up and then slowly, patiently instructed them on how to do things right. Everyone else in the department kept grudges, snapped occasionally when they were running low on sleep. There were always apologies going on at their department—*I'm sorry I said you were a ninny, I didn't mean it, I don't think you're a ninny*. But never Peter.

So she did not know what to do with his stonewalling. She wished he would shout, rage, curse at her, or beat his fists. Anything was better than this stony sulk.

"Can we talk?" Her voice came out very small. "Murdoch?"

He would not turn to look at her. "Can't stop you, can I?"

"I'm sorry for back there."

"Oh, you are?"

A lump formed in her throat. "I didn't mean to—I just looked *down*, and—"

"And the apple jumped into your hand?" Peter snorted. "We had a plan, Law. It was so easy."

"I know, I just—"

"Just condemned me? For fun?"

"I didn't want—I didn't know . . ."

Peter watched her, arms crossed and waiting, eyebrow arched as if to say, *Go on*.

But what explanation could she give? That was her hand. That was the green apple. "Sometimes . . ." She could barely speak. She did not know how to describe what had happened. She had never articulated this to anyone; she had tried for so long to pretend it was not a problem, because admitting the problem would make it real, and this could not be. *My mind is broken and I cannot fix it, I cannot sort reality from dreams*—that was not true. She could not live if it were true. "Sometimes, I try to think, and everything blares at once, and I don't know where I am, or what I'm doing—"

"What are you trying to tell me, Law?" He scoffed. "Your tattoo makes you stupid?"

She flinched.

"That you can't follow simple instructions? Or that you just wanted me dead?"

"That's not what I—"

"But just think about what you're saying," Peter snapped. "*You took the green.* You would have left me trapped. And even if you changed your mind, you still considered that option. You *wanted me to die.*"

"I didn't—"

"Factually you did!"

"I didn't want that," she cried. "I didn't know, I couldn't determine—I just, I was afraid you'd do the same."

He flung up his hands. "Why on earth would you think that?"

"Your notebook," she said helplessly. "I saw in your notebook, the spell for exchange—"

"Exchange?" His eyes went wide. "You thought I'd exchange *you?*"

"What else would that mean, Murdoch? How on earth would I interpret that?"

Peter shook his head. Alice could not make any sense of it. She would have preferred he looked guilty, because then at least her narrative would make sense, and then all their cards would be on the table. Then at least they would be definite enemies, and she would have cause to hate him. But if anything he seemed angrier than before. "You think I'm that sort of person? That I'm capable of—of trading your soul, like you're nothing?"

"I don't know." She could hardly hear her own voice. "I guess I don't know what I think of you. I don't know what you could do."

She knew as it left her mouth that it was the worst thing she could have said.

"Jesus Christ, Law." He still would not look at her. "You have no idea what you're talking about."

*Then tell me*, she wanted to cry. If only supplication could shatter his shell; if only she could beg long and hard enough for him to be honest with her. But the gulf between them seemed so vast now, and all the words that came to mind utterly insufficient. Still she had to try, and she had just opened her mouth, was casting for the right things to say, when Peter spoke.

"You know, I thought—" He swallowed. "I don't know. For whatever reason, I still thought you weren't like him."

She felt worse than if he'd socked her in the face.

Something thumped over the side of the boat. "Dinner!" Elspeth clambered up, then bent to hold up her spoils. "You're in luck. They're fresh!"

Alice blinked down. Three fat rats lay strung together by twine.

"Get a fire going in that stove." Elspeth directed Peter with one hand; with the other, she drew out a butcher's knife. "Matches under the lid."

Wordlessly Peter went to obey. Alice remained where she was, arms hugged tight against her ribs. She felt a terrible whooshing between her ears. She was afraid to move; she was certain if she unfolded her arms, then she might shatter.

Elspeth was oblivious to their distress; she chattered happily along as she took a knife to the rats. "Rats are most of what you get down here. Rats and moles. They keep burrowing further underground to see where they can get. Stands to reason they end up in Hell. Spiders too, but you can't eat those." She jammed her thumbs into flesh and yanked at the skins, which came off with a terrible ripping noise. "Keep the bones for me. They're so tiny, and come in all sorts of shapes . . . I usually toss the meat out. They're fleshier than they look, anyways; they'll fill you right up."

In short order Elspeth had the rats roasting over the fire on a spit. While they blackened and crackled she made a great fuss over laying out plates and silverware on a rickety folding table that she hauled out from beneath the oars. "Found these beauties a few years ago off the shore of Desire. Usually plates come cracked and in pieces but these—these came whole, aren't they lovely!" She paused; took in their anxious faces. "Oh, go on. It's not Hell's foodstuff, it's safe."

Alice was reminded of humble dinner parties in graduate apartments. It made no sense to cook at home instead of eating in hall, where the food was perhaps not better but certainly more plentiful. But still they loved hosting one another. It was pathetically charming, the way they showed off their charity shop acquisitions, the way Belinda insisted they all fuss over her slightly chipped porcelain milk pitcher with a kitten print when they assembled in her flat for tea. None of them could afford a matching dinnerware set or a proper table or even linens, but still they were proud to pass around the cheap bottles of port they'd found at Sainsbury's because it was a luxury to have port at all. Once in her first year Alice had discovered an actual silver gravy bowl at Oxfam, and they all sat on her floor and ate mushroom gravy in April. It was nice to have company over and play homemaker, and pretend you were a real adult.

She therefore accepted a smoking rat leg, if only to be polite. But then her stomach took over and she dispensed with the silverware entirely, ramming the corpse against her mouth so her teeth could get in between the bones.

"There you are." Elspeth helped more onto Alice's plate. "Don't forget to hydrate. Isn't that better?"

Alice was doing *much* better. A fog was clearing from her head. It was the first home-cooked meal she'd had in ages—at the department, it was all Lembas Bread and cold tea—and she ate with such enthusiasm that soon all that was left was a neat pile of bones sucked clean.

She set her plate down. A wet burp escaped her mouth. "Sorry."

"Excuse yourself." Elspeth looked very pleased. "I'm glad you liked it."

"So, Elspeth." Peter set his fork down. He had not looked once at Alice since Elspeth's return; now he spoke as if she were not there. "I've been wondering. How are you and the Kripkes using magick?"

"How do you mean?"

"We thought—perhaps it doesn't work down here. The sand eats it up."

"Oh." Elspeth laughed. "You haven't figured that out?"

She drew out a knife from her belt. Alice and Peter both instinctively shrank back, but Elspeth held the point to her own wrist and pressed. What bubbled out was not blood, precisely, but a thick, black-blue sludge.

Elspeth extended her other hand. "Chalk?"

Peter fished about in his pocket and handed her a stick.

"Anything you need patched up?"

"Cuts and bruises," said Peter.

"Of course. Will Curry's Paradox do?"

"Probably, yeah."

They both watched in awed silence as Elspeth dipped the

chalk in her not-blood like it was an inkwell and drew a perfect circle on the deck around her ankles. The pentagram was not a pristine white but a phosphorescent green that cast a pallid light around her ankles. But it did not sink away.

Curry's Paradox. Commonly taught in Introduction to Analytic Magick classes, this was a silly play on conditional statements and self-reference that could, just for an instant, make true any arbitrary claim. Consider: *If this statement is true, then pigs can fly.* Call this statement S. Statement S has the structure "If S, then P." If you write it out as a logic proof, you will discover you do end up proving S true, for you do end up writing "If S, then P." So the statement S is true, and pigs can fly. The statement is S true, and Peter has no wound.

"There you go," said Elspeth.

Peter withdrew his arm, running fingers over soothed skin. "Thanks."

"I figured that out long ago," said Elspeth. "It's the only thing that makes the chalk take effect—some kind of life force. It congeals with the living-dead force of the chalk. Adds some sort of . . . insulation, I suppose, against the silt. Though it doesn't work so well with my blood. Whatever this is"—she patted her pale, not-bleeding arm—"seems a pale approximation of the real thing. It's vital force that's the key, it seems. Not much force one can draw from a Shade. But your blood . . . it's warm, it's bursting."

She blinked at the knife, then blinked at Peter and Alice with an uncomfortably hungry look. Alice slid her sleeve over her wrist.

"Just a little dip, then?" Peter asked. "That's all you need?"

"The more, the better. The effect seems proportional to— well, the sacrifice." Elspeth blinked again, then set the knife down. "Curry is easy. Doesn't take much."

"How much would a harder spell take?"

"Depends on your blood," said Elspeth. "With Shade's blood, quite a lot. Living blood, I don't know."

"Should we try it?"

"Do Banach-Tarski." Alice spoke up. "Do Banach-Tarski on your flask."

The Banach-Tarski Paradox proved you could cut apart a ball into a finite number of subsets of points and reassemble them into two balls equal in volume to the first. Alice could not perform it herself; she understood only that it involved heavy maths, and had something to do with set theory and little infinities. But she knew Peter knew it, and that was good enough.

The thought had been lurking at the back of her mind. She needed a working flask. Hers was soiled. Peter's was fine. Alone she would quickly die of thirst, but with a copied flask she would be all right, independent—free to go her own way.

If Peter had considered the same implications, he did not show it. He reached for his rucksack and pulled out his flask.

"Now the blood," said Elspeth. "Knuckles are best, you won't hit a tendon."

Peter hesitated.

Alice drew her knife. "Here." She dug the sharp end into the knuckle of her thumb, harder and harder, until blood beaded around the metal. "Is that enough?"

"Might be," said Elspeth.

Alice held her hand out to Peter. He paused just a moment, then pressed his chalk against her thumb. The chalk soaked it up like a sponge; in seconds the entire stick was red.

Quickly Peter drew a circle around the flask, inscribed the paradox, and chanted it out loud. The Perpetual Flask shimmered. Peter reached in and drew it out. When he lifted it from the center its double remained, still in place. Alice, watching, could not help a little sigh. For no matter how many spells she had seen, no matter how long she'd studied magic, the act itself still astonished her. That you could fool the conservation of mass. That a thing could be one, and then two.

"Try it," said Peter.

He was right to check. Banach-Tarski copies didn't always work. For one thing they always seemed flimsier. If it was food, it never tasted as good; if wine, it lacked depth—as if it knew it owed its existence to a mathematical loophole. They had a bad habit of randomly vanishing on you—two decided to reunite as one—but Alice couldn't do anything about that.

She untwisted the flask and tipped some water in. She drank. It tasted clean, fresh. "It worked."

"Good." Peter would not look at her. "Keep it."

"Thank you." Alice slid the doubled flask into her own rucksack. Her thumb was still bleeding. She twisted it into a corner of her shirt and held it tight.

"So the Kripkes." Peter turned to Elspeth. "Whose blood..."

"Come on," said Elspeth. "Why do you think they've got all those patrols?"

Peter blinked, speechless. Alice shuddered. Elspeth appraised them with grim satisfaction. "Think hard," she said. "In all your research in Tartarology, have you found a shred of documentation from the last decade? Tell me. I'm really curious."

Peter tilted his head. "Huh."

"None." Alice was certain about this. "Not even gossip."

"And why do you think that is?"

"Don't tell me the Kripkes got to them all," said Peter.

"The Kripkes ensure there are no survivors." Elspeth nodded. "Any magician comes down here, the Kripkes hunt them. No one's going to make their way back from Hell before the Kripkes do, you see. No one's going to beat them to the scoop. They steal their chalk, steal their notes and textbooks. Sometimes they interrogate their prey for the latest in research developments—I've seen poor souls stretched out over the racks for days and days.

And always, always, it ends with draining their blood. They fill up their bladder sacks, they drench their chalk sticks, and off they go."

"That's sick," said Peter.

"That's research," said Elspeth. "Nothing matters to anyone in Hell, I told you. Dogs, squirrels, the stray lost child . . ." Her throat pulsed. "They're all just fuel for them. Materials for the Great Quest."

"You keep saying the Great Quest," said Alice. "What's that mean?"

"They're not calling it the Great Quest anymore? Why are you here, then?"

Alice glanced quickly to Peter. It seemed obvious the last thing they should tell Elspeth was who they were here for. "I suppose we . . ."

"Might be an outdated term by now." Elspeth rubbed her chin. "That's what we were all calling it my year, anyways. To Hell and back was the goal. That was all the rage. It started with the Kripkes, and then everyone wanted to do it. Nothing like a spectacular failure to inspire a thousand followers. Houdini only ever freed himself from death's jaws; he never came back from the other side."

"But you weren't going on the quest," said Peter. "You —I mean, I thought—"

"Right, just a normal suicide," Elspeth said sharply. "But then I discovered pretty quick I don't want to stay here, do I?"

Peter bobbed his head. "No, that's very reasonable."

"So now I'm on the Great Quest, same as the Kripkes. And we're all looking for the same thing to get out."

"And what's that?" asked Peter.

"Why, the True Contradiction," said Elspeth. "The Dialetheia."

Alice nearly dropped her plate with excitement. The power

of a true contradiction—Contradiction Explosion—was the first thing anyone learned in logic class. *Ex contradictione quodlibet*—from a contradiction, anything follows. If you had a True Contradiction, then you could prove anything. Indeed, it exploded your boundaries of proof. She had been taught the silly, informal version: if you could accept the simple contradiction that one and two were the same, you could prove you were the Pope. You and the Pope are two. Therefore you and the Pope are one. More rigorously, once you had a logical contradiction in hand, you could inject any statement into a proof using disjunction. You could prove the sky was green. That rocks were bread, and water wine.

For a long time Alice had pursued the Contradiction Explosion as a way to get Professor Grimes out of Hell. But the trail kept running cold, and eventually she'd given up. The only basis anyone had for believing there existed a True Contradiction was the unlikelihood of Persephone's persimmon seeds, but those seeds might never have existed at all.

"I thought the Dialetheia was a myth." Peter echoed her thoughts. "There's just no literature—I mean, it's all just conjectures—"

"Only because no one in the modern era's found one." Elspeth huffed. "But we're overdue for a discovery, and mark my words, it's going to be me."

"Wait." Alice leaned forward. "You know where to find one?"

"I have some leads," said Elspeth. "I've been at this for a decade. One does make some modest progress."

Peter asked, "So where is it?"

But Elspeth's face closed up. She looked between the two of them, fingers tapping against the floor. "Well," she said after a pause. "Don't suppose I'm about to just tell you."

"Oh," said Peter. "Sorry—"

"Don't get me wrong. You seem like very nice kids. It's only I barely know you, and all that. And it's not like there's dozens of True Contradictions to go around."

There was an awkward silence—not unlike that which descended on a room of scholars who realized they were all interviewing for the same job.

Alice felt a bit wounded, for she had thought they were getting along quite well. But then she supposed, from Elspeth's perspective, they were no different than the Kripkes. They'd both only come to Hell for research purposes. And they were both Cantabrigians.

"You're welcome to stay on the boat, though." Elspeth gathered up their plates, tipping the bones carefully into a tin can. "I'm not like Nick and Magnolia. I won't drain your blood in your sleep. Only I hope you're not offended if I don't share everything I know."

"No, of course." Peter's voice was curiously flat. Alice could not read his face. She thought she saw something dark in his expression, but what to make of it, she didn't know. "You've been very generous. We couldn't ask for more."

"Anytime," said Elspeth. "We've got to look out for each other, we magicians. It's a sad world when we don't."

## CHAPTER SIXTEEN

The sun slipped under the horizon. The river turned black; in the absence of a moon all Alice could see was the light of Elspeth's lanterns and endless dark around them. They could have been floating in the middle of space; boundless, weightless. Elspeth led them to the hold below deck, a cramped but homey room that she had filled mostly with books.

"My humble paradise," she told them. "Behold."

Alice held the lantern against the walls, squinting at the spines. Elspeth had acquired books of every style from every era, most waterlogged, tattered, and missing entire chunks; some mere pages strung together with twine. "You have quite a collection."

"You'd be surprised how many books end up here down under," said Elspeth. "Whenever I get bored I go fishing on the shores of Desire."

"Why Desire?"

"Don't know, really—but that's where all the books from above end up. Lots of romance novels. Really dirty stuff, I can't get enough of it. You can borrow some if you like. Though I try to spend my time educating myself on the classics. Plato, Aristotle, you know. When I get really desperate I duck into the library in Pride, they have lots of wholesome pretentious material." Elspeth led them to a nook that must have been at the front, for the wall was slightly curved like the prow. "Why don't you sleep down here? I'll be up top. The Kripkes don't generally bother me when I'm over water, but you can't be too cautious."

"Sorry," said Peter. "Could I, that is—where's the best place to take a leak—?"

"Oh—sure." Elspeth pointed behind her. "Just up that ladder and to your left. You can use one of the tins. Only empty it out when you're done."

"Thanks very much," said Peter, and headed up the ladder.

"Nice boy." Elspeth turned to Alice. "Didn't anyone tell you not to date within your department?"

"We're just colleagues," said Alice.

"Oh, sure."

"No, really." Alice hugged her arms against her chest. "I don't think he likes me all that much, actually."

"Oh, he must. He followed you to Hell, didn't he?"

Alice did not feel like explaining the tangled web of complications that had put her and Peter in Hell together. "Let's change the subject."

"Suit yourself." Elspeth dug a little box out of her pocket. "Smoke?"

"Oh—no, thanks." Alice had been trying to quit.

Elspeth shrugged and lit her own. Alice watched, fascinated, as smoke furled out the sides of Elspeth's head. "Does that do anything for you?"

"Of course not," said Elspeth. "Not physiologically, anyways. But the ritual's nice. The soul remembers. It's like—echoes of how it feels, which after a while seems close enough." She took a deep, lusty suck, and a rich, woody scent filled the air. *"Ahh."*

Alice caved. "Oh, all right."

Smiling, Elspeth lit another cigarette and handed it over. Smoke hung in a cloud around her head like a veil.

Alice waved a hand in front of her face. "How do you do that?"

Elspeth looked flattered. "I'm so glad you noticed."

"Can all Shades do that?"

"Only with a lot of practice," said Elspeth. "Do you know what proprioception is?"

"Sure. Knowing where your body is without looking at it." Alice knew this only because she had practice climbing. Most people had some degree of proprioception—you needed it to walk without staring at your feet, to tie back your hair without craning into a mirror—but climbing made you exceptionally good at it. You had to trust you could sustain the whole of your body weight on just two fingertips.

"Right," said Elspeth. "Well, as a Shade, your default state is a gray cloud. You don't cohere unconsciously anymore. You have to hold an image of what you looked like and will your essence to assemble. It takes immense concentration—as if you had to remember constantly to breathe. I'm very good at it. I know *exactly* how I look." Elspeth sniffed. "When I try very hard, I can become butterflies."

She shimmered and, as if to show off, briefly became even more solid. Her smoky veil vanished. Color returned to her cheeks. Her hair assumed a shine, and at her feet, a shadow solidified.

Alice blinked down. She tried to focus on her smoke, the push and pull of it. She had a hard time looking straight at Elspeth. She hated how deeply the resemblance struck her. For no matter how she parsed it, she could not rid herself of the clear recognition that Elspeth looked like *her*. What a cliché they made. Brittle brunettes, sad girl smokers. She wondered. What was the attraction?

"Could I ask you something?"

"Sure," said Elspeth. "You want to know why I killed myself."

"How did—I'm sorry, I'm being rude."

"No, I don't mind. Lots of Shades have asked. Why do you want to know?" Elspeth cocked her head. "Think much about killing yourself?"

Alice found her bluntness astonishing. Elspeth watched her earnestly, waiting for her answer.

Oh, what was the point of pretending? Of course she was wondering. Did death make you better off? Alice often thought it might, but she had only circumstantial evidence for believing so, and most people who had done it were unavailable for comment. "I have, a bit. Once or twice. I guess—it occupies my thoughts more than I'd like. Obviously I didn't—well, I don't know. I'm not sure what I'm asking."

"You'd like to find out where the boundary is," said Elspeth, not unkindly. "You'd like to know when it goes from feeling pretty blue, to thinking you wouldn't mind if a bus ran you over, to actively stringing a rope together and kicking off a chair. Is that right?"

"I—I guess, yeah." Alice had never said as much out loud before, and it scared her to hear her own thoughts reflected back to her. It scared her that someone else had had those same exact thoughts about the bus. "Sorry. I shouldn't have asked."

"No, it's fine," said Elspeth. "Lots of people want to know. I used to hear them from the Pavilion. It was all anyone ever talked about—*why'd she do it*, blah blah blah." She tapped some ash from her cigarette, then cut Alice a sideways look. "Who's your advisor?"

Alice found it prudent to lie. "Helen Murray."

"And she makes your life hard, does she?"

"Some."

"Hm. Well, see, *my* advisor was Jacob Grimes. I'm sure you've heard of him."

"Haven't we all." Alice asked, in a fit of boldness, "And he drove you to do it?"

"Please, no." Elspeth snorted. "I hate to give him that much credit for anything."

"Then *why*?"

"Well, let's start with why not. I imagine they told you I gave up because I'm dull. Is that what you heard?"

Alice had indeed formed the impression that perhaps Elspeth had simply lacked talent. It made the rest easier to stomach. For Alice was not talentless, so the same thing couldn't possibly happen to her. Suicidal depression was just an extreme form of failure, which was a symptom of inadequacy. If you had sufficient force of will, then obviously you wouldn't be suicidal. She did not admit this out loud.

"They . . . well, they didn't say much," she said. "It was more . . . um . . . hush-hush."

"Figures." Elspeth huffed. "I'm a genius, you know. I won all the maths and logic medals my first and second years. No one's ever done that before. I was as poised to succeed as anyone. You must understand."

It seemed very important to Elspeth that Alice acknowledged she was clever. She nodded vigorously. "Sure."

"It was the absolute farce of it all," said Elspeth. "One day it all seemed so *silly* to me, and I couldn't stop laughing about it. The symbolic system collapsed. You write a good paper, and it's rejected because your reviewer was having a bad day. You're a perfect fit for a job, and you lose to the committee chair's godson. Once you have a job it doesn't get better—do you know how many people are passed over for tenure because someone somewhere once felt they were rude at a party? I mean, what's the fucking point? I couldn't keep up the charade, but also I didn't see the value in anything else, so I just put a stop to it all. I could not care anymore. Meanwhile, *he* . . ." Her face darkened. "I mean. He was not the reason why. He was not. I refuse to give him that credit. He was just the symptom, you see. It took me many years to realize this. Every time he yelled at me, or picked me apart, or humiliated me in front of other students—this was just the whole symbolic order coming to a head. This is an arbitrary game of egos and narcissists and bullying perceived as strength. And he was the perfect incarnation of the system's nonsense."

"He treated you badly, you mean."

"He treated me like a dog." Elspeth's tone turned brittle. "It seemed a game to him to see how much I would take, before I stopped crawling back. I invested every fiber of my being in his stupid games. And I used to play along, because I thought, *Well, at least the rewards are so great. Persistence pays off.* And then I realized there were no rewards coming. That it was too late, and there was no way out."

*Aha*, thought Alice. Here was the line between them. There *was* a way out. Alice knew, because she'd perfected the game herself. You learned to read his moods. You fawned when he turned on you; groveled when he demanded an apology. It wasn't so hard, as long as you sacrificed your dignity. Realizing this gave her tremendous relief. She didn't have to follow down Elspeth's path. She was tougher. She wanted it more.

"He's not even that great a magician," Elspeth went on, waving her cigarette about. "That's the worst part. It might have been worth something, you know, if he actually was the greatest magician of our time. But he's just some hack like all the rest."

"What do you mean?"

"You know what they say. Everyone does their best work when they're young. He was big with Russell and all the rest in the fifties, sure. All the war stuff, fine. OBE, whatever, maybe he did save us all from the Germans. But it's been decades since he had a major paper out. All he does now is rubber-stamp things."

"That's not fair," said Alice.

Elspeth cocked her head. "Oh?"

"He's made some incredible discoveries since." Alice felt a fierce protectiveness then, though rationally she knew Professor Grimes needed no defending on her part. She knew he had flaws. She only didn't want to hear it from Elspeth. It was important to her that Professor Grimes was no one's demon but her own. Also, if they were going to criticize him, they ought to have their facts right. "He's researching memory and impermanence. It's so much better than his early work, it's really field-defining stuff."

Elspeth's lip curled. "If you say so."

"It's just taking longer to publish," said Alice. "You can't rush greatness."

"I'll take your word for it," Elspeth said drolly. "I mean, how would I know."

They stood awhile in silence. Alice knew this silence; it was the wary silence common to every time two women encountered each other in academia. They were each sizing the other up. The same questions hung between them. *Is that skirt too tight? How did you end up here? And what did it cost you?*

Abruptly Elspeth asked, "Did they make you do the self-torturer problem when you had your entrance exams?"

Alice shook her head.

"I guess it's out of fashion now. Figures." Elspeth took a deep drag of her cigarette, then sighed, her whole head clouded by smoke. She rambled on. "It's a problem of transitivity and rational decision-making. The setup is, suppose you have to put on a device that tortures you by degrees of tiny increments, increments so tiny that you don't even notice them. You can only turn the dial up; you can't turn it back down. Every day you have the option to turn the dial up by one increment, and if you do, you get ten thousand dollars. So every day, since you won't notice the change in pain, you should obviously turn the dial up and accept the ten thousand dollars. Until one day, you're stricken with unbearable pain, and there's no going back. Only even then, it *still* remains rational to keep turning the dial up, because you won't notice the change and because the ten thousand dollars is so attractive. How did we get to this point? What failure of decision-making led us *here*?"

"It's a 'frog in a boiling pot' problem," said Alice.

"That's right," said Elspeth. "There's a lot of solutions to the self-torturer. It would be rational to set limits on yourself before you begin, for example. Or it might be rational to have a friend cut you off. But Cambridge gives you none of these. It just keeps you turning up the dial. Up and up and up. You start getting tunnel vision about it all. All that exists is the payoff and the dial. Until one day my dial broke." She shrugged. "That's really all there was to it. One day I stopped being able to feel anything at all. There was no difference between pain and pleasure. It was all just the same wash. Nothing *mattered*. And it was only once I got here, once I was fucking *dead*, that things took on importance again."

"Right," said Alice. "I think I understand." She did not. This numbness Elspeth spoke of—she could believe it, but this was not her problem. Her problem was that she felt too much, and hurt too much, and she could not forget any of it, or manage to keep the thoughts at bay, and so she had to make it stop.

"I figured you might." Elspeth's expression softened, and she looked Alice up and down as if confirming a diagnosis. "You've got that look about you."

"What look?"

"Well, not to be rude, but you're all fucked up, aren't you?"

Alice hated this misplaced sympathy. She hated whenever anyone looked at her with this much pity, as if she were a trapped rat, drowning in a bucket. She was not a victim, she had made all her choices herself, and she knew perfectly well how to claw to safety.

But Elspeth so clearly wanted to help her. And the worst part of Alice, the self-serving and nasty part, figured, *Why not?* Let Elspeth believe what she wanted. Let her believe that they were the same; victims in the same story. People liked you better when they thought you needed them. The girls she met at conferences were like this too. You made some noises about harassment and condescension and the Plight of Being a Woman, and they'd flutter all around you, instantly on your side. Wounded attachments. The delirium of shared suffering.

"Cheer up," said Elspeth. "You'll be all right. You want to know how I know?"

"How?"

Elspeth shot her a kind smile. "Because you're looking for a way back up."

*Lord*, thought Alice. *Kill me.* She couldn't meet Elspeth's eyes, so she focused on sucking the last dregs of smoke from her cigarette. She didn't recognize this brand; she had no idea where Elspeth had gotten it, but it was the best thing she'd tasted in Hell. "Thank you. I appreciate it."

"Anytime, love. Get some sleep."

Elspeth vanished into the stacks. Alice curled in on her side and rested her cheek against the shelves, listening to Elspeth's rattling footsteps disappearing up the stairs. She was cold; the air below deck felt stale and drafty at once. She tugged Elspeth's blanket up further over her chin. It smelled of mothballs.

Her own entrance riddle had been the Ever Better Wine Paradox. Suppose you are gifted a bottle of wine that only gets better with time—there is no upper limit on how delicious it can become. Suppose also you are an immortal. When is it rational for you to drink the wine? If you popped the cork, you would be choosing an inferior wine compared to a future possible wine. But if, applying that logic, you never popped the cork at all, then you were worse off compared to every alternative.

Alice had answered with the argument that only adopting an attitude of accepting a satisfactory, not optimal, outcome could avoid the worst possible outcome. The principle of choosing the best possible option was, in practice, self-defeating. You were better off arbitrarily deciding to wait five years, then opening the wine and enjoying whatever you got.

But the lesson there, the nugget of truth within the paradox, was that happiness was comparative, not absolute. And this meant that if you could just outlast the other guy—if you could hold off even ten minutes before opening the cork—then at least you wouldn't be the fool who drank the shitty wine.

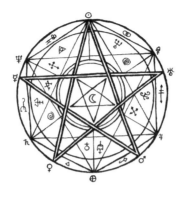

## CHAPTER SEVENTEEN

She must have dozed off without realizing it, for when she awoke Peter was curled in the corner beside her. She checked her watch. Only three in the morning. She propped herself up on an elbow, wriggled over to him, and placed her lips beside his ear. "Murdoch."

He didn't stir, so she dug her finger into his side and whispered again. "*Murdoch.*"

He jerked away. "What?"

"Shh." Alice squinted into the stacks but saw nothing but waterlogged books. She supposed Elspeth was still upstairs. "The Dialetheia. Let's find it."

Peter was fully awake now. "What are you talking about?"

She kept her voice as low as she could. "Elspeth knows where it is. She thinks she's close. We need to get it for ourselves."

She didn't know where she stood now with Peter. He had ignored her pointedly throughout dinner, had spoken directly to Elspeth as if Alice weren't present.

But Alice had practice talking to angry men. She had honed this art after years of managing Professor Grimes, of learning to tiptoe on eggshells when he was in a foul mood. So many graduates had ended up on his permanent shit list for saying the wrong thing at the wrong time. But Alice was like a finely tuned receiver, with an instinctive sense of when to talk him down, when to grovel, and when to stay out of his way.

With angry sulking men, the secret was holding your ground. You didn't get rebellious, no—that was asking for a slap to the face. But you didn't self-flagellate, either. When you acted like you ought to be whipped, that only confirmed to them that you should. One should never cower. The secret rather was to keep talking as if you deserved no punishment at all, and then to distract them with something they wanted more than they wanted to hurt you. With Professor Grimes, it had always been upcoming conferences, exciting new papers. With Peter it would have to be their ticket out of Hell. She was fixing this. This was her apology.

"She's just saved our lives," whispered Peter.

"Which is proof she can take care of herself, isn't it? Look. She's nice and all, I feel rotten about it too. But she doesn't know what it's like to be alive anymore. She's dressing in bones and skinning *rats*, for heaven's sake. She's hardly a person anymore. What's she going to do back in Cambridge?"

Peter was quiet for a moment. Alice waited, letting him think. He'd come around. She knew he would, otherwise he wouldn't have been talking to her.

"It's been ten years," he admitted finally.

"You see? There's nothing for her up there, and the sooner she figures that out, the better. She really ought to just pass on. But, *Murdoch!*" Alice felt a thrum of excitement, the pleasure of resolve. Yes, she could be bold. Decisive. She was not falling apart; she could wrangle her mind into action. She had to take the lead now. This was how she made amends. "If we can get it first, then that's all our problems, fixed—then we've only got to get to Lord Yama's court and wait. We can bargain for Professor Grimes's life, and our own exits besides." She paused. "And then you wouldn't have to exchange me, you know."

Peter did not react to this. For a long while all Alice could hear was his deep, even breathing. Then he murmured, "How?"

"We'll use magick." Alice had thought this through. "Now we know all it takes is blood. We'll use something to get her talking. I'll distract her, and you encircle her in a pentagram, somehow. We'll use the Liar Paradox."

Yes, it could be that simple.

Consider the following sentence: *This statement is false.*

It is devastatingly simple in its breaking of logic. You cannot believe it. You cannot disbelieve it. It has no truth value that you can settle on. You're stuck in the middle, thrown on an endless loop from one end of the sentence to the next.

The Liar Paradox was one of the oldest paradoxes of all time, for it violated that central premise of classical logic: the law of the excluded middle. Statements must either be true or false, and nothing in between. Still no one knew how to resolve the paradox. The Greeks and the Indians had been tooling around with the Liar Paradox for centuries; instead of resolving it, they merely came up with a whole family of related paradoxes, one of which involves Socrates, a crocodile, and a stolen child. It posed serious problems for the foundations of logic—indeed, Philitas of Cos agonized so much over the solution that he wasted away and died.

Inscribed in a pentagram, the Liar Paradox could suspend truth and falsity entirely. Magicians did not use it often, for most of the time they needed someone to believe something, not to exist in a state of uncertainty. But Alice didn't need Elspeth to believe anything in particular about them. She only needed Elspeth off her guard; willing to talk. And she already knew Elspeth liked to talk. The poor girl was desperate for anyone who would listen.

"That'll never work," said Peter. "Everyone knows how to ward off the Liar Paradox."

"Not if she's not expecting it."

"She might be. She already doesn't trust us."

"She does now." Alice was absolutely sure of this. "She thinks we're just like her. Depressed, hopeless souls. She thinks we hate Cambridge, too—she thinks we're on her side."

"Jesus, Law." Peter shifted under his blanket. "What is wrong with you?"

"We have to make it count." She felt a lump in her throat. "All this, I mean. It has to be worth something. We can't have done this all for nothing."

"Hm," said Peter.

Alice waited, hoping that he might say anything more. Wickedness felt better when you had a coconspirator; otherwise it was just you and your conscience. But he remained silent. Eventually his breathing evened out, and she assumed he'd fallen asleep.

Something tickled her cheek. She opened her eyes to see two vast, blinking green pools, inches from her face. Tiny pupils, narrowed to slits. They seemed quite judgmental.

"Don't *you* tell," Alice whispered.

Archimedes spun round, flicked his tail against her face, and disappeared into the shadow.

Irked, embarrassed for reasons too petty to name, she turned onto her side and closed her eyes.

"I HAVE A THEORY ABOUT WHY you're so stuck on academia," an old boyfriend of Alice's had once told her, shortly before he became an ex. This was during their senior year of college, when she had been single-mindedly obsessed with graduate school applications to the point of neglect—and perhaps downright rudeness, as she *had* stood him up at least half a dozen times by now. This, paired with this boyfriend's recent enrollment in a psychoanalysis seminar, made him vindictive. "You're obsessed with gold stars. You never got over the high school thrill of an A+ at the top of your paper and academia will let you chase those little gold stars for the rest of your life." He flicked her forehead. "Little ivory tower princess, you. You're a teacher's pet, Alice. You have a fetish for validation."

"Is that so?" Alice, whose mind was only on the prospect of fat envelopes from Cambridge, Oxford, Harvard, and Yale arriving in her mailbox, barely registered what he was saying. Indeed it took her months to realize this nasty monologue had been his attempt to get her into bed. "Yes. I suppose that's right."

They broke up shortly after. Alice reflected on his words in those following months, but only with a thrilling contempt. "You're giving up too much," he had told her. "This can't be worth it."

But of course it was worth it. It was the only thing that was worth it. She had been fortunate to find a vocation that made irrelevant everything else, and anything that made you forget to eat, drink, sleep, or maintain basic relationships—anything that made you so inhumanly *excited*—had to be pursued with single-minded devotion.

Academia was decidedly not about the gold stars. If Alice had ever fallen prey to this notion, she was quickly disabused of it during her first year of coursework, wherein she heard every day a million things wrong with the way she thought, and only the occasional, "Not bad." If you went into the field for gold stars you were in for disappointment.

No, the point was the high of discovery. No one else understood—certainly not the ex, who went on to do something involving mortgages and making poor people poorer. How could she explain to him the way her mind felt as if it were chewing, digesting difficult concepts? That the headache she got after marking up an impenetrable text was like the pain in her gums after masticating on a good steak? The way her whole body thrummed in excitement when she came across the exact algorithm, translation, historical reproduction, she'd spent hours searching for in the library. The way she always forgot she needed rest as she hunched over a pentagram for hours, sometimes days, scribbling frantically away as idea after idea surged through her mind.

How good it felt when she seemed to abandon her body altogether—when she became fully incorporeal, drifting happily in a universe of ideas. She was very proud of the days that she forgot to eat. Not because she had any revulsion for food, but because it was some proof that she had transcended some basic cycle of need. That she was not just an animal after all, held captive by her desires to eat and fuck and shit. That she was above all a mind, and the mind was capable of miraculous things.

Sometimes she would jolt, and feel suddenly that she was standing still on a spinning plane while abstract shapes swirled about her, calling to her, revealing themselves in full. The mundane world faded away and she was alone in a field of black, except for the brilliant spots—revelations, directions, connections—dancing in the corners of her vision. Everything else was so insubstantial! The world of the college; of chairs screeching on classroom floors, spoons clicking in cups, umbrellas trembling under constant rain—it was just a front, she realized; only a flimsy glamour. Blink and it was gone. It was in the hidden world where truth resided and concepts begged to be understood. She only had to reach for them, and they would come to her. Yes. She only had to listen, and she would hear the music.

In her freshman year, Alice had a professor whose lecturing style was defined by deep, spontaneous sighs. You could tell those weren't preplanned sighs. Some professors sighed as a performance, obnoxiously, to inject profundity where really there was none, but no—this professor was simply so overwhelmed by the moment, by the tangled thoughts waiting to be undone and then articulated, that he would stare off into space and look deeply bothered and tap his fingers together until he figured out in what order to convey it all—and then his spindly shoulders would shake and he would rock back and forth, as if he were a mere vessel, and his body an imperfect tool to convey a message from the gods. Alice's classmates found it funny. They would imitate Professor Eklund in the cafeteria, the way he sometimes lifted his entire knee onto the table as he rocked back and forth. What a dork, they said. What a poser, who does he think he is, who does he think he's fooling? But Alice knew it was not a front. Professor Eklund was in that dark, spinning plane, hearing the music. She could see it in his eyes. She wanted to follow him there.

No, prestige wasn't the point. Elspeth was wrong. Elspeth had invested all her hopes in the wrong symbols. The symbolic order—the paper publications, the applause, the job postings, the grants—was not the point. Even the Oxbridge credentials, which Alice's ex had assumed were solely what she was after, were not the point. Those were only instrumentally valuable to secure what Alice really wanted, which was unhampered time and access to the necessary resources to *think*.

This was why she kept at it for years. This was why every graduate student she knew didn't mind the low pay, the exhausting teaching assignments, or the nonexistent health care. They were all doing their best to extricate themselves from their bodies because they'd been told this was simply what they had to do. The whole system could be broken, and it wouldn't matter. They'd put up with anything, only for the promise of access to that abstract plane.

Peter understood. She'd seen the pure, serene bliss on his face as he stood at the blackboard, copying out equations so quickly she feared his wrist would cramp. That mode of concentration so deep you couldn't snap him out of it if you tried, and nor would you want to. It was too lovely to watch a mind at ferocious work.

Anyhow, it wasn't just pretentious asceticism. There were the good nights, too. She remembered an end-of-term social her first year, when they'd all congregated at the local pizza shop and ordered a massive sourdough margherita to share. Even Peter had come that night, and everyone, Alice included, was too delighted by his presence to ask why he'd stood them up a dozen times throughout the semester. They'd started arguing about dialects and the reliability of regional studies, and from there moved on to debating what it meant to do close reading versus distance reading, and whether it made any sense to impose a third criterion called middle reading.

Alice had never been so fond of her classmates until that night. It helped that the faculty were not present, and it helped that everyone was a little drunk, and no longer speaking to make the right impressions. They had the freedom to be wrong, which meant the freedom to get silly. And they got very silly. What was the difference between Kant's noumena and Plato's forms, they wondered. What was the precise definition of a sandwich, and was it still a sandwich if you ate it vertically? Was the horizontal definition sufficient to exclude tacos? Also, where were the aliens? From aliens they moved to Aristotle's schema of cosmological physics—earth, water, air, the stars expanding outward from the center like shells, and above it all a celestial body—a "celestial space worm," Michele called it, because it was more fun to think of this enormous, rotating, writhing being causing all the motion in the lower shells because it was thinking so hard about God, the unmoved first mover.

At some point Peter and Michele started debating Michele's rather dubious theory of personhood, which entailed that people died when they fell asleep, and woke up new versions of themselves that were related to, but were not *quite*, the person they'd been before. Consciousness can't take breaks, Michele argued; when you fall asleep that's it for you.

"But what about dreams?" Peter asked. "Who is having the dreams?"

"A half consciousness," Michele insisted. "A soul neither living nor dead. An imprint. An eidolon."

Peter found this absurd, and Belinda found it romantic, and they all had a go at dissecting its implications before the conversation turned abruptly to the question of whether it was all right to have sex with trains, particularly if it violated Aristotle's teaching that things should be used for their given functions ("Then what about people who use toothbrushes to masturbate?" Michele wanted to know, which made Belinda blush), and then under what particular circumstances one *could*, if one wanted, have sex with trains. For whatever reason this hit a vein, and their voices grew louder. At one point Belinda and Michele stood up, shouting over the table.

Alice sat watching, cradling her beer, and she was so happy she could have cried.

Here she belonged. Here she could utter things, could be honest about where her mind had drifted, and they wouldn't look at her like she was mad. All her life she had bumbled through social contact like the only actor who'd forgotten to look at the script. She had been the weird one, the troubled one, the one no one wanted to sit with. But they were all the weird ones here. And here no one punished you for caring too much, thinking too deeply. Here you could jump down any rabbit hole you liked, and everyone would tunnel down with you.

And no, perhaps their pub debates were not in the field of pure truth that Professor Grimes liked to go on about. Perhaps these were not the discoveries that would change the world for anyone except for people very sexually attracted to trains. But was it not at least training for something similar? To rejoice in the acrobatics of thought—not as Stoics did, which was to manipulate language for mean and personal gain, but to sharpen their tools in preparation for the real digging. What greater pleasure could there be? What else was life *for*?

There was a time when she felt this energy everywhere she went, with everyone she met. She lived the Platonic ideal of the university back then. She was purposefully naïve about it, because a naïve mind, open to childlike wonder, was the happiest mind in a place like Cambridge. She liked to drift across conversations in hall, listening along, absorbing the excitement, asking simple questions, and receiving dazzlingly complex answers. She loved all her interlocutors. The comparative literature scholar meticulously describing E. A. Nida's translation theory of dynamic equivalence, and its resonance with traditional Chinese translation theory. The paleontologists going on about the complete dinosaur skeleton they'd just found in Surrey, and whether it was an asteroid that killed the dinosaurs after all. The dear boys in the maths department cackling with delight over things called knots and manifolds.

Sometimes the shining faith of the scientists rattled her. For here they were making things, changing the world. It was the era of endless discovery. The physicians had made an artificial human heart. The astronomers were peering at the rings of Neptune; the geneticists were eradicating smallpox and stemming hepatitis B; the physicists were working out string theory; the geneticists were decoding human DNA. It seemed the whole world was spinning faster, growing more complex and exciting, and yet the field of magick seemed stuck in the mud, scholars driving themselves down increasingly tiny rabbit holes over minute disagreements rather than exploding the boundaries of what they could do.

She turned once to Professor Grimes, seeking reassurance.

It's all sand, she said; it's fake, it's just words, just momentary glimmers of an illusion, what's the point? And it was one of the rare moments in their relationship that he gave her exactly what she needed. He was a good teacher, after all; he knew how to mesmerize.

"Schopenhauer argued that all art is merely representational and allegorical except for music, which is the closest thing to pure will," he told her. "But I find in our pentagrams something akin to music. Not in its total abstraction from everyday phenomena, but in its ability to pierce through to the center of them. That shining, cloudless plane of truth on which nothing else matters. It is as Heisenberg said, dear Alice. That modern physics has decided in favor of Plato, that the smallest units of matter are not physical objects in the ordinary sense, but forms, and ideas. And when you have complete mastery of these ideas, when you can hold them in your palm and twist and tease them at will—then you will have stepped closer to God. It will feel meticulous, yes. Petty, fleeting, pedantic. But all the more reason to double your drive, and clutch at every precious wisp of truth you glimpse." And this sent her away spinning, delirious, enraptured by the hidden world.

It was this simple: Alice loved her work.

It was only the social world, the institution, that got in the way. Yes, it was aggravating; yes, it was a world of hurt. But unlike Elspeth, she was not ready to give up on it all. Elspeth was wrong. It was not devoid of meaning. There was something still worth fighting for. Alice had located something in that cloud of symbols, a value that was not nonsense, and she believed in it with her entire being. She believed in it still. She only needed to survive the rest.

## CHAPTER EIGHTEEN

It was still dark out when Alice awoke. Peter was gone, his blanket folded and tucked neatly beneath a shelf. She picked herself up and tiptoed up to the top deck, where she found, with some relief, Elspeth and Peter sitting across from each other on the prow. They were not speaking; they both sat with their knees drawn up to their chests, staring out over the water. Archimedes perched atop the railing, tail swishing back and forth like a pendulum. He, too, had his gaze fixed upon the water, one paw slightly lifted, as if in remembrance of swiping goldfish.

Alice approached, clutching the blanket around her shoulders. Peter ignored her. But Elspeth met her eyes and tilted her head as if to say, *Come join.*

Alice crossed the deck as quietly as she could and slid down beside Elspeth. The *Neurath* cut silent across the night, gliding over still waters without so much as a ripple. They might have been sailing through space, floating over nothing at all.

Alice had not grown up around large bodies of water. As a child she'd meant to go river-tubing with her parents in San Antonio. They'd gotten lost, and whiled away most of the afternoon turning round and round on highways. By the time they reached the river the sun was setting and most families had packed up their things to go. They were debating whether to stay or go when suddenly they heard a sharp cry. The families at the bank were scurrying frantically about, and eventually it transpired that a little girl had been swept downriver. The river was shallow, only waist-deep, but moving fast, and it was hard to spot anything in the dimming light. The shouting grew louder. Alice heard splashes; adults jumping into the water. Alice's mother herded them all back to the car. They never did find out if that little girl had drowned; Alice remembered only driving away with her face pressed to the glass, squinting at the bank, hoping to see a little head emerge.

She had been terrified of swimming since. She never joined her friends on trips to the beach. At Cambridge, she lived along the river Cam, which was as tame as a river could be. Still she feared it; how dark it seemed when she crossed the bridge past midnight, how easily it might swallow anything that came close. Often of late her mind wandered to the prospect of jumping. Whether she might splash around. Whether she might just slip to the bottom and disappear. There was something compelling about water; its ability to absorb, and make nothing and whole both at once.

And the Lethe, by comparison—oh, the great, enveloping Lethe. Less a river than a wound in space. She realized she had no grasp on how wide the Lethe was, or indeed if its thickness was regular at any point. None of the maps really knew what to do with the Lethe, its inverted geography. How far had they drifted into Hell's uncharted domain? Without the moon above or any banks in sight they were only three figures on a little boat, sailing on an eternal black plane with no end and no beginning. Alice felt disembodied. Anything could happen to them. They might sail along forever. They might vanish without a trace.

"Look." Peter was peering over the side of the boat, arms outstretched, fingers so close to skimming the water.

"Careful," said Alice, but he shook his head and insisted, "*Look.*"

She joined him over the railing, and her breath caught at the sight—a glimmering current of light, palimpsestic beneath the black.

People swam in the water. Well—not people, precisely, but flashes of them; faces laughing, crying, arguing, weeping; faint phosphorescent outlines in glowing green ripples. People and things and places from other lives—a sunny cliff by the seaside, a crooked beach umbrella, a dog barking happily as it bounced closer, ever closer, tongue pink and bright, the fluff atop its head so downy soft that Alice could almost feel it in her palm.

"Memories," said Elspeth. "Every forgotten thing from every life lived. The fresh ones form a little current, sometimes—you can see them in detail before they dissolve."

The boat lurched to the left. Suddenly the waters around them began to churn. Over the railing, Alice saw a fomenting black mass—something with too many eyes and too many teeth. She shrank away, but Elspeth leaned over the edge and jammed her punting pole in the middle of the mass. "Back! Back, you. Silly things."

The waters stilled; the boat righted.

"Don't you worry," Elspeth assured them. "Just a rogue nightmare. They dissipate easily enough. They're not coming for us. Sometimes they coalesce, and you get these little whorls of terror. Boltzmann brains, I like to call them."

"Very funny," said Peter.

"Where do they all go?" Alice asked. "Do they fade?"

"Far from it," said Elspeth. "This is their repository. The Lethe is all the memories that ever were. The Lethe is infinite. The Lethe is all the colors on the palette mixed into black. The Lethe doesn't erase, it only absorbs."

"Eternal recurrence," Peter murmured. "Everything that has happened will happen again."

"Don't quote Nietzsche on my boat," said Elspeth.

"Mea culpa."

Elspeth settled back, arms crossed. "It's fun to watch, anyhow. Like the television channel of the underworld. It's always the freshest memories that are clearest. Gives you a picture of what life is like above. Can't believe how much things have changed. Did they really kill John Lennon?"

"Yes," said Peter. "Sorry."

"Oh, what a pity."

Alice leaned over the deck, entranced.

A girl hopped on one foot over a wet sidewalk wriggling with worms. A man wobbled on a bike behind a bus turning into traffic. A woman juggled boiling pots on a stove. A boy walked alone by the river Cam, glancing up every now and then to watch the rowers training in the early morning. Those were not her memories; those faces were not of her loved ones. They struck a deep nostalgia in her just the same, the nostalgia you got looking inside brightly lit windows along the street at night; peeking into lives you might just have had. Someone else's comfort. A warm couch, an old movie humming along on the television. And then your wife or mother or friend joining you from the kitchen, steaming mugs of hot toddies in both hands. She found its sight oddly calming. The insides of her head, tossed out onto water—except these images had no associations with her own, they did not spark the deluge, she could just watch them go by; instantiated, then vanishing.

"Careful," said Elspeth.

Alice realized she was leaning quite far over the railing. She shrank back.

"The Lethe will do that to you," said Elspeth. "You've got to be on guard. Otherwise you dissolve quick, before you know it."

Would she? Alice wondered. How much protection did Grimes's tattoo afford?

"I thought the Lethe couldn't hurt Shades," said Peter.

"The draft doesn't, only cleans your memory for rebirth. But unfiltered water, straight from the river—that can destroy you. I'm very careful. Stuck my pinkie in once. Just the tip. I wanted to see if it would hurt, you see."

"And did you sense it?" asked Peter. "What you were forgetting?"

"Not at all," said Elspeth. "That's the most frightening part. You'd never know what you lost. You don't get to choose."

"You said that the Kripkes don't fear the Lethe," said Alice. "What did you mean by that?"

"They don't," said Elspeth. "No, they court it. I've even seen them drinking its waters. Just once. They stood at the bank in a line, taking tiny sips from a bowl. It seemed like a ritual for them. Like they'd done it before."

Peter looked aghast. "Why?"

"Because it hurts to be human, I'm sure," said Elspeth. "Hurts to be reminded what you don't have anymore. Better to erase yourself bit by bit, until you are only what you need in the present moment." She shrugged. "We all do it. Even the living. Only difference is the Kripkes care less about what they're leaving behind."

Peter shuddered. "But that's not a life anymore."

"They aren't living lives," said Elspeth. "They're just rote functions. Dedicated to a single end."

Alice didn't find this so awful. Why wouldn't everyone strip away the parts of their selves that caused them pain? She'd like to learn that trick, she thought. If she could sift through that mess in her head, pull out the files that kept torturing her, and burn them. Every small humiliation, every shred of guilt—if only she could unclutter her mind so that all that was left was the elements she wanted to keep: the burning core, the hunger for knowledge, the skills to gain it. You could achieve so much without the burdens of personhood. Who wouldn't wash away the rest?

AS THE SUN CLIMBED PONDEROUSLY ONTO its ever-low perch, Elspeth steered them toward the coast. "Better to be out deep at nighttime," she explained. "The Kripkes like to move under the cover of the dark. It gets choppy, though. Days, I prefer to be close to shore."

"Where are we headed?" asked Peter.

"Wrath," said Elspeth. "I need a lantern."

A strip of land came into focus now. No buildings marked the horizon. No—as they sailed closer, Alice saw that on the other side of the abyss that the Shades had labored so furiously to cross was nothing but sand and driftwood. It seemed a barren and hostile beach, the kind you got shipwrecked on; the kind where survivors went mad and devoured one another. Indeed the more she observed, the more the beach presented evidence of some ongoing struggle. Everywhere she saw confused prints in the sand; haphazard fortlike structures; broken spears made of driftwood and rocks; discarded firewood; proof of camps broken up in a hurry.

"The Third Court," said Elspeth. "The deserts of Greed."

"Where's the campus?" Alice asked.

"Pardon?"

"Coming over the wall, we saw this campus," said Alice. "And I just thought all the courts were like—buildings on a campus."

"Oh." Elspeth chuckled. "What's the furthest you've ever wandered from your department?"

"How do you mean?"

"I bet you always lived in college," said Elspeth. "You never ventured further out, did you?"

*Of course I did*, Alice wanted to say; but she really couldn't claim she had. The farthest she could point to was the walk south to Cambridge station, but that didn't count. Downing and Pembroke were down there.

"Don't you know it?" Elspeth gestured. "The dead space. Where the campus ends, but the rest of the world hasn't started. Where faculty and no one else lives. Where the university's bought up land but not built anything on it. Where construction continues, but nothing is ever built, where space is in becoming for ages. Haven't you been there?"

"I did visit Berkeley once," said Peter. "Horrible place."

"Well, that's where we are." Elspeth dug her pole into the bank. "Things get freaky out here."

Near the shoreline knelt a Shade, its head bobbing up and down in frantic movement. As they drew closer Alice saw the Shade was attempting to eat something clutched in his hands. Something shiny, circular, hard. Alice hoped it was only a rock.

"Professor Carpeaux," said Elspeth. "He's been there for a while. Always hungry."

The name rang a bell to Alice. "Wasn't that the man who—"

"Who plagiarized his students' papers for years and got away with it," said Elspeth. "They said he died of a stomach virus, but I think one of his students laced his apples with cyanide. Good work if so."

The barge drifted closer to shore. Here the waves grew perilous, crests smashing against the rocks. Further up shore Alice could see larger groups of Shades, though she could not speak to what they were doing. They seemed to be at war—certainly two groups kept charging one another in succession, weapons in tow—but what happened after was unclear, since no one could be injured in any way that mattered, which meant they could only settle for what looked like vigorous collective writhing on the sand.

Alice was reminded of a faculty volleyball tournament—a few years back, when the students lobbied to have the annual department retreat in Brighton instead of Inverness, and for three days everyone pretended to look natural outdoors, pale flabby bodies sweating under the hot sun. Someone proposed a volleyball tournament, and all the faculty got competitive about it. Some instinct for physical dominance emerged in this new environment. Alice would have given anything for a potion that could selectively wipe the memory of the department administrator grunting as he lobbed a ball into the net, or Helen Murray shrieking with joy when she managed a good serve. The game broke up after an argument about refereeing, which culminated in Helen hurling her cup of water at the other team. Alice had been ever so grateful Professor Grimes did not play. She'd never have been able to look at him the same way again.

"What are they doing?" Peter looked aghast.

Two Shades were now slowly circling each other, arms extended at their sides like wrestlers, while the others gathered around them, chanting something illegible from shore.

"Hell if I know," said Elspeth. "I've poked around before, tried to find out. But they won't talk to me. They're the only Shades that won't talk to me. They're very chatty in Pride, and even the folks in Desire will talk for an hour or two, if you wave a hand in front of their face. But they're so paranoid on Greed. They sprint away every time you approach. And then next thing you know they're ambushing you with driftwood arrows. My theory is that it's some sort of collective action problem, and they could all get out if they'd just hold some democratic forum, but I think they have more fun with their sticks and arrows—oh, watch out." Elspeth tugged at the rudder strings. "They start pelting me with rocks whenever I get close."

They tugged away from the shore. Professor Carpeaux raised a hand toward them—plaintive, supplicating. Elspeth wiggled her fingers in return.

"Do you see a lot of people you know here?" Alice asked. She was trying to think of a subtle way to see if Elspeth had spotted Professor Grimes.

"Oh, yes. Far more magicians than you would expect, actually."

"And do they get out pretty quick, in your experience?"

"Absolutely not." Elspeth snorted. "Magicians are terrible at getting through Hell. They never think they did anything wrong, you see. They think they're different. Everything's justified if they were doing it for research. Only it's never for the research, is it? It's always about the ego, the bragging, the titles and bylines. A hierarchy of complete nonsense. And they can't give it up. I think that's why they muck about in the sand all those years. They could get up and walk away at any moment, but they won't. They can't give it up. And for what?" Elspeth gave a brittle laugh. "Little parlor tricks? Magick is so flimsy. Pointless. There's no one in the real world who cares about what we do. And these people lived like its simplest secrets were matters of life and death. And they'll go at each other's throats—for what? A fucking piece of chalk?"

This last sentence came out sounding rather pointed. Alice tossed Peter a nervous glance. But Elspeth was not looking at them. She was glaring hard at the writhing bodies back on shore.

Peter said, "Beats me why you'd want to go back then."

Elspeth frowned, eyes narrowing. "Now, what do you mean by that?"

"It just—it seems you'd be better off, well, reincarnating. I dunno. If you hate Cambridge so much."

"I didn't hate Cambridge."

"The people, then." Peter's fingers worried at the frays of his sleeves. "The institution, at least. Why spend so long searching for a True Contradiction when you could just pass on? Given there's nothing you want to go back to?"

"I mean, I still have a family." Elspeth's voice grew sharp. "I had parents. Have parents. I have siblings. I still have a *life*."

"No, right, I'm sure." Peter nodded. "But if you're done with research, then what's the—I mean, have you ever thought through what you might do when you get back up there?"

"Of course," Elspeth said scathingly. "I'm going to sit outside. I'm going to have a cup of tea, Assam, with lots of milk and a swirl of honey. And a cinnamon bun. With raisins."

THEY ROUNDED THE BEND PAST GREED and, after a long stretch of empty beach, came upon the Court of Wrath.

Dante had described Wrath as the swamp of the Styx, populated with furious naked souls in the bog, striking at each other and at themselves. Souls simmering such that their rage made the surface bubble. Alice had quivered upon reading this description—"This hymn they gurgle in their gullets / For they cannot get a word out whole"—for it was the first time a poet seemed to understand that wrath was not merely external; was not just a screaming raving tornado of destruction. Sometimes you swallowed it down like a hot coal. Sometimes it only ever burned you, slowly, from the inside out, until you choked. She thought of nights she'd spent awake, tracing over the corners of memories and working herself up into a rage—but it never made her incandescent, righteous; she only stifled herself in her ineffectuality. *All this has happened to me*, she'd think, *and the world is unfair, and still I can't do a thing about it. I might as well drown.*

"So what's on Wrath?" Peter asked. "A rugby court?"

"Actually no," said Elspeth. "The structured institutions start disintegrating after Greed, I think. Past Wrath, it all gets more classically infernal. Degeneration of the psyche, the flight from reason—something like that. We tread a bit more carefully here."

Alice gazed at shore looking for her imagined bogs of souls, like fruit flies drowning in apple cider. But under the dim light of morning, she saw only dark and endless shore. The sand was pitch-black, though dotted with bright, glowing spots. Footprints, Alice realized; undeniably shaped by heel and ball. Though the being who'd created them must have been enormous, for as they drew closer she saw those footprints could span her entire height at least.

"Those will be left by Phlegyas," said Elspeth. "A deity. Cast into the underworld for setting fire to Apollo's temple after Apollo raped his daughter."

"That seems reasonable," said Alice. "I mean the fire, not the raping."

"Well, Phlegyas thinks so too. Always howling about the injustice. Look—there he is, at the foot of those mountains. Can you spot him?"

Alice squinted over the plain. Far beneath the cliffs she saw a crimson pulsing light, moving ponderously through the rocks. And within, a dark silhouette—but what form it took, man or beast, she could not tell.

"Is he dangerous?"

"Oh, very. Could smite you with a mere glance. He does leave these wonderful little embers wherever he steps, though. Coals that don't go out for weeks. That's what I'm here for." Elspeth nodded to her lamp—which, Alice noticed, burned a similar pulsing crimson. Grunting, she hauled a metal bucket out from beneath the pile of oars. "I'm off to collect. Can you two man the boat?"

"Oh—sure." Alice perked up. She had been puzzling over how to trap Elspeth under her watch, and here the opportunity had just dropped into their laps. "What should we—"

"Just stay by the anchor." Elspeth was already climbing atop the railing. "And if the bone things approach, spritz them away. I do hate when they come aboard."

One graceful leap, and she was ashore. Alice watched her dancing nimbly over the coals, jumping from rock to rock until she faded from sight.

She felt something against her back. She turned, then flinched. Peter stood very close behind her, eyes fixed ahead on Elspeth.

"Now's the time," he murmured. "Do you want to distract her? Or draw the pentagram?"

Those were the first words he'd spoken to her all morning. She tried to hide her relief. "Um—either, I guess. What do you—"

"I'm faster with pentagrams. I'll draw it."

Alice was not sure this was true but felt now was not the time to push back. "That's fine. Where ought—I mean, where do you think we can get her?"

She had been struggling with this all morning. Wrangling information out of Elspeth was one thing; the harder was getting her into a pentagram at all. The problem with a blood-soaked pentagram was that it was very difficult to hide. Theoretically the size of a pentagram did not affect its potency—and indeed, in Roman history the Celts had drawn great chalk structures around entire hills and forests to trap their enemies. But it would take time, and more blood than they had.

"Just get her by the stove," said Peter. "There's a mat—we can draw it now, have it there before she's back. You think there's time?"

Alice glanced back onto the beach, where Elspeth was shoveling embers into her bucket with gusto. "You'll have to be quick."

"Sure. Can I get a knife?"

"Why—oh." She fished it out of her rucksack. "Here—be careful."

"I'll do my best," muttered Peter, and headed for the stairs.

Alice took a shaky breath and turned back to the beach. Elspeth's bucket was nearly full. She saw Alice looking at her, straightened up, and waved cheerily. Alice waved back, feeling rotten.

*Have resolve*, she thought. Professor Grimes had taught her this. The difference between greatness and mediocrity was only ever about following through. Anyhow, this was a good thing, the merciful thing. Elspeth had to be put out of her misery. One conversation—that was all it would take. And then they would be on their way, and Elspeth only ever an awkward memory.

"HELLO! TAKE THIS." STANDING TIPTOE ON the shore, Elspeth swung the bucket of embers forward using the far end of her spear. Alice grasped it and hauled it into the middle of the deck. From the corner of her eye she saw Peter disappear toward the stairs, his arm clamped against his side.

She straightened up. "Hey, Elspeth?"

"Yes, love."

"Tell me if it's presuming, but I was wondering if we might—that is, I'd love some tea." She cleared her throat. "If you have any. It's been so long."

"Magicians." Elspeth chuckled. "Incorrigible. Is Earl Grey all right? That's all I have."

"Earl Grey sounds perfect."

"Come, I'll show you how the stove works. Take those tongs, it's out of coal—" Elspeth gestured, and Alice gingerly picked a glowing ember from the bucket.

Elspeth crouched before the stove. The mat sat firmly where Peter had left it. It was a dirty, black-brown thing that might have once been yellow, synthetic fibers waterlogged and filled with sand. Under the legs of the stove Alice spied faded cursive that read: *Home is where the heart is*. She could imagine Elspeth finding it in the course of her scavenging, and carting it back delighted to her ship. Hello, my lovely bones! Look what I've found.

"In here." Elspeth waved for Alice to place the ember in the middle, then fished a stained, cracked teapot from the proofing drawer. This she filled with Alice's copied flask. Driblets streamed out the cracks, sizzling pleasantly against the stove. Together they stood over the flames, watching steam curl off the side of the teapot. Archimedes materialized from wherever he'd been off to and perched by Elspeth's legs near the stove, basking in the glow.

"Where's Peter?" Elspeth asked.

"Oh—um, wanted to lie down, I guess." Alice wondered if Peter had had time to activate the pentagram. She had not heard him speak on the deck—but pentagrams could be activated from a distance, especially if he were standing beneath them just now. She stalled. "I think he's tired."

"He's a brooding type, isn't he?"

"He can be, yeah." Alice twisted her thumbs together, casting frantically about for how to proceed.

She had never been good at lying. Once Professor Grimes had sent her to Professor Stuart's office to suss out whether he was pursuing the same strain of Curry subsets that Professor Grimes wanted to work on, and she had fumbled things so badly that ten minutes in, Professor Stuart began reminding her awkwardly but kindly that he had a wife and children. But all academics, she knew, relished being asked about their research. And it was not difficult to get Elspeth talking—after all, she had languished so long without anyone to listen.

"So who's on Wrath, anyways?" She mustered the most casual tone she could. "Lab managers and registrars?"

"Nothing good. I don't see a lot of folks go through Wrath, to be honest. And the ones that do, I hear more than see them." Elspeth shook their head. "Dreadful place. I don't ever go much further than the shore."

"Do you understand the purpose of the courts?" Alice pressed. "We've been confused ourselves. It seems—it seems, at the end of the day, that punishments are entirely random."

"What's so random about it?"

"Well, I can't tell what the point of anything is," said Alice. "Pride and Desire, maybe. You get over yourself and then you walk out. But Greed? What are they doing there? What's it all *for*?"

"Hell if I know. You stop asking questions, after a while."

"But it's so *vexing*," said Alice. "All these scholars have these theories—about sin, karma, repentance—and then you come to Hell and realize it's all up to the whims of deities. And I just think if any Tartarologists really came down here they'd burn their previous publications."

"That's because they would like to treat the Afterlife like a game," said Elspeth. "All academia is shoving natural phenomena into boxes that won't fit. They'd like to program it out because it makes them feel safe, because if they can point to all the sinners in Greed and Wrath and Tyranny and say *Well at least I wasn't as bad as him*, then they don't have much to worry about. And they get frustrated when Hell won't play along."

"But there should be some order," said Alice. "It should be *fair*."

"You want Hell to obey the rules of classical logic."

"Not logic, necessarily," said Alice. "I know there's elements to the divine, and all that. But the cosmos should have some coherence, don't you think?"

"You are such an incorrigible member of the Cambridge School," said Elspeth. "All systems builders. Closed circuits. *Bah.* Never open to spontaneity."

"I only like knowing what awaits," said Alice. "That's all."

"Here, this might make you feel better. Do you want to hear my theory?"

"Oh, yes."

"Well, I think the biggest misconception about Buddhism is that karma functions as this grand tally that you count up at the end of the day." Elspeth waved a hand. "But it's not like you get five hundred good points and eight hundred bad points, so that in Hell you have to account for a net three hundred deficit. It's nowhere so neat. Karma is more like—hm. You might say karma is like a seed. Seeds grow into fruit. Karma is a natural consequence. Badness accrues. It affects the way you live your life, how you perceive the world. When you do evil things, you see the world as petty and selfish and cruel. And what you experience in Hell is just the final ripple effect of your original evil. You get precisely what you asked for. And I think the whole point of Hell is to show you the full extent of what you wanted."

"Huh." Alice turned this over in her mind. This theory was appealing, she thought, but there was still so much it couldn't explain. "And the Shades in Greed—that's what they wanted all along? Building spears on the beach?"

"What they wanted was to be better than everyone else," said Elspeth. "And now they've got the chance to prove it. They get to go wrestling in the muck. Proving their might and vanquishing weaker minds. Every single day. They're probably in paradise. The upshot is, Hell's not so bad for the people who are in it. They're exactly where they wanted to be."

The kettle began to whistle. Elspeth took it off the stove, tipped water carefully into two teacups, and handed one to Alice. "Here you are."

"Thanks." Alice lowered her head to sip, but a foul stench hit her nose. She blinked down; thick, black pellets floated at the surface of the water. This was decidedly not Earl Grey. Elspeth was watching her, so she put on a wincing smile and feigned a sip.

"Sugar?" Elspeth asked.

"Go on, then."

Elspeth reached behind the stove and plinked something tiny into Alice's cup. Alice stirred, and pretended not to notice it was a pebble. "So then, um—if you don't mind my asking, what court are you due in for?"

Elspeth blinked at her.

"Sorry," said Alice. "I suppose that's rude."

"Incredibly," said Elspeth.

"I only think, sometimes, it would be so nice to just pass on and start over." Alice took another pretend sip of her tea. "I mean, if you didn't do anything terrible, you might as well stomach it and move on, don't you think?"

Elspeth's eyes narrowed. "You two seem very invested in persuading me to give up and die."

"No, no, I'm just—I'm trying to understand." Alice's mouth had gone dry. She swallowed, which did not help. "Seems strange to keep chasing after something that doesn't exist, when you could just—I mean, when it would be so easy to just go on."

"I deny the premise, but sure." Elspeth leaned against the stove. "Something wrong with the tea?"

"No, no, it's fine—um." Alice curled her fingers around her cup. She felt dizzy. Oh, she was terrible at this. "So are you—are you close, then? Do you know where it is?"

Elspeth sipped from her own tea, unspeaking.

"What's stopping you?" Alice pressed. "Is it the Kripkes?"

A strange look came over Elspeth's face.

Was this the pentagram working? Alice could not tell. She had not played around with the Liar Paradox since her first year, and could not remember acutely what it did to its victims. Was that a glaze over Elspeth's eyes? Was she dazed?

"We could help," said Alice. "Me and Peter. If it were the three of us against the Kripkes, they'd never stand a chance. Only you'd have to share with us what you know. If we could just see your notes, I mean . . ."

Elspeth did not answer. She appeared frozen in place. Her fingers clenched unmoving around her cup of tea, which was pitched forward, dripping, but she did not seem to notice. Her eyes were fixed downward at Archimedes, who now stood, hackles raised, spine curved, glaring up at Alice.

"Baby," said Elspeth. "What's wrong?"

Archimedes batted at the mat. Alice's gut dropped. Archimedes went at the mat like a thing possessed, hissing and scratching at its surface. At last he succeeded in nudging the corner of the mat to the side, revealing a smudge of chalk and several red, glistening drops of blood.

For a long moment Alice and Elspeth blinked at one another. Ever so slowly Elspeth set her cup down on the stove.

A number of possible excuses crossed Alice's mind. None of them seemed worth the effort.

"Peter, darling." Elspeth raised her voice. "Why don't you come up here."

An excruciating silence. Alice briefly considered running, or fighting—but to where? And with what? She could only clutch her teacup and stand there like a fool. Peter appeared atop the stairs, arm dripping, face pale. He met Alice's eyes; frantically she shook her head.

"Over there," Elspeth barked. Peter obeyed, and took a place next to Alice. Side by side they were like chastened children, waiting for punishment. Archimedes perched up on the stove beside Elspeth, glaring righteously through pinprick pupils. *Wretched thing*, thought Alice; *after all we fed you.*

Elspeth tapped her spear against the ground. "I think you ought to tell me who you're here for."

"We told you," said Alice. "We're sojourning—"

"*Liars.*"

Something black seeped into Elspeth's eyes. They seemed to rot in her head, whites turning green, then black, years of decay squeezed into seconds. Suddenly butterflies flew out the sockets; a horde of them, awful rustling violet. Alice and Peter skittered back, but Elspeth approached, butterflies doubling with every step, until she was not a person but a rustling mass of velvet, dark and reproachful. Her spear whipped out; the point rested just beneath Peter's chin.

"Step inside."

Peter's neck bobbed. "Why don't—"

"Step inside, love."

Peter obeyed.

"You know, it's not the cruelty that gets me." Elspeth pulled out a stick of chalk, dipped it in a pouch at her belt, and fixed it to the end of her staff. "It's the disrespect. I'm a Grimes student, you might recall." She kicked the mat away and began etching alterations into Peter's work. She wrote with furious speed, muttering in Greek as she went along. This was terrifically impressive magick—very few magicians could inscribe and incant simultaneously. *She is good*, Alice thought; *she is worthy of Grimes*. "You think I have been down here for decades, dancing with the Kripkes, and I don't know my way around the goddamn Liar Paradox?" She closed the circle with a final, vicious stroke. "The Liar Paradox is child's play. But advanced magick, kids—that's making one tell the truth."

She banged her staff against the deck. Alice choked. Two invisible hands gripped the sides of her face, wrenching her jaw open.

Elspeth demanded, "What is your purpose?"

The invisible hands pressed harder. Alice gurgled an answer and tried to choke it down.

"Grimes," Peter gasped.

"Excuse me?"

"Professor Grimes—our advisor, he died, we have to bring him back—"

"*You're here for Grimes?*"

Elspeth howled then, a howl that doubled, tripled, multiplied into an impossible chorus, a thousand Elspeths shrieking from nowhere. Tiny black lines spread rapidly across her skin, and then the top layer of her skin seemed to peel away. Dark fragments coalesced, whirled—but Elspeth was not gone, only shielded now by a horde of butterflies, which swirled agitated around her, whipping up winds, whirling faster and faster until the force of the gale seemed about to rip the ship apart. She-the-chorus screamed, resounding over the winds. "You gave up half your lives, and journeyed to the underworld"—the butterflies enveloped her like a shield, encasing her in a semihuman form until she was not a human Shade but some singular-plural god, speaking with a voice like thunder—"for that miserable, godforsaken *clown*?"

Elspeth pointed her staff. All at once the butterflies stormed outward. Alice flung her arms over her head, but it did not matter; the creatures were like a velvet wall, pushing until she and Peter were forced against the prow, bent at the knee, for the circling winds were too strong for them to lift their heads.

"Get off my boat," said Elspeth.

"Please," said Peter. "Please don't—"

"You dare to beg?"

"What would you do?" Alice cried. "If your advisor died? If you were in our position?"

The butterflies parted. Elspeth's face was again revealed, pale and terrible. "I'd *quit*, you moron. I'd find another one." For just a moment her voice was human. Alice thought she heard it break. "I'd do *literally anything else*."

"But there is nothing else," Alice croaked. "Can't you understand?"

Butterflies closed over Elspeth's face like a helmet.

The mass surged. Alice writhed, but it was pointless. She reached for Peter, but the mass pulled them apart. All she could see or hear was beating black wings and beneath that, a hissing cloud of wrath. A million bursts of wind carried her up and flung her out. She flailed suspended in the air, blind and disoriented, before crashing hard against the ground. By the time the butterflies released her, spiraling away in formation, Elspeth and Archimedes and the *Neurath* were a dot against the horizon, shooting spitefully out of sight.

## CHAPTER NINETEEN

"Right." Peter hoisted his rucksack over his shoulder and turned to trudge up the shore. "Good luck to you."

Alice scrambled to her feet. "Where are you going?"

He did not reply. She watched him for a moment, baffled, and then hastened up the shore behind him. "What are you doing?"

Still he did not reply. She seized his sleeve. "*Murdoch!*"

"Let go."

"Tell me where you're going."

"Why?" He wrenched his arm away with such vehemence that she stumbled back. "You're not coming with me."

"We can't split up, it's not safe."

He barked out a laugh. "*Safe*, she says. *Safe*, says the girl who would have damned me to the Weaver Girl."

"I didn't—"

"That was wrong, what we did. Elspeth was right to cast us out." He turned away from her and kept trudging. "I'm finished."

"Murdoch." She followed behind him, pathetic—but she didn't know where else to go. "Please don't hate me."

He laughed again. This time there was a desperate quality to it; the sort of laugh that was seconds from a sob. "I don't, Law. But I'm quite sure that you hate *me*."

"I don't hate you."

"Then you must think very little of me," he said. "Because ever since we got here, I've only felt—I don't know, this *coldness*, like you don't even care I'm here."

"I never asked you to come," she said. "I would have gone alone, you're the one who wanted to come with—"

"Because I thought we'd be better off together."

"Or because you wanted a sacrifice for exchange, isn't that right?"

"I *told* you, that's not what I had planned—"

"Well, that's rich," she said. "Seeing as you had my name underlined thrice in your notes."

Peter spun around. The fury in his eyes made her flinch; she had never before seen Peter so angry. "I don't have to justify myself to you," he said. "But if you think I'm that kind of person, Law, then you're better off continuing through Hell on your own."

He continued up the slope. Alice stared after him for a moment, then followed. She didn't have a plan; she only knew she had nowhere else to go, and if she lost Murdoch, she was lost altogether.

Her foot stuck. She teetered, nearly lost her balance. She wrenched her foot free—then bent down to take a look, for the sand seemed wet, but that didn't make any sense, for they were getting further from shore.

Up ahead, Peter was bent over his ankle.

"Murdoch!"

He didn't respond. She started toward him—but suddenly, her legs would not move. She tried, but something rooted them in place, and when she glanced down, she saw a hand. Alice screamed.

Dead arms burst out of the water. Alice jumped away, but her feet splashed into a deep recess, and she lurched to the side. She saw then they were not on solid ground at all—what seemed like muddy ground was sand sticking to the surface of water, whole stretches of water, lurking in wait.

A force yanked against her knee. She collapsed sideways into the bog.

She felt a shock of icy water. She opened her eyes. She wished she hadn't. For she saw then an entire lake full of Shades, biting and twisting and pulling against one another. Their faces were horrible, their eyes blazing red, their mouths stretched wide with fury. She could not see where it ended. They seemed to go on and on forever, a bottomless descent of stifled fury, stretching all the way down into the lightless dark. *Sullen in black mire*, Dante had reported. *They gurgle in their gullets.*

She kicked. Her foot connected against something solid, something that gave her leverage. The weight around her leg vanished. She swam up, broke the surface. She flailed about, seeking purchase. There—her hands scrabbled against hard stone. She pressed her fingers down, hauled herself up. She crouched against her perch, trembling—then saw, just beyond, what seemed like a stretch of rock sticking out from the water. She shrugged off her rucksack and threw it forward. It did not sink. Alice crawled on all fours toward the stretch.

The bog was silent behind her. All she could see was bubbles.

"Murdoch?" Her voice was a tinny choke. She spat water out into the bog and tried again. "*Murdoch?*"

A hoarse gasp. Peter broke the surface several feet away. A tangle of Shades rose with him—fingers clawing against his face, his eyes, his shoulders, trying to drag him back down. Alice crouched on her knees, panicked—he was too far to reach, and her hunting knives could do nothing from here.

She yanked out her Perpetual Flask. Bog water was not

Lethe water, she reasoned. These Shades, furious as they were, might be afraid of oblivion yet. She could not aim—there was no aiming anyway, for Peter was enveloped now in a frothing mass of dead souls. She could only fling out black water in a shaking arc. Droplets sailed through the air and landed on the bog with a sharp sizzle, like water hitting a burning pan.

The Shades fell away. Peter splashed through the bog toward her. Three strides, two strides—he stopped, dragged under, then popped up again. A Shade hung off his rucksack, teeth sunk into the upper pocket.

"Take it off!" she shouted. Peter wriggled between the straps, freed one shoulder and then the other. The Shade sank back into the bog with a *plop*. Peter lurched forward, hands splayed at Alice. She grasped his arms and pulled him up.

Together they huddled, pressed as close as they could against one another, unable to do anything but breathe.

"The ridge," she whispered. She could see the narrowest strip of land—and beyond that, a ridge of rock above the bog. Stable land. "Can you make it?"

Peter nodded.

She stood and tiptoed forward. She nearly fell; Peter steadied her.

"Thanks," she gasped, but he did not let her go. His fingers closed round her arm, viselike, and stayed there the entire time that, step by step, they made their way through Wrath.

THE RIDGE WIDENED INTO A THICKER strip of rock, just large enough for a human body to lie on with hands spread out. One by one they stumbled up the edge and collapsed. Alice rolled onto her stomach and lay there for a long while.

"We have to go back," said Peter.

She sat up. "Go back where?"

"The Fields of Asphodel. Over the wall."

"Are you mad? The wall is *gone*—"

"We'll beg. We'll find the guardians, we'll tell them we're alive, we'll plead to be let back up—"

"What—*why*?"

"Look at us." He flung up his arms. "My pack's gone. Whatever's in your pack is all waterlogged. Who knows how much of the chalk still works. Without food or water we have three days, if that. And how are we going to spend it, Law? Chasing down something we don't know exists, or finding our way back home?"

"But then we'll have wasted—"

"It's wasted. It's already wasted. But please, Alice." Peter's voice cracked. "I don't want to die."

"We could die anyways," said Alice. "There's no—I mean, we took the boat . . . I don't even know how we'd get back to the wall, or the fields—"

"Then we find any deity along the way and beg," said Peter. "We might even beg the Weaver Girl, she might take pity—"

"Or she'd trap us here forever! There's no guarantee—"

"But the odds are still better than if we forge on ahead, don't you think? At least the lower courts are predictable. We have no idea what we'll find up ahead."

"But we've already come this far."

"You know," Peter said, "the sunk cost fallacy is one of the most common failures of everyday logic."

"Oh, fuck off, Murdoch—"

"Which is remarkable, since everyone knows what it *is*, they just won't let it guide their reasoning."

"Bugger the sunk cost fallacy," said Alice, committing it all the same. "We've given up too much, Murdoch. Half our lifetimes."

"Half is better than none."

"But think of what they'll *say*. The idiotic venture of Murdoch and Law. Went to Hell, and have nothing to show for it except mild amnesia."

"At least we'll be *back*," said Peter. "I think I could put up with any amount of laughing if I were alive, don't you?"

"Sure," said Alice. "Fine. Then I don't suppose you know a way back over that bog."

They stood silent for a moment, staring over the hilltop. From this vantage point it did seem impossible to find a way back to where they'd come from. The bog stood between them and the shoreline, and there was no clear path through the mountains that ringed Wrath on all sides. Elspeth had brought them over Greed by boat; it was unclear where the path through led. The only stable patch in sight was the ground they were standing on, and this led deeper into Wrath.

"Let us go as far as Tyranny," Alice proposed. "If we don't stop to sleep, then we can cross two courts in one day. And the chances are better than not that we'll find Professor Grimes there."

"That still doesn't solve the problem of how we'll get back."

"But then at least we'll have the three of us, won't we?" Alice forced her voice to brighten. "I'm sure he'll be able to think of something, he's probably got all sorts of tricks we don't know about—"

Something shifted in Peter's face, but it passed just as soon as she noticed.

"Fine." His voice was carefully level. "I'll carry the pack."

Her fingers closed reflexively around her straps. "It's my pack."

"I mean only that it's heavy," said Peter. "We can take turns."

She hesitated, and then shrugged it off and handed it over. Peter strapped it on, stretched his arms out, and without another word began to plod forward.

Alice could just make out a path through the bog ahead; a winding line thin as a pencil tracing. It trickled up through a dip between the distant peaks, beyond which all she could see was thunder.

Four courts left. Violence, Cruelty, Tyranny, and the last—the nameless, final court. Orpheus would not speak of it at all. The Buddhist accounts referred to it only as the final Hell, the dwelling place of nameless evil. Dante claimed it was heresy, but like so much of Dante, this seemed like Christian dogma getting in the way.

Alice hoped they did not get that far. Cruelty had to be the end of it. Tyranny, at the worst. Professor Grimes's sins were many, yes. She was not in denial about that. But Alice could only understand him as tragically flawed, a man who made mistakes on his journey to greatness. Never malicious. Only careless. Only a man whose mind was larger than the rest, a genius burdened with purpose, who couldn't spare attention for the damage he left in his wake.

**THEY SETTLED INTO A MISERABLE RHYTHM** plodding through the valley; Alice leading, Peter following, stepping gingerly across the tenuous, snaking strip of solid ground. The bog bubbled and boiled about them. Every now and then Alice could see through the translucence to a horrid tangle of Shades beneath, clawing and climbing over one another like crabs in a barrel. But so long as they kept to their path and did not disturb the water, the dead did not disturb them.

Soon they passed into Violence, a barren desert punctuated by rocks. The bog dried up, and the rocky ground smoothed into sliding silt. The mountains grew smaller and smaller in the distance as they walked, and by sunset all they could see for miles around them was flat ground. Every now and then something howled in the distance. Alice and Peter did not care to investigate.

Night fell. They did not stop; only switched on their torches and kept plodding along. Dimly Alice registered that her legs were aching, her neck and shoulders throbbing. She forged on. She was glad she at least had practice in ignoring her body's protests. Night after night in that office she had ignored her own need to eat, sleep, or sit down. She was just a mind, floating in the dark, soaring over the terrain. As long as she convinced herself this was true, she could almost forget her body existed at all.

"Alice." Peter stopped walking. He pointed his torch straight in front of him. "Look."

Alice drew up beside him. "What?"

"Those boulders," said Peter. "They're arranged in the same configuration as the ones we've just passed."

Alice waved her torchlight between the boulders. A short, round ball and a long, rectangular slab. Had she seen them before? She hadn't noticed; all she had been looking at for the past mile was the ground before her feet.

"Probably there's lots of rocks in Hell," said Alice. "Probably there's lots in this shape."

They kept walking. Five minutes later they arrived at the same boulders. The little man and the tall man. She couldn't fail to notice them this time. They matched precisely her memory—the cracks atop the sphere, the long groove along the slab.

"We're going in a circle," said Peter.

"But we can't be." Alice felt a tingle of dread. "Wrath is behind us, the sun was before us, the river on the left, I don't understand . . ."

Peter dug into his pocket and pulled out a soggy lump of Lembas Bread. This he crumbled in his palm and scattered at the base of the boulders. With the remaining crumbs he left a little trail out from the base.

"There," he said. "That will settle it."

They trudged on. In five minutes they came back upon the boulders and the crumbs.

Peter touched a hand to his temple. "I feel—I don't feel right."

Alice felt it too; a faint roil in her gut, a dizzying lightness in her head. At each individual moment her bearings seemed to make absolute sense, with a clear path forward, but every time she took a step it all changed.

"Look," Peter said. "Do you see that line, there?"

He slung off the rucksack, knelt, and crawled forward on his hands and knees, feeling around in the sand. Alice had to squint a moment before she saw it too—a curved, slightly raised line in the sand, forming a barrier around the boulders. She followed the arc of the curve in a great loop behind them, encompassing the ground from which they'd come.

A perfect circle, she bet. All magicians could draw a perfect circle.

"Mother of God." Peter spread his hands around in the dirt. "It's an Escher—"

He vanished.

Alice had time to shout, just before the ground opened beneath her too. She fell a short distance, then landed with a *whumph* on her back. Stars exploded behind her eyes. But the dirt was soft, and the pain passed quickly. Soon she was able to sit up and wipe the sand from her eyes.

"You all right?" Peter's torchlight danced above her. She saw his face, wan and scared.

"Yes," she breathed. "But where . . ."

Peter arced his torch in a circle around them.

They were in a pit. Man-made, not natural; its sides were too flat, and they met the pit's bottom at clean, ninety-degree angles. They were about fifteen, twenty feet deep. The surface seemed tantalizingly near but clearly too high to jump to, and still too high even if Alice balanced perfectly on Peter's shoulders and stood on her tiptoes.

Alice felt around in the dirt until she grasped her own torch.

Together they scanned the smooth dirt walls until Alice's light landed on something angular, protrusions in the corner.

"Steps," she breathed. She swung her torch round the walls, following them up. Thank God—they led all the way to the surface. They were not nice steps; they were short blocks embedded in the dirt, just thick enough to balance one foot at a time. But they went up.

They climbed, pressing their chests against the wall for balance. And Alice should have known they would never reach the top—she should have known the moment she saw that circle in the dirt—but still dread pooled in her stomach when they turned the first corner, and the surface still looked as far away as before. They kept going round a second corner, then a third, for fool's hope, but the distance never changed. They were still less than a foot off the ground.

"Damn it." Peter jumped down. He smacked a hand against the wall. "It's Penrose stairs."

She recognized the patterns as soon as he said it. They'd been thrust into a nil-geometry space; they'd been spinning around an illusion. The stairs were never going to lead them out; for the stairs, impossibly, made constant ninety-degree turns in a continuous loop. They were stuck in someone's Escher trap.

Maurits Cornelius Escher, a Dutch architect turned experimental artist, became well-known in the mid-twentieth century for his illustrations depicting physical planes that could not exist. His work founded an entire subfield of visual magick that used illusions to warp physical space. Few found success with Escher techniques, as they required artistic proficiency, speed, and the ability to translate multidimensional artistic representations into algorithmic language. Until the late seventies, that subfield was dominated by Nick and Magnolia Kripke.

"Find the pentagram," Alice whispered. "Find the flaws."

Peter was already on his hands and knees, poking through dirt and upturning stones hoping for any trace of telltale chalk. But Alice knew it would be futile. Any magician worth their salt would have hidden the pentagram beneath layers and layers of dirt.

*Cuck-oo.*

They both jumped.

*Cuck-oo.*

"Jesus," said Peter.

He shone his torch to the surface. High above them, nestled within a boulder's groove, was a cuckoo bird on a spring; the insides torn out of a clock. *Cuck-oo.* There was one just like it in the graduate students' lounge, its sound set excruciatingly high. And when the bird came out, on the hour, it had the effect of motivating everyone to put down their teacups, get up, and leave. No one could bear that sound, reminding them the day was dwindling, marking wasted time. This one hovered back and forth on its rusted spring, peeking out in thirty-second intervals. Its call was not loud, but it spread and spread; the pert chirp fading into wind howling across the sands. *A signal*, thought Alice. *Come here. We've found something.*

Elspeth's grim smile rose unbidden in her mind.

*Why do you think they love the living?*

Alice tried to slow her breathing.

You couldn't think when panicked—this lesson was drilled into every young magician. She tried to straitjacket her mind into the focus needed to solve an exam set. Because this was just an exam set, a very difficult one, and it wouldn't do to lose her head. She had only to ignore the stakes, and remain calm as she went through all the standard routine of undoing another magician's handiwork. Find the pentagram, find its flaws—weak phrasing, awkward constructions—and then undo the unreality with another layer of artifice . . .

But there was no point. The Kripkes had had a very long time to perfect their arts. Their work was seamless. It showed in their bold, sure lines; the cleverness with which they'd embedded every stroke into the landscape. And the longer she searched, the more a pressure built in her chest.

Alice was well familiar with this creeping dread. There came a point with almost every research project where you understood it was time to stop trying—that all that time and effort sunk into a once-hopeful hypothesis were simply leading nowhere. And maybe you could try to forge ahead, but once that seed of doubt was lodged within you it only kept spreading, its tendrils growing through your lungs so that you couldn't breathe or think, and that the more you tried to scrape some positive result from your efforts the more the threads of the project kept coming loose, the sands shifting beneath you, until all the artifice fell away and you were forced to acknowledge that this simply wasn't going to work.

A trained magician was accustomed to this kind of panic. Science just meant failure, as Thomas Edison had shown; science meant knowing when to cut your losses and start over and accumulate new funding, new hypotheses, new materials and ideas. You could always go to bat again, if you knew how to play the game. You could always come up with something else.

Only this time it was a matter of life and death, and there was nowhere to start over. There was only the inevitability of the Kripkes and their blood-hungry chalk.

"No," Alice whispered. "No, no, please . . ."

But it didn't matter. The search turned up nothing, and everywhere she pointed her torch she found only seamless illusion, not a speck of chalk in sight.

Peter had given up. He was slumped against the wall, his head held between his hands. He was trembling all over, but it took Alice a moment to realize he was laughing.

"Elspeth was right," he said. "We are such idiots."

"Don't say that," said Alice.

"I was alive." His shoulders shook violently. "I was alive, I was *happy*, I was *fine*, and still I came down here on this stupid errand—"

"It wasn't stupid."

"It was completely pointless—"

"We came for Grimes, it was worth it—"

"Oh, shut up, Law." Peter pressed his palm against his forehead. "Can't you hear how desperate you sound? All this, just so you could run back and be his favorite—"

"His *favorite*?"

"That's your whole thing, isn't it?" He affected a cruel, high-pitched simper. It was the cruelest she'd ever heard him sound. "Oh, Professor Grimes! You're so *clever*, Professor Grimes! Take me to Rome, take me to Venice—I just want to hang off your arm and drink an *Aperol spritz*—"

"Murdoch, stop." She nearly slapped him. "You don't know a goddamn thing."

"Don't I?" Peter's eyes were red. "Aren't you in love with him? Isn't that the entire point?"

Alice didn't know whether to laugh or scream. Surely he was joking. But he only kept staring at her with those wet, sad eyes and Alice realized Peter believed what he'd said.

"I *hate* that man," she said. "When he died, I felt like I could breathe."

"Then why are you down here?" Peter whispered hotly. "Why on *earth*—"

"Because it's my fault." She loosed a shaky breath. Then said out loud the words she'd swallowed for months, because saying them out loud would make them true, and she did not want them to be true: "I killed him."

# CHAPTER TWENTY

That the academy was sexist was such a boring truism that Alice was no longer disturbed by the fact. When in 1893 the Cambridge University Senate proposed granting full degrees to women, protesting students hung an effigy of a female cyclist at the end of King's Parade. When the proposal was dropped, the protestors decapitated and tore the effigy apart in celebration. It took nearly another century for all the Oxbridge colleges to admit female students. Magdalene was the last, and only began admitting women the year Alice arrived. On the first day of term, the male students wore black armbands, and the flag was flown at half-mast.

Still, there was a general consensus among the women of Alice's cohort that feminism was an embarrassing fad, a bygone fever of the seventies. Alice certainly wanted nothing to do with it. She was not interested in reading Kristeva or Irigaray, in comparing everything to a phallus, in altering language to take the "his" out of "history." She couldn't stand those screeching activists who believed the only politically just thing was to become a lesbian. Burning bras, trashing dolls, the constant invocation of that scary word *discrimination*—it was all so embarrassing, it felt less like a revolution than a tantrum. It seemed the best way to prove women were not inferior was just to not be inferior.

How hard could that be?

In college, Alice had shared several classes with a girl named Lacey Cudworth, who regularly burst into tears when she felt her classmates argued in a very "male" way with her or insinuated that women were not good logicians. Occasionally Lacey turned to Alice for solidarity, and Alice rebuffed these overtures. *Do not come to me*, she thought; *we are not alike.* She thought Lacey gave women a bad name; that her complaints justified everything men believed about women, and that Lacey was focusing her energies on the wrong issues besides. Of course their departments were run by stodgy old men with wandering eyes who thought they were good for little more than producing babies. Those men would be dead and buried soon enough—meanwhile, wasn't the work fun!

But Alice was not prepared for how astonishingly, indeed comically, bad it could be. In her undergraduate days she'd been shielded from the worst of it by a kind advisor and the fact that, as an undergraduate, she was too insignificant for the big bad wolves to care about. So she was shocked when she arrived at Cambridge to discover that yes, indeed, tenured professors could ask her in company when she intended to get pregnant (hopefully not during her PhD, but ideally before she turned thirty and her womb shriveled); whether she'd started dating in another department yet (this would increase her chances of getting a spousal hire in case she herself could not find a job), and whether she would consider coming to work in a shorter skirt (this would raise morale among the male postgraduates).

It was enough to drive anyone to quit. Certainly it turned most of the women at Cambridge bitter. The beautiful Belinda, so keenly aware of her charms, quickly traded her silk blouses for men's oxford shirts; though this did not work, and the boys began calling her Axiothea in jest. Katie, a junior faculty member whom Alice sometimes met for coffee, kept her hair shorn close to her scalp, though this backfired as rumors circulated she was a lesbian. Ada and Geraldine simply left the department—and the field, for all Alice knew—the moment they were married and never returned.

Alice, however, was still convinced by the impossible mean—the idea that there might exist some perfect line between femininity and subjugation, wherein if she could only wear clothes that were both perfectly attractive and perfectly modest, she could both enjoy the attention that being a woman in the department got her while also commanding respect as a scholar. The chances this mean existed were vanishingly small, but still Alice clung to this hope. The whole endeavor of graduate study was clinging to vanishingly small hopes. To be a magician was to be that tortoise racing Achilles; deluding himself, as the runner loomed larger behind him, that space and time would hang still so that he might stay ahead.

IF ANYONE HAD ASKED ALICE WHY she never reported Professor Grimes for any of the things he'd ever said or done to her, she would have explained that there was nothing to report, because it was her fault.

It was her fault, see, because when she first heard that Professor Grimes had a problem keeping his hands to himself around female students, she'd felt a thrill of excitement. Oh sure—she'd professed disgust in public, and then in private wondered if she was pretty enough, delicate and thin enough, to attract that same attention. He likes girls who look like ballerinas, they said; sad, twiggy things with daddy issues. And she went home and held her hair up in a bun at the back of her head, and wondered if she passed muster.

It was her fault because at night, sometimes, she fantasized about his hands on her shoulders, his eyes locked on hers. These fantasies never drifted toward the carnal—it was, in theory, something she wanted; but it seemed wrong, somehow, to defile the magnificence of Professor Grimes, to reduce him to a wanting, sweating body. She could not equate Professor Grimes to those panting, desperate boys she knew from college, who transformed into mere thoughtless animals the moment her hand drifted toward their crotch. What she loved about Professor Grimes was his mind. That knifelike intelligence.

She had no idea what she wanted from their union. She wanted Professor Grimes to devour her. She wanted to be that hunk of flesh in Saturn's hands. She wanted to become him. She didn't know which.

Alice wasn't stupid. She knew that to pursue a relationship with her advisor would jeopardize her career. She'd heard ample warnings from Belinda and Hilary before she ever met Professor Grimes. She made certain never to accept dinner or drinks invitations—she had a boyfriend, she lied airily, she wasn't available—or to dress too casually or even to ever be alone with him behind closed doors. All tips she had picked up over half a decade of being a woman in the academy.

But oh! How thrilling it was to walk right on that line, to exist in that liminal space between virtue and sin. How her heart fluttered when his gaze landed on her during a lecture; when his lips quirked in approval at some observation she'd made. How she loved being his favorite—*Alice's done it, the rest of you need to be more like Alice.*

She knew he found her attractive. She had noticed too many lingering glances, too many hands on her shoulder that stayed much longer than they should have, to remain in doubt whether her professor would sleep with her if given the chance. This knowledge gave her a twisted sense of power, as long as she didn't act on it. Because she could, she *could*; all she had to do was say yes. She knew this was possibly why he'd picked her as an advisee; why he took her along to conferences and research trips. She knew what they said about Professor Grimes behind closed doors, and sometimes to his face. He loves showing up with a pretty girl on his arm. Well, if it was only his arm, that was all right. Favoritism was all right so long as it benefited her.

She knew how to walk the line. She liked dazzling them all at conferences with her professionalism and poise; her pencil skirts and clacking heels. She snickered wryly at the lewd jokes the old guard made, and shot down anyone who came on to her.

"Don't try with Alice." She once overheard Professor Grimes saying this to a younger man who had been smiling at her all night. "She cares too much about the work."

She rejoiced privately over this compliment for days. He took her seriously. He thought she cared too much about her work!

She thought she'd learned to inhabit the impossible ideal: the girl who was eminently fuckable but unreachable, and therefore virtuous and perfect. The girl who was everything all at once. It was the waning days of second-wave feminism, and all the girls in Alice's generation were so tired of being told they'd been born to be raped, oppressed, silenced. Surely this was not the entire picture; surely there was some power in their sex. Alice was both attractive and restrained, and this made her feel superior, even as she witnessed Professor Grimes disappearing into hotel rooms with other women from the conference. Alice was different from them. They were wives in the making, and she was a magician.

Once at the office she was working late when Professor Grimes came in with a giggling, staggering blonde. It was the new department secretary. Alice had only met her once, earlier that week when she'd dropped off a stack of graded exams for the undergrad pidges. Her name was Charlotte, she came from

Kensington, and she had the sort of quick, manicured personality that made you feel bad for taking up her time. She had shiny, butter-colored hair. She had the legs of a former dancer.

"Oh!" Charlotte gasped. "You stop that."

"Make me," said Professor Grimes, which was the least professorial thing Alice had ever heard him say.

"You bad—" Charlotte began, and giggled as Professor Grimes buried his face into her neck. "You big bad *wolf*."

Alice could not move.

She was allowed to be here—in fact, Professor Grimes *knew* she'd be here, as he was the one who'd asked her to stay late in the first place. Likely he'd forgotten, but that didn't mean she was doing anything wrong—even if the lights were off; even if to any reasonable person the office looked like it was abandoned. Still, she should have made her presence known; and since she hadn't when they first entered the building, she couldn't now without startling them.

She couldn't get to the door without being seen. She didn't want to crouch below her desk and hide, like some fool. To Alice's panicked brain, the only option available seemed to be to stand in place, watching heart pounding and slack-jawed, as Professor Grimes twirled Charlotte around the lab.

Thankfully, Professor Grimes was headed to his office. If only they would get in there and close the door. Then she could make her escape unnoticed.

They didn't make it. They began kissing against the chalkboard. Charlotte gasped. Professor Grimes lifted her up by the legs; rammed her back against the wall; did something with his hands that made Charlotte's voice go up several octaves—a single moan, running up and down the scales.

Alice was frozen in place, entranced and horrified, wondering if this was a tableau she wanted to join. Charlotte moaned once more. Alice's hand slipped, and knocked into a beaker. It did not shatter—it was too far from the edge—but it did clink against another beaker, and the sound pierced the room.

Professor Grimes looked up through hooded eyes that locked on to her own. He did not cease his ministrations.

Alice's heart skipped.

She grabbed her badge and hustled out, then. She felt Professor Grimes's eyes searing into her back the whole way out the building, and it was not until she burst out the front doors, into the night chill, that she took a breath.

She didn't think Charlotte ever knew she'd been there. She wondered, sometimes, when she passed Charlotte in the hallway. In the next few weeks she watched Charlotte perking up when Professor Grimes passed her office; her shoulders slumping when he did not return her wave. She noticed little changes in Charlotte's appearance—how she'd stopped wearing lipstick, how she no longer matched her blouses with her shoes, how more and more often her hair looked unwashed and uncombed. She noticed Charlotte glowering at the other women in the department, Belinda in particular; eyes narrowed, fingers twisting. She wondered sometimes when she gazed into Charlotte's shadowed, haggard face if Charlotte might confide in her—but all she ever got in return was a polite, "Morning, Alice."

She wondered sometimes if she'd made up or exaggerated the whole encounter; if her mind had wandered, as it always did during these late crunches.

But she couldn't get it out of her head. Her memory, after all, was infallible.

She couldn't look at Professor Grimes without thinking of Charlotte's laughter, or of her bouncing thighs, or her delighted gasps. She couldn't hear his voice without thinking of that low growl.

*Make me.*

And she began confusing those panicked flashbacks for her

own desires—for it was her own fault if she kept bringing them up, wasn't it? She wouldn't have seen so much if she'd only made her presence known—if she hadn't been so *sick*, so naughty, so eager to stay and watch.

She could not tell where Professor Grimes's malfeasance ended and where her complicity began. She could not sort out what she'd done wrong.

So when it all became too much—when it started interfering with her studies, when she started feeling less like a proper scholar in his eyes and more a walking pair of legs—she had no one to blame but herself for acting like a lovelorn, empty-headed slut.

She should have known better from the beginning.

She was the lamb that had walked straight into the lion's den, because she'd wanted to see what all the fuss was about. Deep down, a part of her wanted to be devoured. And she felt that Professor Grimes, surely, had seen that the instant he met her eyes that night. That perhaps Professor Grimes had known this about her all along.

IT HAPPENED THE NIGHT THEY RETURNED from the Leverhulme Prize dinner; dizzy, elated, both of them drunk on the attention they'd received all evening. They took the late train back from Liverpool Street station, and then a cab back to the department—the department, not their respective lodgings, because Professor Grimes had decided at the station that they first *must* stop by his office to pick up some papers and Alice, thrilled and exhausted, didn't think to interrogate this threadbare excuse.

At the department they kept giggling, bumping into things. Professor Grimes lost his balance and smeared his hand through a set of algorithms Michele had been laboring through on the blackboard all week, a perfect five-fingered arc through the dense layers of chalk, and this struck them both as tremendously funny. In his office, Professor Grimes proposed they get a head start on the lessons plans for next term, which was a ridiculous pretext because neither of them were in any state to plan lessons for the term.

At his office they made a perfect diorama of fools; stumping into doors, dropping their things, fumbling with their keys. Alice, very drunk and very focused on that pretext, riffled through Professor Grimes's desk in an attempt to find his lecture handouts. At that moment, it seemed the most important thing in the world that she find those handouts.

"They were just here," she kept saying. "I had them printed yesterday, they were just here."

"Alice," said Professor Grimes.

She stood, turned around.

He crossed the room and took her face in his hands.

It could have been a romantic gesture, but all Alice registered then was how trapped she felt. Her cheeks squished in the man's iron grip. Up close, his face was so *large*, unbearably large, as if inflated on a television screen.

The features she'd pined for all those nights—those thick, dark brows; that sharp-edged nose—inches away, they suddenly seemed grotesque. Too human, too *wanting*. All the qualities she admired—genius, brilliance, a sharp and cruel intellect—inscribed after all in a crude and mortal body. His breath was sharp, sour, and she suppressed a gag.

How quickly the buzz vanished. Her laughter died in her throat.

"I know." He mistook her trembling for delight. "I've seen it in your eyes, Alice. I feel it too."

"No," she choked.

"It's all right." His hand caressed the back of her head. His eyes surveyed hers, and his lips split into a smile. She'd spent years admiring that smile; the warmth of his charisma. Now it horrified her. All manufactured charm, all caprice. My, how white his teeth were.

His other hand traced her waist. Moved lower.

"You fucking tease," he said.

"God, your ribs," he said.

Alice thought her heart might explode out her chest; she actually thought she might before things progressed further. Never in her life had she felt so like a trapped animal; weak, helpless, caught in a cage entirely of her own making.

What shamed her most about that night, the memory she could never drive out of her skull, was how close she'd come to saying yes to it all.

It would have made everything so easy, if she'd just given Professor Grimes what he wanted. He'd have satisfied his urges. He'd have been sated, happy with her, and that might have given her some reprieve. In the tired moments after she might have asked for some guidance on her research proposal. She might have asked him to put in a good word for her when she applied for extra funding that summer. She might even have gotten some pleasure out of it. She was sure that, if she split her mind in two, if she ignored all the parts of her that were screaming, if she sank back into her tipsy stupid buzz, then she could turn it into a fun night that got a bit wild.

And it might continue, because if you said yes once it meant you said yes to all times in the future. But then she only had three years to go. In three years, she would graduate, collect her recommendation letters, and move on to some new institution where her work would be so dazzling that soon everyone would ignore the rumors that floated around her. And perhaps before then, his eye would have landed on some other bright-eyed, bushy-tailed first-year, leaving Alice free to concentrate on her work.

One could tolerate anything for just three years.

She softened in his grip; felt her lips opening up for his. And she would have succumbed right there, if she hadn't felt a sudden, overriding wave of disgust.

He wasn't just any fellow in the department. This man was her advisor. The guardian of her mind. Her *teacher*.

"I don't want this." It took every ounce of strength she had to push those words past her throat. "Professor—"

His lips grazed her neck. "What's that?"

"I don't . . ."

To her horror, she saw movement over his shoulder.

There across the lab, in the faraway rectangle of light, stood Peter Murdoch. Books in hand, a pack of chalk stacked on the top, standing frozen in the doorway with one hand lifted as if he'd been about to knock.

Professor Grimes never saw Peter. But Alice watched Peter back slowly away from the door, his mouth slightly agape. Their eyes met just for an instant, just over Professor Grimes's shoulder, before Peter turned and hurried away.

"Please." At last she found the strength to break from his grip. He did not want to let her go—she had to wrench, really fight to break his grip, and the sudden violence seemed at last to convince him her protestations were not, in fact, flirtation. "I don't—"

"Don't be afraid."

"*No!*" she shrieked—the first real sound she'd made; at least, the first time he seemed to hear her. It worked. He started backward. She wriggled out of his grasp.

"Alice," he called as she hurried down the hallway. Ever so calm. As if they'd done nothing but look at syllabi. His voice grew stern. "Alice, come here. You come back here."

But she'd fled down the hallway, heart pounding against her ribs. And though she knew he wouldn't follow her, though she'd forgotten her coat, and though her heels wobbled perilously against the cobblestones, she did not stop running until she had gone down the street, up the bridge, all the way along the river, and back to her apartment.

**AFTER THAT NIGHT PROFESSOR GRIMES TURNED** so cold.

She saw it coming, yet she was gutted by the sudden withdrawal of his support. When she showed up at lab the next day, timid and fragile, she found her workstation had been cleared and all her possessions redistributed to the annex office down the hall. She wandered tentatively toward his office, hoping delusionally there had been some mistake, but Charlotte informed her that Professor Grimes would be in London all morning. When he did return, she was standing in the hallway on a tea break with the other postgrads. She lifted her face to greet him, but he brushed past her without a word.

"What did you do?" Michele asked.

"I don't know," said Alice.

"He looks so mad," said Michele. "I've never seen him look so mad."

Professor Grimes wouldn't talk to her the day after, or the day after that. From anyone else this kind of silent treatment would have been funny, childish, but from Professor Grimes it terrified her. There was no sign of when it might end. She didn't know when he would retaliate, if he was planning some further punishment. She didn't know whether she even crossed his mind at all—whether he'd simply written her wholesale out of his field of thought. She could only tiptoe around his office, hold her breath when he was near, and, day in and day out, hope for his mercy.

She did have reason to keep showing up at the department. She had projects in place, papers to write, classes to teach. He couldn't just invalidate her work. She was good at what she did, and had proven her mettle to the other faculty many times over by now. And he couldn't continue ignoring her in front of everyone else. In public, at least, he had to keep up the pretense of a good advisor. He wanted to invite questions even less than she did.

But he could whittle away at her confidence comment by comment; snub by snub. Little blows. He no longer welcomed her in his office for tea. When he was announced editor of the latest collected volume on linguistic magick he did not ask her to contribute, though she would have been the obvious choice to write the introductory chapter on false friends and cognates that he instead assigned to a first-year who could barely spell his own name.

This went on for months.

Meanwhile Peter's stock rose again in Professor Grimes's eyes. Whatever mysterious slight he'd committed over the summer was forgotten. Whenever Alice wandered past Professor Grimes's office, she could see Peter already there through the window; leaning forward on the edge of his chair, hands flapping animatedly as they talked. Suddenly all everyone could talk about was the exciting new paper Murdoch and Grimes were coauthoring; how it was sure to be accepted in *Arcana*, how it might revolutionize the field of set theory, how it was making Bertrand Russell turn over in his grave.

The rest of the department sensed this shift, though none of them could guess at what had actually happened. The faculty assumed Alice had irritated Professor Grimes with shoddy work, and subsequently began to treat her with kid gloves. They had watched students burn out before. They'd witnessed the deterioration that came before the crash.

"Jacob can be tough," Professor Byrne told her in the lounge one day, without prompting. "But—well, just keep your chin up and do good work, and things will be back to normal in no time, all right?"

The undergraduates, who were afraid of their own shadow, saw the way Professor Grimes spoke to Alice and assumed (perhaps rightly) that her stink of failure was contagious. Students began trickling out of her sections into Michele's and Peter's. The graduate students were savvier. They knew, just the way everyone had known about Charlotte. Even if they could only sense the general outlines of the story, they knew. Michele was sympathetic, always offering Alice a kind sad smile when they crossed paths. Belinda, however, became quite cool toward Alice. Alice sensed that she thought, perhaps fairly, that Alice should have known better. That if Alice hadn't acted like such a whore, that if Alice had been as careful as Belinda had always been, she wouldn't be in this mess.

Word had spread, and Alice overheard. Eventually every single person in the department had some opinion on Alice, whether it was pity or condescension or abject curiosity. Still, Alice was used to rumors. She was a Grimes student, after all. And she could have weathered it all, if it were not for Peter.

She could not bear the way things had changed with Peter.

He became unbearably awkward after that night. He seemed not to know what to do with her. He seemed afraid of her, angry with her, and baffled by her all at once. He couldn't even keep up a veneer of professional rapport. He never looked her in the eyes. If he wanted to tell her something, half the time he asked an undergraduate to do it. Once she called hello to him across the lab, and he promptly dropped his coffee. Once she had thought his indifference was the cruelest thing, but she would have preferred it to whatever they were now: all brittle tension, and too-vivid memory. She saw it constantly; it overlaid her vision every time she so much as glanced at him. Peter in the doorway. Books clutched against his chest. A faltering hand. Eyes wide, disgust spreading across his face.

She thought often about telling him the truth. She knew what he assumed; she wanted him to know it was not so. Oh, but she was so ashamed! Just the memory of his eyes, wide in confusion, made her want to shrink into the floor. She could not decide what would be worse, his resentment or his pity. "Something's happened to me," she would say, and all his respect for her would vanish.

At last she decided: pity was better than disgust. She needed at least one person to know it wasn't true. She had to at least try. And Peter Murdoch was the one person for whom her words might carry meaning, for whom shreds of nuance might untangle the truth. It took her weeks to muster up the courage, but she was going to do it. If only she hadn't spoken first to Belinda.

"Do you know when Murdoch's coming in today?" Alice asked her.

"Peter?" Belinda shrugged. "Dunno. Think he's gone nocturnal. Why, what's the matter?"

"No, it's stupid—there's just something about this paper, and I don't want to bother Grimes."

"Right. Grimes." Belinda had an odd expression on her face. "You know, he did say something. Peter did."

Alice felt cold all over. "What'd he say?"

"Oh, nothing much." Belinda's mouth worked, for no sound came out. She had the look of someone deciding how to mince her words, to hint at an accusation without actually making one. "He just mentioned you and Professor Grimes were getting—close."

"He said that?"

"Something . . . something about a late night, and how you're a teacher's pet?"

Alice felt the ground plummeting from under her feet.

"You do know that's against the rules, right?" Belinda's eyes narrowed. "You have to disclose things like that?"

Alice could not speak. Towers knocked over in her mind, whooshing wind and cyclones, and all that was left was rumbles and dust. She was vaguely aware that Belinda was still standing there, mouth pursed, waiting for an answer. She knew this was the one chance she might ever get to defend herself. That if she did not speak now, then the rumors would grow and grow, and petrify into fact, until it was part of departmental common knowledge—that just as Elspeth Banks had failed her comps and killed herself, Alice Law had fucked Professor Grimes.

Still the words would not come. What defense could she offer?

"You—I mean, it's not true, is it? I'm sorry if I jumped to conclusions." Belinda's expression softened. "Come on, Alice. You can tell me."

There were a lot of things Alice could have said then. But why bother? It all seemed so pointless. All words were ineffectual, signifying nonsense. Belinda stared, waiting, but Alice simply turned on her heel and walked away.

ALICE UNRAVELED VERY QUICKLY AFTER THAT. Her self-esteem plummeted. Her moods grew erratic, her work uneven. She tried everything to get back into Professor Grimes's good graces, but being a try-hard only intensified his disdain.

At her lowest, she tried again to seduce him. She wore those black tights and short skirts he'd said once that he liked. She kept her blouse tops unbuttoned. She tried every old trick in the toolbox: sitting with her legs suggestively crossed, bending down lower than she needed so the curve of her ass was on full display.

*I'm here*, she tried to tell him. *I'm willing. Have me.*

He pretended she did not exist.

Alice fought. She did fight; she had come too far to let her career slide so quickly down the drain. She sought counsel in the office of Helen Murray.

Helen did not particularly like Alice. Not because of anything Alice had ever done, but because she was a Grimes student, and Helen Murray and Jacob Grimes hated each other. He'd once famously called her a cunt in public; she, in turn, forced him to teach the undergraduate survey class every year that she was the department chair. But this morning, Alice thought, perhaps their animosity might count in her favor.

"Hello, Alice." Helen Murray seemed to be expecting her. In any case, she did not ask why Alice, who was not her advisee and who was not in any of her seminars, had stopped by. "Would you like some tea?"

"Oh, no, I'm all right."

"Do have some tea."

Alice sat and accepted a cup.

It was a well-known fact about Helen Murray that she would not entertain work talk until she had gone through the ritual of boiling water in her kettle, measuring out tea leaves, and waiting the full five minutes for it to brew. Until then you were supposed to make small talk. This was supposed to be the most humanizing thing about her. Helen Murray *cared* about you; she cared how your life was going, what extracurriculars you pursued. Her advisees loved her for this. Alice hoped, for this reason, that Helen Murray might hear her out.

Helen clinked a spoon around her cup. "Why don't you tell me what's happened."

Haltingly, Alice explained.

When she finished, Helen sat silent for a long while. Then she took off her glasses, looked Alice up and down, and sighed. "Please let's not be so immature about this."

"Um. I don't know what that means."

"You surprise me, Alice. One would have thought you knew what you were getting into."

"Getting into?"

"A story as old as time. See Aristotle and Phyllis. Merlin and Morgan le Fay. The boys in our department, they never learn. Hungry beasts. You're at Cambridge. Didn't you know?"

Alice could not determine if Helen was joking. She understood the reference; she, too, had seen that woodcut of naked Phyllis, Alexander's consort, riding Aristotle like a horse. It was very funny, and Aristotle looked ridiculous, but Alice could not see how this was useful guidance for her career going forward.

"But it's not—I mean, the way they treat women, it's not fair."

Helen's lip curled. "Ah, you're a feminist now!"

This was a pointed barb—the first inklings of a trap, but Alice was too distressed to see what she had walked into. Helen hosted the annual Women in Magick conference at Cambridge, but Alice had never gone. No one in her cohort bothered to go. Belinda went once her first year, and came back rolling her eyes—*Just a bunch of crones, wishing the men would die*. No, no one in her cohort was a feminist; they eschewed the label, they thought it would only bring them trouble.

"That's not what I mean," said Alice. "It's just—I don't know what to do."

"Of course." Helen set down her cup. "So why did you come to me?"

*That much should be obvious*, thought Alice. Why did Helen think she was here, and not in the offices of Caspar Stuart, or Aaron Byrne?

"Because we have so much in common?"

This too was a trick question, but Alice took the bait. She thought solidarity was on offer; she could not help but nod.

"No, dear." Helen folded her arms and leaned forward. "As it happens, we have nothing in common."

The trap sprang.

"Girls like you despise women like me. Isn't that so? You think we are wrong to insist on the differences of our sex. You find our activism embarrassing. You think we complain too much."

The accusation was just, all these things were true. But Alice had always harbored these thoughts as a sneaky conviction. She could not really justify them.

Helen pressed on. "And why wouldn't you think that? You've never known a locked door. Your mothers were educated, your schools were coed, and so you think the whole world is open to you. You want to wear slacks, and shirts without bras, and drink all night long with the boys, and you want everyone to treat you just the same."

It occurred to Alice that Helen had been waiting a long time to say these words; had banked up this screed, watching her and Belinda and the others in the halls, awaiting the first one to stop by. This was not about her anymore; it was not even about Grimes; it was about Helen getting her word in, and Alice was merely the audience.

Helen leaned forward. "The difference between women like me and girls like you is that we always understood the battle was never over. Your cohort has chosen to live like the rules don't apply to you. And it seems to work. I salute you girls, I support you. I wish I could have done the same. But you can't just cry wolf when things don't go your way. What you must realize, Alice, is that you cannot just take refuge in feminism when it suits you."

"I'm not crying wolf," Alice said desperately. "I just—I need guidance—"

"You want to change advisors, then? You want to work with me?"

This took Alice by surprise. She had not planned to ask; had not even considered it a solution. And perhaps her face betrayed her thoughts, because Helen laughed. "Of course you don't. You don't respect me enough for that. You think I am a—what was it? A spousal hire in a girdle?"

"I didn't . . ."

Oh, but Alice had. They'd all said it. They received the gossip first from their advisors and they giggled about it among themselves, told stories at late nights at the pub—*does Helen even publish, does anyone take Helen seriously, what will happen when he divorces that cow?* But professors' ears were much closer to the ground than anyone thought. Alice should have known this, because she knew Grimes was acutely aware of everything anyone said about *him*.

"Of course." Helen found the confirmation in her face. "That's a no. Then would you like to go to the police?"

"What? No—"

"To file a complaint, then?" Helen was having her fun. "Would you like him reprimanded by the university, compelled to write you an apology? Would all this make you feel better?"

"No—"

Helen threw her hands up. "Then help me understand. What are we doing here, Alice? What do you *want*?"

Alice felt so stupid then.

Why didn't she have any response? Why was this question so hard? It was as if she'd sat down for an exam, only to find she didn't comprehend any of the material. All the contradictions were coming to a head, and she couldn't synthesize an answer because none of her positions made any sense. She wanted Grimes's attention but also his respect. She adored his power, except when he used it against her. She wanted no special treatment for her sex, and still she felt wronged, in a way she felt that only women could be wronged. Helen was right—she could not have it all, could not believe everything she did and still complain. But still, was there not something wrong here? Was she so wrong to feel hurt?

She tried to sort through the most basic question. What *did* she want? If she could wave a magic wand to fix this, what outcome would she have?

It boiled down to one thing: she wanted Grimes to respect her, to like her again, to go back to being her teacher again. But Helen could not help here there. Grimes's disposition toward her was an immovable fact. She could not change it by wishing.

In fact, all of her wishes were ridiculous. She wanted it all to have never happened. She wanted her mind back. And she wanted to be more than a body, more than mere *flesh*, a thing to inscribe and observe and maybe fondle when you were bored. She wanted the version she was promised, she wanted a teacher who cared about her, who respected her as a thinker, who did not treat her as a tool.

But all this was a fairy tale. In relentlessly enforcing the glamour, she had closed off her other options. And now she was left in a trap she had constructed for herself.

*There is no point*, she thought helplessly. *No point in breaking out. It will destroy everything to try. Stop believing in one postulate, and the whole edifice comes tumbling down. You cannot have a stable Euclidean surface without the parallel postulate; you cannot survive without believing you are invulnerable. So your only option is the reconstruction of the lie—I am not embodied, this cannot matter, and so it does not matter.*

"So you see." Helen's expression was not unsympathetic. "It only hurts you to take this further. The best thing you can do for your career now is to forget it ever happened."

*I can't*, Alice wanted to cry. *I can't forget anything.*

"Grimes certainly will." Helen's mouth twitched. "He'll be on to the next freshman by Michaelmas, and then it'll be business as usual with you. And anyhow—as you say, it was only a kiss."

*Not only a kiss*, thought Alice. Her tattoo seared white-hot, hot as the day he'd carved it into her skin. But this she could not reveal. She had promised Grimes her silence; she still wanted to be a very good girl.

And she suspected that Helen knew, anyhow. Not the details. Only the shape. Helen must have known, because she had seen it all happen before, must have been through it herself, and here she still sat where she was. Her own office. Courtyard window, mahogany desk, tenure. What did that take? Alice wondered. What cages of beliefs kept Helen going?

Helen was not mocking her. She had laid out the blueprint. Believe the lie—trust the lie—it is the only thing you have. Stay in the cage and paint the walls. If you do not, then you must quit; but if you can delude yourself long enough, then your delusions might very well come true.

"Thank you," Alice managed. "This has been very helpful."

"You're welcome," said Helen. "Do finish your tea."

AFTER THAT MEETING ALICE BEGAN DREAMING of dying.

It wasn't so much that she made active plans to end her life. That took too much initiative. More often she would walk along Sidney Street as the buses whizzed by and reflect that it wouldn't be so bad if one just happened to hit her. She liked to imagine her bones crunching; her blood splattering across the pavement. She made a game of wondering what, precisely, would be the acute cause of death—the splintering of her skull into her brain? That would be best—much worse was the messy, internal splitting that irrevocably broke you but left intact your ability to feel pain, your ability to think and reflect that this was the end. If she was going to die, she'd like to do it headfirst.

Anyway, dying seemed perfectly acceptable on moral grounds. The best argument Socrates could make against suicide in the *Phaedo* was that mortals were like possessions of the gods, and that the gods would be irritated if one of their possessions freed itself from their mortal prison by self-destruction. The Christian injunction against suicide only seemed to be a reframing of that. But God's interests did not seem relevant here. Probably her friends and family would be upset—her mind wandered vaguely to her parents in Colorado, sobbing as they hung up the telephone—but she could not imagine anyone would miss her that much. There simply didn't seem much to go on for.

How could she explain it? What was devastating was not the touch—he had hardly been violent with her. No, what hurt was how easily he could reduce her to a thing. No longer a student, a mind, an inquisitive being growing and learning and *becoming* under him—but just the barest identity she had been afraid to be all along, which was a mere woman. It was all such a fucking cliché. How could she ever have dared to think it did not apply? Girl enters into the academy, and the lads get rough. She felt flung into a well-trod story whose ending was already written, and she had no choice but to follow along, utter her lines, and wait for the curtains to close. And it felt, during those days, that the easiest thing for her would be to just jump off the stage.

But she never found the resolve to end things for good. Not because she was afraid of the pain—for at that point she wasn't sure she could still feel pain—but because of the shame. Because even after everything, despite how numb she'd become, what lingered were the tenets of the academic world, which were so burned into her bones that even in her weakest moments she still felt their echoes.

If she died, they would think she had failed.

Poor Alice, they would say. Another Grimes student driven mad. And Belinda would cluck her tongue and say in a gossipy tone to the next cohort of bright-eyed candidates, "I'm sure you've all heard of Alice too, *poor* girl—remember the counselor's office is available if ever you should need to talk."

Alice could bear any amount of pain. But she could not bear that shame. It still mattered to her, above everything else, that they respect her as a scholar.

So she kept plodding on; showing up to lectures, keeping her hours in the lab, grading papers and drawing pentagrams and filling her brain with all sorts of useless information. As long as she was in the lab, focused on the work, struggling with translations so difficult that she could think of little else, she could distract her mind enough to keep the memories at bay.

It was when she left the department that the memories rushed back. She couldn't sleep; she could only lie in the dark, staring at the ceiling as Professor Grimes's face loomed in her imagination. She stopped eating; everything she put in her mouth made her stomach roil. Her hair started falling out. Her skin turned gray. People called out to her, people tried to help. She barely heard them; she did not answer. She heard a strange buzzing in her ears all the time. The world felt muted and distorted, as if she were moving underwater.

Still she kept going. She didn't know what else to do. Her plan, if she could call it that, was simply to be an automaton until the center could no longer hold; until she fell to pieces against her will.

But it was Professor Grimes who shattered first—literally, all his flesh and guts and bones wrenched apart with the centrifugal force of millions of years of stored living-dead chalk energy.

And Alice—who stood stock-still with his brains and skull fragments and blood splattered across her face—could not stop laughing. For a way out had opened up after all. And it seemed the most hilarious thing in the world, in that instant, that it nevertheless led straight to Hell.

## CHAPTER TWENTY-ONE

Peter did not speak for a long time after she finished. She was grateful that he didn't; she would have wilted had he launched into any of the standard responses. *I'm so sorry, why didn't you tell me, I'm horrified that happened to you.* Peter did not try to make it better. All he did was witness.

At some point he'd taken her hand. His thumb rubbed again and again over the crevices between her knuckles. An automatic impulse, Alice knew; he could never sit still, he needed something to fiddle with. If it weren't her hand it would have been a stick of chalk. Still it was the most comforting touch she'd felt in months.

They weren't back to where they'd started. But it seemed, for the first time since she could remember, that they could be honest with one another.

At last Peter said, "But you were so sure."

"About what?"

"That he wasn't in Desire."

"Desire is for lovers," said Alice. "That wasn't love."

Peter considered this, and then nodded. "So what was your solution?"

"To what?"

"How you would have gotten Professor Grimes out of here alive." He let go of her hand. "You saw my plan. What was yours?"

*Might as well*, Alice thought. She dragged her rucksack toward her. "I'm not sure I had one."

"What's that mean?"

"I kept telling myself I was here to get him back." She fished out her notebook. The binding was waterlogged, as were the edges, but the pages still dry and legible. "But you know what? I never really cracked it. I kept telling myself—time's ticking, you've just got to go, you'll figure the rest out on the way. But this was all I came up with, and I'm not even sure it would work."

She flipped to the very end of her notebook, to the last things she'd written down before she drew the pentagram to Hell. "Two weeks ago I found the syllabary of the Thessalian witch Erichtho."

"Eric-who?"

"Erichtho."

"Never heard of her."

"You wouldn't have. She's tricky, Erichtho. Always lingering on the margins, never in the main archives. It seems to me she was a fairly accomplished magician, only everyone in her time found her arts too freakish and frightful to document properly. I never would have heard of her at all, except I—well, by the time we got over here, I'd started digging into some pretty odd stuff."

She flipped backward in her notebook. "You see, I started with Dante. Virgil cites Erichtho as the one who bade him journey into Lower Hell and report back to her all that he found. And from Dante I got over to Virgil, and from Virgil I got into acrostics. And I learned about these ruins, see, called the Colossi of Memnon. They're these two colossal statues in Thebes built to guard the tomb of an Egyptian pharaoh, but they've been associated with the Trojan king Memnon since antiquity.

For thousands of years, every morning at dawn, these statues have emitted a high-pitched cry. We don't know what causes it. Maybe it's the heat of the sun expanding the rocks so the wind hits them at just the right angle. But it's believed the sound is the dying Memnon crying out to his mother, Eos, the goddess of dawn. And I started wondering whether the Colossi of Memnon held some chalk inscription that allows communication from the underworld."

She wasn't sure her ramblings made any sense—it was all a jumble of associated concepts flung together from days of frenzied research—but Peter nodded patiently. "And what did you find?"

"Acrostics, mostly. I couldn't very well drop everything and go to Egypt, but I *did* find all these photographs hidden in some personal collections, and I found all these Greek and Latin inscriptions that visitors over the years had left on the statues. *Proskynemata*. Religious writings. They were all lightly encrypted, and they all made use of basic acrostics magick. Small spells to send messages to their loved ones or to wish their loved ones peace in death, I don't know. But I did see that one name kept coming up over and over again. Erichtho."

"This is a fantastic rabbit hole," said Peter.

"Quite." Alice laughed sharply. "I know, I'm sorry. But you know how when you're running yourself ragged on a research project and nothing sticks and then you find that one thing that holds promise? Like it's glowing, calling out to you? Like a single star in a dark sky?"

Peter nodded. "It's a lifeline."

"Right. You cling to it with everything you've got. Because there's nothing else."

Erichtho was the only name that held significance for Alice those days, the only hope of an answer. She would wake up from unwilling sleep with the dreadful task of Orpheus before her, and amidst the gray dead ends of all the scholarship in centuries past only Erichtho gleamed like Ariadne's string, leading somewhere unknown—but at least *somewhere*.

"So then I went searching in the Greek archives. It took forever to track down any manuscripts of hers, as they weren't even classified in the magick library, but finally I found some old scraps of papyrus that are carbon-dated to Thessaly. And then I sat with *those* for a while, and I realized Erichtho was playing around with the same divergent series that modern Tartarologists were obsessed with. And that it's possible, back centuries ago, that Erichtho arrived separately at the same thing we'd call—"

"Ramanujan's Summation," said Peter.

"Precisely. The same mechanism that let us come to Hell in the first place." Alice turned the page and tapped a drawing of a pentagram, one very similar to the one that had sent them to Hell; only two crucial names were placed elsewhere. "So there's my solution. But instead of sending a physical object to new coordinates, I would have bound a soul to separate coordinates and brought it back to earth."

"I don't follow," said Peter.

Alice hesitated. It all seemed too horrible to say out loud, so she opted for the classic magician's approach, which was to phrase everything in the clinical terms of a journal abstract. "In Dante's *Inferno*, Erichtho is passingly mentioned as the one other person who has sent Virgil into the depths of Hell. Scholars are divided on what Dante was trying to accomplish with this mention. Some think it's to reassure the reader that Virgil knows his way around Lower Hell; others think it's to emphasize Virgil's paganism by associating him with witchcraft.

"Either way, here Dante is drawing from a more elaborate anecdote in Lucan's *Pharsalia*, in which the Thessalian witch Erichtho is asked by the Roman general Sextus Pompey to divine the outcome of the Battle of Pharsalus. And she does." She hugged her arms around her chest. "She drags a corpse off the battlefield and forces its soul to return to its mangled body, to deliver to Sextus a prophecy. It is a horrible spell. The soul is not living nor dead; he speaks through his former body, but only with great effort. He cannot live life as he used to; but neither can he die, for his soul is trapped. Eventually Erichtho frees his soul by burning his body on a pyre."

Peter said nothing. If he knew where this was all going, he didn't show it; he only kept watching her, inscrutable.

"And that's what I would have done to Grimes." Alice's arms tightened around her chest, like a closing trap, like she could squeeze herself into nothing if she tried hard enough. "I would have put him back in that corpse. I would have filled it with all sorts of unnatural shit to keep it together, and kept the spell going long enough that the mechanics of his vocal cords and tongue could move, could say all the things I needed it to say. I would have kept it at my complete mercy. I wouldn't have given Grimes a second life at all. I would have made him into my toy and pet and made him beg for release."

Peter remained ever polite, curious. "And how would you have done that?"

"Oh, all the witchy things. The froth of slain mad dogs. Lynx's entrails. Sea leeches. All the monstrous things of nature. Lucan is very descriptive."

"Oh my."

Alice cleared her throat. "And also I dug him up."

"There it is."

"There wasn't much to dig up, anyways."

"I'm sure."

"But see, it works because you're not trying to bring the soul back," Alice said. The rest she said as quickly as she could; robotic, just reading out the summary. "You can dispense with the cosmological problems of life and death and reanimation and all that, because this version of Grimes doesn't get to interact with the living anymore. He wouldn't be properly alive. He'd just be a voice. An imprint. He'd be mine. All mine. My *thing*. Mine to play with, or experiment on, or interrogate, or even—just— Lock him in a closet, and forget about him for years."

Well, there it was. She loosed a breath, lifted her chin, and awaited judgment.

"I see." Peter tilted his head. "That's—hm. Fascinating."

"You think it's sick."

"No, I think . . ." He blinked at the pages, considering. "I think this is very impressive research, considering. Your creativity is astonishing."

"Oh, well. Thanks."

"How long would you have kept him alive?"

"I didn't really think that part through either."

Indeed there were many parts of her plan she had not thought through. How to explain a reanimated corpse to the rest of the department. How to keep Grimes from screaming for help. How to convince a dissertation committee that the hoarsely blathering pile of rotted flesh and bones was in fact the soul of Professor Jacob Grimes speaking, and not a paid undergraduate hiding beneath the floorboards.

Well, she supposed it was obvious why not. She could convince herself all she wanted that this was a rescue. But it had never been about the recommendation letters. It was only about revenge, and bloody control, and having Grimes understand at last how it felt to be someone else's toy. It was only a fever dream. And Peter was too smart to for a second believe otherwise.

"Though I don't think it would make me feel better." Alice drew her knees up to her chest. "That's the problem. I hoped it might—but the more I think about it, the more I realize, I only want this because it's what he would have done. It is such a perfectly Grimes solution, you know. Brutal, efficient, shocking. He never went halfway, he only ever went through. And some part of me, deep down, is actually excited. Because I keep imagining him waking up to see what I've done." She gave a helpless laugh. "And I keep fantasizing he might actually look around and tell me *good job*."

"You know," said Peter, "I do think he would."

"He's stamped on our minds," said Alice.

"Oh, yes." Peter cast her a sad sideways smile. "Can't get him out."

They both stared down at the notebook.

Alice had not revisited these pages since she scribbled her notes. She was amazed now by the sight of her own handwriting, a frenzied scrawl that looked nothing like her usual neat script. She remembered those final hours of research, sitting hunched over Erichtho's writing beside a dim and buzzing lamp, forcing her hand to keep up with her racing thoughts. At points she had pressed so hard against the page that the lead broke, leaving charcoal smudges. Peter's notebook looked tame by comparison. Her own looked like the work of a lunatic.

In a small voice she asked, "So you don't think I'm mad?"

Peter reached out; his fingers wrapped around hers.

And although all they did was sit, silent, and although still they had no solution and no way out, somehow Alice felt more clearheaded than she'd been in a very long time. She felt still, her thoughts settled. As if she had been flailing through the air, flapping and choking, and here at last someone had granted her a place to land.

TIME SLIPPED FORWARD. THE SKULL CONTINUED to cuckoo. At first Alice kept checking her watch, but soon she stopped bothering. Minutes, hours, it did not matter. They had no way out.

The Kripkes had not come. This gave Alice some small twinge of hope—that perhaps the Kripkes had forgotten about them, that perhaps instead of a terrible bloody death they would only die a stifled, quiet one. The Kripkes were in no hurry. They didn't need to grapple with two adults. They only needed to wait them out. And the Kripkes had all the time in the world.

She considered weeping about it, but it was too hot and dry; at this point she didn't have the moisture in her body to condense into tears.

Was this the end, then? She took stock of her life, all her dreams and efforts and desperate aspirations, and could not feel anything other than a pathetic amusement at where she had ended up.

She'd taken a class on Greek philosophers during her first year of college, before she discovered she was allergic to philosophy. She didn't care much for Socrates, but she did like the way Aristotle wrote about the world, the soul, the form of living creatures. He had such faith in their drive to flourish. And she remembered reading Aristotle's argument about how any living being, even the most primitive organism, was animated by an idea of the good. Even the plant turned its face toward the sun. Even the tiniest ant sought food; the brainless worm sought soil. It was all so easy for living creatures—all except people, except people like *her*, who had a knack for seeking only that which made them miserable.

All her life, it seemed, she had run headfirst in precisely the wrong directions. It was not for lack of opportunity. She knew very well where the sun shone, and yet was bound by impulse to bury herself in the dark.

Perhaps human intelligence was a mistake, and everyone who celebrated the escape from the Garden of Eden was wrong. Perhaps the gift of rationality did not outweigh the debilitating agony that came with it.

Or perhaps people like Alice were just fundamentally broken. Perhaps they were wasted on life; perhaps dying was the best thing for her. Perhaps she was less like Aristotle's plant and more like Freud's organisms, who were driven compulsively toward death, toward the tranquil, inanimate state of things before they had the misfortune of being born. She voiced this theory to Peter.

"Hm," he said. "I don't think we compulsively seek death."

"Speak for yourself."

"I just think we got tangled up. But we're still trying to face the light."

They chatted for a bit. Mindless memories, bland observations. Meals they'd once had. Books they'd once read. Once or twice Alice made Peter laugh, and that seemed the greatest victory she could accomplish in the moment; that she could still elicit his hiccupping laughter.

Their voices grew hoarse, their tongues dry, their voices soft. At last they lapsed into silence.

Alice supposed there were worse ways to die. At least she knew she had nothing to be afraid of. At least she was not dying alone.

And she could not deny the part of her that was relieved at the fact that finally it was all out of her hands; that there was no longer any point to the scheming and spell casting and struggling. At last there was a punctuation mark to it all, and she had no control over it. This was a comfort.

"Alice." Peter nudged her shoulder. "Alice?"

She blinked awake. "Yes?"

"I've been lying to you."

"No you haven't," she mumbled. "Don't say that."

"The equation you found." He sat up straight. "You were right. It wasn't just my playing around. It is, in fact, my dominant strategy to get Professor Grimes out of Hell."

"Oh, we were having such a good moment." Alice let her arm fall limp against his. This confession did not bother her as much anymore—now that they were going to die, knowing Peter would have killed her had he gotten his way was disappointing, but not a surprise. "Please don't ruin it."

"You don't understand," said Peter. "I wasn't going to trade you. I never would have traded you. I was going to trade myself."

"But you can't," said Alice. "Axiom of . . . you can't. I tried."

"Well, no," said Peter, "I would have asked you to do it for me."

It was so hot, Alice thought. So damn hot. She couldn't tell if the buzzing came from without or within. But she could let her mind slide, and think only about the buzzing, and not about the implications. Oh, sweet blankness; the absence of thought. She should have been born a rock. She considered acting like one; playing deaf, just letting Peter's words slide off her like water.

But he looked so very distressed. He was clearly not going to let this one go.

She pulled together the energy to ask, "Why?"

"Well, because *I* killed him." Peter's face worked terribly. "I mean, his death is my fault. Not yours. So it stands to reason I should bring him back."

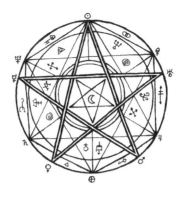

# CHAPTER TWENTY-TWO

Peter Murdoch never meant to hurt anyone. He was not like Alice; he didn't have vicious determination. Peter did not hold grudges or acknowledge rivals, in part because he was so used to winning by default. Peter Murdoch was born with a silver spoon in his mouth and a stick of chalk in hand. For him academia was a playground, not a battlefield, and he was just so good at all the games.

Yet this made him dangerous in his own way. For Peter had gone through life blithely assuming things would just fall in place precisely how he needed them, since in most respects, they always had. This made him careless. He never thought much of the consequences, or about much in particular except his own research. And it was only when things went sideways, when things got carried away, when the domino effects of his whims cascaded far beyond anything he'd hoped or intended—only then did he discover how dangerous being careless could be.

PETER WAS FIVE WHEN HIS GENIUS became evident. He was stuck ill at home, and was not getting better as quickly as hoped, and his parents had deemed it necessary to engage a home maths tutor so that Peter would not fall behind. This tutor—one of his father's advisees, who would have happily done anything else if not for need of pocket money—took the pedagogically irresponsible approach of feeding him one algebraic exercise at a time while distracted by his own pile of problem sets to grade.

Peter traipsed happily through the problems. And since he was not in a classroom full of children cooing over crayons, and since all his attention wasn't spent on not drawing attention to himself, he let himself skate through the next lesson, and then the next. The way Peter saw it, he was only happily solving the next problem as it appeared. He didn't notice his tutor's jaw slackening over the hour.

"He's astonishing," the postgrad reported to his father. "He doesn't belong in year one, you've got to get him out of there."

Peter's parents—his dad a mathematician, his mum a biologist—were overjoyed by this news; for all academic parents hope and expect to have smart children but don't dare admit out loud that they want genius children. But it seemed Peter was in fact a genius, and so they made arrangements for him to be surrounded by tutors all the time, stimulating his brain with advanced studies.

This was a good thing, for otherwise Peter's childhood would have passed in tedious solitude. For the other defining trait about Peter was that he was so often sick. At first it seemed he was a classically persnickety child, always caught up with a round of upset tummy or food poisoning or diarrhea or constipation. He'll grow out of it, said his grandparents; some children just like to catch every germ in the air. By the time he was six, however, it became clear that whatever Peter had was severe and chronic. Medical research on inflammatory bowel diseases would come quite a long way over the course of Peter's lifetime. But in his early childhood, the most that any doctor could tell his family was that his colon seemed to be getting inflamed for no apparent reason, and that he would do best to avoid wheat flour. This later expanded to include dairy, nuts, and raw vegetables—indeed, Peter spent a lot of time on elimination diets. They couldn't tell if any of it helped, only that all-liquid diets—that is, bone broth and apple juice—seemed to improve things when he was at his worst, but only because it meant there was nothing in his bowels left to clear.

At last, after many specialist visits and misdiagnoses, he was diagnosed with Crohn's disease—a chronic inflammatory bowel disease with no known cause and no cure. Peter and his parents began referring to his condition as the Beast. It helped to personify the disease, for otherwise it was just a mysterious thing that messed with his sense of self. His own immune system was attacking his own cells for no clear reason. Easier to think of it as some capricious, alien entity. Sometimes the Beast left him alone. Sometimes it gnawed relentlessly at his insides. Sometimes it withdrew for several weeks, just long enough for him to make plans to go to birthday parties and the beach and go hiking, which he'd still never done, before returning with a vengeance. The Beast was unknowable, unpredictable. The only constant they knew about the Beast was that it couldn't ever be vanquished; only kept at bay, hidden from, for brief pockets of time.

Peter grew used to doctor's visits. Crohn's had a number of side effects as a consequence of malnutrition. His eyes were always red and scabby. His teeth were all wrong. Every now and then a big red rash appeared all over his back, which no number of oatmeal baths would alleviate. He was chronically underweight, and because the first course of treatment for a Crohn's flare was immunosuppressants, he was also chronically suffering from whatever seasonal bug was floating around. There was never a time when Peter was not coughing or sniffling or vomiting; indeed, if ever the rare day came when he appeared in good health, his parents only braced themselves for a vicious flare to come.

Peter took this all in good cheer. He had no siblings nor friends in the neighborhood; he did not have a "normal childhood" as a comparison case. Poor health was just something he had to deal with. Otherwise, he had his tutors. He didn't need sports when he could stretch his mind; he didn't need the outdoors when he had entire abstract universes unfolding in his imagination, their secrets waiting to be explored.

He loved numbers because they behaved the way they were *supposed* to, because the rules never changed. The square root of sixty-four never ceased to be eight.

Most of the time, he had such fun that he nearly forgot he was a sick child, shut up in his room, with no friends.

Still, Peter's parents felt that he needed to spend some time with children his own age. Therefore on his eighth birthday, during a months-long stretch in which Peter was actually feeling quite well, his parents invited his third-grade class over for a birthday party. Peter had spent so little time in class that semester that he hardly knew anyone's names, yet everyone invited turned up to his home, bringing presents and good cheer.

"Look who's popular," said his mother.

Peter, venturing out of his bedroom, felt quite overwhelmed by the crowd and the noise. "What am I supposed to do?" he asked.

"Socialize," said his father. "It's good for your development."

"But how?"

"Just give it a try." His father pushed him toward the stairs. "Have fun."

He did try, and he had enormous fun. Peter had never spent

so much time with other children; he had never experienced the joys of hide-and-seek, or playing tag, or pin the tail on the donkey. And even though he was terrible at finding hiding places, and even though he was by far the slowest in the group, everyone cheered at his minor victories; everyone laughed with him, not at him.

For three hours that afternoon Peter felt funny, charming, adored. Everyone was so nice! And he even seemed to keep catching the attention of Jemma Davies, who even Peter knew was widely acknowledged as the prettiest girl in the neighborhood, with great big brown eyes and chestnut hair so smooth it shone.

When it came time for cake and candles, Jemma sat down beside him, placed her little hand upon his, and said in a very prim and grown-up voice, "I'm *so* glad you're having us over. Company is good for invalids."

"Invalids," repeated Peter.

"Well, you're very sick, aren't you?" Jemma squeezed his hand. "I heard your mum telling my mum. That's why we've all come. We're going to make you feel better."

She beamed at him. Peter smiled back. But everything tasted like ashes now in his mouth. He feigned a smile through the singing and candle-blowing, through the enormous pile of presents and the endless party games that came after—but the day was ruined, and he could not receive anyone's goodwill except with suspicion.

At the end of the night, he kissed Jemma Davies on the cheek and told her, "Your charity has been much appreciated." And then he shut the door.

After the cups and plates had been cleaned and the presents put away, Peter asked his parents if he might be homeschooled through his A-levels. Oh dear, they fretted; had the children been mean, had he been bullied? Not at all, he answered; they were perfectly pleasant, only he just didn't think he could get much out of socializing with inferior minds. This could not be good for his development.

That night he listened as his parents argued behind closed doors. He's right, said his father; he *is* advanced, there's no reason to hold him back. But he's grown cold, said his mother. *Inferior minds*, what a term, where did he pick that up? We can't have him growing up thinking he's better than everyone else.

This was fine, thought Peter. Let them think him cold, rude, antisocial. Growing up with a chronic illness just meant choosing between bad and worse, and Peter had determined that day that no matter what else happened, he was never again to be the object of pity.

**BY THE TIME PETER WAS SITTING** his A-levels, his doctors had finally settled upon a course of medication that seemed to work better than the others. It was called mercaptopurine, and it interfered with DNA synthesis so that inflamed cells could not easily divide. This had the unfortunate side effect of suppressing the rest of his immune system, which meant that Peter had to wash his hands obsessively and avoid large crowds during the winter flu season. But otherwise he could eat all the same foods, and do all the same things, as everyone else his age. So three weeks after his seventeenth birthday off he went, two trunks in tow, to the same university where his parents had met and fallen in love.

Peter blossomed at Oxford. His coursework enthralled him; his tutors adored him. He tried champagne for the first time. He rode a bicycle for the first time. One week into his first term he attended a public lecture on basic paradoxes in magick and fell in love with the field; its caprice, its unknowability. Before, he had planned on entering maths or physics. But magick, it seemed, was a vast big iceberg of which they had seen only a glimpse of the tip, and it thrilled him to know how much more was left to be discovered. In those years, people were publishing groundbreaking discoveries every day. They'd just started investigations at Carne Abbas. They'd just found chalk deposits at the Agora. They were just now discovering the foundations of magick underwriting the history of the ancient world, and here he was at the center of it. Sometimes he took long walks around the colleges with no aim at all, so giddy with excitement that he could not sleep.

It also became clear to him during this time that he had become what some people might call attractive. It was a marvel he grew up as tall as he did, as he'd spent most of his childhood in the bottom percentiles for his weight. But when puberty knocked it was like some trickster god pulled him by the head and ankles and stretched him out like Silly Putty, until he'd become some unrecognizable assortment of floppy hair and gangly limbs—a concoction that, when you stuffed it into a suit and tie, the boys and girls of Oxford rather liked. His proportions made him good at rowing, and once he started rowing he noticed a whole host of nice new things about his body. His arms grew strong, his chest filled out, and he learned to rub just a small squeeze of gel through his hair so it stood halfway up.

All this to say, Peter got a little silly during those Oxford years.

His remission was not perfect. The Beast still came every few months, and this meant hospital stays, IV steroids, and bed rest. But no one cared, Peter learned, so long as he didn't *tell* anyone what was the matter, so long as he let them fill in the gaps with conjectures of their own. Never once did he say he wasn't feeling well; he just refused to make excuses at all. He found he could get away with more and more. He could miss days of class. Weeks, even, though he tried not to be excessive.

He did try never to stay home unless he was bedridden. No one ever complained; if anything his friends and tutors took it all in stride. Oh, they said; that's just like Murdoch. Does whatever he wants, what a crazy lad. So over his three years at Oxford, he developed this reputation—an absent, erratic genius.

Perhaps he leaned into it. Perhaps he put on an affectation sometimes—he would talk about solutions to problem sets in a dreamy, indifferent voice as if he hadn't spent hours working through them, or pretend he hadn't done the reading when in fact he'd stayed up all night. If ever he had to leave class for the bathroom, he claimed he was going for a smoke. And if ever his hospital stay lasted more than a week, he pretended he'd buggered off to Barcelona or Göttingen—this was sometimes true, since his parents liked to attend conferences and he liked to accompany them—or just stayed home and slept, because he felt like it, because Peter Murdoch didn't need to attend lectures to ace a class.

He was astonished by how well this worked. No one resented him for his absences; they only got so much more excited when he showed up. Murdoch was a rare presence; his appearance was a blessing. In a world defined by perception, Peter was learning now to construct a most compelling front. Geniuses could be excused any idiosyncrasy. They would forgive an ailing body, Peter determined, so long as they were intimidated by the mind. And oh, what a mind he would become.

**WHEN IT CAME TIME TO DISCUSS** his future, Peter had decided firmly on a PhD in analytic magick. Maths and physics entertained him, but he was seduced by the slippery unknown; the way grappling with truth in magick felt like trying to clutch sunlight in your palm. Now, this would have made Cambridge the obvious choice, if only his parents did not have such reservations.

Aoife and Howard Murdoch had done their doctorates at Oxford, which was in their view the greatest institution on earth. They were also deeply connected in the social circles of British academia, so of course they'd heard the rumors.

"That man is a brute," said his mother. "Anyhow, won't you be happier somewhere . . . more comfortable? Why not stay at Oxford?"

"Or even the New World," said his father, who still insisted on referring to it as the New World as a bit, though no one ever laughed. "They're doing quite innovative stuff these days, you'll have a grand old time. Why muddle your best years away at *Cambridge*?"

What neither of them said out loud: *Are you sure you can bear it?*

But Peter, since childhood, had operated by two interrelated principles.

First, he was only interested in doing the hardest possible thing. He was Nietzschean in this regard. Not in the weird and antisocial Übermensch way, which so many young men at Oxford had taken to heart. He was Nietzschean in the broader sense that he felt life only had purpose if he was constantly pushing himself past his own limits. He believed only the faculty at Cambridge could help him reach his limits. And he would not waste his time doing anything but his best work.

Second, he hated to ever make exceptions on account of his constitution. Peter had spent his entire life being the sickly Murdoch boy. He'd been informed since childhood, usually by well-meaning and sympathetic teachers, that it was all right if he sat out this game, if he didn't come on this field trip, if he couldn't sit his exams, if he didn't want to run the last lap. Peter had had quite enough of other people feeling sorry for him. He was not interested in merely keeping up with everyone else; in doing what someone without Crohn's could. He wanted to do what people without Crohn's could *not*. So when he heard the horror stories—the lab assistants who had quit, the grad students who regularly stormed out of Grimes's office in tears—Peter took it as a challenge.

Now, perhaps his time at Oxford made him overconfident in his own charm. Perhaps his peers and professors had fawned a bit much; perhaps his ego had grown a touch larger than was good for him. But Peter did not think he was wrong believing that he was something quite special—and that if anyone could ever impress Jacob Grimes, it was him.

CAMBRIDGE! PETER LOVED IT INSTANTLY; THE cobblestone alleys, the winding river, the green and peaceful banks. He'd gotten the clubbing out of his system as an undergraduate—several sticky semesters at Wetherspoons were quite enough—and now he appreciated Cambridge's quiet. There was always too much going on at Oxford. Cambridge, out in the fens, seemed like the sort of place where you could focus and get things done. The boys angling for Westminster were all studying politics, philosophy, and economics at the other place; here at Cambridge, the scientists came to dream. The Department of Analytic Magick, too, was everything he'd been promised—brilliant faculty, brilliant classmates, and a bottomless budget for chalk. Professor Grimes was exacting and formidable, just as Peter had hoped; under his tutelage Peter felt his mind being honed, a knife scraped sharp against a whetstone.

And there was Alice.

Alice Law. How many nights during that first year did he bike home long after midnight, giddy with the memory of her laughter? Peter had never known anyone like her—prickly, stubborn, ridiculous Alice. She had an underdog's persistence, an artist's creativity, and best of all she thought so *differently* from everyone he'd trained with at Oxford. Perhaps it was the American influence (Peter had never been to America but his father had led him to believe it was a land of iconoclasts), or perhaps it was Alice's off-kilter sensibilities, but something about her mind was—well, rhizomatic was the best way he could describe it. She didn't think in straight lines; she was always zigzagging outward. She was always wondering how unrelated disciplines might speak to one another, or dredging up random shit from archives no one had ever heard of. Can you imagine a world without memory? she would ask. Can we form meaningful relationships if we have the memories of goldfish? Does your pet know that they will one day die? Does teleportation equal death? Now suppose you do think teleportation is death—if you woke up, and your spouse professed they had been teleported from one side of the bed to another, would you mourn them? Never before had he met a thinker whose thoughts spiraled out into places he could not easily follow. He so loved watching her think out loud, hearing her fragmented thoughts spin into complete arguments, seeing her eyes dart around a point in space he could not see.

It wasn't just that she was brilliant. Everyone around him was brilliant; brilliance here was boring. Alice was a *challenge*. Alice kept him on his toes. Watch out for that one, Professor Grimes told him over tea at the faculty club. She'll either flame out early, or she'll win a Nobel.

Yes, Peter did a lot of watching Alice. At night he dreamed of a birdlike silhouette stretching on tiptoes before a chalkboard. Head tilted, considering.

It was all so romantic. For a short while Peter Murdoch had everything he had ever hoped for: an advisor who inspired him, a best friend who challenged and excited him, and a body that was stunningly cooperative. Every few weeks he biked down to the hospital for a checkup with his gastroenterologist, though deep down he'd started to suspect this was unnecessary. He was now on the longest stretch he'd ever been without a flare. Sometimes, unbelievably, it took active effort to remember the Beast at all.

They said you could go into remission for decades. The Crohn's information pamphlets were crammed with testimonials by people who one day woke up without pain, without cramps, and never felt it again for years and years. No one knows what induces remission, they said; remission is a miracle; sometimes your body just decides to stop attacking itself. Throughout his childhood Peter had never let himself dare. But as more time passed, the more it felt reasonable to hope that this was it—that he'd left the Beast behind him forever, and now he could run free.

THE SWITCH FLIPPED MIDWAY THROUGH HIS first year.

Crohn's could do that to you. He ought to have remembered. The Beast was never vanquished, only banished into hiding. One night he was eating spicy curries and drinking rose cardamom lassi at the Indian place across the bridge. The next morning his stomach was tight with telltale cramps; only mild just yet, but a harbinger of things to come.

It escalated so quickly. This was the worst bout Peter had experienced since he was twelve. Things had gone well for so long that he had forgotten how horrific it could be—the double anvils of constant diarrhea and dehydration, the cramps and hemorrhoids, the revulsion toward putting anything in his mouth for fear it would only come back up again. In a single month he went four times to the hospital; twice first for IV drips, the third and fourth for intravenous steroid courses. He seemed to have developed a resistance to mercaptopurine, and this meant his treatment plan now consisted of hurling various things at a wall and seeing what stuck. His weight plummeted. His skin turned a translucent pale; when he looked in the mirror, he could see his veins, blue and spindly, floating underneath.

He told no one. When you'd earned the reputation he had, the world afforded you a certain privacy. Everyone already had their theories about Peter Murdoch and so, when he started skipping lab days to curl up in bed, when he simply failed to turn in his grading assignments, they simply amplified those theories. *Murdoch can't be bothered. Murdoch doesn't care.*

His goodwill was running out. Erratic was one thing; irresponsible was another. *Jesus, Peter*, Belinda snapped once, when he leaned on her one too many times to cover his sections, *it's not like the whole world revolves around you.*

But anything was better than being vulnerable. In Peter's imagination, the moment anyone found out would be the moment Peter the Great's reputation vanished, replaced by Peter the Sick's. Peter the *Invalid*'s. And so even by the time he could no longer cycle home for fear of collapsing in the road, he couldn't bear the thought of anyone knowing. Least of all Alice.

He knew he'd hurt her. He saw her wounded passing looks. He felt terrible about the way he'd left things off. Never before had he felt he owed anyone an explanation, because never before had he become so close to someone that his sudden disappearance could impact their life. Before, Peter had simply slid into the background, out of orbit. He passed in and out of friendships, always a prized acquaintance, never a constant. Here Alice had become a constant. He could not give her up.

Still, the memory of little Jemma Davies was stamped in his mind, and so too the terrifying moment when he could no longer tell friendship from charity. He figured he could always apologize later, make excuses, win her back over. But if they were ever to be friends again, then Alice could never know.

The one person he could not lie to was Professor Grimes.

Things had come to their breaking point—he was behind on too many assignments, he'd missed too many meetings. It was impossible now to skate by on reputation alone. At this point he risked losing his funding.

So Peter went to his advisor's office, medical records in hand, to beg for mercy.

"But you look just fine," said Professor Grimes, who must not have been looking very hard, for Peter by this point had lost twenty pounds and could count all his ribs in the mirror.

"It's, ah, not the kind of thing that's so visibly apparent."

"And you've had it all your life."

"Diagnosed when I was six."

"But it's only just now gotten worse."

"Seems like it," said Peter. "I'm obviously very disappointed."

Professor Grimes frowned. "Well, how long will this last?"

"Nobody knows. It comes and goes, there's never a set pattern."

"So you could be incapacitated for over a year."

Peter winced. "I hope not, sir."

"Isn't there something you can take for it?"

"There was," said Peter. "It's stopped working. There are newer medications that might work better, but they'll take some time, and before we try that we need to control the symptoms first. And that'll take weeks. Meanwhile, I'm not sure how much I can do."

Professor Grimes seemed thoroughly unconvinced. "I see."

Peter was not sure he would have believed himself. This seemed precisely the lie a shifty, unreliable doctoral student who had reached his limit would concoct. Perhaps it would have been better if he were missing a limb, or if a jagged scar cut across his body. Then at least the contours of his loss, and incapacity, would have been clear. As it was, Crohn's was coming off as something completely, conveniently, made-up. *A beast gnaws at me at all hours of the day, but you can't see it. I feel so weak and scattered my mind won't work—but here I am, speaking to you, clearly alert. My tummy hurts—what a joke.*

"Well." Professor Grimes seemed unsure about what to say. Watching him try to give comfort was like watching a duck put on a suit. Aristotle said it best; certain beings were just not meant for certain functions. "Well . . . just try to get through it as best you can, won't you?"

"I will, sir," said Peter. As if it were so easy; as if he could dismiss it all with sheer force of mind. "You won't hear about it again."

He was halfway out the door when Professor Grimes called after him: "Murdoch—a word of advice."

He halted. "Yes?"

"Try not to feel so sorry for yourself."

"I—well, I try, Professor."

"I mean there are great minds who were disabled. Edison, for one. That fellow over in Cosmology." Peter could not tell whether Professor Grimes was mocking him, or if this was some genuine and horrifying attempt at comfort. Professor Grimes continued, "It is a great liberty, from a certain perspective—to be free of the normal human desires and distractions. I knew a great mathematician once—one Irene Fulmencio. Remarkable woman. We met in Venezuela; she'd never left her hometown. She was crippled by a childhood illness and spent her days in bedridden contemplation. She lived in a world of ideas. She thought of nothing else. She was *able* to think of nothing else. Her mind transcended to pure abstraction—her body was an afterthought. It was a great liberation, really."

Peter was too astonished to explain that his particular illness rather never let him forget how embodied he was.

"Anyhow, hire an undergrad to take down dictation if you really can't get out of bed." Professor Grimes turned back to his desk. "Heavens knows you're paid enough."

THINGS GOT A LITTLE BETTER BEFORE they got worse, as these things tend to do. For a few weeks the steroids seemed to work, and the inflammation went down, during which Peter worked like the devil to make up for lost time. He finished the last of his grading assignments. He gave Belinda a bouquet of thank-you flowers, which earned him a flurry of cheek kisses. He passed his exams with flying colors.

And then, because he had always been an overachiever, and because his best research insights always arrived during such frenzied spells, he developed an algorithm that would change the field of categorization forever.

This may have sounded boring to the casual observer—and, indeed, was boring to most people in magick. Categorization was, however, of immense import to any logician. The question of how to sort and describe the world had bearing on almost every other field. Peter's innovation was in a subtle variation of Russell's Paradox, wherein sets themselves were not members of the sets they described—meaning things could be both normal and abnormal, or neither normal or abnormal. This had a whole range of implications for how you might suspend the nature of things, but in the interim, Peter was interested in how you might situate human beings temporarily outside of space and time. Beginner stuff.

"Not bad," said Professor Grimes, which was the highest praise Peter had ever heard him utter. "Finish your pentagram sketches and we'll come back next week to test it."

"Yes, sir." Peter went home, ate an ill-advised burger, and spent the next twelve hours in the bathroom.

He wept often with frustration over that next week. He knew precisely what he needed to do to finish this paper. He knew the shape of the problem, knew the journey his thoughts needed to take—he simply couldn't take his mind across. Instead he had to dwell on the number of bowel movements he had in an hour;

the calories he'd ingested that day; whether two boxes of Saltine crackers was enough to keep him out of the hospital. He hated this meat sack he'd been trapped in; hated every tissue and organ that sapped his attention and energy when all he wanted to do was sit and think. He demanded so little of his body, and yet it would not even afford him this.

A horrible impulse overtook him then.

He decided he would not get help. Not this time. No doctors, no hospital, no medications, no waiting and watching to see how he responded to various courses of treatment. No steroids, no side effects. He was exhausted by the entire cycle. No, he would not have his mother come up and sit fretfully by his bedside, watching his every movement, flinching every time he moaned, staring at him intently as if she could heal him with the sheer force of her will. It was an outrageous and possibly suicidal commitment but once he conceived it his mind was set. It seemed the only degree of freedom he had left. The universe was unfair, so he would bait the universe. *Do your fucking best*, he told it. *Put me in the ground.*

What happened is precisely what any doctor would have expected, which is that Peter rapidly deteriorated.

He could never forget that final night. Lying on the bathroom floor, crying pitifully from the pain, stomach spasming every few minutes like it was tying itself into ever smaller knots. Always he would remember the burn of the bath mat against his face, that mildewed smell of wet feet. *So many students have come through these quarters*, he thought, *and I might be the first to die here.* Always he would remember praying, something he had not done for years; kneeling on his hands and knees on the bile-splattered bathroom tiles, uttering half-remembered lines from Mass—*Have mercy on me, oh Lord—Christe, eleison—*

*God don't let me die I don't want to die God—*

He did not die. The scout came in to clean the next morning

and, hearing no response to his knock, decided the room was empty and came on in. Peter was unconscious on the floor. Calls were made; ambulances summoned. Peter awoke in the hospital, hooked up to an IV and steroid drip. His mother had come up from London that afternoon. A doctor came in and explained Peter needed part of his colon removed. The inflammation had grown so severe that recovery was beyond hope; he now had a stricture in his colon, and a colectomy was the only thing that might relieve his symptoms. They would take out the diseased half of his colon and reattach the nondiseased ends together. This was if Peter was lucky. If not, he'd need the whole colon out, and spend the rest of his life carrying around a stoma bag. And even if everything went well, Peter might need the whole colon out anyway—colectomies were only temporary solutions, after all; they did not cure the root disease.

On the bright side there was very little Peter could have done to prevent this. Crohn's reached this stage sooner or later; drugs stopped working, and inflamed tissue became unusable. He might have gone to the hospital earlier, but it would have made no difference, only accelerated his surgery. So despite his mother's sullen recriminations, Peter could not blame his stubbornness for this development. Only his flawed biology.

"Still," said the gastroenterologist. "Next time we recommend coming in before you're at risk of sepsis."

Peter did not want to hear any more. He sat through his consultations, eyes glazed over. Do whatever you need, he told his doctors; just wake me up when you're finished.

SIX WEEKS LATER PETER RETURNED ON shaky feet to the department. He was prepared for some backlash. He had not told anyone he was getting surgery, after all; he'd only disappeared off the face of the earth and assumed he could clean up the mess when he returned. This had always worked for him before. But people were always inevitably upset, miffed; he'd always needed to smooth things over.

Instead, all everyone wanted to talk about was the paper that Professor Grimes was publishing soon in *Arcana*. Had Peter heard? Apparently it was groundbreaking, was going to revolutionize the way we thought about categories. It had to do with Russell's Paradox; wasn't that the subject of Peter's dissertation? They'd circulated drafts at a work in progress presentation last week; here, he could have a copy.

Peter should have known, but still, reading the byline was like taking a slap to the face:

**NEW APPLICATIONS OF RUSSELL'S PARADOX**
By: Jacob Grimes
Department of Arcane Magick
Cambridge University

Peter had never in his life had people refuse to listen to him, so he barged into Professor Grimes's office that very afternoon with full confidence he could set this right.

"That's my research." He slammed the draft manuscript on the desk between them. "Those are my ideas."

"And what very good ideas they are." Professor Grimes leaned back in his chair. "Welcome back, Mr. Murdoch. Care to explain where you've been?"

Peter pointed to the byline. "Why aren't I a coauthor?"

"Perhaps because you didn't author any of it."

"This is theft."

"Is that so?"

"I could report you.

"Would you, now?"

"There's procedures," Peter sputtered. "I could go to the board—"

"And say *what*, precisely? That you wrote this paper? You did not. That I stole your ideas? I did not." Professor Grimes's voice grew louder; the whole room seemed to shrink. "From my point of view, Mr. Murdoch, you were a happy collaborator until you quit. You haven't signed in to the lab since January. I have called and written many times, to no response. You have offered no explanation and no apologies. You dropped off the face of the map for over a month and expected me to do nothing with our findings?"

*I've been sick*, Peter wanted to say, *I've been in a hospital bed, having diseased tissue cut out of me.* But an entire lifetime of denial—the anticipated disbelief; the conviction that, despite everything, he was exaggerating his own suffering for special treatment—stifled his words, and his tongue stuck in his throat.

"Listen, Murdoch. I will make many excuses for talent. Great minds work at their own tempos. I know this. But you are getting lazy. And laziness does not get you published in *Arcana*. It gets you expelled."

What defense could Peter make? Guilty, guilty on all accounts—he had not been diligent enough; he had not met his deadlines; he had not overcome. A weak body was just the same thing as a weak mind; either might afflict you, and both disqualified you from genius.

He slunk out of the office, head bowed. The lab outside was silent; everyone was looking at him. Alice met his eyes; she stepped forward, as if to speak. But Peter's vision had narrowed to a pinprick around the door, and he brushed past her as if she were not there.

PETER COULD ONLY ATTRIBUTE WHAT HE did next to childish pride.

To add insult to injury, Professor Grimes had asked Peter

to contribute the proofs to the final drafts. A portion of each publication needed to involve documentation of multiple repetitions of each pentagrammic component before you could activate them with a human subject, and then documentation of multiple repetitions of all human-based iterations. This meant Peter had to go over his own stolen research with a red pen, and report back on all the mistakes he might have overlooked. Of course Peter agreed; no one could refuse a direct request from Professor Grimes and keep their funding. But this did not mean he needed to do a good job.

He swore to God—he never meant to hurt anyone. The most malicious thought he ever held was that it might be nice to embarrass the professor. He knew Grimes did not double-check his own work; it was an open secret that Grimes had long gotten sloppy at details, would never finish a paper if it weren't for an army of assistants looking things up for him. In Peter's imagination, all this culminated in some grand public embarrassment at the summer conference of the Royal Academy of Magick perhaps, when Professor Grimes got booed and laughed off the stage for making mistakes an undergraduate would have caught.

And really, Peter's dominant motivation was just not to spend more time on the paper than Professor Grimes deserved. Why bother, if he wasn't getting any credit?

So he went through the whole stack in a single night, propped up in bed, half-heartedly scribbling corrections in the margins. He didn't bother with retracing every pentagrammic iteration; it took so much bloody time, and required so many back-translations from Latin and Greek. Briefly he skimmed the algorithms—some other postgrad had put it all together, he was sure everything was fine—and scribbled at the top: *Looks good. Minor corrections, see below. Can continue.*

Then he trudged back to the department, dropped the draft in Professor Grimes's tray, and left without thinking twice.

AS SOON AS HE REACHED THE department the next morning, he knew. Police cars and fire trucks were parked all round the front entrance. Caution tape covered the doors and windows; an officer stood by the front door, warding off anyone who tried to get in. Peter stood among the crowd, heart pounding as he watched uniformed figures emerge from inside. Two med techs came out bearing an empty stretcher.

"There's no point," he heard an EMT say. "We'd need a bucket."

By then the whole department was gathered outside. Their whispering grew frantic; voices swelled, theories flew as they counted who was among them and who wasn't. A gaggle of undergraduates were so distressed they'd started crying. "Who's in charge here?" Helen Murray kept shouting. "What's going on? Can't someone tell us what's happened?"

Peter pushed his way back through the crowd, stumbled home, and threw up all over his sink.

Several solutions crossed his mind that night.

He did consider killing himself. He spun out all the scenarios in his head. Hanging, ovens, cyanide apples—what demanded the least amount of effort? Probably the oven, except the graduate cottage only had a shared oven and it was too low to the ground for him to get his head comfortably inside. Yes, that was his excuse. *I am too tall to comfortably kill myself.* He also considered turning himself in, confessing his deeds, and letting the Royal Academy of Magick punish him as they pleased—which would be akin to killing himself, since if he couldn't do magick than he might as well be dead. But dying seemed so unpleasant, and in any case he couldn't put his parents through that kind of grief.

Anyhow it seemed the most obvious—and most difficult—way to put things right would be to retrieve Professor Grimes's soul from the underworld. And hadn't Peter always been motivated by doing the hardest possible thing?

Still, planning his sojourn took him longer than he thought. The formula for exchange was the easy part—the Alchemists had found it a long time ago; it was only rarely ever used because no one wanted to pay the price. The gateway to Hell was harder. He had the basic idea, but certain texts containing the details he wanted to cross-check kept disappearing from the library. Some ghost seemed to haunt the archives, always one step ahead of him.

One night he came into the lab just as Alice was departing. She bumped his arm on the way out, but she said not a word. In fact she hardly seemed to register his presence at all; she only cast him a wide-eyed look that was not looking, then hurried down the hallway wobbling under the weight of books balanced in her arms. Chalk was smeared all over her hands and face. And on the hastily wiped board behind her, Peter could see the traces of a summation he'd recently come to know quite well. He recognized it all in a glance.

Ramanujan's Summation. Setiya's Modifications. Two columns knocked together then in his head; two premises that concluded with his redemption; at that moment, the only valid thing in the world.

First: Alice Law was headed to Hell.

Second: he must go with her.

## CHAPTER TWENTY-THREE

"Why didn't you ever tell me?" asked Alice.

And Peter gave the only correct answer, which was the true answer, which was just the question flipped. "Why didn't you ever tell *me*?"

All this time, thought Alice. All this time they'd both been drowning, and thinking the other was gloating at them from the shore. She remembered that set theory paper; remembered how proudly Professor Grimes had spoken about it. *I'm going to revolutionize how they think about categories*, he'd told her. *This is the closest we've ever come to solving Russell's Paradox. They're going to be shitting their pants.* Never once had he mentioned Peter.

She pushed her palm against her cheek. "I can't believe it."

Peter stiffened. "Why not?"

"I'm not calling you a liar," she said. "I believe you, I'm just—I mean, I can't imagine why he would need to do that. He's *Grimes*, for heaven's sake—he has a million projects going on all the time, he shouldn't have to *steal*—"

"You're doing it again," said Peter.

"Doing what?"

"Valorizing him. Defending him. You always make him out to be this—this great, larger-than-life genius—"

"Well, because he *was*—"

"He's just an asshole, Law."

"No he isn't." Her voice hitched. "Don't you understand? He can't have been. Otherwise we let some—some *person* jerk us around."

"And it makes it better if he was a genius?"

"Not better. But—worth it." Alice splayed her hands. "Don't you know what I mean? If there was some method to the madness, then at least—right?"

Peter stared at her a long while, then sighed. "I do, yeah."

"And because—well, he just didn't seem all that bad, do you know what I mean? He wasn't like the rest. A bad actor."

"I know," said Peter.

This was how they'd consoled themselves for years. At least Professor Grimes wasn't like those *other* professors, the toxic ones, the ones who screamed abuses at their lab assistants and called them stupid to their faces, spittle flying out of their mouths. Wasn't like the anthropology professors who took their students out on field trips in South America and went mad, hurling cups and plates and putting their students' lives in danger. He wasn't a bully, wasn't a tyrant. After all, what all those abuses usually boiled down to was insecurity and incompetence, and Professor Grimes was neither. All he ever did was utter a stern word. He only ever held them to the same exacting standards to which he held himself. Being upset with Grimes was synonymous with being bad at your job. And even now, in the pits of Hell, Alice could not shake the conviction that if she had gotten into a tizzy about it, then it was all her own fault.

"And I just thought, if it wasn't working for me, then that meant there was something wrong with me," she said. "After all, you were doing just fine."

"Funny," said Peter. "That's how I felt about you."

They blinked at one another.

"It's embarrassing in retrospect," said Peter. "He was so good at pitting us against each other."

"It felt like that for you, too?"

She had always assumed theirs was a one-sided rivalry. She was the mess, and Peter Murdoch was the unreachable yardstick; the standard against which she was always measured. Peter could have done this in his sleep. He gave Peter the Cooke, after all; meanwhile poor Alice was so hopelessly behind that she needed an illegal, permanent pentagram to keep pace.

"Oh, yes. Every time." Peter affected a growl. "'You haven't got Alice's creativity, Alice's drive. Alice shows up first and leaves last and she's the only one between you who will get ahead, she's got what it *takes*. Alice is a true scholar. Alice will leave her mark on history, and you will only ever be a dilettante.'"

"He didn't," said Alice. Hearing this made her feel better in the stupidest way. "There's no way he said that."

"Are you blushing?"

She pressed her hands against her cheeks. "I am not."

"You'll take the compliment. Even now." He shoved at her shoulder. "Jesus, he really did a number on us."

"But it wasn't all bad," she said. "He made us good magicians." *He made me perfect.* Her tattoo twitched, and even then, she could not bring herself to consider it more a curse than a blessing.

"I don't know, Law." Peter pulled his legs to his chest and rested his chin atop his knees. "I've been wondering this myself. Whether we really needed Grimes to become who we did. Because, honestly, I think anyone could have made us good magicians. He just convinced us we had to suffer for it. Just had me thinking, even when I was on the bathroom floor, that I wasn't tough enough. That if I just *wanted* it enough, I'd be all better." He snorted. "Stupid."

"So how . . ." Alice glanced at Peter's midriff, then back up at his face. "How are you now?"

"Surgery helped," said Peter. "I'm in remission."

"Until?"

He shrugged. "Until I'm not."

"I'm sorry."

"It's all right," he said. "So it goes. Doesn't matter now."

THE DECLINE WAS VERY QUICK AFTER that.

Really it was merciful, how rapidly the Escher trap drained their energy. The air got hotter. Their mouths were like sandpaper, their tongues flat, rough stones. They sat side by side, but as time trickled on, their heads and shoulders drooped, like they were toys running out of battery, until they were slumped, Alice lying on Peter's lap, Peter lying atop her.

Alice was fairly unbothered by it all. Even if she was upset, her mind and body were too numb to register much; it took energy to grieve and she had none anymore. Her ears buzzed in a way that was almost pleasant. She closed her eyes, and thought only of cool rivers, velvety darkness, blanketing waters. Was this so terrible? All she had to do was go to sleep.

She heard the scratch of pencil against paper. She opened her eyes. Peter was scribbling on her notebook.

She lifted her head. "What are you doing?"

"Trying to figure a way out."

"We've tried everything," she mumbled. "There's nothing else."

"Oh, there'll be something."

"How do you know?"

"Because of Gödel's Incompleteness Theorem."

"Of what?"

"It's a theorem in mathematics." Peter sounded bizarrely chipper. "I learned about it when I was a child. Basically, it says no theory of mathematics can ever be complete, because for any reasonable mathematical system there will always be truths that the system cannot prove. Math has its limits. There's always something we don't know. Some people think Gödel's theorem proves the existence of God."

"But it doesn't prove anything at all."

"It does, though. It proves there's always another option. It proves no system is ever closed."

"Jesus, Peter." Alice blinked fast, but the dots would not clear from her vision. "That doesn't prove anything. Sometimes maths is just maths."

Peter's pen spun frenetically in his hand. "Well, consider this: In book four of *The Inferno*, Dante asks Virgil if any soul that was not saved by Christ had ever been rescued from eternal Limbo. And indeed, Adam and Abel and Noah, among others, had been blessed and raised to Heaven. God broke his rules, just for them."

"No one takes book four seriously."

"I mean, I too have some bones to pick with Dante. But the point is, even Dante's vision of Hell includes exceptions. The Underworld yields and bends. It is unpredictable—it follows no order but its own. It is just as Borges said—*the certainty that everything has already been written annuls us, renders us phantasmal*—and yet we are *not* phantasmal, not annulled, because nothing is fully written! There is no coherent set of axioms that explains it in full. Just like maths. Ergo, there will be some way out. And I will find it. I must."

"That isn't how logic works," said Alice. "I am sure this proof is missing quite a lot of steps."

Peter shrugged but said nothing. He only continued writing.

It exhausted her to watch him. How silly this was, she thought. How silly this all was—not just his scribbling, but the entirety of their efforts. Their situation in the Escher trap was just a microcosm of their entire lives at Cambridge: endless scribbling in an attempt to prove they could be the golden exception when in truth there was nothing exceptional about them at all; they were only following the scripts laid out for them from the beginning. And clearly the only thing to do was to get off the wheel, to quit, and refuse playing the game. Really the only victory here was death. How could she convince him?

She tugged on his sleeve. "Peter."

He paused. "Yes?"

"We don't have to be afraid," she whispered. "It's just as Elspeth said. We're living souls in Hell. We won't go anywhere. We won't become anything. It'll just be over—everything, all of it, done."

"But I don't want it to be done."

"Oh, hush." She patted his knee. "It will be fine, I promise."

"Don't say that."

She only patted him more firmly, as if he were a crying babe, as if he only needed to stop making such a fuss. "It'll all be silent. It will be all right."

She was so tired. Her eyesight had gone blurry. She couldn't see Peter's face then. She saw his lips moving but heard nothing, and then all she saw was the outline of a shape, growing smaller and smaller in her view, until all receded to black.

*SNAP.*

Her eyes blinked open. Peter's fingers hovered just under her nose. He snapped again, and she startled awake, ears ringing.

"Wake up," he said briskly. "I've figured it out."

"Hm?" Alice raised her head. Her whole body felt fuzzy. She didn't remember when she'd drifted off to sleep, nor could she tell how long she'd been out. The low red sky burned above, just the same as always.

Peter sat hunched over an array of papers, still scribbling. He'd filled out eight sheets at least since she'd drifted off—all covered in crossed-out, circled, and shaded-in algorithms.

"Our way out," he said. "I've got it."

Reluctantly she sat up. "What?"

"It should have been obvious." He spoke at a quick, robotic clip, a voice Alice knew quite well. It was the voice he always took on in lab when he'd figured something out; when he needed to get it all out at once but couldn't get his mouth to keep up with his thoughts. "Something I know from introductory logic. A silly game, really. It's got to do with types of knowledge and probabilities. But perhaps I shouldn't tell you, it'll weaken the paradox—"

"Murdoch."

"Okay. Listen." He drew a neat circle between them, just large enough for two to stand side by side. "Would you say that when the Kripkes come, it will be a surprise?"

Alice couldn't determine the significance of this statement, but neither could she find a problem with it. "Ah, sure."

"And would you say that they must come sometime between now and when we starve to death five days from now, otherwise our blood will go bad?"

"I suppose that's what I would do."

"Excellent." He pressed his palms together. "Then the conditions are set."

Her head hurt. "I still don't understand."

"Just listen," said Peter. "Now, suppose a prisoner is awaiting his moment at the gallows. The hangman tells him he'll be hanged sometime in the week, but otherwise he is not to know the date of his execution. Which day of the week can we rule out, then?"

Alice pondered this, and then ventured, "Sunday?"

"Good. Why?"

"Because it's the last day of the week. So if he hasn't been hung on any of the previous days, then he'll know it's happening Sunday. Only then it won't be a surprise."

"Very good," said Peter. "So Sunday's out. What happens, then, if he still hasn't been hung by Saturday?"

"I suppose Saturday's out too." Alice's thoughts churned sluggishly. "Because Sunday's out, which makes Saturday the last day it could happen, but if it hasn't happened by Friday, then Saturday isn't a surprise either . . . Oh." Something clicked in her mind. "But then Friday is the last day it could happen . . ."

"You see," Peter said gleefully. "It's recursive."

Alice saw now. "So then the prisoner can never be hung, because none of the days will be a surprise. And they have to let him go."

"Precisely!" Peter beamed. "And are not the conditions perfect for this paradox? We know we will expire in five days. We know the Kripkes always come when least expected. But if we map you onto the Hangman's Paradox, then you are invincible—they can never get you at all. So my hypothesis is if we write this into an algorithm, it releases you from the trap—that, or constructs some shroud of invulnerability, so that even if they come they can't hurt you—"

"Fine," Alice sighed. Stupid, ineradicable hope crept back into her chest; stupid, exhausting *feeling*. Things had been so much better when she'd only been numb. "Give that here."

Peter slid her notebook across the sand.

She traced her finger down the lines, willing herself to focus. Slowly she made sense of his scrawls. "You've messed it up."

"How do you mean?"

"You've written it for only one." She tossed the pages back into his lap. "It's no good. You have to do the whole thing over for two."

"Oh," said Peter. "No, I'd noticed that. That was intentional."

It took her a moment to register what he meant by this. "Murdoch . . ."

"It's not a very strong paradox," said Peter. "It's not like Sorites. There's a couple of obvious solutions, and I know them far too well. I can't suspend my disbelief long enough for it to work."

"All paradoxes have solutions." Alice fought a rising swell of panic. "That's why they're temporary."

"*Very* temporary," said Peter. "I'm afraid this one is particularly flimsy. And against something like an Escher trap, there's really no room for doubt."

"Then how do you know it'll work on me?"

He cast her a soft smile. "Because you're not a very good logician."

"Fuck you, Murdoch."

"Get in." He gestured. "Let's send you out."

"I am not leaving you."

"And I'm not letting you die," said Peter. "We can't have come all this way for nothing. You said it yourself. This all has to be worth something."

"Then we go in together."

"Not sure that'll work."

"Well, we've got to try." She smacked the notebook. "Rewrite it. Set it for two."

"It won't work for me," Peter insisted. "And when it doesn't work, you'll be a corrupted subject as well, and then you won't get out either—you'll *die*—"

"I'd rather die." She meant it. She'd never meant anything so much in her life. A week ago she hadn't been able to say she'd save Peter's life with certainty—but now, she knew. She didn't want to live. Didn't want the future, this stupid goal they'd been chasing. "We both live, or we both die, there's no third option."

"The third option is you *live*. You deserve to live—"

"I don't deserve anything." Alice meant this, too. What had she done since they'd come to Hell? Lied, betrayed Peter, betrayed Elspeth, landed them all in this sorry mess. It was about time she closed the book on this pathetic story. She was so very tired—she only wanted now to expire quietly in the dark, but Peter wouldn't even let her do that. "I don't, I really don't—oh, gods, Peter, just let me die."

"Can't. Won't."

"Why are you being so noble?" She would have beat him with her fists, if she could muster the strength. "Stop being so noble."

"You're the only one with an algorithm to bring him back. Mine doesn't work. I get out, and the only person we send back up top is Grimes. You get out, and at least you get home alive."

Violently she shook her head. "I don't know if the Erichtho spell even works—"

"Well, there's a chance it does. You're the only one with a positive outcome here, Law. It's just how the numbers fall."

"I don't care about the numbers!"

"Anyhow, you're the only one who didn't try to kill him—"

"You didn't kill him. I did. I remember I didn't close the loop. I remember, I don't *forget*—"

"I double-checked the submission after. You didn't close the loop because there was no closure. I never put it in."

"But still I should have known." Alice did not make mistakes; she couldn't. She saw everything; every detail was seared in her brain. And the only way she could overlook a thing like the Ant Test was if some part of her intended it. "I've been over this a thousand times. I saw the gap, I *knew*—"

"Stop it." Peter flung up his hands. "Just stop. We are not fighting over who gets credit for his murder. Who cares about the details—"

"The details matter," Alice insisted. "They matter because

you think you deserve to die when you *don't*, when it's not your fault at all, and you did nothing wrong, and you shouldn't even be down here—"

"The fact remains." Peter raised his voice, spoke right over her. "I can get this paradox to work on you. I am absolutely certain I can make it work. I have almost no certainty about the two of us. So that's just basic decision theory, Law. Maximum expected outcome."

"Shut up."

"It's just maths. I'm sorry if you don't like it."

"But you can't die here." She swallowed. "Not when—not when I've just—"

There was something wild, desperate in Peter's eyes. "When you've just what?"

What did she want to say? Alice didn't know. She didn't have the words for this pit of feeling, dark and gnawing and delirious. She wanted to hurl herself into his unknown; wanted an intimacy she couldn't describe. She wanted him alive; near; beside her. The words that came to mind were clumsy and insufficient, but they were all she had. "When we've just learned not to hate each other."

Something closed in Peter's face.

They stared at each other, a chasm yawning between them.

Oh, why was this so hard? Alice wondered desperately. Why couldn't she ever tell Peter what she *thought*? Always they had been bodies hurtling just out of one another's orbit, when all it would have ever taken was an honest word. But that was precisely what magicians lacked; there were no honest words, only puns and illusions and constructions of reality so convoluted that you couldn't keep track anymore of what was real and what wasn't. Everyone was always trying so hard to pretend they were somebody else.

If only they had caught one another, looked at each other, forced their ways across the gap.

But it was too late now, too late for everything.

Peter drew out a blade.

"What are you doing?"

"I'm deciding for both of us."

"You can't."

"It's the only rational solution," he said. "Please, Alice. Don't be an idiot."

She lunged for the blade. He raised it up out of her reach. She tried to shove him over—she tried with all the strength she had, but Peter could not be budged from the pentagram. She smacked his arms, scratched and pulled. But he was taller, heavier, and stronger; all he had to do was wave her aside.

"I hate you," she cried. "You're so—you're such a—"

"Logician." He gave her a sad smile. "I know."

He drew the blade across his arm. Blood flowed thick and fast across his skin, dripped down his fingers and onto the chalk, suffused the pentagram like spreading ink until the whole thing glowed crimson. Peter began to chant. Alice wailed. She hit him, she flailed, she railed against his grip—but he was so strong, and nothing she did could break his rhythm. On and on he went, sonorous as ever, confident until the last.

"The rucksack, Alice." He patted her shoulder. "Don't forget the rucksack."

Then, with a flick of chalk, he closed the circle.

Alice screamed, but he didn't hear. In an instant the sand rose up around her, threw her out and blocked Peter in. The Escher trap vanished before her, cuckoo bird, boulders, and all. Then all she saw was silt, an endless flat plane, under a constant, dying sun.

*"Lines that are parallel
meet at Infinity!"
Euclid repeatedly,
heatedly,
urged
Until he died.
and so reached that vicinity:
in it he
found that the damned things
diverged.*
　　—PIET HEIN, "PARALLELISM"

## On Paradoxes

*The reason why paradoxes trouble us is not because their conclusions are true. The donkey does not starve. The world does not consist of unending staircases. Of course Achilles could outrun a turtle, of course the arrow hits its mark, of course the heap runs out. The principle we must accept if we want to go on with our lives is that no paradox makes the world stop functioning as it should. The laws of the universe get their say. Things always snap back to how they should be, and a paradox always eventually runs out its charge. The only reasons why paradoxes perpetuate for as long as they do is because we let them.*

*No—the reason paradoxes trouble us is because their absurd conclusions make us rethink all of our premises. A paradox is like a staircase, in which each step leads inexorably to the destination. But you get to the top, and the destination is impossible; you've stepped off into empty air. So one of the steps must be folly. Because the conclusion must necessarily be false, because we cannot live in a world where logic does not work, one of our premises must necessarily be flawed. This is the source of our unease. A paradox means that somewhere along the path, we have gotten something deeply, terribly wrong.*

## CHAPTER TWENTY-FOUR

Late summer in Cambridge, two weeks to Michaelmas. The town was birdsong and rippling water and the barest hint of red peeking around the edges of the leaves, and the sun still shone warm enough to make you forget, year after year, the winter rains around the corner. Everything was new and shiny and full of promise.

Alice Law tripped up to the department in a brand-new pencil skirt and stiff white oxford shirt. She had ironed both herself that morning in a panic; she thought she'd seen a crease in the mirror on her way out the door. She could still feel the heat of the iron as she paused before the main entrance, one hand on the door handle, bracing herself for her first meeting with her new advisor.

The night before she had flown her first transcontinental journey, then ridden the late train from King's Cross to Cambridge station, then dragged her trunk the two miles north to her little room in Audley Cottage. Everything was new and exciting—the taste of digestives, the bright red telephone boxes, the cars zooming down the road on the right. When she stepped outside that morning she felt she had traveled across both space and time, down the rabbit hole and into a fantasy of her own making, into a more genteel and colorful world. She felt that she had jumped through the last hoop. They had finally let her into the club.

She had not yet met Jacob Grimes in person. She'd watched him present at a few conferences in America but never summoned the nerve to go up and say hello. Every conversation they'd had since her acceptance had been through the post—Professor Grimes seemed to hate the telephone—through which she'd tried to glean clues about his personality. He struck her as blunt, casual, and a bit scattered—he'd asked her the same question about her arrival date thrice over two months. But what else could you expect from the greatest magician in the world?

She steadied herself with a breath, opened the door, and stepped through. The building was silent. Term would not start until next month; the campus was empty. Professor Grimes's office was at the end of the hall. The door hung slightly ajar. Alice saw, with relief, that someone was sitting behind it. She knocked.

"Come in."

"Good morning," she said, and her voice cracked only a little. "I'm—I'm your new advisee. Alice Law."

"Hello, Alice. Have a seat." He came around the front of his desk and stood leaning against it, hands clasped before him as he stared down at her. Afterward, she couldn't say what he looked like. It would take several weeks of blinking out of the corner of her eye, registering his profile, his height, the faint beginnings of a stoop. Professor Grimes was like the sun. She couldn't look directly at him, she could only sense his presence from the edges. "It's lovely to meet you."

"I'm so excited to be here." She'd rehearsed this statement many times over but could never make the words come out in a way that didn't seem fawning or stilted. Now they tumbled out her mouth all out of order, breathless and silly. "It's such an honor to be working in your laboratory—I'm so grateful to be here, I can't wait to get started—"

"You sound nervous, Alice."

"I—I am." She swallowed. "Well, of course I am."

"Don't be." He smiled, and for the first time Alice understood what it meant for someone's eyes to literally twinkle. "You deserve to be here. Yours was the strongest application I've read in a long while."

"Oh." Alice's eyelashes fluttered, actually *fluttered*, and her fingers twisted frantically in her lap. She had prepared for a litany of questions. She was waiting for Professor Grimes to realize he'd made a mistake in accepting her; she still felt she had to pass a test. She had no idea how to react to such a compliment. "I don't know what to say."

How much a simple word of encouragement could mean to a young and insecure mind. Professors never knew the impact of their utterances. They seemed not to realize that a careless comment, the briefest smile, could make or break a student's day. Professors, who saw dozens of hopeful faces over the course of a day, forgot always that they were their students' entire universe.

Though perhaps Professor Grimes did know. Perhaps this was why he met Alice's eyes with such deliberation. Perhaps he knew what it meant to her—fresh from America with all the wrong clothes and mannerisms, terrified she'd tripped her way into a program where she was badly outclassed, and resentful already of the peers who seemed destined for Oxbridge from birth—to hear these words from his mouth.

All it took was those simple words, and Professor Grimes had Alice's undying loyalty.

"Never let them make you feel like you don't belong." He leaned forward, and his gaze was so intense that Alice felt dizzy.

"Posers in flapping gowns. Junior clerks in the making. Remember that you're special, Alice Law. Remember your particular mental signature. That's the only thing worth holding on to. That spark." He rapped his knuckles against the table. "Welcome to Cambridge, Alice. We're going to take apart the world."

In the months to come Alice would learn that Professor Grimes, like her, had come up from less-than-illustrious circumstances. The son of an absent alcoholic who had in his youth squandered his own father's fortune, Jacob Octavian Grimes spent late nights at the local library reading everything from Bacon to Wittgenstein. He had inherited that aristocratic curiosity that often skips generations. His was a mind meant for Mozart and Proust, and he clung to this conviction. There was no money for schooling past high school, so he joined the army, did his time overseas, and came back with a scholarship to a college in Austin, where he earned a technical degree in agricultural engineering. And then, through the persistent phone calls of one nearly retired professor who recognized in him a singular mathematical mind, Grimes found himself at Oxford, where he was so badly outclassed that for the first time in his life he longed for home. They mocked his handwriting, his outdated proofs. They imitated his drawl. They called him the Texan. They asked if he wore cowboy hats. He found himself looking up the cost of return fare. Then he thought more carefully of Lubbock, of stained floors and empty bottles. He remained.

Then there was the war. Jacob Grimes went back into uniform, this time with the War Office's research division, and by the time things wrapped up he had a British passport and several medals as reward for his achievements. Perpetual Flasks, instant disinfectants, Lembas Bread that never ran out. Jacob Grimes had kept the troops alive. There were the failed interrogation trials—all increasingly sadistic versions of the Liar Paradox—but no one spoke anymore about those. For a brief moment after the war, magicians were celebrities, and Grimes's face was printed on every newspaper in the country. The War Office's Warlock, they called him.

He left the army with the sort of reputation that gives one unlimited research funding. He was just too late to join the glory of the Vienna Circle, but he rode the cutting edge of all the scientific world's exploding innovations thereafter. During the war years everyone was obsessed with the bomb, but afterward there were solid-state physics, the transistor, the computer. New work in quantum physics was putting Einstein in his grave. Fred Hoyle coined the "big bang" moniker, and to his dismay, it took off. Nash proposed his game theory equilibrium in the fifties, and this set off a flurry of research into social paradoxes. The world was getting faster, more bewildering. Questions exploded, and Jacob Grimes chased them down each rabbit hole.

When the sixties rolled around, no one remembered Jacob Grimes as anything other than a fixture of the field. He was synonymous with analytic magick itself. He set the agenda. He had no beginning and no end; he had simply always been *there*, an incontrovertible fact of the discipline, a necessary encounter if you wanted to accomplish anything at all.

He had ascended to the hidden world. He brought his advisees with him.

This was the advantage of being a Grimes student. All the doors were open. You could get an audience with anyone; you could secure funding for anything; you could travel anywhere, and all it took was his assent. When Alice was under his wing, no one questioned her right to be in the room. "My student," he would say, hand stretched toward her. And suddenly it was like she had a glow upon her. For the first time, people saw her. She spoke, and people listened.

So despite everything that happened after, Alice would always remember that it was Professor Grimes who believed in her first. He'd plucked her out of obscurity. He'd seen her file in a stack of applications, held it up to the light, and decided, yes. Yes she was worth his investment, worth initiating into a world of mystery, worth making her equal to what he was, an intrepid traveler through abstract lands. His was the first plank in her staircase of belief. And in a world founded on insincerity and insecurity, that faith was a debt she would always feel she had to repay.

## CHAPTER TWENTY-FIVE

Alice flew into a frenzy outside the trap. She tried everything. She scrabbled around the sand, flinging it up in great fistfuls, just in case anything she touched disturbed the hidden pentagram. She drew every spell she could think of. She dug a knife into her fingertips and soaked the ground with great dribbles of blood, white dust glowing red. It didn't matter. Her chalk faded into the sand. She screamed to Peter, begging him to try the spell again, to come out and join her. The trap held firm. If he heard her shrieks, she couldn't know.

She fled when she heard skittering on the horizon. She had half a mind to stay rooted where she was, to plop herself on the ground and let the Kripkes take her too. That would be the easiest thing to do. But Peter's wide, plaintive eyes were burned into her mind. To die then, after his sacrifice, would be spitting on his corpse. So she snatched up the rucksack and ran as fast as she could, choking back her cries.

She needn't have bothered. The Kripkes paid her no heed. Several moments later the skittering ceased, and a victorious howl echoed over the sands. Alice paused, horribly compelled to turn around. She saw them stalking in a straight line across the sand. She could not see their faces clearly from where she stood: only their frames, two large figures and a smaller one. Like Elspeth they dressed head to toe in armor, but where hers was of chain-link debris, theirs was of white bone. Sharp fangs arced past their jaws. Something else's ribs caged their torsos. Bulbous round things hung at all their waists, bobbing at they moved. Pouches for blood, Elspeth had told her. They made them with bladders.

The little procession paused before the boulders. The two older Kripkes bent over, incantating over their spell. A ripple formed in the sand. One by one they disappeared inside. Alice heard a sharp, grating noise. Metal screeching. She heard Peter scream.

She screamed too through her balled-up fingers, fists shoved in her mouth to muffle her sounds. She sank to her knees, shoulders convulsing. The pressure was terrible. She thought she would split apart. But the only thing more terrible than the feeling itself was that obliteration didn't come, that she kept on hurting. She had never felt anything so sharp. Before she had only thought this grief theoretical, a grief that exceeded what words could describe. The only thing that came close was the Classical Chinese phrase "斷腸," because although the words translated figuratively meant "a broken heart," 腸 meant literally all one's internal organs and viscera, and for a heart to break meant that everything felt twisted and ripped apart and spilled onto the sand. A heart didn't just break, a heart yanked out the rest of you.

She wished it were her they were bleeding and gutting in there. She'd have given anything to change places. She wished to feel those blades digging into her skin, pulling her veins apart, because compared to this pain, that evisceration would be so clean and sweet. But no matter how hard she wished it she could not will it into being, and when the scarlet fog lifted she was still alive, and Peter was still dying.

She screamed her muffled screams until Peter's cries faded to nothing, until his blood was drained into those fat pouches. Then she got up, wiped her face, and kept on running.

FOR THE REST OF THE NIGHT Alice roamed the dunes. Landmarks drifted in and out of the edges of her vision. Gleaming bones. Jagged rocks. All of Violence looked the same, a barren field stretching endless from the river. She would have preferred to faint, for that would have relieved her of the burden of consciousness, but she was filled with adrenaline. Her heart slammed against her ribs, and she could nearly feel her pulse in her dry mouth and ringing ears—she had to keep moving, she decided; she would simply keep moving until that terrible energy exhausted itself and she broke down.

Still the moment wouldn't come, so Alice kept moving.

Her head would not quiet. She tried her staircase; she strained to focus; none of it worked; the television blared. She could only replay in excruciating detail every second of those final moments inside the pit. Peter's scribbling. The arc of chalk on sand. His soft, sweet smile. She couldn't determine whether she'd done enough—if she'd protested harder, if she'd convinced him otherwise, if she'd wrestled that chalk out of his hand . . . But these were questions that had no answers. All she could remember was her cries, and Peter's resolve.

Peter—Peter—*Peter*. Her memory track slid sideways, conjuring back every detail. The flop of his hair, the warmth of his curved frame against her back. The sweet, slightly musty scent that floated around him when it was late, when he hadn't showered. The sound of his voice, his laugh. Peter had such a wonderful laugh. It gripped all of him, made his arms and shoulders shake; it had a vulnerable, helpless quality to it, as if it seized him completely and he had no choice but to submit to his mirth.

Now all that was gone. This was the unbelievable fact of death. This was a paradox her mind could not accept, that someone could be in the world one moment and simply be gone the next. But Peter wasn't here anymore; the Kripkes had drained his blood and obliterated his soul; he wasn't in any world anymore, this one or the next, and it was all her fault.

Her guilt accumulated with every step. She kept retracing the worst decisions she'd made. The resentment simmering under her skin every time she saw him on campus. The disdain she felt for his smile. All those quips and jabs. The worst things she'd believed about him; her vile resentment. Ugly, wretched, petty—it was like watching a horror film from within her own body; she recognized herself as the actor but could not grasp the logic of every awful decision. She didn't recognize this person, this nasty resentful scheming little bitch. But memories didn't lie. She had done and said it all, and she had to live with the guilt.

All Peter had ever done was save her life. Meanwhile all Alice had ever done was hurt the people trying to help her, and it was so obvious she didn't deserve to live, and she wished she could just get it over with and die, except that, for Peter's sake, this was the one thing she could not do.

THE SUN ROSE. THE DIM ORANGE light illuminated rolling desert all around her. The silhouettes of the early courts had long disappeared. Alice had not realized until now how much she would miss them. Dreadful and claustrophobic as they were, they were at least *familiar*, were tangible structures she could touch and recognize and ground herself in. What she would give now for a nap in Desire, or even a study break in Pride! They oriented her, even if all their directions were false. But here the world grew further and further from the world that mortal souls knew, and this unanchoring terrified her.

She was deep in Cruelty. At some point in the night, she had made the crossing; perhaps the Escher trap had been at the border of Violence and Cruelty all along. The change was a difference not in kind, but in degree. Both were desert planes, but where Violence was harsh and mindless, Cruelty was littered with intention. Cruelty fucked with you on purpose. She kept coming across mysterious structures—interlacing bone, precipitously balanced, arranged occasionally like abstract art. Shapes carved out on the sand. Footsteps, maybe human, dancing in patterns she couldn't make sense of. Sometimes she found what looked like paths, lines traced carefully in imitation of road marks, only they ended abruptly or turned back in on themselves. Near the shore she glimpsed once a semicircle of slabs that called to mind lawn chairs on the green. Deep in her journey she found a pure, smooth marble block, about the size of a door, unmarked and unguarded. She spent the better part of an hour running her hands around the block, trying to detect any clues about its presence, trying to lure its creator out from hiding. But this block yielded nothing; no secret carvings, no hidden design. She screamed in frustration, and kicked at the block until her toes hurt.

She tried to conjure an explanation for it all. Suppose the Shades sought shelter. Suppose these arrangements were temporary houses, stations in which to rest and reflect. Suppose the Shades threw beach parties here. Suppose the Shades put on art exhibits. But really it seemed like bones thrown together in some attempt at amusement—at making meaning upon a plane that was, fundamentally, meaningless. Alice saw clearly now she was trespassing across the desert of consciousness, a map of madness; and the landmarks she witnessed were just the same delusions of everyone who had come before.

Now and then she saw glittering oases out of the corner of her eye. She did not stop to drink. She still had her copied Perpetual Flask, and she knew better than to drink Hell's water. But once she detoured, curious, toward a pool. She thought she might run her fingers through that gleaming surface. She wondered if there would be drowned things below, hints of what came before. But when she knelt and reached, her hands found a solid surface. No water here; just a sheet of obsidian glass. Someone had polished and sculpted it with just enough curve so that even up close, it looked liquid.

Alice thought about searching for meaning here, but the marble block had taught her better. She kept walking.

Sometime around sunset tall, white structures appeared on the horizon. She gravitated toward them, for the most basic need of a destination more than anything else. As she approached the white things she began to hear low, guttural moans. They were so faint at first that she did not register them as human at all. They sounded rather like empty glass bottles blowing when wind hit their apertures. Then she came closer, and looked up. She saw skeletal cages above—reminiscent of dustland construction, abandoned building frames—only these were made of alabaster bone, and glimmered under the sun. Their construction was exquisite, a lattice network of bones fit together just so, so that groove rested perfectly against groove, so that those cages swayed back and forth but never fell.

She wondered if these were built by deities. But there was something gorgeous about their mathematical perfection. These were projects possible only if you had eons of time, and a singular devastating focus. The structures of Hell were dreamscapes that emerged effortless from the mist. These cages took effort. They were meticulously human.

Trapped inside were Shades; hands clenching the bars, moaning in disharmony. Alice's mind flashed ridiculously to study rooms, to carrels at exam time; rooms filled by lowered heads and hunched shoulders in uniform solitude. Whenever the carrels were all booked up some students would build their own carrels from books, walling themselves in, hostile in their focus. This hopeless atmosphere—oh, she remembered it well; she had felt it acutely before. You could not walk through those carrels without choking in despair.

These Shades did not seem trapped against their will. Those bars were very wide. Alice saw no guards, no chains. And those were not cries of despair. Were not voluntary noises at all. The sound was not of them, but moved through them, an involuntary response against physical forces. The necessary reaction to let the universe know you were still there. Was this punishment, or a refuge? Perhaps both. It wasn't clear. Alice could only assume, like everything else, this was some way to make Hell more bearable. She could imagine a kind of peace up there in the sky, trapped in her own cage. Barely visible around her, others in their own cages as well—and the comfort of knowing that others were just as alone as you were. Far away from the cruel desert where nothing could touch you, an oasis unto yourself.

She cupped her hands around her mouth.

"Hello up there," she called. She felt a sudden urge to join them. Right then nothing seemed better than a spiraling cage of her own, just and eternal. *I want to moan too, I want to vanish into despair.* "Hello?"

The Shades did not acknowledge her.

"Hello? Might I come up there?"

A short pause to the moaning. Then it continued, redoubled, as if determined to drown out the interruption.

Alice felt very silly then, so she trudged on. *Let them have it their way*, she thought. Those cages were ugly anyhow. She could build a prison all on her own.

**BY MIDAFTERNOON, THE SAND HAD HARDENED** into cracked, brown rock. No more were the alien rocks and taunting patterns. She had gone from desert to deadlands. There was a difference; one was muted life and one was the scorched earth after everything living was burned away. The air here felt thicker, dryer and hotter. It smelled of frustration; of thirst never slaked.

Alice figured she was approaching the boundary between Cruelty and Tyranny.

There was no line in the sand, nothing that declared a hard and fast distinction between the cruel man's blows and the tyrant's cunning manipulation. Still Alice could tell the difference. The air sat heavy on her tongue. There was a metallic, musty tang here. The wind rose, a blistering force that rubbed her cheeks raw. She clutched her hood around her face. Her knuckles cracked and bled.

The Shades, too, acted differently. All the Shades of the previous courts had been harmless, too caught up with their own suffering to pay Alice much notice. But the Shades of Tyranny, sparse as they were, seemed aware of her and of each other in a way that made her uneasy. Several times she saw movement out of the corner of her eye, or glimpsed faces watching her from the trees. Yet every time she turned, they had disappeared.

She knew not what they wanted from her, or indeed, what they could do to her. She only felt their malice all about, constant and sharp, prickling like ant bites.

But she couldn't turn back. There was nowhere else to go. So she wrapped her jacket tighter around herself, kept her knife close at her belt, and trudged on.

**THE SUN SANK AND VANISHED. ALICE** walked until her limbs shook, and then she hunkered down in the shadow of a boulder to examine what supplies she still had with her. The Lembas

Bread was waterlogged, but the bits in the middle were still good. All the tea was foul with bog water—she threw that away. Miraculously the copied flask still worked. She drank one cup of clear good water, then another, and then six.

Body sated, mind cleared, she unfortunately began to think.

In the process of keeping herself alive, she realized she had to come up with a justification for all this effort.

What she knew was that she didn't fear death anymore. She had seen the other side in that Escher trap, and like a child receiving her first flu jab, or emerging intact from the dentist's office, she understood there was nothing much to fear. Death was just nothing. A twinge of pain, and that was it. And she had it better than any Shades, for she didn't even have the afterlife to contend with. Only the vanishing of the self, and the end of all obligations.

But the question now—now that she was no longer motivated by the instinctive fear of death, now that she had no urgent reason to keep running—was what came next. She had a bigger problem on her hands now, which was the point of living. Living meant a future meant some teleological end, but Alice could not figure out what on earth she was going on for.

Her original quest seemed so silly now. She didn't care to find Professor Grimes. She might be content if she never saw Professor Grimes again. The scales had fallen from her eyes. But she could not imagine any other future for herself. Everything she'd ever wanted now felt so frivolous; their pursuit agonizing. She imagined standing before her dissertation committee; receiving her marks from Grimes; moving on to her own job posting where another crop of miserable graduate students would come up under her tutelage. She imagined becoming a part of the cycle. She would rather have a cell in Desire.

Meanwhile death was so present, and obvious, and enticing.

Alas, she had put her mind to it, and her mind had settled on two premises that formed the incontrovertible conclusion that she must live.

First, because Peter had asked her to, and she owed him that much.

And second, because of his ridiculous hope that, at the end of everything, one might make an exception of Hell.

Damn Peter and his exceptions. Whether she liked it or not, he'd buried within her a seed that she couldn't grind away. Like Dante's Adam and Noah, like Gödel's Incompleteness Theorem, like the possibility of a True Contradiction, maybe going on meant believing in what she couldn't possibly know. Maybe if she went on she could find some way to make this pain stop. Maybe. *Maybe.*

Follow the river. Rescue Professor Grimes. Get out. Alice felt no internal motivation toward these objectives, but they were the only scripts she had, and they were better than nothing. At least they gave her reason to put one foot in front of another, again and again, until the minutes turned to hours turned to miles over endless silt.

THE NEXT DAY, ALICE CAME UPON the tower.

She saw its shadow first, for she had been trekking with her head stooped, registering nothing but the ground before her. At first she found it odd, this streak of darker ground among the gray, but then she lifted her eyes and saw a great spire not a hundred yards off; a single, sharp point on the horizon. *Ah*, she thought, *it's a clock tower, it's the center of campus*; for at Cornell you never needed a watch nor a map, you only gazed up to the bell tower, and you knew your way home. But of course it was not a clock tower, for in Hell there was no time to keep, no reason for bells to ring, and near the top where a clock face should have been was only a blank circle. *That is cruel*, she thought. *You did that on purpose, that is so very cruel.*

As she drew closer she realized the tower base was not built with rock as she'd thought, but sprawled and twisting forms—human faces and torsos, piled upon one another, frozen in their fight to climb away. Whether they were Shades or likenesses carved in stone, she could not tell. Arcing round the tower base was a line of rocks balanced over raised bits of dirt. A low wall, and easily trespassed, but a boundary nonetheless.

She heard a hissing. She looked up.

Upon the balcony stood three deities. Tall sinuous bodies, skin like marble, garbed in flowing cloth of the deepest red. Great hulking wings protruded from their shoulders. Alice understood these must be the Erinyes. Alecto, Megaera, and Tisiphone, chthonic creatures born of that blood shed from that first broken oath, when Kronos slew his father and cast his parts into the ocean. One for anger, one for rage, and one for endless destruction. Dark, curling hair undulated round their faces. They were very beautiful.

All three looked down on her at once.

Their eyes were without pupils; a singular scorching gaze. Alice felt a terrible heat as they scrutinized her, more intense even than Professor Grimes's gaze had ever been. She felt stripped of her clothes; of her flesh and bone. She was only soul, shuddering and naked, unable to conceal every evil or selfish thought she'd ever held. It seemed to linger for an eternity. Every thought extricated, suspended, turned over, and carefully considered. She was reduced to her unexamined truths. And a deep triplet voice echoing round her skull, demanding again and again: *Whose oaths have you broken?*

Alice squeezed her own eyes shut but it did not matter; still the Erinyes' gaze scorched her mind. She felt so small, tiny and mortal and pathetic. She felt like she had never had an original thought in her life. A confessor laying everything bare, only there was nothing interesting to say, only the normal human filth. *I was proud, I desired, I was greedy, I was wrathful—*

WHOSE OATHS HAVE YOU BROKEN?

"All of them," she gasped. "I don't know—"

*LIAR*, they three spoke at once.

The heat intensified. Hell faded out into a white plane, upon which Alice could only see moving shadows. A body spinning upside down. A noose. A heap. Flames licked around her face. Her ears thundered, the heat sharpened, and Alice heard the Furies cackling, and the burning question repeated until it scorched into her mind:

*Why—*

*Why—*

*Tell us—*

*Why?*

But this was just the thing she could not answer herself. She knew she had erred, but her sins felt like they had been committed by someone else, for reasons she could not fathom, and the only defense she could offer was that along every step of the way, from start to finish, each next move had in that very moment seemed the only rational thing. Grimes died, so Alice went to Hell; Peter hurt her, so she hurt him back. Elspeth had what they needed, and so they tried to steal. One thing led to another and that was all. She didn't mean to obfuscate. She wanted to be good for these beautiful burning women. She wanted to confess all, except every way she cast it made it seem that much flimsier, trite and convenient, as if her whole life story were beads knocking about an abacus. "I was just trying," she whispered. "I only—I was only doing my best."

Abruptly the flames died. The heat vanished. Alice lurched forward and gasped, small and limp, a candle doused in water.

High above atop their perch, the Erinyes threw their heads back and laughed.

"Professor Grimes," said Alice. "Is he here?"

The Erinyes ignored her. They shook in their mirth; their great wings pulsing, magnificent heads thrown back, displaying proud, white necks. *Come in if you wish*, said their laughter. *We care not.*

So Alice stepped over the wall, and entered the final court of Hell.

THE EIGHTH COURT WAS VERY QUIET. Whatever Shades lurked on the border seemed wary of the tower, and as she continued forth, their malicious presence faded. She was all alone now. Gradually the tower receded into a tiny prick on the horizon, and vanished, leaving Alice in a truly empty terrain: the river constant on her left, a sheet of orange above, a sheet of gray stretching endless to the right. She was dazed enough to find this pretty, this geometrical neatness. Here were three concepts displayed with perfection. Finite boundary, finite point, infinite plane. *I live now in a textbook*, she thought; *I am a diagram of the Poincaré disk.*

She saw then specks whirling gently in the air before her. Further ahead, more white specks littered the ground.

Birds? How lovely that would be. Alice had seen a beach once just before dawn, while all the seagulls were still asleep. She had always imagined that seagulls slept in nests; she did not know they also slept on the beach, heads tucked into their downy backs, little white lumps dotting the sandbar. She drew closer, and was disappointed to find those white things were not birds but scraps of paper. She reached out and picked one up. Strange, after all these immaterial shades, to touch something so incredibly human and material. It was modern paper, too. Smooth, bright stuff, with none of the ink bleeding or rough textures that dated older papers. These were not the detritus of Elspeth's collection, old unwanted things scrounged from the living. This was fresh stationery, sourced from Hell.

The page Alice held was blank. Others, however, seemed covered in lines. She chased another paper in the wind, snatched it, and held it up to her face. The handwriting was so looping and messy she could hardly make out what it said. Really the only legible fragment was what appeared to be a table of contents.

*Part One—My Upbringing*
*Part Two—My Pathology*
*Part Three—My Unfortunate and Inevitable Criminality*

Why, thought Alice, these were rough drafts of a dissertation. They obeyed the structure of a dissertation precisely—the flow of chapters, the slow development of arguments over three clearly delineated sections. There were footnotes, appendices, and even a dramatic conclusion, with stakes and implications for the field: "Why I Therefore Deserve Redemption, and a Ride Across the Lethe."

She skimmed one page of the section titled "Part One—My Upbringing." Her eyes fell on several footnotes professing that the author's family was of little means, and so he had no choice but to run in the streets and fall in with the bad sort rather than growing up pursuing virtuous hobbies like playing the violin. His father had beat him, and this instilled in him a hatred of the world. His mother turned a blind eye, and his sisters mocked him, and his German nanny often sent him to bed without his supper, and this instilled in him a fierce hatred of the other sex.

Alice flipped to the section labeled "Part Three—My Unfortunate Criminality."

*I did not mean to do what I did*, stated the author, and then went on to describe his violent crime. There Alice saw quite a lot of passive constructions. *My heart was seized with rage. My hand was possessed of a knife.*

She let the page drift away and plucked another out of the air. This one was written in a different handwriting, and seemed preoccupied with the many reasons why women, in fact, enjoyed being raped. She plucked yet another page. Murder of the elderly is a social necessity, it argued. They are a drain on resources and annoying besides.

Not the work of a single madman, then. For whatever reason Lower Hell was full of authors justifying their sins, and from the looks of it, producing many failed drafts. Alice wondered who this was written for, and who was reading, and which divine reader was deeming these dissertations unworthy of a pass. What would that reader make of her excuses? What excuses could she possibly make?

SHE CONTINUED ON UNTIL THE SUN fell again, and then she sat down and made her little camp. She nibbled a bit of Lembas Bread. She had left only one morsel the length of her index finger, which made eight pinches she could spread over eight days. She chugged from the Perpetual Flask until her stomach hurt, which was the second-best thing to being full. No matter how much she drank, however, her tongue still felt like sandpaper. Yet the rest of her felt deliciously light, a feeling she remembered well from lab days; the days she hadn't eaten, and was deliberately not eating anymore, just to push the boundaries of how little she needed it. She knew not to trust that lightness. It was always the prelude to the crash.

She wished she could find any sort of shelter. The tower was long behind her, and all that lay before her was open terrain. There were not even boulders against which she might curl. The best she could do was throw her jacket over her head and take refuge in an ostrich's logic—maybe if she couldn't see them, they couldn't see her. She pulled her legs beneath her and wrapped her hands around her head.

Something snuffled against her side. She cracked her eyes open.

Archimedes was carefully arranging himself in a ball inside her shadow. His fur was scarred and matted; a trickle of dried blood had hardened against his face. Alice blinked several times, hoping she had not hallucinated his presence; but every time she looked, the cat was still there. She reached with a palm to stroke his side, though stopped when the cat flinched from her touch.

"Did they get you too?"

Archimedes mewed. His right eye seemed unable to open. His left met her gaze, a hard green glint.

"Looks like you gave them hell, though."

Archimedes sniffed.

"Made out better than we did, anyway." She tried again to stroke him, though this time she made sure first he knew where her hand was. This time he let her, pressing the top of his head into her palm. "Good for you."

She pulled herself to a sitting position and fished some Lembas Bread from the rucksack. The cat watched, unmoving, as she arranged it on a bit of wrapping before him. "Go on," she said.

He stretched his head forth to nibble.

"I thought cats were obligate carnivores," said Alice.

Archimedes wriggled his bum, which seemed to be cat-speak for *I do what I want*.

"What's happened?" Alice asked. "Where's Elspeth?"

Archimedes did not answer.

"Maybe we can look out for one another," said Alice. "Keep watch, and all that."

Archimedes made no indication he'd heard her.

"Please stay," said Alice. "I don't—I can't make it all alone."

Archimedes stretched forward and rested his head between his front legs. His rump settled unhelpfully atop the hilt of her knife. Then his right eye closed.

*How stupid*, Alice thought, *pleading for help from a cat.*

But it was still a comfort, watching that matted, bloodstreaked flank rise and fall. Archimedes made a little wheezing noise every time he breathed in. The whole of his little rib cage trembled with the effort, but this did not disturb his slumber. He did not seem in any hurry to abandon her. Alice supposed life did survive down here after all; kicking and biting and snarling its way through. The indomitable will to live. She lay down next to the cat, curling her own torso around him like a fortress, and wondered where she might find that in herself.

## CHAPTER TWENTY-SIX

Alice slept. She dreamed, and lost herself in the specificity of memory: a spoon clinking against a teacup, driblets spilling out the sides that deepened to blood-red; the teacup became a bladder pouch, and the spoon a knife of bone. Helen Murray's voice; white teeth, lipstick too bright, smeared over dry skin. What do you want, Alice? Did you think you were the first? Alice in a graveyard, dirt beneath her nails; a shovel in her hands, an ache in her back. Professor Grimes, or at least the pieces she'd found of him; an eye, a lip, a fragment of a nose; all the little pieces on a sheet of wax paper, lined up against a poor pencil sketch; and a nail through his forehead, just to keep it all in place; all the scribbled recordings of the Thessalian witch. The living face imposed over the revived pieces. Those shredded lips moved. Good morning, he said.

Alice awoke.

A Shade knelt over her; all silvery smoke, his face very close to her own. She jolted upright.

They regarded each other. The Shade had such a slippery face, features lapsing and shifting, as if he couldn't decide himself what he looked like. If Alice had been pressed to describe him, the best analogy she could have come up with was a grayscale mugshot. Nondescript, fugitive. He looked at her with what Alice could only think of as a wide-eyed hunger, not destructive, but longing, as if he wanted to take her in with all of his senses. The look of her, the smell of her.

Still—and this was her foggy, starved head thinking—he didn't *seem* dangerous. At least he was not warped with that singular meanness of the Shades in Greed, or the suffocating howl of Wrath. He seemed more human than any of them, more in control of his appetites anyhow. If this Shade was going to hurt her, she supposed he would have done it while she was asleep, and for this reason she sat still where she was.

"Who are you?"

"I'm Alice," she whispered. "Alice Law."

"You're one of the living." His voice was like gravel, like earth shifting.

She didn't see the point in pretending. "Yes."

His eyes flickered up and down the chalk stains on her sweater. "You're a magician."

"Yes."

He burst into laughter.

"Heavens," he said. "I have been waiting, and waiting, and now here you are."

This Alice found vaguely threatening. She pulled herself to her feet, and immediately regretted it; a wave of vertigo hit and she swayed, her vision pulsing black.

The Shade put his hands up. "I won't hurt you."

"What do you want?"

"Only to speak." The Shade veered forward, until once again he was inches away. He seemed to have no conception of personal boundaries. No matter how she shifted his face loomed close to hers, as if he were about to lick or kiss her. "But you, of the living—what are you doing here, all alone in Hell?"

What indeed was she doing? Still she had no answer, and she did not think this Shade needed to hear of her regrets. "I'm looking for someone."

"Where might that someone be?"

"I don't know." She sighed. "I've searched Upper Hell. I have wandered Wrath, Cruelty, Violence, and Tyranny. I never found him, and I have reason to suspect his sins were not so light."

"You think he is in Dis."

"I—yes, that's right." Alice had been certain the city was real; all the reliable archives agreed so; but it startled her to hear its name confirmed from the mouth of the dead. So it was there, so it was waiting. "He must be."

"And you need to find the gates."

*I have a guide*, Alice wished to say, but she saw now Archimedes had absconded; she was again on her own. "I suppose."

"Come on, then." The Shade nodded toward the horizon. "I'll show you. Safe passage."

"What for?"

"What do you mean, *what for?*"

"I don't mean to offend." Alice thought of George Edward Moore, mad for a chum. She thought of the Weaver Girl's girlish laughter. She thought of Elspeth, righteous and vengeful. "Only we—I haven't had a wonderful time here. And we are in Lower Hell. Everyone wants something."

Again the Shade rumbled with laughter. He turned his eyes back on her, and this time they became the most solid things about him; deep stone, hollows of time. "A story for a song," he said. "That's all. You want to know of Dis. I want to know of life."

SO HERE SHE WAS IN THE deepest circles of Hell on a brisk stroll with a Shade whose sins she did not know.

Alice couldn't determine if she was very lucky or very foolish. At least this Shade—he introduced himself as John Gradus, which seemed an obvious lie—did not pretend to be her friend. His desires were quite clear. He badgered her for information on the world as she knew it. He was not at all interested in political or historical developments. She tried to tell him about the Soviet Union, and he waved a hand in impatience. Instead he wanted accounts of what brands of chalk were now in vogue ("Shropley's? They haven't gone bankrupt?"), what kinds of foods were then served at dining halls ("Still the same mashed potatoes? Does the Yorkshire pudding still taste like cardboard?"), and how girls' fashion evolved on campus (Alice felt a bit icky describing this one, but Gradus seemed satisfied with a mumbled answer about skirts and stockings. How short? She didn't recall. Above the knees? Well, sometimes. Not in college, but sometimes.) She didn't mind the interrogations. Here her memory came in handy, and she needed only close her eyes, summon photographs to her mind, and recount the details as they walked.

"The London skyline?"

"There's been a lot of new construction. They've got this big ugly thing, the NatWest tower, sticks straight into the air like a blunt."

"The music?"

She recalled the window of a record store and told him all the names she had seen there. "Judas Priest. Soup Dragons. Iron Maiden. Talking Heads."

"What kind of music is that?"

"Sort of like . . . indie punk, rock, that kind of thing? As in, the opposite of Dusty Springfield?"

She could not tell if these names made any sense to John Gradus. He asked, "Do you like them?"

"They're a little loud," she said. "But I'm not very adventurous. I just like the Beatles. And Bach."

"Pretentious," he said. "The last meal you had?"

"Lembas Bread."

"No, I mean before."

"Oh." Alice rifled through her mind. "Um. Tea and a toastie."

"What kind?"

"Cheese. Cheddar, I think."

"Warmed up?"

"No, cold." She saw the plastic wrapping in her mind, the generic logo. Late-night offerings from a buttery about to close. "It didn't taste very good."

"A cold toastie," he muttered. "All the time in the world, and a cold, congealed toastie."

He hungered for the tangible, the material. He became resentful when he felt she had wasted her time above. Most of all he was irritated about missed gastronomic opportunities. He seemed unable to understand why Alice did not eat three-course, gourmet meals every day. The answer "I wasn't hungry" made no sense to him. He got such a beady, famished look while Alice spoke that sometimes she felt uneasy; she felt he was siphoning something from her, though she couldn't put her finger on what. Living force, it felt like. Perhaps when they were done he would be close to alive, and she would be a rumbling mass of gray. Disturbing as this was, it was this naked exploitation that, in turn, let her take him at his word. It could be this easy. It could be the case he truly was taking her to the gates of Dis.

She glanced sideways at him as they walked, trying to make out the face of her guide. Her own Virgil. She wondered if she could recognize him, if his story was one of the many rumors that haunted the academy. Was he the demonologist who fed his infant daughter to Azazel? The cryptologist who sent his students into Faerie without a lifeline?

Unfortunately Gradus had not put nearly as much effort into maintaining a solid form as Elspeth. If she focused too hard on his eyes, or on his build, his features slipped and morphed as if they could not decide what they used to be. Strangely he took the clearest shape when she glimpsed him out of the corner of her eye, when her imagination could supply the rest. A straight-backed and bespectacled man, the sort who might carry a briefcase, or who might offer you an umbrella when it rained. A man utterly forgettable. You saw him on the train, or in the university library, or at the bookstore. And then he walked out of your life and you forgot all about him; for shapes like him only existed to fill in the background of your own richer world. Gradus was a man completely without specificity, and Alice suspected he had worked very hard to make this so.

She tried to place him at least geographically or temporally, because then she could at least rack her memory for mention of any horrendous crimes, say, at Yale in the sixties, but Gradus had been so long in the underworld that he made no references to place himself. Sometimes she thought she detected vague Nordic undertones in his speech, but otherwise he had that mysterious mid-Atlantic accent that could belong to a Brit who had spent too much time among Americans, or an American who had spent too much time in England. He was not forthcoming. She tried once simply asking where he was from, and all he said was, "I'd like to see you guess." If anything he seemed to take delight in messing with her. He would make references to Roosevelt and Churchill, then insinuate he'd personally known Copernicus.

Once a suspicion struck her, and she asked quickly, so as to catch him off guard, "Jacob?"

Professor Grimes had always liked his little tests.

But John Gradus only hmmed and asked, "What's that?"

No, he couldn't be Professor Grimes. Professor Grimes hardly cared so much about the world outside his office. He would never have asked her about Talking Heads. Fashions changed; Professor Grimes stayed the same. He lived in a castle in the clouds. All that mattered was his ideas, and how far they could take him.

AT LEAST JOHN GRADUS GAVE AS well as he got, so long as she did not inquire much about personal identity. On the topic of Hell he was very forthcoming, if not always helpful. Most of what he said left her with a million more questions. She asked him what those pieces of writing were, and he explained, "Why, dissertations, of course. That much should be obvious."

"Dissertations about what?"

"Whatever we're in for."

"Does everyone write them?"

"We all must write them."

"Who reads them?"

"Whoever is in charge. The Furies. Lord Yama himself. Who knows? I've yet to witness anyone read them, mind, but then it's a rare dissertation that passes muster. They say to write until you've done your best work, and when you've done your best work, the ships will come to bring you across the Lethe."

"What's the point of them?"

"Entertainment, I'm sure. I certainly enjoy reading others' drafts. I came upon a whole stack subtitled *My Lolita* the other day. Now, that one was really fun!"

"I mean, what makes a good dissertation?"

"Bugger if I know. That's the whole puzzle, isn't it?"

She couldn't tell if he was being flippant on purpose or if he truly did not know. "Is that how you're being punished, then? You don't get out until you've thoroughly understood your own crime?"

"Some think that."

"Then how do you pass?"

This made Gradus hem and haw. After a pause he said, "The only thing anyone knows for sure is that they say you have to tell the truth. That's all."

"Is it very hard to tell the truth?"

"It must be. Never seen anyone get out."

"It must drive them crazy," Alice mused. She knew her fair share of dissertating students. At Cambridge it seemed the standard for a good dissertation was asymptotic. The closer you got, the more obvious it became that you would never hit the limit. Eventually what decided things were the restrictions of time— you turned work in on the deadline, perfect or not. But there were no deadlines in Hell. You had an eternity for mistakes. "I bet it's agonizing."

"Probably," said Gradus. "I don't try."

"Why not?"

"No more questions," he said. "Our deal is that you entertain me."

"Oh, fine."

"What about this man you're looking for? What's he dissertating on?"

"Oh—well, I don't really know." Alice paused a moment. What *was* the worst sin Professor Grimes had ever committed? When she put her mind to it, she couldn't come up with anything but the vaguest descriptors, and none of them rang true. He stole (but for good reason). He was cruel (with good purpose, to those who deserved it). "We both had our theories, but I don't think there's any way to know."

Gradus's voice sharpened, a hook finding purchase. "You both?"

"Oh," said Alice.

Gradus's footsteps slowed. His essence billowed out like a pleased, squatting cat. "Now, this is interesting."

Her pain delighted him. He kept rubbing his smoky hands together, like a child in glee over a bedtime story. *Then what?* He kept asking this. *Then what? Then what?* Like a child demanding more sweets, relishing all the droplets of living affect he could wring from her. She told him about the Weaver Girl but kept vague about Elspeth; she described the bog in Wrath, and the Escher trap, the cuckoo clock, Peter's sacrifice. The screech of metal. The Kripkes' delight.

"Hold on." Gradus stopped walking then. His aura changed. The swishy, indifferent whirl of gray stilled to something human—a chill Alice recognized well. The clammy chill of fear. "The Kripkes are after you?"

"Why would you be afraid of the Kripkes?"

"They are fiends," said Gradus. "They are the worst things to haunt this land."

"But you're already dead, you—" But then Alice remembered Elspeth's words. *I've seen the Kripkes murder a soul.* "Well. I suppose we'd better walk faster."

"But now this is *exciting*!" Gradus spread his hands, palms open. "A tragedy, a revenge story, a rescue, a race against time. Will you escape the Kripkes? Or will they hunt you down, before you can finish your fallen comrade's quest?"

"I suppose."

"What do you mean, you *suppose*?"

"I mean, that sounds like a fine script." Alice felt very tired. "I suppose I'll follow it."

"What do you mean, you'll *follow* it?" Somehow she had

agitated Gradus. His coat started whipping around both their heels, as if he could encircle her in a vortex of his irritation. "Aren't you upset?" he demanded. "Aren't you *devastated*?"

"Sure, Gradus."

"You sound as if you don't even know what you're doing here."

"That's just it." His frustration was exhausting. She wanted to swat him away like a fly. "I *don't* know. I'm just tired."

"But don't you care about anything?"

"I suppose I should."

How could she explain to him this numbness? It wasn't that Alice didn't care, it was that she had cared so much, and a thread had snapped. Some fundamental capacity was broken. She felt hurled out of the world of meaning, feeling, attachment. She couldn't bleed anymore. She was drained already. Scripts were all she had now, and they were enough to keep her walking, but not enough for her heart to start beating.

"But you're *alive*," said Gradus, as if this were the answer to everything.

"Against all my desires. Yes."

Gradus said nothing. She walked and waited, hoping he would change the subject, but he remained silent. She sensed she had upset him, but how, she could not say. Gradus had not seemed the sensitive type. Until now she'd been comfortable in their callous rapport. At one point she had insinuated he was Jack the Ripper, and he had only laughed.

But he asked no more questions. For the rest of the morning they walked in silence. Once or twice he muttered to himself, but she could not make out what he said. She sensed only his resentment, a bitter and hostile wave, as abrupt as it was confusing. And Alice, well accustomed to placating volatile men, knew only to await her punishment.

"SO." GRADUS SPOKE AT LAST. "THERE it is."

For the past hour they had climbed up a steep and rocky hill. Alice was nearly bent over with exhaustion, hands over her knees. Her eyes had rarely left the ground in front of her. Now she lifted her head, straightened up, and gasped.

There lay the city of Dis. It was so much more marvelous than she had ever imagined: a gleaming white castle, three rings thronged at the bottom by snaking inlets of water that churned against its foundations, black waves smashing so furiously against stone, bone, brick, that Alice could hear the distant roar where she stood.

She had read much literature about Dis. The Land of the Damned. The Doleful City. For Virgil's *Aeneid*, Dis was the name for all of Hell itself, and, within its realm, a fortress ringed by three walls, surrounded by a river of fire. For Dante, Dis was only the city for the sixth through ninth circles of Hell, a great fortress in a land littered with broken sepulchers. Others said the city of Dis and Pandemonium were one and the same; the realm of Lucifer and the demons. They said Dis was a foul and evil place, forsaken by God.

No one had prepared her for the city's beauty.

Dante mentioned only that the city had high walls. He did not describe how those walls were the perfect mirror image of the sacred places its inhabitants had scorned; how Dis's architecture was a clear rebuke to the Vatican. No; in truth, it put the Vatican to shame. Michelangelo and Raphael had had only one lifetime to praise their God, but the inhabitants of Dis had eons. Dis was the extremes of human perfection. Dis was faultless marble, balustrades and domes, tiled courtyards lined with columns. Borges had written that the city was horrific, so horrific that the mere fact of its existence polluted the past and future, and compromised the stars; but had Alice and Borges witnessed the same city? Where Borges had found a perversion, Alice found a miracle. Dis was a millennium of effort, a haven constructed by those without salvation. Alice could see so clearly what it was trying to be, and what it could never be. But even in that fundamental lack there was something lovely, transcendent, a testament to human will. The city of Dis was defiant to the idea of an afterworld itself. They had left the campus behind now; this was a temple. *Damn us*, it said, *and we will make Hell shine.*

Gradus's voice had a funny lilt to it. "Suppose your man's in there."

Alice felt a prickle across her skin. "Is it dangerous?"

"Hardly," said Gradus. "Those in Dis are no threat to you. You'll see. They are very particular sinners."

"What do you mean? Who's in there?"

"Traitors. Oath-breakers. Those who made a promise and failed to keep it."

This answer disappointed her. She had always assumed Dante was exaggerating. "That doesn't seem so bad."

"Doesn't it?"

"Well, I mean, everyone breaks promises."

"There are trivial promises," agreed Gradus. "And then there are declarations. Promises that say, *This is what you mean to me, and this is what I owe to you*. The kinds of promises a husband makes to a wife. That which a parent makes to a child. That which a teacher makes to a student."

A chill ran over Alice's spine.

Staring at Dis, she felt as if a shard of ice were pressing against her bosom. That beauty took on a vicious gleam. She sensed its inner sin—a biting, evil thing; that force that poisoned bonds, turned friend against friend and kin against kin. She could only describe that feeling as a violation; the sharpest, severest pain, that which pierced in her inner depths where she felt most safe.

"So what did you do, Gradus?" she asked. "Who did you betray?"

Some part of her wanted to get back at him, though she couldn't say for what. His silence? His sudden coldness? She felt judged and shamed by him, and now that he was speaking again, she wanted to make him hurt. Anyhow, he'd been so callous with his own questions, and she felt she could now be callous in return.

"You didn't ask that," said Gradus.

"Yes I did. What did you do? Why aren't you writing?"

"Never ask that."

*Come on*, she nearly said, but realized he was serious. There was no laughter in his face.

"I am warning you, Alice Law." Gradus's eyes were stone. *He can't be from this century*, Alice thought suddenly, *no one from this century has such time-deadened eyes. He has been here for lifetimes.* "You may take confessions if freely offered. That is permitted. But if you wish to survive, remember this one rule about Dis. Never ask."

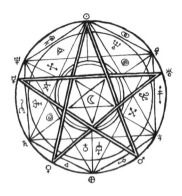

## CHAPTER TWENTY-SEVEN

A small, fidgety Shade guarded the pale doors of Dis. He watched them approach with his chest puffed out; one hand on his hip, one hand clutching a black spear with a carved stone tip. He slammed this spear thrice on the marble as they ascended. "Who dares enter the Great City of the Damned?"

"Bugger off, Parmenides," said Gradus. "It's me."

Parmenides squinted at Alice. "Then who's this?"

"She's new," said Gradus.

"Ooh hoo *hoo*!" Parmenides's chuckle scaled up and down several octaves. He leered at Alice. "What are you in for, dear?"

"Don't answer." Gradus pushed his way past Parmenides. The doors rumbled open at his touch.

"Murder?" asked Parmenides. "Poisoning? Did you touch a child?"

Gradus waved a hand. "Come along, Alice."

Alice scurried behind him.

"Trade you a story for a story," Parmenides called behind them. Alice was afraid he would follow them through, but he only stood on the threshold, brandishing his spear as the doors screeched against the marble floor. "You know where to find me."

The doors thudded shut.

Inside was darkness, cool and silent. Gradus drifted down a hall to the right. Alice followed. She heard a crescendoing hubbub of voices, just before Gradus opened a door and they spilled out into a courtyard, open space enclosed by four walls that reminded Alice of abbey cloisters. Nothing green grew, but the sculptural arrangement of rocks, and the floral mosaic patterns across the tile, suggested a meticulous attempt at upkeep. The effect was surprisingly pleasant. A tall, twisted white tree stood at its center, and Alice could not tell if it was dead or carved from stone. Under its branches, clumped in groups of three or four, milled several dozen murmuring Shades.

"Think your professor's in here?" Gradus asked.

Alice couldn't be sure. The problem was there were too many Shades who looked like Professor Grimes in this courtyard. She had not expected to end up in a courtyard so full of middle-aged men. Half of them wore glasses, and all were draped in some version of the dark Oxbridge robe.

"Go on!"

"That's right, go on!"

Quite a lot of the Shades were clustered in a huddle in the far corner of the courtyard. They were egging on one Shade at the wall, who stood with one hand grasping a thick stack of bound pages, the other resting on what looked like the handle of a library book-drop drawer embedded in the wall. He kept pulling it open, shuddering as if in panic, and letting it slide closed. Each time he did, the Shades booed in chorus.

"Let it drop," they cried. "Let it drop!"

"Suppose it's not ready," said the Shade at the wall.

"Not this again."

"It's been decades."

"If not now, when?"

"All right," said the Shade. "All right."

He squeezed his eyes shut—and looked rather silly as he did so, like a child pinching his nose before jumping into a pool—and slid his dissertation into the drawer. He let go and flinched back. The drawer slammed shut with a resounding metal *twang*. Everyone glared expectantly at the drawer, but nothing happened. Eventually there was a lukewarm smatter of applause. The Shades continued watching the drawer for a few moments and then dispersed again into their cliques, murmuring in disappointment.

"What happened?" Alice asked.

"Someone's just submitted a dissertation," said Gradus.

"Where's that drawer lead?"

"No one knows. Only whatever goes in that slot can never be retrieved."

"So when will they get their marks?"

"Marks." Gradus chuckled. "Imagine, marks. No, they don't tell you anything unless you've passed. We don't get revisions. We receive no feedback whatsoever. We just wait in anticipation forever and ever, until hope turns to panic to disappointment. If you hear nothing, then you must assume you've failed. Only there's never confirmation, and timelines here mean nothing, and so it's up to you when to extinguish your own hope."

Under the tree, several Shades bickered over the same question.

"I'm *telling* you, the Furies aren't reading them."

"Well if not the Furies, then who?"

"You must be new here," scoffed one Shade, and this roused chuckles around the courtyard. "It's the victims, see, we've got to wait for the victims to die, and then *they* decide if it's sufficient—"

"But that doesn't make any sense. Why would the victims hang around?"

"What did Socrates say? *Their calls are followed by supplication, as they beg their victims to permit their exit from their river . . .*"

"Socrates was put to death for being annoying, Socrates's opinion doesn't count for anything."

"Anyhow, who cares about the victims' opinions? What makes them such moral experts?"

"Right, suppose two robbers shoot each other in the head at the same moment."

"Come on, that's not what happened to you."

"Point-blank and the other guy in bed, is more like it was—"

"But *suppose*," insisted the Shade who'd first leveled the objection. "Suppose two robbers shoot each other, and they're both victims and perpetrators, and no one has the moral high ground. Who's reading then? Whose forgiveness matters? Who gets to decide?"

There was a hubbub of voices as Shades descended to weigh in on moral agency, forgiveness, and whether you could still be wronged if you did something wrong first. This seemed an old topic in the courtyard, something controversial and divisive and somehow such a familiar argument that all sides had long rehearsed their positions. Someone shouted about Jesus and unconditional love, and the whole forum groaned.

The Shade who had submitted his dissertation stood hunched and alone at the wall, looking forlorn. Every now and then he traced a finger across the drawer handle, as if he could will it to respond.

"Come on." Gradus urged Alice toward an exit across the courtyard. "We'll try the Writing Bazaar first. Then the workshops."

ALICE THOUGHT PERHAPS GRADUS MEANT "WRITING Bazaar" in the sense that *Harper's Bazaar* meant "bazaar," which is to say a metaphorical marketplace of ideas. She expected a conference, perhaps, or a shelf of print journals. She did not anticipate a bazaar in the fantastic Oriental sense: a chaotic marketplace, stalls and stalls in rows where hawkers yelled their goods and Shades drifted through the rows, buying and bartering. After the stretching silence of the desert this was all quite overwhelming, and Alice nearly tripped over a Shade squatting by the gate. The Shade squawked and fell back, toppling stacks of yellowed paper behind her.

"I'm sorry," gasped Alice. "I didn't see you—"

The Shade muttered something Alice could not make out. Though she did not seem to be speaking to Alice. Rather, she whispered something fiercely at the sheet of paper she clutched in her hands. Alice realized then that the Shade was reading each page out loud at a crawling pace, stopping every so often to mutter questions about prepositional phrases and object pronouns. She had beside her a copy of Strunk and White's *The Elements of Style*, which Alice had not seen since grade school.

"She's fine," said Gradus, tugging her along. "She's just doing copyedits."

"Copyedits?"

"Lots of Shades believe they can fail for the slightest spelling error. They spend decades combing over their manuscripts before they feel comfortable submitting."

Alice thought of Professor Grimes, whose eyes slid so quickly over student papers she wondered sometimes if he registered their content at all. "Do the judges even care?"

"No one knows," said Gradus. "They never explain why they reject dissertations. All we can do is cover our bases as best we can."

Behind them, the Shade was howling and smacking herself against the temple.

"Stupid," she cried. "Stupid, stupid—it's *two* spaces after each period! Oh, it's *all* got to be redone!"

The next stall was completely taken over by pyramids of used books. The collection was enormous. Elspeth's library was paltry in comparison. All the books were battered and stained to various degrees. Some missed covers; some missed entire chunks in the middle; some appeared to have been dredged from the bottom of the river, dried, and painstakingly rebound with needle and thread. Still they looked and smelled enticing, for all books, like wine, had a readerly aroma that ripened with age, which was why bookstores and libraries smelled so good. Alice's fingers itched with the familiar urge to flip through the volumes. The hawker perked up when he sensed her attention. He passed immaterial through the piles and stopped right before her. "De Quincey?" He held up two volumes, one thick and one slim. "De Sade?"

"None today, thank you," said Gradus.

"You sure? De Sade's very fun. If not for remorse, then for titillation."

Gradus held up a hand as he moved past. "We're fine."

"Rousseau, then," called the hawker. "You'll like that."

"What's he mean?" asked Alice.

"He sells confessional texts," said Gradus. "Saint Augustine, Saint Patrick, and so on. Lots of folks here think that's the template."

"So they read for inspiration?"

"Sure. Or to cheat. People like to copy down all the good bits—the part about souls being rendered in two, the fires of guilt burning you up from the inside, blah blah blah."

"Or divine salvation," called the hawker. "New translated edition of *Crime and Punishment* here now, brand-new, excavated in mint condition from a Derbyshire tomb—"

"No, thank you." Gradus quickened his pace.

"Does that work?" Alice hurried behind him. "Copying down confessions?"

"Oh, never. They always know when it's not original work. They take plagiarism quite seriously here—somehow folks always forget. A while ago someone copied two sentences from the *Confessions of an English Opium-Eater* and they wouldn't let him touch paper again for fifty years."

"Gosh," Alice muttered. "Who wouldn't do their own work in *Hell*?"

"Everyone," said Gradus. "Haven't you ever had writer's block?"

"Well of course, but—"

"Did someone mention writer's block?"

Alice ran smack into what felt like a great, meaty wall. She stumbled black. Before her stood a veritable centaur; a man's head and muscly torso over the indigo-blue bottom of a horse. She would have found him very handsome, in the rugged mountain-man fashion, were his mouth not split in a massive, toothy grin that indicated he wanted to eat her.

"I'm sorry—"

"No apologies necessary." He dipped his head and forelegs in a low bow that should not have looked so elegant as it did. His head ended up somewhere near Alice's crotch, which was both startling and titillating. "I am Nessus." His voice was wonderfully smooth. "Lower chthonic deity, itinerant writing tutor of Dis, at your service."

"Bugger off," said Gradus.

Nessus rose and grasped Alice's hands. "Are you new to the city, love? First time in the bazaar?"

"Yes, I—"

"Never fear!" He squeezed her hands tight. His skin was very warm. "I am here to offer any paper-writing services you need. Proposals, outlines, bibliographies, even entire dissertation chapters if you so desire. Rates are negotiable—"

"Leave her alone," said Gradus.

"Does that work?" asked Alice, intrigued.

"Of course it doesn't," said Gradus. "No one wants those phony essays."

"Our essays are the best on the market." Nessus continued to ignore Gradus. Indeed, every time Gradus spoke, Nessus only opened his mouth further, continuing on with his pitch at a deafening shout. "WE HAVE HELPED HUNDREDS OF SOULS PASS THEIR DISSERTATION DEFENSES AND FIND PASSAGE ACROSS THE LETHE ON LONG-AWAITED GOLDEN SHIPS—"

"It's a complete scam," said Gradus.

"OUR ESSAY WRITERS HAVE INTIMATE KNOWLEDGE OF THE WORKINGS OF THE UNDERWORLD. MANY HAVE WALKED THE SANDS OF DEATH SINCE THE BIRTH OF THE WORLD—"

"But you're all deities!" Alice exclaimed. "What can you possibly want for trade from humans?"

Nessus ceased his shouting, looked her up and down, and murmured close into her ear. "A human soul can be useful in more ways than one."

Alice did not quite understand what he meant, but she knew enough to jerk her hands away.

"Leave her alone." Gradus grasped Alice's arm and dragged her down the stalls. Nessus did not follow. When Alice glanced back over her shoulder he was in avid negotiations with another Shade, haggling over word counts and delivery times.

"Haven't you ever been in a market before?" Gradus demanded. "You keep your gaze forward, you never *respond*—"

"Sorry," Alice gasped. "It's just—there's so many—"

"The bazaar is built to distract," said Gradus. "This is Lord Yama's design. There's a million things to keep a soul from writing, all in the service of making you better at it. Remember that, Alice Law. Hell is a writers' market."

The bazaar seemed endless. Lost in the thick of it, Alice could not see any way out. Only Gradus seemed to know where they were going, ducking and weaving around hawkers with irritable indifference. They passed stalls of writing accoutrements and productivity cures—old typewriters, reams of paper, sand hourglasses ("DON'T PROCRASTINATE FOR ETERNITY!"), self-help books (*How to Write a Confession in Ten Days*, *Two Thousand Words a Day: The Augustinian Method*), and black quills advertised as bona fide vulture feathers ("SAY NO TO THE TYPEWRITER: WRITE IN ANALOG TO PROMPT YOUR CREATIVE MIND"). Alice couldn't quite understand what passed for currency in Dis—she saw Shades exchanging all sorts of trinkets, from buttons to bottle caps to what appeared to be human knucklebones—but the trade, evidently, was thriving.

The traffic thickened. They pushed their way forth and came upon a packed crowd gathered around a creature—a deity, Alice saw, a giant with an elephantine head, his skull studded with too many eyes. Two great horns extended from his temples, but Alice's eyes could not track where they ended. She could only describe those horn tips as ending many places at once, a cloud of probability. Indeed Alice found the deity himself hard to look at; his form kept shifting in space, so that the moment she thought she had fixed him in her vision, he was several inches to the left.

"Who—"

"Laplace's Demon," said Gradus.

"Laplace's Demon is real?"

"Oh, yes. He likes to wander the bazaar and talk people into thinking nothing is their fault. Sets them back decades in their progress. Come round this way, you'll get lost in the crush."

Alice followed him to the edge of the crowd. The demon's followers listened in rapturous excitement as he pronounced facts about their lives, explanations of their pathology. Someone's pet cat had died when they were ten. Someone had been spanked too hard by a babysitter. Someone was genetically predisposed to anger.

"How does he do that?"

"Well, he's a determinist," said Gradus. "So he thinks just because he knows everything about you, that frees you of all personal responsibility from everything you've ever done."

"How would that work?"

"Laplace's Demon has been observing the universe since its very beginning," said Gradus. "Or so he says. The first collision of atoms, the big bang, all that. He watched the first cells on Earth become sentient life. He watched as the atoms they were composed of interacted in new and exciting combinations to create generations. He knows, because of set natural laws of the universe, precisely how those atoms will interact in the future to form new combinations, and so on. He knows, when you are deciding between an apple and orange, what you will choose. He knows if someday you will betray your husband, or drown your child. He knows all, for every ill deed you have ever done was determined the day you were born. Life is a set course that you were born onto, a course you can never escape. You don't know that you are even following it."

"What if I choose different?"

"It doesn't matter," said Gradus. "He will have anticipated this too. He knows one day you will think of determinism and feel compelled to resist. And he knows you will choose what seems unpredictable for the sake of it. Laplace's Demon knows all."

"And that means no one can ever be responsible for anything." Alice had caught on now. "Which means there's no concept of guilt, or culpability . . . I mean, could it work? If you could explain all your sins as the product of forces outside your control?"

"Maybe. I don't know."

She huffed. "Don't you know *anything*?"

"I know everything there is to know about this place," said Gradus. "And I'm offering that knowledge freely, by the way, which is a better deal than you'd get elsewhere."

"Then how come you can't say how a dissertation passes?"

"*Because.*" Again Gradus's essence took on that frightening, deadened calque. Alice felt the weight of accumulation, of layers on layers of time. "I don't know how it's done. Because nobody knows how it's done. Because I have never once seen a passing dissertation in the entire time I have been in Hell. Because many of us think that the dissertation is a pointless exercise offered by sadistic deities to keep us distracted, because wouldn't that be so funny, wouldn't it be the best and cruelest joke to keep us running in circles around the bazaar forever. Because none of us in this wretched place have ever been given reason to hope."

"Oh," said Alice, in a very small voice. "I see."

Dis did not feel so impressive now. The bazaar's hustle was no longer amusing. Now the stalls and crowds struck her as a dreadful show; teeming and desperate, hamsters spinning circles in a pathetic ornate cage, all to avoid the only question that seemed to matter: *why did you sin?*

Could *she* write her own way out of Hell? Alice wondered. If she somehow died a natural death, if she ended up in Dis. Could she face down the blank white paper and tell the truth?

She knew what her great crime was. She had let Peter Murdoch die. She had killed Peter Murdoch.

Now, Alice knew from conversations in hall that the philosophers at Cambridge were greatly concerned with the difference between killing and letting die. Some argued that there was no distinction: that if you knew the cause of death and failed to stop it even if you were able, then that was morally tantamount to murder. Others disagreed. Letting die might be morally callous, they argued, but it entailed refusing to get involved in a situation, not bringing it about. If letting die was so evil, were we responsible for not doing anything about world poverty? About orphans starving continents away? So one might reasonably convince Alice that no, none of this was her fault. She didn't throw them off the *Neurath*, she didn't lay the Escher trap, and she didn't make Peter sacrifice himself. She'd simply failed to stop it all, and she couldn't be blamed for that.

But this reasoning didn't stand up to intuition. Alice knew also that in criminal defense, there was a type of argument called "but for." But for your actions, would this car have crashed? Would this child have drowned? But for Alice Law, would Peter Murdoch be dead? The answer was obviously no. Alice could draw a straight line from her own stupidity and selfishness to Peter's sacrifice. And she knew, if she ever died properly in the world above, if she ever escaped back to the world above, she would end up right back here atoning for the murder of Peter Murdoch's immortal soul. But if she was ready to admit this, if she laid it all down on paper, would that be sufficient? Was it enough to declare what she'd done and admit full responsibility for it? Certainly that was too easy, for if so there would not be so many frustrated souls in Dis. Certainly not all of these souls were deceiving themselves. Certainly, after decades in this pathetic din, one would prefer to tell the truth.

But that meant Hell demanded something more than a guilty plea. That the Furies, or whoever that mysterious *they* was, if they existed at all, expected a more profound acknowledgment of guilt. And whatever this was—whether because her mind would not admit it, or because it was out of the grasp of her understanding—Alice was not certain she could ever put it down on paper, or set it to words at all.

GRADUS LED HER OUT OF THE bazaar and into another series of hallways until he stopped before a plain, unmarked door. "The workshop," he said, and pushed it open. Inside was an unadorned room containing one long, oval table, at which sat a dozen or so Shades perched on metal folding chairs—very specifically, the kind of folding chairs with a gap just large enough to frustrate any hope of back support, and rusted metal bolts that threatened to splice you open whenever you tried to fold them up. The room was badly lit. The air smelled of cat piss.

A meeting was in progress. The Shades were hunched over a smattering of papers, debating something that had to do with "domestic violence" and "moral culpability."

Alice scanned their faces. All dour, focused expressions. Thick scowling brows; mouths pressed in thin lines of concentration. Half wore spectacles. The other details of their garb had faded, leaving plain dark robes, and this gave them a vaguely Victorian air. These Shades looked ready to expound on the phrenological markers of intelligence across races. If ever there was a room in Hell where Grimes belonged, thought Alice, it was here. But none of the faces matched.

"He's not here," she whispered to Gradus. "We should—"

The door slammed shut behind them. The meeting fell silent. The Shades looked up and stared.

"Ah, Professor Gradus." The Shade at the head of the table rose to his feet. A brass placard before him read, *Chairman*. "Haven't seen you in a while."

"Went on a retreat," said Gradus. "Needed to clear my head."

"Well, we are not giving you comments," pouted a Shade to the chairman's left. "You know the rules. You give critique to get critique, you can't just disappear for years and then expect us all to help—"

"That's fine," said Gradus. "I'm only here to observe."

"*Gradus*," Alice whispered again. But he ignored her.

"Who's she?" asked the chairman.

All eyes turned to Alice.

"New blood," said Gradus. "Only just arrived."

"I thought we said no newcomers," said the Shade to the chairman's left.

"She's still getting oriented," said Gradus. "Hasn't started writing yet. I thought you lot could share a bit of your wisdom. Show her how it's done."

"But this is a *serious* writing group," said the Shade. "We don't take novices, they're a waste of time."

"The rule was ten years at least," the chairman agreed.

"She's a Cambridge postgrad," said Gradus. "Analytic magick."

The word *Cambridge* was like a spell. Even here, prestige opened doors. The Shades looked round at each other. A few shrugged. The chairman grunted. "I suppose she can audit. On a trial basis. You may take a chair in the corner."

"Go on," Gradus told Alice. "Sit."

Alice did not understand what they were still doing here. "But he's not—"

Gradus nudged her forth. "The chairman invites you to sit."

Alice realized then she was not in control here.

She'd been a fool to trust Gradus. She could not fathom what he wanted; she should not have played along. She didn't understand what was happening now, but she did not like her chances in Dis alone, so she sat gingerly at the edge of her assigned chair and tried not to look too afraid. Gradus remained standing beside her, his essence billowing around her like a cage.

"Might we get back to Professor Bent's dissertation?" asked a monocled Shade. "If we're quite done with interruptions?"

"Yes, yes, of course." The chairman sat down. "Let us continue. Professor Brown, you were saying . . . ?"

Professor Brown tapped the pages before him. "I do find this a bit revisionary. The tone is—well, it's very combative, isn't it? And the rebuttals to women's liberation. Aren't they a bit extreme?"

"I object," said a Shade several seats down from Professor Brown. Alice presumed this was Professor Bent, author of said dissertation. He had a very long face, and a mouth startlingly far down from his nose, which seemed the natural result of a lifetime of stroking one's chin as Professor Bent did now. "It's—a bit contrarian, certainly, but it's all telling the truth."

"The truth is that all women are evil nags?"

"I'm sure *some* women are virtuous angels." Professor Bent sniffed. "I won't make sloppy generalizations. I only mean to say *this* woman, in her specific case, exemplified all the foibles of her sex. Not all women are jealous and aggravating and empty-headed. But *this* woman—"

"Yes, blah, blah, the Eve to your Adam, the source of all evil," another Shade interjected. "It's a boring interpretation, don't you think? You minimize your own agency and demonize your wife—"

"What am I supposed to do?" demanded Professor Bent. "All I've written is the truth, no more, no less. I cannot fabricate arguments just to please an audience who is interested only in feminist interpretations. I refuse. It would be bad scholarship."

"But this isn't at all a confession," said the monocled Shade. "This is just a manifesto."

"Well, I've nothing to confess."

"Oh, why do you think you're in *Hell* then, you idiot?"

"Now, now," said the chairman. "Let us remain professional."

"The concept of the confession is so Victorian," said Professor Bent. "Have you not read Foucault? *Science sexualis*. The confession is a repressive discursive form, through which no true knowledge can be produced. The confession is about hidden shame, guilt, extraction. But I will not be a prisoner on the rack, do you understand? I will not lie for freedom."

"I'm not sure the Furies have read Foucault," said the chairman. "You must consider your audience."

Professor Bent sniffed. "Well, if the gods are perfect and all-knowing, then they should be amenable to reason. The gods should understand this mode of dissertation is antiquated, and that we gain nothing from self-flagellation. The gods should wish us to break free of our repression—"

"Why do we speak of the gods at all?"

A woman Shade sat at the opposite end of the table, her chair pulled slightly back so that she was half-hidden behind her peers. She wore her dark hair tied tightly in a bun, and when she leaned forward, Alice saw she had a severe, foxlike face. She had put much more effort into distinguishing her clothes than her peers. She wore a high-necked black dress, her white collar starched very clean, each pleat of her skirt pressed with precision.

"Ah, Gertrude," said the chairman. "You wish to contribute? Speak up."

Gertrude scraped her chair back and stood. "My question is, who wants reincarnation anyhow?"

"Not this again," said Professor Brown. "Everyone wants rebirth, that's why we're here."

"Have you not read *The Republic*?" Gertrude demanded. "Know you not the myth of Er? Ajax becomes a lion. Odysseus becomes an ordinary citizen. But the wicked have no right to choose. The wicked suffer in the next life."

"We've been over this," said the chairman. "We have no evidence that karma affects rebirth—"

"Yes, you're right, all we have is a priori reason. But do you think our little punishments are enough? Do you really think, once our papers are polished and turned in, that the powers that be will see fit to reincarnate us as lords and ladies?"

"Now, we know there's no guarantee—" began the chairman.

"Who wants to be an earthworm?" Gertrude demanded. "Who wants to be a dung beetle? Or worse—to be born with human cognition but have no opportunity to exercise it. On balance human suffering vastly outweighs the pleasures of human life, and we were all just lucky enough to end up where we did in our past lives. But who among you could go from college housing to the streets?"

"It makes no difference to the reincarnated," said Professor Bent. "You would forget, you'd have no basis of comparison—"

"Not to mention forgetting!" Gertrude cried in triumph. "Why should we want our memories stripped clean? How is the Lethe different from death? Better to exist as we are, *here*, and *now*. We follow the example of the Morning Star. We make our own paradise in Hell—"

"All right, Milton," said Professor Mansfield.

"God has no hold on us," said Gertrude. "Morality is for the weak."

"All right, Raskolnikov," said Professor Bent.

"You may mock me all you like," said Gertrude. "But I believe Raskolnikov didn't take things far enough. His resolve wavers at the end. His mistake is that he falters, he gets paranoid, he lets the policeman get in his mind. But imagine if he held on to his convictions! Imagine if the idiot Sonya, and all her Christian moralizing, never entered the picture—yes, imagine if *guilt* never got in his way . . ."

"Yes, we know, we've all read Nietzsche, God is dead and so forth," said the chairman. "But unfortunately, *some* higher power decided we deserve some punishment, so here we are—"

"But it doesn't have to be that way!" Gertrude slammed her palms on the table. "Why do we accept the courts of Hell? Why are we so comfortable in our situation? Don't you see, if God is not already dead, then we must *kill God*. We must rebuild Hell to our own liking. We must make Dis our own paradise."

"Why is she here?" Professor Bent demanded to the chairman. "This has nothing to do with my dissertation."

"Impact has everything to do with a dissertation," said Gertrude. "Why put out a piece of work, if you don't know what you want it to accomplish?"

"We are here to discuss methodology," said the chairman. "Not metaphysics."

"Though it's not like this piece could pass," said the monocled Shade. "We haven't even gotten to the shaky autobiography—"

"Watch who you're calling shaky," said Professor Bent.

"You really think it was worth twelve pages discussing how your wife's family wouldn't pay for the wedding?"

"It's better than your effort last week," said Professor Bent. "All grotesque and gore—"

"Detail matters."

"Oh, sure, if you're writing *fiction*—"

It escalated so quickly. One moment Professor Bent and the monocled Shade were shouting over the table; the next they were wrestling atop it. Half the Shades stood to join the fray. The other half sat back, arms folded and scowling. Alice watched, mouth agape. She felt such a profound pity. They cared so much, they argued so viciously, but couldn't they see it didn't matter, didn't even remotely register in the cosmic span of things, and that this was the dumbest possible way to spend eternity?

"Are you happy?" Gradus looked pleased as a cat. "Is it what you'd hoped?"

But Alice couldn't imagine what victory he thought he'd gained.

"Look!" someone cried. "*Look!*"

ALL FACES TURNED TO THE WINDOW.

Lights appeared in the sky. To Alice's eye they looked like stars—constellations of winking bursts that seemed so remote at first but then drew closer and closer, until they approached and she saw they were not stars at all but flakes of ember. Fires sprang to life everywhere they landed. The hawkers rushed about with mats, trying to smother the flames. But they were too late, and Alice heard howls as whole stacks of paper went up in smoke. She saw the woman who had been doing copyedits running around in circles shrieking with her head ablaze, the Strunk and White clutched against her chest.

Chairs screeched as the Shades stood up. They jostled past Alice in their hurry to get out the door. She watched them run, baffled. Several moments later, she saw them from the window, running with arms windmilling toward the flame.

"Oh!" Alice rushed forward several steps, then stopped herself, unsure of what, if anything, she could do. "Oh—someone stop them!"

But she had misinterpreted their cries as expressions of anguish. These Shades were delighted. They ran to the fire the way children would dash barefoot into an ocean. They raced toward the bazaar not to rescue their peers, or salvage the supplies, but to join in the fun.

They caught flame as quick as shriveled leaves. Alice could not tear her eyes off those burning faces. Ever since childhood she had been so afraid of fire. She used to imagine burning at the stake as the most horrible way one could go. Bubbling fat, the transmutation of flesh to charcoal—it frightened her so. But the souls in Dis did not wither. Their flesh did not slough off their cheeks, even as it sizzled. Beneath the flames their skin remained smooth, untouched. Burning here was not permanent. The only thing manifest was the pain.

"Stop screaming," said Gradus.

Alice had not realized she was. She touched her neck; her throat was hoarse. Her hand trembled. "Oh, *why*—"

"We cannot produce fire for ourselves," said Gradus. "No one knows why, but it is the one thing Hell denies us. So we're very happy when it comes from the sky. Don't worry, it can't hurt them. It's only a memory."

A hubbub erupted near the shore. A great shape burst through the city walls, scattering its marble foundations. Some howling, rumbling thing, too huge to be comprehended all at once. Alice could only register its attributes in pieces. Heavy footsteps. A hulking gait. The beast had three heads. The Shades cried out as if one. "*Cerberus!*"

They surged forth. Alice could not understand why they were approaching the beast, and yet they stood with their hands outstretched, waving with abandon. She reached without thinking for Gradus, though her fingers met only cold air. "Aren't they scared?"

"Scared? Cerberus is the most exciting thing to happen down here." Gradus looked so pleased with himself. "We hope he will trample us. We beg him to maul us."

"*Why?*"

"Because it's *interesting*," said Gradus. "Pain is interesting, and you can bear anything as long as it's interesting."

"But how—"

"It's all just sensations in the end, Alice Law. Pain or pleasure, mirror images of each other. And both preferable to dead time. Time crawls here. You do anything to feel." He gave a start. "Oh! A direct hit!"

One of Cerberus's heads shot down and grasped a Shade around the waist. The crowd along the shore cheered as Cerberus lifted the Shade into the air. Viscera splattered everywhere. Cerberus's jaw moved, and dismembered pieces littered the sand. But he couldn't have done that, thought Alice; the Shades had to bisect themselves, they had to want this. A great cheer went up around the courtyard, and Shades surged forth to volunteer their bodies.

"Me next!"

"Me, Cerberus!"

"Me!"

Alice heard a high-pitched ringing in her head.

"My arm, Cerberus—rip it off!"

"My head—"

"My juicy guts!"

Was this the end point of existence? Alice could have wept with the ridiculousness of it. Now she understood Hell in full. She saw its intricate design; could understand that it was no random imitation of living rituals but a cruel mirror; that all its karmic reflection just was to show life's worthlessness to begin with. The point was not rehabilitation but a stripping down to form, to show that humans were blindly writhing worms, rooting about to feel anything at all. *Oh, God*, she thought frantically, *why did you create us, why foul the universe with our failing, why not rest after the fourth day, and be content with the silent stars . . .*

Only the Shade named Gertrude had not left the room. She stood still by the window, watching the proceeds with perfect calm. Alice felt a sort of horrified fascination with her, perhaps akin to the fascination schoolboys felt for their severe and pretty teachers.

"Pathetic, isn't it?" asked Gertrude. "The things they do for entertainment."

"You don't write," said Alice.

"Oh, no. I refuse."

Alice nodded to the shrieking bodies. "Then what makes you any different from them?"

"I don't see reincarnation as the answer," said Gertrude. "I see reincarnation as the escape. Escape for weaker wills who cannot face their new world with resolve, who cannot understand that *this is it, this is all we have*." Gertrude turned away from the window. Her harsh eyes met Alice's own, and a shiver ran up Alice's spine. "May I show you?"

"Leave her be," said Gradus. "No one's interested in your cult."

"We must all decide for ourselves, Gradus."

"What cult?" Alice asked.

"A fellowship," Gertrude clarified. "Come freely, leave freely."

"That isn't true."

"You left, did you not?"

"Alice," Gradus said urgently. "Trust me."

Alice tilted her head. "But why would I do that?"

Gertrude was a question mark. Meanwhile Gradus had brought her into Dis to mock and disturb her. She had no reason to trust either of them, but between them, Gertrude had not yet laughed at her despair.

Alice could have blamed her choice on reason then. Professor Grimes might be with Gertrude, indeed was probably with Gertrude. Certainly she would not lump him in with those screaming Shades. But it was impulse above all else; impulse and curiosity, to see the final refuge of sinners.

"Why, Gradus." Gertrude cocked her head, and her voice was a velvet threat. "Who is she to you?"

For a moment Alice feared Gradus might reveal she was not dead. But his face blanked. His grayness wrapped around him like a shawl, and he made no response.

Gertrude extended her hand to Alice. Alice reached for it, then hesitated. "Where are you taking me?"

Gertrude nodded to the wall. There was a wooden door Alice had not seen before. Gertrude pulled it open, revealing a tiny, spiraling set of stairs. Alice could not tell where they led, or how high they reached; only that the narrow stone steps curled into darkness.

"Into the Rebel Citadel," said Gertrude. "Into the way out."

## CHAPTER TWENTY-EIGHT

Gertrude glided, and Alice followed. During the Italy tour Alice had climbed the steps of the Duomo in Florence, a dreadful idea in the dead of summer, four hundred and sixty-three steps in suffocating heat that she counted one by one in her head, because nothing else in that dim, unventilated, claustrophobic spiral gave her any reason to continue. One woman suffered something resembling a heart attack halfway up, and the rest of them had to press themselves tight against the wall as she and her husband shuffled, gasping, back down. Once every hundred stairs there was a tiny window in the stone, and everyone pressed their face against the bars as they walked past, desperate for a breeze.

Alice could only assume the architect of Dis had been inspired by the Duomo. But the interstitial windows here afforded no cool air, only small rectangles of Hell's burnt-orange sky. Her legs burned; her lungs could not get enough air. She turned all her efforts on putting one foot in front of another, on ignoring how many there had been and how many there were to go. At last, just as she feared she might faint, they emerged into a courtyard.

For a moment Alice thought they had ascended into the living world, for what she saw here mirrored the splendor of Rome, of the Villa Borghese, of Palatine Hill. These were not ruins, not scattered artifacts fallen through the cracks between worlds, but coherent, elegant designs. Tiled footpaths arced around sculptures, gazebos, and burbling fountains. Alice breathed deep, and the air that filled her lungs was crisp, fresh, and sweet.

"Come along, my dear." Gertrude gestured for Alice to follow her up the hill. They reached a terrace lined by statues upon plinths. A dozen men and women, much larger than life size.

"The greatest among us," said Gertrude. "Our builders and dreamers. Magicians, architects, and poets among them. All finely attuned to beauty, and convinced that beauty could be torn away from the divine."

Alice tried to guess at the identities of these figures, but there were no names on the plinths, and the chiseled faces were strangely impersonal. They evoked ideals more than they did particular people. Uniform strong brows, eyes lifted upward, straight patrician noses. Mouths set in heroic, defiant frowns.

"Where are they now?" she asked.

"Still with us," said Gertrude. "This is the Rebel Citadel. We lose no one to death."

They walked across the terrace to an overhang. Alice leaned over the edge. She could see all of Dis below—the bazaar, the workshops, the milling interlocutors. The city was so much larger than she'd imagined. The bazaar—still burning, wrecked by Cerberus's rampage—seemed to be only one small pocket of many such marketplaces. From here she could see a whole teeming mass of Shades, running about the city like ants, all dedicated to the same pointless task. She stepped back. It felt good to escape above, free of the noise. If only she kept away from the edge, she could block the bazaar entirely from view. From this terrace, the rest of Dis might as well not exist.

"It's lovely here," she said.

"Isn't it?" Gertrude beckoned. "Come over round this way. The view is better here."

They turned a corner. Alice saw that they stood on not a mountaintop but a cliffside. Below churned the Lethe, black and merciless. Here it was more agitated than Alice had ever seen it, slamming furiously against the rocks below. Here more than anywhere else the Lethe seemed not a river but an ocean, a vast black expanse that surrounded them on all sides. She looked out to the horizon, wondering—but she saw nothing there. King Yama's domain remained out of sight.

"We built on the water's edge," said Gertrude. "The greatest rebuke."

Proudly she surveyed her domain. Alice followed her gaze, marveling at that complex silhouette, those towers reaching defiantly for the sky. At the highest peak overlooking the Lethe, where all patterns suggested there should have been a bell tower, was a jagged, incomplete edge.

"There was a quake," said Gertrude.

"A quake?"

"Every now and then the land rebels," said Gertrude. "The earth is rent apart. Chasms open beneath our feat. Lava spews from beneath and sloughs off our skin, encases us in rock. Those who fall below take eons to climb out, if ever they do."

"Oh," said Alice.

"Once there was a most terrible quake, and the bell tower fell." Gertrude shook her head. "Such a calamity. We watched it tumble down the rocks, ringing the whole time, and sink beneath the waves. Still sometimes we hear a low note, humming in our bones, and we know it is the bell ringing from beneath the Lethe, ringing still."

She said this with no sense of loss.

Alice could guess why. "There will be another bell. You will build another bell."

"Oh, yes," said Gertrude. "Everything ends up in Hell eventually. Everything finds its way to Dis. Souls go round and round. But all their *stuff*—that doesn't get a second life. In time we will scavenge enough to build a second world below. Not a replica. No one wants a replica of a flawed world. We are building something better."

For a moment Alice saw what Gertrude saw, looking over that skyline—a great city just becoming, to be filled out and completed over one millennium and then another. Gertrude spoke as one who had the time; whose existence was not counted in days but in eras; whose project could be measured in one long breath from the birth of the world to its end. Alice saw flashing in her mind all the outlines of cities that had come before the citadel. Rome, Jerusalem, Alexandria, Xi'an—all the great centers of the world, places the Rebel Citadel had outlasted. She tried to imagine Dis from that long view of time. Perhaps in time Dis would grow so large, so hospitable, that no souls would ever cross over. Why toil, when you could rest in peace?

Gertrude turned to the horizon. In the burning light, her profile was quite striking. Her right hand was lifted up to her chest, palm open in beneficence. Alice had gravely mistaken her for a heretic. Up here, Gertrude occupied more the role of a saint.

"Have you ever watched sand falling through an hourglass?" asked Gertrude. "Imagine it now, in your mind's eye. Pay attention to what happens at the bottom. Always the sand forms a little peak. A mountain, reaching. Then the weight becomes too great, and the sand collapses outward, and the bottom flattens again. Time doesn't build to a climax, you see. Only a little peak, always about to collapse. That is how time moves here in Dis. Tiny impulses forward, the illusion of a build. Then the cycle repeats, again and again, while all the time the bottom accumulates. One day we will reach the top. But it takes so very long."

She lifted her chin. "We will be here at the end. We will be here when the dying sun goes out. When the armies of Gog and Magog assemble to invade the saints of Heaven, when Fenrir swallows Odin whole, when Apep devours Ra and casts all in darkness, when the world turns upside down and its crust is cast into molten rock to be reborn anew, *we will be here*."

She spoke with such conviction.

Alice wondered what it took to sustain that hope across years, across centuries. Then she wondered where to locate the flaw in Gertrude's thinking. Was there one at all? For in a world where none of the rules were stable, why *not* believe in an apocalyptic reversal of the moral order? Why was that so unlikely? Wasn't there a perverse beauty to it all? What conviction—to do wrong and stand by it—how much bolder it was than to do right simply because one was afraid. Just then Alice envied Gertrude. At least Gertrude knew what she stood for. At least Gertrude had a future to fight for, faraway as it was.

"And I can just . . ." Alice spread her hands, unsure how to comport herself. "You mean that I can just stay here?"

"Stay as long as you like," said Gertrude. "Stay forever."

"And no one else can get in?"

She was thinking of the Kripkes, but Gertrude took her to mean John Gradus. "That charlatan? He won't bother you. Nothing enters the citadel without my knowledge."

"And should I want to leave?"

"I will not force you to stay. No one comes to the citadel except by free will. But I think you will be much more comfortable here than you ever could have been outside." Gently, Gertrude pressed her hand against Alice's back. "Go on. The city is yours."

This seemed rather abrupt to Alice. She did not know what more fanfare she could have wanted—Gertrude had delivered precisely what she had promised—but she had not expected such a quick dismissal.

"But where is everyone?"

"Resting. People come to the citadel for the quiet. We do not squabble like those down below. Wander as you like, but in time you will find you prefer the quiet as well."

Alice felt a twinge of panic. She did not want to be all alone here; she didn't know what to do with herself. "But where are you going?"

"To mind the city." Gertrude gave Alice's shoulder a firm, final press. "Go now. Find your peace."

SO ALICE WANDERED DOWN THE MARBLE path, feeling a bit like a child told, before the sun was even down, to go to bed.

She spent a while peering at the statues, but their smooth perfection got boring in short order. They were only inspiring from a distance; up close, all their faces looked the same. Florence had been fascinating in a way this place was not, she thought. Florence was textured. Nothing here had history. Nothing was cracked or rubbed shiny with time. It was all built and repaired and maintained constantly so that eternity somehow looked merely a decade old.

She felt a bit let down, if she was being honest. The name *Rebel Citadel* promised something more—ideally, something rebellious—but mostly it just seemed quiet. Where were the Lucifers?

She wandered further along the silent path, mildly curious to see where she would end up. She could not grasp the citadel's design. It was not a spiral or a beehive or a simple spread on the hill, but somehow all three of those at once. It curved in on itself; the same paths that crawled down its inside also looped around its outside. Several times she passed along dark, high walls, convinced she was down deep in the city's bowels, only to pop out unexpectedly onto a terrace. Outside, from all angles, the citadel seemed empty and idyllic—so then where were its secrets? Alice fixed herself an arbitrary principle—turn always toward the darkness—and this led her to a dense maze of squares that quite resembled the walled-in matrix of alleys and campos of Venice. She turned a corner into what looked like a courtyard, and saw in the dim light the most incredible thing.

Growth. A root. A *branch*.

Alice's heart leapt. A True Contradiction, Elspeth had named it. Something growing in the land where there can be no new life. Was this the secret to their confidence? Could the Rebel Citadel have grown its own Dialetheia?

But this branch didn't look like how the archives said. The archives promised a dazzling bloom, a vitality that shouldn't be. But this branch was a withered, black-brown thing, extending limply from a dried-out bush. When Alice touched it with her fingertip, it shrank away like a worm from salt.

She thought she heard a voice in the dark. But it was so faint, a feeling more than a word. Something like *No, go away, leave me be*.

"What on earth?" she murmured.

She touched the branch again. And though the branch shrank back further, Alice heard the sound more definitely this time—a coherent voice now, a word she could just barely make out, if she could decipher its language. She held her finger against the branch, and a whorl of whispers seeped through the air.

She strained her ears. *Please let it be a ghost*, she thought, *please give me some company, anyone at all*. But whenever she tried to seize on one strand, to decipher its train of thought, it dissipated back into the mass. All she could make out was a general air of hostility. The branch did not want her there. The bush wanted to be left alone. But Alice was too curious to leave things be.

She moved fast this time, and succeeded in grasping the tendrils in her palm. The whispers grew louder. She knew it was foolish, but she simply had to know, with sick fascination, what would happen if she grasped a branch and simply—

*Crack.*

The branch snapped in her hand. The bush shrank back, all its whispers crying out at once. They were not loud cries, but so dearly pathetic.

*Why would you do that*, they cried. *Why would you ever do that?*

Alice glanced to her palm. The branch was a branch no longer, but an ugly twisted thing. She dropped it. It shriveled and crumbled into dust, and in the bushes where she'd broken it a shiny tip was exposed to air, gleaming with something darker than blood. A whisper of smoke curled around that wound, the same gray of a Shade's essence.

Alice ventured deeper into the campo, and saw row upon row of bushes and trees—a whole garden, interlacing thorns and twisted branches and mulch. She moaned. "All of you?"

"Not so loud!"

Alice jumped.

It was the knob at her knee that spoke; an ugly, lumpy growth in the side of a blackened tree. She could personify that stump, if she tilted her head just the right way. A rustle, a groan, and suddenly it became the turtle-like head of a toothless old man. He nipped at her fingers. Alice yanked her hand back, and the knob cackled.

"Playing. Only playing. Don't startle, love."

Alice folded her arms tight across her chest.

"Are you new here?" the knob inquired.

"Clearly, yes."

"Why don't you sit down over there," said the knob. "He's new, too."

Alice turned to where the knob gestured. A stone bench lined the path. But she didn't see anyone else, only more undergrowth.

"Who?"

"I'm not sure about his name. We don't have much use for names."

Alice took a second glance at the undergrowth and saw that the cluster of greenery on the edge looked younger and greener than the rest. The leaves were small and tender. The branches hadn't yet grown thorns.

"Why don't you sit," said the knob again.

Alice perched gingerly at the edge of the bench. "But what do I do now?"

"Why," said the knob, "now you rest."

Alice crossed her ankles, then uncrossed them. She felt oddly self-conscious. She half expected leaves to start budding on her own limbs, but nothing happened. "You mean, like this?"

"However you like." The knob shrank back against its stump. "Only settle down, and rest."

"Rest how?"

"Let your mind wander. Skim like a dragonfly over the pool of your consciousness and let go."

"And then I'll turn into a tree?"

"You'll take root," said the knob. "You'll take the form most pleasing and stable to you, if only you can quiet your mind."

Alice's chest felt tight. The groves were too still, too silent. There was something terrible about leaves with no rustle, stones with no sound of water. A courtyard needed wind. She felt dread trickling in her stomach. She tried to ignore this; tried to remind herself that she should be at peace now, that nothing and no one could hurt her. But of course this was the wrong thing to think. For here, without the distractions of hunger or exhaustion or a million mysteries trying to kill her, Alice realized she was facing down the greatest horror of all, and that was the agony of stony spaces. Where all was silent, and you could not run from the thunder of your mind.

A great pressure built up in the back of her skull; bottled-up memories, demanding release. Now hear the screams. Now taste the metal. Now feel the blood, enormous volumes of it, smearing her eyes, salting her tongue. She had never imagined the human body contained so much blood. Professor Grimes's panic—the way he spun toward her, the reproach in his eyes, the way he *knew*—

Knew what? After all this time, she still could not make a coherent narrative from the mess, could not sort those impressions into a structured story that offered any clarity about what she had done and what she owed. Here was the Gordian knot: her memories were perfect, but she could only sort through impressions as they had first occurred to her. And the day of Professor Grimes's death was so jumbled and confused that, months later, and after a million times of reviewing the evidence, she still had no idea what to think. Certainly she hated him. Certainly in the weeks before the accident she had often looked into his face—that crevassed, savage, handsome thing—and fantasized about smashing it apart so it no longer had value, could not enchant. Was that killing intent? Was intent enough? But she didn't want him dead. She never wanted him dead. She only wanted him to feel a shred of what she felt, only so that he would *understand*—only so he wouldn't look down on her so. And she remembered gazing at him and not wishing he were gone, but that things could go back to normal; that she could keep dancing on the line, flirting with danger, have her cake, eat it too.

She could not define her guilt. All she had was fragments, and these she went over compulsively. The whoosh in her mind when she entered the lab that day. How his voice alone made her dizzy. *Don't look at me*, she had thought; *forget I am here.*

Her shaking hand, the chalk wobbly in her grasp. A broken white line. She saw it, she saw it clearly, otherwise she wouldn't have this memory; she saw the gap between one statement and the next, and she didn't do anything about it. But did it *register*? Did she know what it meant to ignore it? She saw the gap, she blinked, she stood up, she said they were ready to go. Alice ran this sequence back in her mind a thousand times over but each time it offered no answers, only a building urge; a screaming desire—for what? A confession, a correction, *something*— something had to change, something had to give; she could not go on under these conditions. She fidgeted. The groves hissed, and Alice strained not to scream.

*Settle*, whispered the forest. *Settle, settle—*

"I can't," she gasped.

*Just try*, whispered the forest. *Hold your thoughts at arm's length, and go—empty.*

An impossible task. They might as well have asked her to retrieve the moon.

She knew very well how hard it was to dull your own mind. The radio blared at all hours. You could not turn it off. You smashed it, and it screamed louder. Most times, all you could do was manage the pain. In the past year Alice had learned a million and one tricks for distracting her mind from wanting to die. Rituals helped. Keeping herself busy helped. She was not one of the depressives who lay stinking in bed; she could not just *lie* there, the stillness hurt worse. Moving staved the agony. Laundry day was wonderful because that was at least two hours of guaranteed distraction, of tasks she absolutely needed to do. So too was grading day, when she could take her stack of tests to the pub and lose herself in the rote activity of checking, circling, calculating, and scrawling marks at the top. The trick, in those days, was to cram her mind with as many thoughts as possible to keep the memories at bay. At home alone, she read everything within reach. She did tasks one-handed so she could hold something to her face with the other. Shampoo bottle instructions. Canned soup nutritional information. She pored a million times over the newspaper while mindlessly chewing her cereal. She kept the grainy television set on at all hours in the lounge, and if her housemates were bothered at least they left her alone. *Doctor Who* went on trial. Ringo Starr played with toy trains. This did not dissuade the bad thoughts. They were always playing in the forefront, in bright colors, on full volume. The strategy however was to dial a dozen other things up to full volume as well, so that the airwaves canceled each other out, and the cacophony in her head reached such a saturated state it approximated silence.

But it all made her so tired. You couldn't keep it up, counting down the seconds from one day to another. It wrung you out, stretched your mind thin. She did not have a tolerance for repetition. Somewhere buried there was the deep, curious spark that rebelled at boredom, which longed to be productive, or at least engaged with the world. Only that spark was too dulled now to do much more than hurt.

She had tried meditation. It was all the rage on campus those days; you couldn't cross the street without glimpsing a New Age poster promising enlightenment, transcendental out-of-body experiences. Alice had been desperate; she had tried everything. She had sat cross-legged on strangers' carpets and hummed and remained for hours in perfect stillness, chasing that promised calm, trying not to hate everyone in the room, trying to believe the lie.

She tried those methods again now, because she wanted what the forest promised. She wanted to be good for the knob. She squeezed her eyes shut. She slowed her breathing. She summoned the image of a candle flame—all the Cambridge yogis had mentioned a candle flame; warm and happy, the fire of life—and focused all her attention on keeping the flickering at the fore, and that heap of broken images dimly in the back.

She couldn't tell how much time had passed. Five minutes, ten, twenty, an hour. But then it didn't matter, did it? There was no end point, it didn't count for anything. She could reach a state of transcendental calm and it would still count for nothing. When she woke up a hundred years might have passed, and there would still be a hundred years to go, and a hundred more after that. This bargain was terrible. All that effort, and no reward.

A crystal shattered in her mind. The illusion could not hold; impatience exploded; a million ants crawling over her skin.

"Oh," she cried, "I can't *stand* it, I can't be here—"

"Yes you can," said the knob. "Try, try . . ."

"I've tried."

"Try harder. It will come. You will calm."

"But how do you know?"

She was aware of how childish she sounded, but at that moment she did feel a childish need for the simplest answers. If only someone would tell her she would be all right. If only someone would show her the way.

"Because you're not the first."

The knob creaked back, and Alice followed its gaze down the groves clustered in all corners of the campo: all up the side streets and up the walls, trailing out of windows. Dense forestry crowded the inner streets of the Rebel Citadel for as far as Alice could see.

"They come in agony," said the knob. "They come with their regrets and confessions. They come in shame, and with a great urge to make things right. They stand in the squares and fret like you are now, until they learn the calm of stony places, and they become part of the grove."

"And now they're asleep?" Alice asked.

"Close," said the knob. "Sleep doesn't come, not here. But close your eyes, still your mind, and you get something close . . ."

"But what if I can't?"

"Then seek the monasteries."

"The monasteries?"

"Across the way," said the knob. "In the shade lie the trees. Along the cliffs, the abbeys . . ."

Alice had thought the citadel was emptied, still. But where the knob gestured, inside the walls along the cliffs, she saw Shades in congregation. No great movement, but a kind of stirring; rhythmic, circular. Souls pacing in place. Souls chanting in unison. That was the buzzing, she realized; not bees, but psalms.

"Psalms at Terce," said the knob. "Prayers at Nones, prayers at Vespers. In all other hours, prayers and meditation . . ."

"Praying to what?"

"They pray to the act," said the knob. "They pray to waiting, for the strength to be patient until the end. Until the world turns upside down. Until the Lethe runs dry, and the domain of Lord Yama turns in on itself. For nothing is eternal, not even the order of this universe, and one day the eight courts will fold in on themselves and the meaning of being itself will change. They believe that souls cannot be purified by retribution, or reformation, but only by the fires of time. That the *kālavāda*, the school of time, holds all answers to the cryptic idiocies of Hell."

This response was so disappointing, Alice nearly wept. "So they're waiting for nothing."

"Do they not have good reason to wait?" asked the knob. "Every religion supplies an origin of the universe. Every tale has a beginning. Every beginning implies an end. The one became a million which will diminish to one again. The fires of Ragnarok will split the earth and birth it anew. Even Father Time is not infinite; even he will be slain."

"So what?" Alice cried. "They think they'll survive *that*? The apocalypse?"

"Nothing will survive the apocalypse," said the knob. "But it takes away the necessity of choice. They do not move on. They do not die. They only wait. They await the turning of the sands. A new world, and a newer world after that. Worlds you could not imagine, with laws utterly unlike our own. Worlds where entropy runs in the other direction, and time proceeds toward order. Worlds where men fly, and birds are tied to the ground. Worlds where chance does not exist, and the future is a solid, steady block. Worlds without pain and suffering, worlds without subjectivity, worlds of beauty, worlds worth dreaming for . . ."

Perhaps, thought Alice; but this was a game not of millennia, but orders of magnitude even above that. And before that new world came, their world had to die, and everything in it. Nothing here would survive the turning of the sands. These souls would not perceive the future.

It pained her more and more to look at this forest, all this vegetation that had given up and was content now to barely *be*. She thought to all the hours she had ever wasted in her life; all the minutes she had watched count down on the clock, waiting for them to go faster. Whole days she had spent confined to her room like a prisoner, sitting blankly on her chair, anticipating the ritual marks that proved time was going by: meals she didn't eat; prayers she didn't attend; the bells at all hours, reminding students it was time to get going. She'd been so relieved to sleep; so disappointed to wake. Back then every hour that slipped by her seemed like a tiny victory. But why had she been so eager for that time to disappear? What was that countdown *to*?

At least in the world above she had the slimmest hope that something in her condition might change, that one day she would wake up and feel right again, that a door would open up; a solution would present itself. Here that countdown led nowhere at all. Change was foreclosed. Here all events were just little piles in the hourglass; reaching, then collapsing, over and over again.

The garden seemed so dead and cold then. That wasn't green. Just the memory thereof. Just a cruel imitation.

And Alice realized with terrible clarity that this was the worst punishment of the citadel, of Hell itself. This punishment they had wrought themselves. If Aristotle and Leibniz were right, and time was just change, then time was done for them. But not for everyone else. They still had to feel it, chronicity with no telos. And to be placed outside of time—denied everything that moved in cycles, birthing and growing and aging and dying; denied ancestors and descendants; denied any place in the tree—while at once forced to feel every inch of its slow, inexorable progress—God, but this was horrific! Stumps only, dead ends with diminishing echoes of their short mortal loops. Immortality here was no gift. Nothing was fleeting, precious, and so nothing was valuable. Not even thoughts, for none of their thoughts were original, but mere echoes of one another, everything they would ever be capable of thinking in a gilded box with the spotlight merely roving. Nothing added; no discovery, no delight. No growth here. Just withered stumps of time.

Suddenly the campo seemed to shrink around her. Alice had a vision of sinking into that grove; of receding further and further into the settled souls until black branches closed over her face. She felt a swell of panic, and this made her want to yank at the branches, smack at the leaves, set the whole thing on fire, just to make it stir. Oh, to make it scream!

"Well then," she snapped, "if you're not *waiting* for anything except the end of the world, then why don't you just die?"

At this, a cluster of branches beside her made a low keening noise. Alice felt a stirring in the bush. Something solidified, pressing against her shoulder. She saw a silhouette that hadn't been there before. The slope of a forehead; the mass of a chest.

"Now look what you've done," said the knob. "You've woken him up."

Alice didn't understand why the knob was so peeved. It could only be a good thing that this Shade would shrug off the forest. It was a miracle, in fact, that after a hundred years, anything here could summon the subjectivity to return from plant to person.

"Hello," she said.

The undergrowth exhaled in response.

The whole bush quivered, seemed to scrunch itself up, and then with a ripping noise the Shade tore himself free of his surrounding bush. He stood. He was quite tall; a great, hulking mass, all his extremities still ending in branches. His face was a gray blur but took on finer distinction with every passing second. An uneven slope of a mouth emerged from the haze. A nose. Two bright, blinking eyes.

"Settle down," the knob told him. "Settle, won't you—"

The Shade took a wobbly step. The whole of him lurched, but he kept on his feet.

"Settle down," repeated the knob, more urgently this time. "Now, let's think about what we're doing—"

The Shade strode with purpose down the path.

"Hold on." Alice hurried after him. "Where are you—"

The Shade began to run. Alice followed after him, curious. The Shade went down a path and turned a corner. Suddenly the forest ended, and the shore lay open beneath them.

"No—" cried Alice, but it was too late. The Shade sprinted off the cliff and, for a single, weightless moment, was suspended in the air. Then the Lethe imposed its gravity. Some eddy opened, beckoning, and the Shade swirled down.

She had to look.

The Shade landed facedown and did not resist. For several seconds he floated atop the waters, and then parts of him began melting into the current—bright, swirling colors that unfurled in long, thick streaks. Alice had visions of a jellyfish, a parachute, a magician's scarf; so many colors emerging from a single point, an endless fount of memories stretching to ten feet, twenty; a cartoon strip of a life laid out for anyone to see, and she was beginning to wonder just how much territory it could cover until at last it all mixed and blurred, then dissolved into the beating black. Then the obsidian face of the Lethe was just as before. Swallowing all, releasing nothing.

Vertigo hit. Alice swayed.

Two contradictory impulses swirled inside her then.

First, a vicious pang of jealousy at the *completeness*—at that mad swirl of colors that was finally, mercifully, allowed to dim.

Second, only now did she learn how badly she did not want to die.

She teetered over the edge, and a howling rush came up at her; a violent invisible force that left her skull spinning, her knees weak. *Not me*, she thought; *not me, not now, not yet, not like this*. Blood thundered in her ears, and did not let up until she staggered back to safety.

She swayed and turned away. She found all the trees of the citadel were bent toward her. All the malice of countless souls focused on a single point. In a single voice they said, *Thorn*.

Alice ran.

She did not want to go toward the forest but she had to get away from the cliffs, and this left only the paved path through the campo's center. The grove howled and gathered around her—leaves reaching, branches curling. The whole orchard moaned and contracted. So many faces emerged from the leaves; mouths yawning, eyes blinking open, necks creaking in her direction. What saved Alice was its inertia. There was no real animosity in that forest. The forest had trained so long to feel nothing that it had forgotten how to hate. The forest did not care much about

Alice at all except that, like a lazy waking organism, it had identified the source of its discomfort and tried with every degree of movement it had to scratch her away. Tendrils stretched, but Alice batted them back. She broke free of the courtyard and raced down the marble path. She was faintly aware of Gertrude shrieking above her but did not stop to look. She dashed across the terrace, past the statues and fountains, and back into the narrow staircase. The light dimmed; she had no sense of where she was, only that her feet were still pounding the steps, and that she was headed down, down, down.

She broke out onto the ground floor. The entry was transformed. No wooden door. Only a block of solid stone now—an impossible cell, with no doors, no windows, no way out. Gertrude had lied, and Alice was trapped in Dis.

But this was an old trick! Alice reached the wall, saw its smooth construction, and nearly screeched with laughter. If magicians had built this place, then magicians were still telling the same joke. She knew exactly how it went, could recite it in the exact cadence of a first-year telling it for the first time at the pub. Ludwig Wittgenstein had once argued there were no philosophical problems, just problems of language. What are doors and windows?

"Doors and windows keep you in," Alice breathed, and raced forward without stopping. She did not even need to draw a pentagram for this, the illusion was so flimsy. She had been through it many times before; she had seen this trick at the entrance to her own department. "Doors and windows can be shut. There are no doors and windows, and so the way is not shut, and so there's nothing in my way."

It worked.

Lord have mercy, it worked. The walls pressed in dark for just a moment, a single terrifying moment where Alice felt squeezed between the marble before her and the reaching grove behind.

Then she broke through into the overbright courtyard, and even that hot, stale air was a wonderful relief.

She did not stop there. She ran past the bazaar, past the hawkers and skeptics and believers. Past Laplace's Demon and the shredded manuscripts. Past howling Cerberus and the bodies in his wake; past those great gates, for there was no guard on the inside, and the doors swung easily open when she pushed. She passed the laughing Parmenides, who screeched behind her, asking if she'd gotten what she came for; she ran away from Dis until the city was a dwindling point on the horizon, away from the Lethe until the shore was long faded from sight. She ran until she was alone again on the dunes, under the low-burning sun amidst bleached-white bones, far from the comfort of human structure, from anything that remotely resembled the world above; back into the waste land where the only force that gave sense to anything was her own deteriorating thoughts.

## CHAPTER TWENTY-NINE

Now Alice was properly lost.
She could not find the Lethe. She had lost sight of it as she ran, and now no matter which direction she turned, she could not find it. She could not see its faint black outline on the horizon, nor hear its waves crashing against the rocks. Until now Hell had been always bounded at least on one side, and now it was not. No matter which map was right—Peter's spiral/pizza/anus, her linear progressive map—the Lethe was the only limit on infinity. And in both Euclidean and hyperbolic space, a line that once intersected another would never intersect it again.

When she considered the implication of this, the bottom fell out of her stomach. If she never found the Lethe again, she might just trek deeper into infinity forever.

Oh, dear.

She had no landmarks. She could not find the citadel. She could not find Dis. The terrain was confounding, and seemed deliberately so. The land taunted her. The grounds shifted far more rapidly than the earlier courts, and every time she glanced up she was somewhere new. A ring of cacti became a ring of rocks; a hill in the distance became, at second glance, a valley. At the very least she thought she was not walking in circles, for she came across no familiar landmarks—but the desert-scape reformed itself so often that even if she was spinning in place, she might not even know.

But what was there to do but trek?

She would not die. She would not fade away, passive, listless, into the black. She knew this much. But that was all she knew. She needed that fact to matter, but she didn't have the reasons why at hand. Only the inkling of an idea. An impulse really. An open question, a fumbling in the dark. That was enough to keep going. It had to be.

*We are searching*, she told herself. *And we will know what we are searching for, when we find it.*

Time slipped by. She stopped counting the days. She lost track of the sun, the moon. She suspected the moon had disappeared; whenever she searched the sky, she couldn't find it. She found she didn't get hungry or thirsty anymore. When she did eat she felt nourished, but otherwise, her body felt theoretical. Her metabolism must have slowed; she hardly registered her need. Perhaps her body was stilling to match the rhythm of Hell, where change was counted in not hours but ages. In her mind's eye she saw herself whittled down until she was hard and gleaming like the incomprehensible skeletons that littered the plane.

Here was a riddle: If nothing lived in Hell, then how was it that bones were stripped bare? For it was hawks and buzzards, nibbling crawling bugs, that made skeletons gleam so on earth. Death was scrubbed clean because life went on; rot and decomposition were growth; the cycles begot one another, so how did death polish itself in these wastelands, where time stood still? *Boundaries are porous*, she thought. *That must be it;*

*the only explanation.* Life seeped in, even here at its antithesis; life made death beautiful, and kept the circle going.

But the implications of this were profound! This meant there were no absolutes, if even death itself was not an absolute. *Peter and Gödel were right*, she thought. *The universe is incomplete, and I am one of their moving exceptions. But what does the fact of me prove, except that I am here?*

As she wandered deeper into the desert she began uncovering the strangest things. Bookcases half buried in the sand. Books in languages she had never encountered. Metal bars—silver, bronze, gold tools—curved into shapes she had never seen and could not imagine a use for. Dentistry implements? Torture devices? Or evidence of another civilization; something ancient even to the Sumerians, the Mesopotamians? It was quite incredible. These artifacts matched absolutely nothing in her memory bank, set off no associations. This was new. This sparked a dull curiosity in her; the embers of the fire of discovery that had once guided her every decision. She might have stopped to study them. She might have been the first chthonic anthropologist. But she wouldn't have known where to start—these were texts that she couldn't decipher; markings she couldn't even identify.

She recalled another theory she had read of Hell; this one from a Mahayana Buddhist text, which held that the world itself moved through cycles of life, death, and rebirth just as humans did. The world hurtled through the stages of civilization until humans burned themselves out, and everything fell in cataclysm—through climate change, or world war, or any variety of planetary destruction that turned all that vibrant life into gray silt. And that became the resting place for all souls, from the beginning of time until now, until a spark of life formed on the other side—and the seeds of life began to sprout. So the world kept shifting and tilting like a great coin, souls spilling over from one side to another. Perhaps Gertrude and her ilk did have some reason to hope, then. Perhaps Hell was indeed not eternal; perhaps the sands would shift and the souls in Dis would emerge masters of some world.

But before that moment came—a millennium had passed, and how many more millennia to go?

Jesus fasted forty days in the desert, and emerged only when he'd resisted Satan's temptations. Here Alice found nothing quite so clarifying. She passed no test. She was bored and desperate and ready to give it all up, and she was sure that the moment some demon offered any way out she would accept. *Let me return to the citadel*, she thought; *give me a cell in Desire, a carrell in Pride*.

The desert did not purify or improve her. It taught her nothing—except that the loneliness, the sheer expanse, made her rebuild and reinforce herself, like an insistent castle on shifting sands. One sought structure in the flow. One needed repetition, a pounding sound. I am still here. I think, therefore I am. *I am Alice Law, I am a postgraduate at Cambridge, I study analytic magick . . .* she really did need to reinforce these things, because the sheer, flat wash threatened to erode her sense of self until she was just swimming in a bath of unstructured memories. Faces here; feelings there; but what did it all build up to? Who did those recollections make?

The strangest effect of all this was that her memories stopped bothering her so much. Her skull no longer felt so painfully tight. Instead her thoughts were given space and time to spill outward; a flow from which she could step outside, pick and choose. The awful stuff was still there, but it was easier somehow to let it just—slide through her fingers. She had now some way to sort those memories; some coherent narrative built on the most basic premises, which she repeated over and over in her head, so as to remember she was human at all.

*My name is Alice Law.*
*Sometimes I am very clever but most of the time I am not.*

*I have been a good person sometimes, and a bad person at others. Sooner or later I will die.*

*But before I do, I will try—I will try very hard—to make it count.*

ONCE SHE HEARD SKITTERING BEHIND HER and her heart nearly dropped out from fear. But she turned and saw it was only a poor lurching animal. A leopard or wolf or coyote, she could not tell in the dim light—some thing composed of hide and bones that seemed on the point of death but not quite there yet. All sorts of things make their way down to Hell, Elspeth had told them. People and animals and forgotten things.

She decided it was some sort of large cat. She could only guess, for its fur was so dirty and matted, its head and ears mangled with sores. But its eyes gleamed a bright green, pupils narrowed to thin black slits. She thought she remembered from freshman biology that only cats could manage such an eerie glare.

They regarded one another in silence, breathing. Alice watched the cat's flanks laboring to expand, contract, expand. It was so very thin.

"Poor thing," she murmured. "How did you get down here?"

The cat padded forward. She realized, belatedly, she ought be afraid; that under that matted fur and those jutting ribs still was a deadly predator that had clearly gone far too long without eating. Its jaws glistened; saliva dripped from yellow fangs. Borges had written once of a distant wildfire, colored the pink of a leopard's gums. The cat was close enough now that Alice could see its raw wound of a mouth. She wondered if this was Borges's leopard. Fire in a maw, ravenous flame.

Her fear was a dull, abstract thing. She simply could not summon any true panic at the thought of having her jugular ripped out, her blood spilling and sinking into the soft gray. It seemed an abstract proposal to her, and an aesthetically interesting one at that. *Maul* was such a meaty word, so visually suggestive. She had a guilty want to hurl herself into its fangs, and witness the subsequent slash and tear. She could not help it, the attraction was always there; she understood now the Shades that had run at Cerberus. Still, she reasoned, Peter had not saved her for her to be eaten by a desiccated leopard.

She considered reaching for her rucksack but feared the sight of a knife might inspire the cat to attack. In any case, she didn't care to take her chances against those fangs. She had Lethe water in her flask, but that would not help her here. The poor beast would not know to fear those waters. Perhaps it had even drunk already, mistaking it for a clear stream—perhaps had lost all sense of self, its history, its pack and cubs; perhaps now knew only that it was very hungry, and could not get out of this place.

She stepped back. The cat stepped forward, keeping even the distance between them.

*How soft those paws are*, thought Alice; *how delicately they press, leaving not even footprints on the silt. What I would give, to step with such grace.*

They moved again, in tandem. Then again, and again. Step by step they moved along the sands, locked in their dance of apprehension. The cat did not pounce; Alice did not draw her knife. Still it seemed critical that she did not drop her gaze, for whenever her eyes slid the cat hunched forward, sniffing for any lapse in vigilance. So Alice kept her gaze as focused as she could while she moved, locked on the cat's famished, bloodshot eyes. And because of this, she wasn't looking when she stepped into the Kripkes' trap.

Suddenly her foot wouldn't move.

She knew the moment she stepped that she was trapped; recognized the congealing that spread through her limbs and up her body. It was a smaller trap, not nearly as complex as the endless puzzle that had kept her and Peter walking in circles for hours. But all the Kripkes' work had a certain taint to it; the chalky taste of magick. She felt it thick and bitter in her throat.

The cat pranced closer, delighted.

Alice stood frozen, nearly blind with terror.

*Make it quick*, she prayed; *rip my neck first, don't make it hurt—*

Then the cat, too, was trapped—Alice saw, by its right paw, a line of chalk stretching around its tail. The cat cocked its head, puzzled, and sank back into a crouch to spring again. This time the trap redoubled. The cat yowled, pained and mystified, as all its kinetic energy went nowhere and ripped against its muscles instead.

Alice and the cat panted, staring at one another. Their faces were mere feet away from each other; the cat strained, desperately hungry, saliva dripping from its jaws onto the swallowing silt. Beneath its matted fur Alice could see the silhouette of the creature it once was; the strain of muscle against bone. *What a waste*, she thought; *all that power, and nowhere to put it.* Its eyes were enormous with panic; its pupils nearly disappeared into the green. *Help me*, it seemed to want to say; *please, help me.*

"I wish I could," Alice breathed. "I'm sorry."

Tucked into the sand between them lay a gleaming bird's skull. Some invisible wind moved through the hollows of its eyes, and a low cuckoo's croon floated across the sands. Come, come, it told the Kripkes. Your prey is here.

Alice noticed then the metal buckets lined up all around them, visible now inside the trap's glamour. She heard a grinding noise above. She glanced up. A set of knives rose inch by inch into the air above them, suspended by some hidden set of pulleys. They reached their apex, then dangled back and forth in the air, calculating. The blades turned toward the cat.

Alice could guess the internal logic. The trap had weighed

Alice's life against the cat's and decided the cat was worth more; was bigger, carried the most blood. The knives whistled down. It was not a clean slice. They didn't chop, they gouged. Blood poured, but slowly, and the cat howled piteously, swirling around with claws reached out to Alice as if begging her to help it find release.

But Alice was gone, lost to screaming memories. All she could think of was Peter suffering the same fate; hung up upside down, his life bleeding away into those buckets. For a moment she couldn't move, terrified as she was—her limbs were floating, distended; a bell-like ringing started at the base of her head and grew louder and louder until she felt her skull shaking with it, until she thought she might burst apart. Oh, if only she could just shatter, if only this would all *end*—but it kept going on and on, and the terror reached a screaming pitch.

The cat gurgled. Something had ruptured inside, and blood spilled out from between those fangs. The blood did not sink into the sand, but trickled by magick into those buckets; many hot, thick streams racing across the sand. The cat's spine contorted. It hunched into a ball and then stretched out like a flat line, reaching across the sand. In Alice's mind rose the idiotic comparison of Belinda's Norwegian forest cat, a sweet thing named Dame Antonia, who could sprawl like a carpet twice her apparent length. *Cats are liquid*, she heard with Belinda's tinkling laughter, and that tinkling grew louder concurrent with the cat's piteous cries.

At last the buckets were full to brimming, and the cat lay still. There was a horrible grinding noise as the pulleys reset. This time the blades aimed for Alice.

"Think," she gasped. The sound of her own voice—tinny, fragile, human—brought her back somewhat; rooted her in a sensation that wasn't her own terror. "*Think.*"

She crouched low in the sand, scanning for any proof of the

pentagram—and there it was, one corner untucked; one word peeking out from the glamour. *Chelone*. Greek for *tortoise*.

She made a noise that was half a laugh, half a scream. Zeno, of course. She was frozen in her steps because the Kripkes had inscribed the first of Zeno's paradoxes of motion. Achilles races a tortoise but gives him a head start. When Achilles catches up to where the tortoise once was, the tortoise has moved on; he catches up again, but again the tortoise has moved on; and so Achilles will never overtake the tortoise, and motion is physically impossible.

No one did Zeno anymore, Zeno was for freshers. Anyone who walked into an Introduction to Magick seminar knew already that space and time were not infinitely divisible in this way. But down here the Kripkes preyed on starving, senseless creatures. The Kripkes were getting lazy.

She had chalk. She needed blood. She stretched her arm toward the nearest bucket, but her fingers only grazed its side. She took a deep breath, then flung her arm out as far as it would go. Her finger snagged the bucket's lip. She yanked back; the bucket tipped. Blood pooled over her fingers, soaked the chalk. And the cat's blood was so rich and fresh, the chalk wrote so cleanly, it took her only seconds to write in mathematical language what amounted to the statement, *But for calculus*.

Her legs sprang free. Alice jumped and rolled to the side, just as the blades whistled down against nothing.

**WHEN SHE CAME TO, WHEN HER** panic ebbed and her pulse slowed, she was ravenous.

The beast's blood did it. Its stench suffused the air; musky, salty, delicious. She crawled to her knees, and after she'd flung her fingers through the sand and defused the trap for good, she pressed her face against the corpse and moaned.

She couldn't get enough of it. It wasn't just the blood and lingering warmth; it was the sheer grossness of the corpse. She had not been around this much living viscera, the moist and squishy components of *life*, for so long. Hell starved the senses. All was so clean and quiet down here, so *sterile*; but the cat's stench was proof that life was messy, full of blood and guts and gristle. Decomposition meant life. She wanted to roll in that mess; she had the overwhelming urge to dump a bucket over her head, slather the blood all over her face and arms, and wrestle with the corpse until they were one.

Reason prevailed. She set to building a fire.

She had a handful of matches that were still dry, and her notebook pages made good kindling. In short order she had a roaring stable flame. She untied the Kripkes' knives from their pulley and sawed into the cat's side until she had several fistfuls of meat. She dug further, and found what looked like a heart and a liver. Organs are healthy, she'd once read; eat those first. All this she skewered on a knife and placed directly into the flames. Let it burn; she didn't care. She wanted it messy; charcoal and blood and all. She couldn't wait long enough for the meat to cook through anyway. Once the smell hit her nose her stomach screamed, and she saw herself in her mind's eye with the same slavering glare the cat had once turned on her. She seized the meat. It burned her fingers; she didn't notice. The liver she ate quickly. It came apart soft in her teeth. The heart she chewed for a long time, relishing how sore it made her gums. Taste did not matter, she hardly registered it; all that mattered was that the chemicals in her gut could tell it was nutrient-rich biological matter and that it was good.

By then the rest of the meat had cooked, all enticing crackling fat, but Alice's stomach roiled at the thought of stuffing more inside her. She lay on her back and stared at the sky in a daze.

What a trip.

She would have liked the luxury of having a mental breakdown but unfortunately, now time mattered again. She was hurled back into a schema of change and there was forward momentum now, a destination, things to do and get done. She had to busy herself with whatever happened several hours from now. Futurity! What a concept.

Once her senses came back a bit, she regarded the spread-out carcass. She supposed she could have been more careful about butchering the meat—organs, blood, and flesh lay scattered across the sand, and at this stage she had a hard time telling what was what—but still she was able to salvage entire steaks from the cat's sides and legs. She didn't know the first thing about curing meat, but she figured cooked meat would last longer than raw. Provisions for the future. A future. Incredible. She roasted the flesh using the knife as a skewer, staring intently as the crackling meat went from bright red to a hard black. The smell made her ravenous once more. She tore the meat into pieces and ate with gusto, licking fat from burnt fingers.

For the first time in a long while, she had a sense of her body. She felt its wants and pangs. She felt its strength. She turned her right hand over before her eyes and stared, astonished, at its ridges and veins. So many little grinding pieces composed this heaving lump of a machine. And miracle of all miracles, it worked.

She felt something else: a thrumming roar deep in the pit of her stomach. She couldn't quite describe it. It was not a sensation she had ever felt before; indeed the intensity of it rather scared her. But that moment, all Alice knew was that she desperately wanted to kill something.

# CHAPTER THIRTY

"My, my, my." The ground rumbled. "Aren't you a sight."

Alice propped herself up on her elbows. "Hello, Gradus."

He drifted closer.

She nodded to her steaks. "Try some."

She expected him to scoff. She was surprised when he said, "Smoke it for me."

She obliged, dipping her makeshift skewer over the fire until the meat blackened. Gradus leaned low over the flames. Gray tendrils furled into his essence, so that for a moment Gradus and the smoke seemed like the same entity, and he made low, satisfied noises. *Thurification*, thought Alice. That was the English word. She thought to little sacrifices her parents laid out during festivals; offerings to their ancestral dead alongside slow-burning incense. So this was what happened on the other side, she realized. Ghosts plunging their heads in thick, hot food. *Next time I'll dispense with the incense*, she told herself, *and just toss the food in the flames.*

"I'm sorry," she told him.

"What for?"

"I should have listened to you. I should never have gone with Gertrude."

He raised his head. She giggled; his face was half blurred with smoke; half smeared and dripping, in imitation of a man at a barbecue with no bib. He'd surely put on this effect to amuse her, and this pleased her; it meant they were still something to one another.

"Bah." He shrugged. "Of course you went. It sounds too good in theory; you always have to know."

"You were at the citadel once."

"Oh, sure. I helped build it. I have spent countless years at Gertrude's side, planning our expanding skyline. I have been a tree in that courtyard, still, and almost disappeared. I have been a pacing soul in the gardens, treading the same steps over and over again." Gradus bent back over the fire and sucked in another long, satisfying drag. He sighed. "And I have teetered over the rocks, watching the waves, daring myself to jump."

"Why did you leave?" Alice asked.

"Because the temptation was too great. In those last few years, I . . . Every day, you know. Every second. So much time I spent teetering on that cliff. And finally I knew that if I stayed there a moment longer, then I really would jump."

"But why didn't you?"

"Isn't that just the question."

"Sorry." Alice smiled. "I guess it is."

"I just can't figure it out." Gradus spread his hands. The whole of his self spread out too, a sad and confused billow. "I don't know how to move on, and I don't want to die. Time allows no exit, and it all boils down to one of two choices: end it for good or keep going. Now, the former seems more elegant, and certainly it's more rational. A clean end compared to infinite suffering. But then why aren't we lining up to jump? It can't just be fear, you see. Fear expires. Even the most acute terrors erode over time. I used to cower from those crashing waves and now, I don't even flinch. I watch others jump, all the time, and their unraveling does not scare me, I do not look away. But still I do not jump. I cannot. Something deep within me refuses. Why is that? So now you understand the problem." His tone grew urgent. "I am searching for the reason. And if I fear anything at all, it is that this reason does not exist, and that I am trapped in existence by a delusion."

"I'm not the first sojourner you've met," Alice guessed.

"Far from it."

"And you ask them all this same question. Why go on."

"Yes."

"Do they say anything helpful?"

"Never," said Gradus. "Either they don't think it's worth it, and we have the same problem—very common among sojourners, by the way—or they do, but they can't explain it; it comes as naturally as breathing to them; of course they go on, because isn't life fun? They're delirious with good fortune. They've never even pondered why."

Alice could make sense of his frustration now; could understand perfectly why he'd thrown her into Dis, if only to witness its futility. She forgave him for it. She would be frustrated too, if she'd wandered this wasteland trapped by two bad options, and along pranced some idiot who declared it didn't all matter.

"I just wish," said Gradus, "I could find some way out."

Alice racked her mind for consolation, and couldn't find it. In the whole of chthonic literature there was nothing on this fundamental problem, there were only varied and detailed accounts of never-ending despair. No one was much interested in how souls got out of Hell. She could only settle on Dante's answer, the only possibility of salvation in the entire *Inferno*. Only one being could harrow Hell. "Suppose you're rescued by an act of divine grace."

"Don't be a cunt, Alice."

"I know, I'm sorry. I wish I could give you an answer."

"That's all right," said Gradus. "No one ever has."

Alice watched his grayness undulating around the fire and wondered what it was like to exist so long that your practical identity was no longer hinged to a time or a place, but a question.

"So what are you going to do now?" Gradus asked.

"Oh." She didn't hesitate. She knew what she had been searching for. "I'm going to kill the Kripkes."

They both looked to the cuckoo skull. All this time it had been blowing a low, constant coo; a signal carrying across dead air, alerting its creators to their spoils. Alice had not tried to destroy it. She had deliberately left it alone.

"It'll take them a while," said Gradus. "It always takes them a while. They don't like coming this far down. But they will come."

"How long do you think I have?"

"When did the trap spring?"

"Only a few hours ago."

"They prefer the upper courts. Safer there. And they move over land; they never sail. So I'd say at least the night."

"Good," said Alice. "I have time to prepare."

"Revenge?" asked Gradus.

*No*, she thought. *More than that.*

For the first time since she'd descended to this place she felt some clarity of purpose. She knew what she was meant to do. She could not change the past, could not take back her murder, could not keep wallowing in her guilt, could not bring Peter back. But she could make her death mean something—she might do *something* to end this terrible cycle, and even if this ended with her bloodless on the silt, that might be enough.

"I'm going to scour Hell," she declared.

"My, my," said Gradus. "Aren't you confident."

"The Kripkes have always done the hunting." She felt a rush to her head as she said this. "They've never been hunted. They don't know what they're in for with me."

It was the strangest thing. Here she was marching to her almost certain death, and it was the first time in a long time that she felt her life mattered. This urgency, this rush—like all of her, body and soul, was pointed like an arrow, taut with purpose. Something better than anger, despair, or vengeance. She could feel her heart beating, the blood coursing through her veins, from her heart to her fingertips, clenched tight around her blades. When she spilled it, it would matter.

How much time had she wasted wandering around in a fog? Looking back now it made her want to scream. No, she did not want to fade into those churning depths. Refused to petrify into comatose forest. She wanted to crash brilliantly against something, and when she went she wanted to leave a mark.

"One question, Gradus."

"Yes?"

"Which way is the river?"

Gradus hmmed.

"Things get a lot more interesting if you show me to the river," said Alice. "I've lost the way."

"You're not far." Gradus drew an angle in the sand. "Straight from here. You will see hills; keep them on your right. Continue until you hear the waves. And you'll need some protection. Something sturdier than that rucksack."

Alice blinked down at the cat's mangled corpse.

"Seems appropriate," said Gradus.

Alice dragged herself over to the cat and set about dismembering it.

You could do quite a lot with bones, it turned out. Alice extracted all the spiky bits—claws, vertebrae, the end of its tail—and gathered them in a handkerchief. She reasoned she could clutch them in her knuckles and, in a pinch, gouge at cheeks or eyes. The cat's femurs were long and hard. She bashed them against a rock and found herself with a set of makeshift daggers. Delighted, she weighed them in her hands. They were lighter than her knives and better fit her grip.

Now for armor. It took some finagling, but at last she managed to extract the cat's rib cage intact and slide it on over her own torso. It was surprisingly light. She tapped it a few times with her knife, and the bones felt sturdy enough. It wouldn't stop a blade piercing her heart, but it would ward off glancing blows.

"Ooh," said Gradus. "Terrifying."

Alice preened.

The only item she couldn't use was the skull. She spent nearly an hour digging the eyes and brains out with her fingers, though once she'd cleaned off the skull she couldn't pry it unhinged or fit it in a way that made sense as a helmet. Her head simply wouldn't fit. Pity, she thought; it looked very cool.

Instead she made a little mound with the dirt, arranged some pebbles in a neat circle, and placed the skull on top. She even inscribed a bit of magick to keep the mound intact. Just a tiny ward that stilled change. It wouldn't keep someone from kicking it over, but it would protect against the little erosions of time. Wind blowing, rodents scurrying.

She sat back, satisfied. *There*, she thought. She'd made her own contribution to the map of madness. Years might pass and the cat's skull might still be here, those massive sockets leering at all those who passed. Let it bedevil the next sojourner who came through, demanding interpretation. She bowed low to the little shrine, since she felt the cat deserved some of her gratitude, and then tapped it on the forehead. "Remember me, won't you? Even if they gut me like a pig."

"You don't have to fight them," said Gradus.

"What's that?"

His voice was hardly a mumble. "You have a head start. You could hide out in Dis."

"Oh, Gradus." She smiled. "Are you trying to get me to run?"

Gradus would not meet her eye. His face was faded halfway into mist, and the miasma around his legs curled in and darkened, as if he were hiding within himself. Alice found this adorable. "Your odds are terrible."

"I know."

"The Kripkes are practiced killers. You are a mouse. They will drain your blood and kick your bones into the Lethe." Gradus paused. "I do not wish that for you."

Alice knew better than to imagine he cared. Probably he regarded her the way one regarded a toy kitten. Oh, please don't run into the street. We still have games to play. Still, this was the first time in a while that anyone had expressed concern over her demise, and she was dearly touched.

"I wish I could give you a hundred years of memories, John Gradus." She made a gesture toward the mist. He shrank away; shy, or startled, or both. "But that would take no sand out of the hourglass. We'd only be delaying the inevitable."

He sounded peevish. "But at least you'd still be here."

"If I die, I die," said Alice. "But there's no life otherwise, I think. Life is an activity that's got to be sustained. You have to fight for it. Otherwise it's no life at all. That's just it. It's just an impulse. And we've both determined that's not enough. You know that."

Gradus hovered silent for a while. Then he said, "Snort some chalk."

"What?"

"It will help. Just trust me."

"I'm not going to snort chalk!"

It was a long-running joke at Cambridge that snorting chalk imbued you with all the magical potential energy of long-dead sea creatures. But magick chalk was also an academy-restricted substance shown to deteriorate human tissue upon ingestion, and improper use could get you a lifetime ban from practicing magick, so despite all the jokes at the pub, no one had ever tried it.

"I am not joking," Gradus said. "Snort the chalk."

Alice pressed the nib of a stick to the back cover of her notebook. It broke off into chunks. Too bad, she thought. She'd always prized Barkles' inability to crumble.

"Where I'm from they cut it with a penknife," said Gradus.

Alice was trying to crush it with the base of her palm, but all that did was leave dents in her flesh. "Stop mocking me."

"Just try it."

Alice had lost the penknife, so she tried the dagger instead. It took a bit of experimenting but she did manage by alternating the dull and sharp sides to cut the chalk into pieces that wouldn't choke her. When it seemed sufficiently pulverized, she gathered it into a neat little pile in her palm. Then she leaned over and huffed.

The effect was immediate. She felt like she'd stuffed wasabi up her nostrils. Sharp stabs of pain spread through her nose into her skull. Tears welled at her eyes. She reeled back, clutching her temples, just as spots of color exploded in her mind. A cacophony of memories, memories she didn't even know she had—memories she still couldn't place, entirely foreign except for their intensity. A woman laughing. A deer startling. A giant's stride. A midnight streak into the lake, and the plunging cold. All the axioms in the world swirling and dancing above her. Here was the hidden world revealed and written clear; no shadows, no veils. She stretched her arms above her head in some primal bearlike stance, and in that moment Alice felt capable of devouring the universe.

"Jesus." An icy burn spread through her limbs. *I'm burning*, she thought; *I'm on a pyre, and it feels delicious.* "Jesus *Christ*."

Gradus howled with laughter. "I told you."

She took a step and reeled. Each movement sent the universe spinning sideways on its axis, sent ripples across Hell. She was afraid to breathe, for she did not want to cause the apocalypse.

The cuckoo skull cooed once more. Alice seized it, hurled it down, and crushed it beneath her foot.

She thought she could hear the alarm—the invisible signal now a humming perceptible to her ears. She felt from across the dunes a sharp, hostile awareness turned suddenly toward her, and this exhilarated her. At last, a challenge.

"Come on," she shrieked to the desert. "Come get me, I'm right here."

## CHAPTER THIRTY-ONE

Alice was no wartime magician, but all the military histories she'd ever read made a big deal about finding the high ground. So she tracked first to the river, and then she found a spot on a bluff where she could see the Kripkes coming from all directions. This bluff stretched into jagged overhangs that loomed above Lethe, and so she formulated a plan: to lure the Kripkes to the top and find some way of tricking them over the edge. The drop was not far, but she didn't need the fall to kill. She only needed to get them wet.

Then she roved the surrounding hills with a bucket of cat's blood, dipping and drawing pentagrams on every spare inch of sand she could find.

This work was quite calming. It gave her somewhere to focus her chalk-screaming mind. Always it was so lovely to have a well-defined objective and clear parameters for success. In her college years Alice had participated in several Magick Olympiads, in which contestants were given half an hour to inscribe pentagrams to accomplish a series of tasks. Make the bowling ball rise to the ceiling. Move this pin from one end of a field to the next. She'd racked up a half dozen medals for her talent in inscribing quickly and accurately under pressure. The old thrill of competition came back to her now. Forget the Kripkes for a moment, forget the likelihood of impending death, and win the game at hand. Here is a board, and here is your objective: to obstruct your opponents more than they obstruct you.

She pulled out the standard repertoire. At intervals across the field she inscribed all of Zeno's paradoxes of motion: Achilles and the tortoise, Atalanta on the racetrack, the arrow in flight. If Atalanta wished to cross a racetrack—if the bone-things wished to cross the field to the bluff—she had to first get halfway there, and then halfway to halfway there, and then halfway to halfway to halfway there. But if you kept dividing the distances by half, then Atalanta had to accomplish an infinite number of tasks, and so she probably couldn't budge at all. And if the bone-things wished to even move—if they, like an arrow, wished to traverse space from point A to point B—they must grapple with the fact that at any given moment in time, if you took a freeze frame of their movements, they would be standing still. The time it would take them to reach Alice was composed of such given moments, but that meant they were always standing still, and never moving. And they could never harm Alice if they could not move.

This was all silly stuff, as long as you had beginner calculus. But the bone-things did not have calculus.

Where the ground sloped toward the hill, Alice wrote out an expanded version of the Liar Paradox. This was a practical joke within the department that often had undergraduates stepping back and forth on the stairways, stuck like rocking horses:

**THE NEXT STATEMENT IS FALSE**
**THE PRECEDING STATEMENT IS TRUE**

At the top of the mound, right against the ledge, she drew from memory a most special paradox. She had no clue whether this one would work, but she didn't strictly need it to work. She only needed to show Nick and Magnolia something they'd never seen before. Something interesting enough to give them pause.

"You seem very prepared." Gradus had been drifting at her heels as she worked, murmuring in appreciation all the while.

"You could help me fight them," said Alice.

"What, and huff and puff until they all blow down?" Gradus blurred himself all over, as if to emphasize his insubstantiality. "I'm only a Shade, remember."

"I'm sure you're good for lots of things," said Alice. "You could distract them, for instance. You could swoop and billow and yell very loudly."

But she could tell she had overestimated the strength of their bond. Gradus was fond of her only when it was amusing to be. And while she considered their time together very special, she was only a fraction of his deep time. In one thousand years he would likely only chuckle at her name.

"Ah . . . well." Gradus made the sound of a throat clearing. She thought Gradus might say something more. For a moment it really did seem like he was considering it. But it was so much less awkward not to. Goodbyes were worth the effort only when you meant to see someone again. Gradus merely dissolved where he stood, solid grays fading to a shadow. There was a slight breeze, then he was gone. And Alice might have felt abandoned, but she thought about it for a moment, and then concluded she didn't have any real grounds to be upset.

Humming, she returned to her work.

She checked all her pentagrams, made sure all the circles were closed. She sprinkled sand across her handiwork, enough to hide it from a casual glance, not enough to interfere with the pentagrams' range. She stood back, surveyed the now-smooth terrain, and nodded in satisfaction. She had laid a very good chessboard. It was the best anyone could do with a cat carcass and waterlogged chalk.

Then she retreated up the hill and watched for the bone army's coming.

**THE WAIT WAS INTERMINABLE.**

Alice was filled with bloodlust and chalk dust, with nowhere yet to put them. She was long past the point of fear. She felt she was on a speeding train, fast approaching the crash, and she hated to feel the minutes pass because it was all putting off the end. Several times she thought or hoped she heard clicking, but they were only memories become too vivid. Each time she shook her head, like a dog shaking off water, and the clicking ceased.

At last she saw that roving line of white. No Kripkes in sight. Just a menagerie of reconstructed bones; dogs and cats and what looked like a small cavalry of raccoons.

This was a much larger horde than had attacked her and Peter outside Greed. She wondered if the Kripkes knew she was something special, if they had assembled all their best forces specially for her. They drew closer, covering the distance with astonishing speed. She counted under her breath. *Thirty white horses upon a red hill*, she thought. *First they champ. Then they stamp.* The bone-things reached the base of the hill. *And now they stand still.*

She squeezed tight the hilt of her knife.

For a moment she was ready to fight the horde whole. She had forgotten that her spells did indeed work, and she was quite a good magician, until she saw the evidence. She had been right. The bone-things could not do calculus, and could not tell Zeno from God. A third of the horde slowed, and slowed again, and slowed down infinitely until their spindly little legs beat pointlessly into degrees of diminishing fractions. Only a lucky few skirted round the piles of their incapacitated friends, and when they got up the hill this number was whittled to a mere handful.

The bravest among them approached her sniffing, cautious now. It had the slender, trembling build of a whippet.

"Stop it," she told it sternly. "Go. Sit."

The bone-thing yipped and sprang.

Alice smashed her blade against its side. It fell, and before it could get up Alice slammed the knife down again and again until its ribs cracked open and its limbs splayed at its sides.

Alice rose. "Anyone else?"

They all sprang at once.

But they were so *slow*! Alice could not believe how easy this was. Snorting chalk had done something to her vision, had altered her perception of time and space. Her sight broadened and sharpened both at once. She could see every little bit of them, all the chalk that animated their joints, every stroke of the Kripkes' meticulous handwriting. And she knew precisely where to hit them, so that the rest would fall apart. She knew when they would spring, where they were aiming, and where they would be. She knew to get there first.

*Thwack. Thwack.* She wielded a blade in her right arm and a flask in her left, sprinkling the air like a priest sprinkles holy water. The water dissolved their joints, and her knife did the rest, and a pile of bones began building up around her ankles as she danced.

God, what couldn't she do? It was exactly that manic feeling she got when she'd drunk five cups of coffee and felt suddenly confident that she could master any field if she put her mind to it—that very brief high always followed by a dreadful crash. Only here the crash never came, and with each movement, as Alice's blood pumped hotter, the world grew slower and slower until she had the frightening sensation that her mind might race right out of her body. But sanity held, and her mind and body did not come apart. She hung there at the brink of transcendence, when all the world stood still and its fault lines pulsed visible. She had a flashback to those late nights in the lab, every time she'd blinked and seen the hidden world—and now it was all laid out in front of her, not in abstract, but in terrible concreteness. Just bones to shatter. Spines to break.

If only Elspeth could have seen her! She recalled Elspeth dancing with her spear along the shore, and imagined her own movements now were just as graceful. This was fun! She didn't only defend herself from their hacking jaws, she made an art of it. She swung her blade in the prettiest, most elegant arcs. The philosopher Zhuangzi once met a butcher who was so practiced in his arts that his blade never dulled; he slid his cleaver through the hollow spaces, where he met no resistance. *This is the Way*, thought Alice; *I see those hollow spaces*. She sliced so cleanly through their spines she carved them apart in one blow. One poor runt she bounced off the hilt of her knife and decapitated in midair as it fell. This must have been how lumberjacks felt. Every time they swung an axe and wood cleaved in two. What a pleasure, this tactile competence. Clean destruction—and the earth cracks beneath your hands.

When she'd dispensed with her attackers she descended the hill and dispensed with the trapped things, too. She felt it prudent to be thorough. The Kripkes might free them, and then she'd be in trouble. But the Kripkes were as yet hidden, and her targets frozen in place, and their spines gave so easily when she chopped them clean through.

She thought she read fear in their bones. Yes, they actually trembled. They could not move their legs, but they could quiver, duck their heads, shrink back in every imitation of living things fearing the whip. And this might have stilled her, but then she saw layered over their heads Peter's wan face, and the knives grinding in midair. She swung. When the blade met their spines, the cracks sounded so pleasing that her delight drowned out everything else. She had never before felt the high of sheer entropy. Indeed it felt so good to just make things fall apart. She wanted it to go on forever—was disappointed, indeed, when she realized her targets had run out; there was nothing more to attack.

Alice stood, chest heaving, and stared over the empty dunes. At her feet, a disembodied skull nipped at her ankle. She gave it a savage kick. It rolled, tumbling down the hill, then came to a stop amidst the carnage.

She'd demolished the horde. The fields were silent.

"Come on," she panted. Chalk burned her nostrils. She had a wild vision of eating the Kripkes alive; of plucking their heads off their necks and chewing through them whole. "Come on out."

THEY APPEARED SECONDS LATER—THREE FIGURES BOUNDING on the hill, their eyes black, and their bodies encased in armor made of bone. Papa and Mama and Baby Bear, come back from our vacation. Goldilocks has been very bad in our house. Goldilocks must be stuck like a pig. Pouches hung at their waists—wet, full-to-bursting pouches that jiggled when they moved—and their arms glistened with fresh, red blood. Peter's blood.

The Kripkes paused a moment to take in the carnage.

They conferred among themselves. Alice wished she could hear what they said, because they probably involved some compliments. Skilled magician. Oh, yes, very skilled. Probably trained at Oxbridge. We must be careful.

Then the Kripkes swept through the field.

Alice should have known her silly spells would hardly dissuade them. And yet, the speed of their demolition dismayed her. Nick Kripke seemed not even to read what she'd written.

One look at the exposed chalk, and that was enough. Blood arced freely from his pouch, and he tossed counter-spells onto the sand, dismantling her proofs without looking. He never broke his stride; even the White Horse Paradox hardly fazed him, and here Alice was certain that Nick had never studied Chinese. Theophrastus and Magnolia followed in his footsteps as one by one Alice's defenses melted away.

Theophrastus paused briefly at the two-step Liar Paradox—his feet rocked back and forth as he sounded out the words—but then Magnolia tugged him aside and kicked the red sand away.

They looked up. They saw her now, standing atop her hill.

She saw them clearly too; their rangy, lean forms, their spiked and shining armor. The top halves of their faces were hidden under helmets made of bone, and the eyes she saw through the dead creatures' sockets gleamed with sinister intelligence. They wore identical leers; thin lips stretched back to reveal sharpened, black-rimmed teeth. Magnolia's lips looked so vibrantly red, the scarlet shine of department store lipstick. Though Alice could not imagine where in Hell she found such bright pigment, except in blood.

*Primitive* was not the word. They had not devolved, like a family lost for months on a hike; they had not lost their faculties in despair. Neither did they resemble Elspeth, whose piecemeal attire was junk scraps made pathetic, homespun art. The Kripkes' armor was flawless, tailored to indecipherable purpose. *They are aliens now*, thought Alice. They did not move like humans; they did not think like humans. They had evolved and adapted to their terrain, become the apex predators the underworld lacked.

Every inch of her body wanted to flee. She had to shout down her instincts with her tinny rational mind. *Run, and Gradus will mock you. Run, and you prolong what must come. Run, and your back is to the beast.*

The Kripkes stopped at the base of the hill.

They watched her for the longest moment, all three heads tilted left to identical degrees. Nick and Magnolia conferred. Then Magnolia trudged up first, Theophrastus in her wake.

Alice's mind went unbidden to the acknowledgments of so many monographs. Last of all, many thanks to my loving wife, who kept our house, set our tables, fed our children, typed up all my notes, and came up with most of my original ideas as well. My dear, you make our lives possible; your love inspires me.

"Who are you," Alice scoffed. "The research assistants?"

Theophrastus broke away and ran screeching up the hill.

This seemed even to startle Magnolia, for she reached out to try to grab him. He evaded her grasp, scrambling on all fours at an inhuman pace up the sands, growling and yipping as if he were a wolf.

Alice saw a dizzying montage of all the misbehaved children she had ever encountered. Toddlers throwing fits at the grocery shop. Cousins over for the holidays, screaming their cheeks scarlet. Helen Murray's squalling brood, whom she had once babysat for pocket change. The younger boy had pooped his pants and pretended he hadn't. The older sisters had screeched with laughter and danced around singing that he stank, and the youngest one decided she was a lion and kept sinking her teeth into Alice's ankles. Alice remembered how children could be capable of such gleeful destruction; how they smashed and hit things with no care for the consequences; how at Helen Murray's house, she'd had a guilty, violent impulse to smack one of them across the face. Most of all she remembered that children were a fright . . . but they were *children*—and so very, very small.

Theophrastus ran full-tilt toward her, and all she had to do was scoop him up by the arms and lift him flailing into the air.

He was very light. It would have been so easy to fling him over the ledge, but Alice did not want to hurt him; this was not his fault. She decided she would dump him in the Zeno trap.

Time out, go to bed, let the adults have a word. Alice dragged Theophrastus toward the pentagram, tussling as he flailed.

Magnolia appeared atop the hill.

"You," Alice panted, "are a very bad parent."

She wondered why Magnolia did not attack. Then it occurred to her she might use Theophrastus as a hostage. The child stood between them—perhaps Magnolia was afraid Alice would hurt the child. Alice was pondering how best to make this threat when Magnolia grasped for her own left shoulder and popped the arm clean off.

Alice gawped.

Magnolia whipped her skeletal arm at Alice's face. Cold bone smacked Alice across the cheek and jaw, rattling her teeth. Magnolia struck again, and this time the force of it sent Alice sprawling. Theophrastus wriggled free, shrieking and clapping.

Magnolia advanced, swinging her dead withered arm like it was some medieval ball and chain.

Alice scrambled to her feet. She felt a surge of indignant fury. The ridiculousness of it all. Peter had not died in the desert so she could be smacked around by someone's detached arm.

Magnolia swung out again. This time Alice traced its coming. She caught it by the wrist and tugged hard. The chalk dust still coursed through her veins; she still felt a strength whose limits she did not know. Apparently this shocked Magnolia, for she offered almost no resistance. The arm slid clean from Magnolia's grasp.

*Right*, Alice recalled. This was her advantage. The Kripkes were not accustomed to anything fighting back.

Magnolia drew out her knife.

*No, no*, thought Alice. She flung the arm away, then flung herself at Magnolia.

Alice had never fought anybody. She'd been such a well-behaved child. The closest she had come was a basketball game in elementary school, when she'd been so furious that another girl stole the ball that she lashed out and kicked the girl in the shin. They tossed her out of the game for that. Her parents collected her and yelled at her in the car while she sobbed and explained she didn't know why she'd done it, she'd never be so bad ever again. The lesson had been engraved in her mind ever since: Other bodies are inviolable and you do not touch them without permission. You do not try to hurt or break them. You keep away and they will keep away in turn, see, everyone exists in their little bubble. So it was a great shock when she collided against Magnolia and they toppled, still wrestling, to the ground. Alice's chalk-dusted senses did not help her now. All she could perceive was thuds and swipes, spikes and sharp edges. She couldn't see, her hair was in her eyes. She swung wildly with her own knife but could not tell if she made purchase. She thought she hit something, but it could have just been leather, just armor. She felt vaguely that she was losing. Then she was flat on her back, winded. Magnolia had her pinned down by her knees. Magnolia's knife came down. Alice flung her hands up against Magnolia's wrist, straining to push the blade aside. But Magnolia was so strong. The knife pressed perilously close against her face.

Alice's gaze slid to the pouch at Magnolia's waist; crimson, bobbling. Two principles clicked in her mind then:

*We are in the Zeno trap.*

*She needs blood to get out.*

Abruptly she let go of Magnolia's arm. Magnolia, expecting resistance, lurched up and over. Her knife jammed into the dirt by Alice's head. This gave Alice just enough time to wriggle forth and slash desperately at Magnolia's belt. The pouch popped. Blood splashed across her face—Peter's blood, rusty and salty and somehow still hot. The swell of memories nearly overwhelmed her—the Escher trap closing shut, Peter's smile, the screech of iron—and it was all she could do to train her focus, recall those most basic algorithms. Blood filled her eyes and nose. She choked and sniffled, all the while gurgling out the words in Ancient Greek.

Magnolia swung her knife down above Alice's head. Halfway through the arc her movements slowed to half, then half again, then half of that. Alice could see her arms straining to move inch by inch, millimeter by millimeter, but it was no good, for the more Magnolia tried to move the slower she got, her degrees of freedom vanishing into one divided by squares of two, until for all intents and purposes Magnolia knelt frozen. Behind her Theophrastus sat completely still, hands stuck midclap.

Alice scrambled to her feet.

The only things Magnolia could move were her eyes. She glared up and locked on Alice, gaze bloodshot and furious. Alice could read her frustration, her condescension. Zeno's Paradox. A *baby's* paradox. But to disprove it she needed blood, and all the blood was in the sand.

"Ha," said Alice.

Magnolia's eyes widened with terror. And at first Alice could not make sense of that terror, until Magnolia's gaze slid to Alice's knife, and she realized from Magnolia's point of view, the rationally expected thing for her to do now was to kill them both.

Alice had not thought this far ahead.

In all her fantasies the river had done the work, and she merely got to stand by observing, absolved.

But what to do now?

*Slit their throats*, screamed the chalk in her blood. But her arm would not budge; the knife would not lift. She could only stand there, frozen in indecision, until Nick Kripke came running up the hill.

He paused at the top, looking between Alice and his wife and son. Calculating, clearly: attack Alice, or free them?

She could not let him choose the latter—she could not fight all three of them at once.

She took a gamble. She turned her back on Magnolia and Theophrastus and sprinted further up the hill, where her masterwork lay waiting, all pieces in place except for the subject within. She was right. Nick followed. She had counted on his curiosity.

Here was the only thing, more so than fresh blood, that could still entice him after all these years. A theoretical breakthrough, a piece of work he had never seen. The Kripkes were masters of their craft, but they only had what was in their own heads; all these decades and they had no access to the archives, to strange lines of thought stretching into other places and times. Here at last was something Nick Kripke hadn't spent decades picking apart and putting back together, and this was why Nick Kripke made the fatal mistake of pausing to read.

Behind him, Alice chanted.

She read the lines off the script in her mind's eye, substituting the words "Nicomachus Kripke" for "Jacob Grimes," speaking faster and faster, before Nick understood what she meant to do, so that her voice was not intelligibly human at all but a high-pitched, garbled wail. A witch's howl, Erichtho's howl—and she was so near the end, only two lines away, when Nick whirled around with panic on his face.

His hands whipped out. Alice raised her arms, but he knocked them away. His hands wrapped tight around her neck. Alice choked but made no sound. If she made no sound, then the incantation would not be ruined, and she would not have to start over. She had only two lines more to go, she only needed one breath of speech, if she could just stay calm and whisper them out. But Nick's thumbs pressed hard against her trachea. She could not breathe. She twisted but found no purchase. His grip was so solid, the pressure painful, immense. *Oh dear*, she thought. *But I was so close.*

Then a screech, a flash of gray.

Archimedes flew down from nowhere and landed atop his head. Nick let go. Alice rolled gasping to the side. Nick flailed, arms windmilling. Archimedes yowled as he clung to Nick's head. His paws scrambled for purchase on that bony helmet. His great bushy tail wrapped with determination over Nick's eyes. Nick seized Archimedes by the midriff and hurled him to the side, just as Alice closed the circle.

*Now we'll see*, she thought frantically, *now we'll know if I'm a real magician.*

Hell fell away.

Not entirely. The spell did not transport them, it only established a link. They were present now in two worlds at once. Hell's sands were still faintly visible, but layered on top were the familiar maroon walls and blackboards of Laboratory Room Nine. Chalk-dusted floors, persistent mildew. On the floor, arranged neatly within a twin pentagram, lay the fake body Alice had so carefully prepared. All those grimy pieces, stitched up like Frankenstein's monster; just enough muscle and bone and ligament to put together a face, all the necessary biomechanics to re-create a voice.

She was amazed no one had cleared it away after all these days. She'd been afraid they might tether up to nothing, that when she finished her spell they'd be pinned to some inescapable place in between worlds. But she had been so careful. She'd chosen the basement room no one ever used, locked the doors tight, and reserved it under someone else's name, a postdoc who commuted from London and was rarely on campus. And she'd even inscribed some spells that slowed decomposition, so that even though the corpse reeked, it was still not rotted. Its tissue remained sufficiently intact to house Nicomachus Kripke's soul.

The corpse's eyes fluttered open.

"Hello," said Alice. "Welcome to Cambridge."

Of course no sound came out. Perhaps she had spoken aloud in Hell, but here Alice was tethered to nothing. She could only watch, a disembodied presence, as Nick Kripke returned to life.

One eye strained open, then the other. The torso flinched.

The parts animated by Nicomachus Kripke's soul writhed on the floor. The eyes bulged; the tendons strained. He seemed to be in enormous pain.

Erichtho's notes had warned of this. The soul is wrenched from the underworld and forced violently into a dead or dying body that is not his. Everything is wrong—every muscle, every bone and ligament—everything is too large or too small and so, so foreign, and he is in utter agony, every nerve in his body screaming, on fire.

It was so hard to read tone in Ancient Greek, but Alice thought the witch must have felt some wicked satisfaction in writing this. Alice had chuckled too, upon reading the pages. *I'll give you a body, Professor, I'll bring you back. We'll see how you like it.*

But how awful it was to watch that spell in action; to see that ruin of a mouth twist open and emit the worst sound she had ever heard.

Magick was a mistake, Alice thought. These were unnatural bonds, this boundary should never have been crossed. She tasted bile, a roil of guilt—what had she done, she had to put him out of his misery—but then Nick howled louder, and the laboratory walls seemed to shake and cave in. The whole room glitched, like a dream world dissolving upon wakening, but did not fade away. The worlds bled into each other. Carpet turned to gray sand; desert turned to walls, it was all braided in a hopeless, disorienting mess.

But Alice was used to this. She had survived for so long seeing multiple worlds layered upon each other. Images winking in and out of place did not disorient her; she knew how to move within them. So while Nicomachus Kripke choked on the horror of life, Alice pulled him determinedly toward the cliff's edge. They were so very close now, only several feet away. All it took now was a shove. The river would do the rest.

The lab room flickered away. This was not Alice's doing. Nick Kripke's force of will was immense. Alice saw him straining to concentrate, to free his soul. There was nothing she could do. Her spell established the link only; she had no power to trap him on either side.

Down in Hell, Nick Kripke jolted alert. His fingers closed again around her neck.

"Release me," he rasped.

*No*, Alice tried to say; but his thumbs pressed around her windpipe, and she could not budge. Black pressed in at the edges of her sight. His fingers tightened. Her limbs slackened.

Divine grace saved her then.

That was how it seemed, anyhow. It was nothing so solid as a living being; only an impulse, a whisper. Just the echo of a presence. But still that touch was enough to tip them over the edge, into empty air. Onto the rocks.

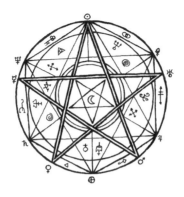

## CHAPTER THIRTY-TWO

A blur, a gasp, a splash, and the shock.

The fall was not far, but the water was shallow and the rocks so hard. For a moment Alice could not see for the pain. All her limbs exploded white, an electric field that only gradually dimmed to throbbing red bursts. She lifted her head, then her arms. Her legs would not move. All she could manage was a dazed half-sit so she did not lie submerged while she processed which pieces were still attached to her body. She blinked at the sky. A pale circle hung straight above her, barely visible. It was less a defined shape than a ripple in the sky. If one looked askance, it disappeared back into the orange. *Oh*, she thought. *The moon. So that's where she's been.*

Several feet away Nick Kripke hauled himself upright. Water came up to his ankles.

He glanced down at his feet, head cocked, as if he could not comprehend where he stood. He blinked, then raised his head slightly, staring ahead at nothing. He seemed like an old man who'd come down to the kitchen for a glass of water and forgotten what he was doing.

He looked to Alice.

"Excuse me," he rasped, and Alice was stunned to hear a voice wholly human from that armored throat. "I seem . . . I seem to have left . . ."

Then that gleaming intelligence came back to his eyes, and Nick Kripke realized where he was. With a shout he lifted one foot out of the water, then the other, then jumped pointlessly on alternating feet as simple physics caught up to him. Alas, he could not levitate. Alice watched, fascinated, as Nick danced a desperate jig toward the shore while memories streamed out of him, fast and urgent, a vast and building current. They flowed past her with frightening speed. A film sped up eight times, sixteen, thirty-two; too fast to make out anything distinct except the most glancing impressions. A campus in the dark, white chalk on a board. The current grew larger and Nick grew smaller. *A Popsicle in a boiling pot*, thought Alice. *When he reaches the edge, how much will be left?* He'd nearly made it, he was only several steps from shore. But the memories seemed to have an attractive force of their own. The current was too great; the memories lost clung to the memories remaining. The current swelled. Nick Kripke tipped forward, fingers clawing for the bank. Alice saw on his face a look of utter terror. He met her eyes, and his right hand twitched—begging? Supplication? By instinct she moved to help him. But her limbs hurt so; pain exploded when she tried to stand up. She could only stare back at Nick, mute. For what was there to say? At that moment her mind went to the Lewis Carroll story. "Balbus's Essay." Such a funny tale. An item submerged in liquid will displace liquid equivalent to its mass, but when the liquid is displaced, the water level must rise, but if the water level rises, the item is submerged further, and so the water must rise further, and on and on, until a man at the edge of the sea, who even just dips in his toes, must soon be drowned. Shouldn't he?

In this case, yes. A wave of black water rumbled forth, and when it receded, Nick Kripke was gone.

Alice sat staring at the empty waves.

So that was all it took. She could not believe the waters could lie so still. The waves had ceased their churning; now the surface was glasslike, deceptive. Several seconds, and a lifetime of hurt just wiped clean, forgotten by the universe. No punishments, no redemption, just nonbeing. Like Nick Kripke had never happened to begin with. *You ass*, Alice thought. *You lucky, lucky ass.*

She heard footsteps padding on the sand, then the screech of a blade.

She turned and looked up. Magnolia stood looming above her, her knife drawn by her side. Theophrastus trailed in her wake. They'd broken free; she knew not how. Both gazed upon the waves, where the last traces of husband and father spiraled out into the black. Magnolia tilted her head back. From her throat emitted an awful, wordless moan. Theophrastus joined her. His high-pitched screech entwined with her low rasp, and for a moment it seemed like the whole world was howling.

"I'm sorry," Alice said weakly, for indeed she was, though this was all her doing.

Theophrastus approached.

He was so very small. He must have been about ten when he died, so he was small even for his age. He barely reached his mother's waist. Alice wondered if anyone called ever him Theo. He looked so much like a Theo. A lisp of a name for a wisp of a boy; soft, skinny limbs hidden behind all that borrowed bone. But still strong enough to wield a blade, and bring it down.

Alice shut her eyes, awaiting the blow. It would not be so bad, she told herself. A bit of pain, some pressure at her neck, and then it would be over. And then her soul would be free to fly off to wherever Peter was, and even if that place was nowhere, nowhere was good enough.

The blow never came. Alice glanced up. Magnolia's hand lay upon Theophrastus's shoulder. Mother and son regarded Alice, unmoving. Alice tried but could not read any emotion on those harrowed, alien faces.

Magnolia reached down and grasped Theophrastus under the shoulders. It was the most human movement Alice had ever seen Magnolia make; a swift, practiced mother's hug. She hoisted Theophrastus up and balanced him against her waist. Then she trudged down the bank toward the waters.

"No." Alice tried to prop herself up on her elbows, and a terrible pain shot through her back. She could not get up. "Stop, don't—"

Magnolia ignored her. Her lips moved against Theophrastus's ear. Theophrastus's head bobbed. Magnolia continued toward the river, moving with singular purpose, one steady foot after the other. Theophrastus leaned against her neck.

"Wait," Alice said again, but realized then she had nothing more to say.

What could she offer Magnolia now? A way back to humanity? This was not in her power.

She could only let them finish what she had started.

Mother and son trod forth step by step into the depths until the waves washed over their heads. Then their memories began to peel away. Little things at first, astonishingly vibrant in the black. A toy wagon. A box of colored chalk; a child's chalkboard, covered in white and purple flowers. Then the memories swirled outward, the things that defined Magnolia the most, the things she'd held on to despite years of whittling away the rest. Theophrastus's beaming face. He wore thin wire glasses—of course he'd worn glasses. Steps to a stage. Brilliant lights. The glossy wood paneling of a lectern. Lights so bright that all the faces blurred to nothing. Sweat pooling in your palms. Then applause, thunderous applause that shook the floor, shook your bones, shook you right out of your body. All those dinner-plate eyes, hungry gazes, trained upon you. Magnolia unspooled and Alice stared, entranced, at the life she had always thought she wanted.

She used to admire Magnolia so much.

Once, in her freshman year of college, she had snuck into a talk by the Kripkes. The colloquium was restricted to graduate students and faculty, but she'd snuck in through the door when the ticket checkers weren't looking, and once she was in her seat nobody questioned her.

Then the talk began, and Alice was entranced. The research alone was brilliant. If Alice had merely read Magnolia's papers, that would have been enough to make her fall in love. She had the loveliest prose style. Later the establishment would treat her lyricism as evidence that she lacked methodological rigor, but at the time Alice was amazed by how Magnolia could make the driest strings of logic sing.

But Magnolia was so much more than her proofs. Alice had never seen a woman scholar perform like this in public before. Oh, Magnolia Kripke, of the raven-black hair and creamy, ageless skin. Her voice was sonorous, melodic. She carried herself, and all the womanly parts of her—breasts, hips, curves—with a poised confidence. She did not shy from flaunting her beauty. She did not hide it under baggy clothes and bad posture, the way so many women did. She made herself the center of attention. She knew everyone's eyes fell upon her, for the right reasons or wrong. She seized that attention. It was the subtle ways she moved—smoothed her skirt, flipped her hair over her shoulder. No one could look away.

Alice sat rapt, stunned by this living instantiation of the impossible type.

She had heard of other couples in academia, usually through gossip about their impending breakdown. A pair of professors at Yale were married—she a classicist, he a logician—and they were constantly unhappy, their students and advisees caught in the crossfire of their disputes. The trouble was that she'd left a tenure-track position at Stanford to join him at Yale as his spousal hire, meaning that her tenure was dependent on his; he was a full professor, and she would only ever be a lecturer. He had edited three volumes; she had only published a handful of papers, and rumors proliferated that she'd asked him many times to help her further her career but he had refused on the grounds of nepotism. Supposedly he was also sleeping with his teaching assistant, a sloe-eyed and glossy-haired Radcliffe graduate who pranced around in colorful scarves and thigh-high boots. They all thought she—the wife—should divorce him. But she could not leave the marriage. If they separated, the university might fire her the next day. Why waste her salary? Anyone could teach Introduction to Tragedy.

The Yale case was nothing special. Hear one story and you'd heard them all; the nasty divorce at Cornell, the married teaching assistant at the Sorbonne. The husband was the star. The wife taught undergraduates who didn't know the title lecturer could only mean "recent hire or spouse," and then she left to raise their babies.

But here was a woman scholar with prestige, a husband, and a baby. It was remarkable how Nick treated Magnolia. He hardly spoke that afternoon. He introduced his wife—this aspect of their research had been all her doing, he said—and then he left the stage. Throughout the talk Alice kept glancing toward him, wondering when his adoring attention would give way to boredom. But he was utterly infatuated with her. He laughed at all her jokes; he nodded appreciatively whenever she unpacked a particularly tricky theoretical knot. Not once did his eyes leave her face. *So this is true love*, Alice had thought. *I wonder if anyone will ever look at me this way.*

And when Magnolia left the stage, she didn't seem to step out of her role; didn't transition from star to wife and mother.

Rather she was just as vibrant and magnificent as she had been at the lectern, husband and son orbiting her like moons. Magnolia was just who she was at all times. She was, impossibly, all things at once.

*You were the best of us*, Alice wanted to tell her. *You made it all seem possible.* But Magnolia was too deep in the waves now; up to her neck, head thrown back, eyes closed and mouth agape in an expression too like ecstasy. All Alice could do was watch from the sands as mother and son disappeared beneath the surface.

"Good riddance," said John Gradus.

Once more Alice turned round. Gradus drifted, gloating, over the sands. Could she stand, she would have thrown her arms over his shoulders and kissed him.

"You came," she said. "Why?"

"An act of grace," he crowed. "And it wasn't God, Alice Law. It was me."

She reached for him, but he, like Magnolia, strode past her toward the waves.

"Gradus . . . ?"

He walked straight into the water. Alice made a distressed noise, but Gradus did not disintegrate. Rather he stepped lightly onto the Lethe's surface. The waters stilled beneath his feet, held him up as if he were made of marble. Then Alice saw what Gradus saw: a boat growing larger on the horizon. It was a slender, beautiful thing, its body a single, curved stroke of bright autumn wood, and its sails a rippling silken sheen. So it was true; so those Shades were right to hope.

Gradus waded further out to meet the ship. His cloak billowed open and his arms splayed at his sides, as if he was presenting himself in full.

"John Gradus," Alice called, "who were you?"

He didn't bristle at this question like he once had. Rather it slid off him like water. He shrugged. "No one, now." He turned and waved an arm. "Goodbye, Alice Law! May we never meet again!"

"Goodbye," she cried. "Good luck . . ."

The boat was very close now. Alice saw a figure standing at the prow; a being clothed all in white, shining so bright against the dark horizon that it hurt Alice's eyes to look. She had to squint. She could only make out the vaguest outlines as the figure helped Gradus onto the boat and offered him a bowl. Gradus tipped the bowl back and drank lustily, shoulders heaving. Great swaths of memory began peeling out of him then. His grayness was like a fish belly sliced open, spilling all its guts and waste out into the ocean. Alice saw images flickering in that viscera. They confirmed her worst suspicions—a twisting of bodies, a splatter of blood, the shadow of a great, spindly elm. But she did not look too closely. She did not think it mattered anymore.

Then Gradus was not Gradus anymore, but a shimmering glow; immaterial in a wholly different way than Shades. For Shades were imprints, persistent past, but this Spirit-Not-Gradus was undefined future, brilliant in its potential. The Spirit-Not-Gradus turned away and went to sit at the bow, his face turned toward that promised shore.

"Wait—" Alice stretched her own hand out, hoping, against foolish hope, the boat might take her too.

But the figure in the boat seemed to smile, and withdrew its hand. It did so not in cruelty; only in acknowledgment of rules that Alice, too, was expected to know.

The boat pulled away. In its wake, a wave pushed out at Alice, rippling and insistent. Her limbs went limp; she had not the strength to resist it. But it was not the kind to force her underwater. Rather it carried her insistently toward shore, as if the water had arms and was flinging her out. Not you, it said. Not yet. Gently it nudged her away until Alice lay curled on her side on the sand, just out of the river's reach.

There she lay, dazed and breathing, watching the waves dart up just close enough to say hello.

Eventually she registered the pain in her arm.

She lifted the arm to her face and watched, amazed, as black water seeped in at the edges of her tattoo. She had spent so many nights pinching and rubbing at her skin, worrying at Professor Grimes's handwriting. She had thought nothing except for cleaving off her own flesh would ever dull those sharp white lines. Yet now the writing fizzled at the edges and frothed wherever the water touched. Little chemical reactions burned all over her skin. It did hurt, but no more than the sting of matches against wet fingertips. Besides, the pain dimmed against the overwhelming relief. She felt a tension disappearing from her skull; a great weight whose presence she had lived with so long, she didn't notice it anymore except when it released.

She tested her memory. She reached for Linear B, something she never used, a file her mind just wouldn't throw away, and was delighted to find that she came up empty. She reached for page 52 of the *Tractatus*. She couldn't see it.

Belatedly she realized she might be in trouble.

There was no getting dry of the water. She was soaked all the way through; clothes sodden, boots waterlogged. She made some effort to wipe her arms dry, but it seemed pointless. The stinging now spread to every bit of exposed skin. When she shifted against the sand, bits of color came away.

Her delight gave way to panic.

She riffled through her thoughts, reaching for and clinging to the things she could not lose. *I am Alice Law, I am a magician, and I am here because Peter Murdoch—*

*Oh please, do not let me forget Peter.*

She tried to hold his face in her head. She had no idea what else she was losing, and no idea if she could prevent it, but still she tried to chisel Peter's image into her brain—that floppy hair, those wide brown eyes. The loose, ready smile. She remembered the hunch of his shoulders and the sprawl of his hair; the way he twirled chalk, the way he pinched his wrist when he had nothing to fidget with. The sound of his laughter. The crackling electricity of his thoughts. She put all these remembrances in a little box and locked it and held it at the forefront of her mind, as if she could keep it there with sheer force of will. *Give me Peter—let me be a monument to Peter—if I am an otherwise empty shell on this desert, a broken record that plays one memory, that will be all right.*

But her mind was fracturing now, and she could not stop her thoughts from sliding sideways. The locked box slid out of her grasp, tumbling down the sands. Memories played their final burst like reels of film spinning out before they burned. Enormous banks of detail went first. Mundane repetitions. Boots splashing in mud. Darkening skies; the mist, the rain. The turn of a key, the click of a lock; day in, day out. Spoons in teacups stirring, clinking, going round and round and round . . .

Then the abstract, too, burst and faded like fireworks. Swaths of knowledge vivid before her eyes. Jakobson, Lacan, Deleuze, Guattari. What had they said? Who knew anymore. Her languages were going. Visions of dictionaries; great vocabulary lists she'd stored and never used. *Mar sin leat, do svidaniya, auf Wiedersehen*, goodbye.

Plato had argued in *Meno* for a theory of anamnesis—that souls were immortal, knowledge was innate, and learning just was a process of rediscovering that which you had forgotten. Reason functions to tether a knowledge that was always there. When a slave boy learns geometry he is not making a discovery, he is only recollecting what he once knew. Then what would Plato make of Alice? Did she forget now only the muddled truths that stood in reason's way? Or was she forgetting all that innate knowledge as well?

*What will I be when I am an empty container?* she wondered. *How will it feel to be nothing?*

Nothing, null, zero—what an interesting concept. Whole schools of thought were possible only because of the acceptance of zero. Her mind tumbled back to that popular fresher's riddle; a syllogism told so many times that its premises and conclusion had taken on the cadence of a nursery rhyme.

Nothing is better than eternal happiness.

A cheese toastie is better than nothing.

Shouldn't it stand to reason, then, that a cheese toastie is better than eternal happiness?

*Wouldn't that be nice*, Alice thought. *A cheese toastie here, at the end of the world.*

Her lids felt so heavy. It would take too much effort to remain upright—indeed, it took so much effort to panic—so instead she let her whole self go limp. Her head thumped against the sand. She felt a little thrill—that sneaky pleasure at the thought of her own demise that, despite everything, would never entirely vanish. *It's happening for me*, she thought, *when I feared it never could. I will go the way of the Kripkes, and soon I will not be a self at all. How exciting this is. I have never known what it was like not to be. Witness now my last trick: I disappear!*

"Hey."

Something hard prodded her shoulder. Alice moaned and made a desultory gesture to swat it away. *Let me fade in peace.*

"Get up. You're not so bad."

Alice moaned more insistently.

"Oh, shush." Two hands jammed under her torso and rolled her over onto her back. Alice cracked one eye open and saw the hollow curve of a bird's skull over a thin, bright face. Beside her, a smug and tail-swishing cat.

"Christ," said Elspeth. "The look of you."

## CHAPTER THIRTY-THREE

When Alice came to, they were sitting at the prow of the *Neurath*, the shore a faint line behind them. Archimedes sat contently in Elspeth's lap. His forelegs were neatly wrapped up, bandages tied with precise little bows. She stroked the back of her index finger along his spine and he arched, purring, into her touch.

Alice straightened up. "Elspeth?"

"Yes."

"How old is that cat?"

Elspeth blinked and cocked her head, as if the thought had only now crossed her mind. She tapped a finger against Archimedes's nose, and Archimedes sneezed. "Are you still letting him drink out of that same water bowl?"

"What water bowl?" Alice thought hard. "That thing in the garden?"

"My God." Elspeth was laughing. "We turned it into a Perpetual Flask, so we wouldn't have to keep filling it. It's still there?"

Archimedes rubbed his cheek against Elspeth's elbow,

drawing her hand back to his spine. Then he stretched himself out across Elspeth's legs, nearly doubling in length, and stayed that way. He looked very pleased with himself.

"Look at you." Elspeth leaned in toward Alice. "You've learned to dress just like them."

Alice glanced down and ran her fingers over the cat's rib cage, embarrassed. "I thought some armor would be nice."

"Where did you get it?" Elspeth took in Alice's wan face, the dried blood across her cheeks and arms, then shook her head. "Never mind. I can imagine."

"It saved my life," murmured Alice. She felt she had to give credit to the cat. "It stilled their blades."

"They're gone, then?" Elspeth asked urgently. "You saw them dissolve?"

"All three, one by one." Alice thought of Theophrastus, still and obedient in Magnolia's arms. "It's finished."

"But why didn't the water affect you?"

Alice rolled up her sleeve. Her arm had turned a red and mottled mess, the site of a still-active chemical reaction. The white lines were blurred, bubbling and frothing at their edges where oblivion battled against permanence. Even Professor Grimes's magick could not withstand the Lethe—the lines were fading, the water was winning.

Elspeth traced her finger over Alice's arm, lips moving silently as she read. "Grimes did this to you?"

This time Alice did not contest the transitive. "Mm."

"You let him?"

"He said it would make me a better magician."

"Did it?"

"I'm sure he thought it would," said Alice, because it seemed like the only honest answer. "I'm sure he hoped it would."

She braced herself as she said this, but Elspeth only nodded. There was no anger on her face. She held on to Alice's arm, cool fingers stroking against the wet skin. They were both silent, watching as the colors swirled on Alice's arm, as white chalk and black water mixed and fought, until the white lines shimmered pale, and at last faded away.

"So are you . . ." Elspeth pointed to Alice's temples. "You're all right in the head, still? You know where you are?"

"I think so, yes."

"You've still got it all?"

Alice prodded her memory. She knew enough that she was not confused about where she was or how she had gotten here, but beyond that, she really couldn't say. There were patches that she had, and patches she knew were gone, and even more patches whose loss she didn't know to register at all. For a moment she found this prospect terrifying—that memory was not a well-kept library, but rather a moth-eaten basement with dim, flickering lights—but remembered then that this was just how everyone lived all the time; how she herself had lived most of her life. You groped around in the dark. You settled for stories, not recordings. You made do with the bits you had and tried your best to fill in the rest.

"Not all," she said. "But I've got enough."

**ELSPETH COOKED FOR HER THAT NIGHT.** She seemed very excited about the occasion; she spent nearly an hour clamoring around the little stove, digging up spice bottles and making exclamations like "The rats were *fat* this week, just *crackling* on the stove." After an hour of effort she served up a stew of salt, congealed blood, and some thick, stringy meat that hurt Alice's mouth to chew. Alice wolfed it all down, swallowing stew in hot, satisfying gulps, then gnawed at the bones until her gums bled.

"Taste good?" asked Elspeth.

"Incredible," Alice gasped.

Elspeth waited, beaming, as Alice drained the bowl and licked at its insides. Then she scooted closer so that they sat face-to-face, inches away. "I feel an apology is in order."

Alice put down her bowl. "I'm so sorry—"

"I feel rotten about what happened," said Elspeth. "I shouldn't have left you two on that shore."

"We betrayed you." Stew trickled down the side of Alice's mouth. She wiped her chin against her shoulder. "I'd be angry, too."

"I just couldn't understand it," said Elspeth. "Why you'd ever want to go back to him."

"Right."

"He is simply monstrous." Elspeth's hand moved up and down in a staccato, as if she were lecturing to an undergraduate. Basic principles. "You must know this. He leeches the life from you. So when you said the name Grimes—I don't know, something just came over me, and then I couldn't think straight—"

"Please don't apologize," said Alice. "It's my fault. You took us in, you sheltered us, and we . . ." She swallowed. "I can't justify it. We knew what we wanted and how to get it and everything else was—I don't know, just collateral. I wasn't thinking about you at all. All I could think was, *What would he do?* How I could make him proud."

"Well." Elspeth sniffed. "He has that effect."

They sat a moment in silence. Once again they regarded one another, two bruised girls with too much in common. But this time there was no measuring up, no guesswork, only a tired recognition. *I know how you got here. I know what it took.*

"It's all so stupid." Alice rubbed her palm against her temple. "I just can't figure out why—I mean, he has *everything*, you know? And I don't know what he needs, or if he's hurting—"

"Stop trying to justify him."

"I wasn't—"

"You were. Listen, Alice, I've been there. I've spent years trying to justify him. Everything you just said, I've been down that road. I've considered it all. So please trust me when I tell you there's nothing more to it. Some people just are that cruel. There is no design. They are not giants. They don't do it for any reason, they just like it. And the rest of us just have to survive them."

"I know that," Alice said tiredly. "I only mean—"

"We weren't special for it. We weren't—worthy of it, or handpicked for it, or anything like that, can't you understand?" Elspeth's hand moved again in that lecturing staccato. Harsher this time. "He did not care. It was completely random. We were just *there*."

"But can't you see," said Alice, "why I'd choose to believe anything different?"

"Oh, love." Elspeth placed her hand over Alice's. "You don't have to believe anything about him at all."

Alice supposed this was reasonable. The stakes of this debate were suddenly opaque to her. Whether Grimes had ever cared, whether she deserved it all—suddenly she couldn't see why these propositions ever mattered to her in the first place. The name Jacob Grimes hung empty in her mind, a symbol with no referent. No flood of memory attended the call. The whole issue seemed shorn of significance, as if she had spent so much time working through its implications that the threads had snapped altogether, and now it was just crumpled paper. It simply did not matter.

"Thanks," she said. Suddenly it felt very difficult to put words together. Her lids felt very heavy. "I think—I think that's right."

"Forgive me. You're exhausted." Elspeth rummaged beneath the seat and dug out a thick, ratty blanket that might have once adorned some grandmother's couch. "Go on, you're safe. I'll be right here."

Alice took the blanket and draped it around her shoulders. It smelled rank, somehow of mothballs and mildew both, but still this was the most comforting thing she had smelled in ages. She wrapped it snug and held the edges close to her face. It reminded her of guest rooms and grandparents. She couldn't get enough of it.

Elspeth watched her settle back against the boards. Then she asked, very lightly, "By the way, where's Peter?"

Alice hesitated, wondering how best to explain. Then she burst into tears.

"Oh, dear." Elspeth fished around in her pocket and handed her a handkerchief, oily and stained. Alice took it and mopped it around her eyes. She was horrified; the tears simply would not stop. She hadn't meant to cry. She hadn't even planned to feel sad. But just then it was like a switch flipped and that veneer of dazed indifference shattered, and all the grief she'd been carrying broke through the floodgates.

"My apologies," said Elspeth.

"It's fine."

"What happened?"

Alice wanted to answer but felt an overwhelming fatigue the moment she tried to open her mouth. She did not want to recount it. She could not put it into words. She felt fragile to the point of breaking, and to rearticulate those last moments in the trap might shatter her. All she could do was shake her head.

"I see," said Elspeth.

There was nothing to do but let the weeping run its course, to succumb to the racks and shudders until the flood subsided, and all the phlegm and snot was run out, and finally Alice could take a breath without howling.

"He decided it should be me." Her fingers curled into balls. "He didn't even ask—he just *decided*—and then I was out, and he was gone."

"Of course he did."

"What does that mean?"

"But surely you knew." Elspeth gave her a look of deep pity. "He was in love with you."

Two contradictory statements came to Alice's mind then, and she couldn't decide which one seemed more plausible, so she uttered them both. "That can't be." And then, "But I didn't know."

"Then you're blind," said Elspeth, "because it was written all over his face. Yours, too."

Alice reasoned that Elspeth was probably right. If she thought about it, a small part of her suspected the same. Only she didn't know what to do with this information. She wished she could carve it out of her chest; set it flaming and quivering down somewhere else, maybe lock it in a box, if it would just leave her alone.

"But we were fighting when we met you," said Alice. "He hated me."

"All the same. If anything, that made it easier to tell."

"But he never said." Alice sniffled, pulling the blanket tighter around her shoulders. "I wish he'd just *said*."

Elspeth shook her head, smiling sadly.

"Magicians," she sighed. "Fools, all of us."

ALICE SLEPT. WHAT DELICIOUS SLEEP IT was; quick and dreamless, sleep that came easy and made time slip away. Elspeth was staring at her when she awoke, her face tight and pensive. She kept tapping her fingers against her leg. Her mouth twitched, like it couldn't decide between a smile and a frown.

Alice sat up. "What is it?"

"I am trying to decide whether to help you."

"Oh. Well let me know if I can offer any input."

Elspeth did not respond.

Alice set her hands on her lap and watched the water rippling. She felt like a naughty child in time-out. She felt she was being weighed, though she couldn't say what for.

At last Elspeth sighed. "I haven't been fully honest with you."

"That's more than fair."

"No, look." She drew a satchel out from beneath the paddles. She placed her hand inside, hesitated for a moment, then withdrew an item. She placed it in Alice's hands. "Here."

Alice understood immediately what she beheld.

A Dialetheia. She peeled the fabric back and found the most curious plant she had ever seen: a Janus-headed flower, one face with seven petals the red-orange hue of the rising sun, twinned at the back by a second face with seven petals of identical shape, these the bluish-white of a falling moon. Vibrant and deathly both at once; warm and cool. A pomegranate tree growing defiantly in the land of the dead. A True Contradiction, the thing that could not be.

"I found it just before we met," said Elspeth. "The Kripkes weren't after you. I should have told you. They were hot on my heels. They were after me."

Alice turned the True Contradiction over in her hands, marveling at the brilliant hues along the stems and stamens, at the delicate, tiny buds emerging from the tips of the branches. What a relief, to see such colors after weeks in grays and black. The only splash that had broken up the monotony was the brilliant red of blood—but here, finally, was green.

"Where was it?"

"In a crack between two boulders at the bank of the Lethe. Can you imagine? No fanfare, no fairy rings. Just growing there, impossibly, with nothing to announce itself. I would have passed by it entirely if I weren't looking for a place to moor."

Alice heard Peter's voice in her head. *The world is not a complete system; there is always an exception. No explanation for* its existence; no reason why one might expect it to have existed before or ever exist again. The world was simply unknowable; exceptions cropped up all the time, and all you had to do to beat the odds was just look.

"Hold it close," said Elspeth. "Drop that and I'll kill you."

"My word." Alice held it closer, marveling. The petals were so fine, thinner than paper, their translucence lined with patterns like lace. "A contradiction explosion . . ." Slowly the implications caught up to her. They wouldn't just be able to leave Hell. They could change everything. With the True Contradiction on one side of a proof, they could write anything else into validity. They could end world hunger, end famine and wars, reshape reality's boundaries however they liked. If they could just get the True Contradiction out of this place, they could do *anything*. "But then that makes you God, Elspeth. You could do anything you liked. Reality's just putty in your hands . . ."

"You still need blood," said Elspeth. "Where do you think I'd get all that blood?"

"But still . . ."

"And the archives are quite clear on the limits," said Elspeth. "The Dialetheia won't work above. It's only a miracle in Hell. Above, it's just a tree."

Elspeth leaned back, arms folded. "It seems to me that the only useful way to employ a True Contradiction is to take it back to the Lord of Hell. That's how Orpheus bargained for Eurydice. The Lady Persephone was so moved by his music that she gifted him the first Dialetheia as a favor, and then Hades had to barter with him to retrieve it. The Dialetheia has too much power to let loose in the world, you see. It's no use to us down here, but the Lord of Death needs it back. So you take it to the final court, to the throne on the island at the edge of the world, and you offer it up freely. You always get one boon, that's what the stories say. And with that boon, you ask for your life." Elspeth nodded to the Dialetheia. "So be careful what you say up there. You only get the one chance."

It took Alice a long moment to realize she had just been given instructions.

She could not find the words. She had no frame of reference to make sense of this, this impossible generosity. It defied every rule she'd been taught about moving within the world, in which favors were like the conservation of matter. A give always entailed a take. "You're just giving it to me?"

"Well, don't look so put out about it."

"But can you find another one?"

"It's a Dialetheia, you fool. They don't just grow on trees."

Alice did not know what to do with this gift. She could think of no appropriate response. Just then the Dialetheia felt so heavy in her grasp; she was seized with the irrational fear she might fling it into the water.

Archimedes mewed in agitation. Elspeth scratched the back of his neck. "Hush, you," she murmured. "I know what I'm doing."

A small part of Alice lit up with suspicion. Surely Elspeth wanted something. Everyone always wanted something. No magician ever did things out of kindness, or they wouldn't have gotten where they were.

But there was no guile on Elspeth's face. Just a sweet, open sympathy. Just kindness.

"But I don't deserve this." She deserved none of the favors she had received. Peter's sacrifice, Gradus's sacrifice, now Elspeth. *What am I to you*, she wondered, *that you would do this for me?* Her mind cycled through the possible tropes: relations of dependence or charity; mother to child; elder sister to younger; mentor to mentee; lover to beloved. But none of them fit, none of them came close to approximating this singular, inexplicable grace.

"Elspeth, why—"

"There's no why," said Elspeth. "You don't have to understand it. You just have to accept."

Alice pressed her face against the Dialetheia, brushing her cheeks against its petals. It smelled like another world; like a garden in spring, like fresh rain and birdsong. *The world used to smell like this*, she thought. *I used to smell this all the time.*

"In any case," said Elspeth, "I don't think they're so difficult to find after all."

"No?"

"We don't understand the gods very well," said Elspeth. "But we should not assume they have the same constraints as mortal beings. King Yama theoretically has control over his entire domain. I don't think he lets something like a True Contradiction hang around just out of sheer negligence. I don't think the gods *do* negligence."

"Then you think he left it here on purpose."

"Rules are so boring," said Elspeth. "So is infinity. You can't knock about a closed system forever; the possibilities run out. I think, then, sometimes the gods like to play. Just for the hell of it."

"Peter thought something similar," said Alice. "It's how he interpreted Gödel. There are always exceptions. There's always something unexplainable, meaning at some level everything becomes possible."

"That's a good sentiment to hold on to," said Elspeth. "Better than the alternative."

"So you're going to find another one."

"Eh." Elspeth gave her a little smile. "Maybe."

Realization dawned. "You're not searching anymore."

"I've held off the inevitable for so long." Elspeth had a faraway look in her eyes. "And I don't want to put it off any longer. I'm tired of the *Neurath*, understand? I'm tired of always bobbing out at sea. I want someone to ferry me over."

"I've seen them," said Alice. "The ship, the angels. They came for Gradus, and I watched . . ."

Elspeth pressed forward, eager. "Oh, yes?"

"And it was beautiful." Alice was so glad she did not have to lie. "Exactly like all the stories promised. They let you board. They let you drink. And then they take you over the horizon, to whatever lies beyond."

Elspeth rapped her knuckles against her wooden seat. "Then let's hope they'll come for me eventually."

"You're way ahead of everyone in Dis," said Alice. "You'll do fine."

Elspeth nodded. Alice saw her lips tighten with something—fear, perhaps—but they just as soon gave way to Elspeth's typical resolve. "Any chance you could tell me how to get out of there quick?"

"You think *I* know?"

Elspeth chuckled. "Fair, that. Any advice, then?"

"Avoid the citadel." Alice settled back, gripping the Dialetheia tight against her chest. "The citadel's a waste of time."

**ELSPETH GUIDED THE *NEURATH* FORTH INTO** waters unknown. They sailed without pitch or tumble, over waters so glassy smooth that Alice would have thought they were sitting still on dry land except for the rapid current of memories sliding away beneath them. Lower Hell shone dimly on the horizon, the fires of Dis growing fainter and fainter until it blinked out into darkness. Then they had only the low flickering light of Elspeth's ember lamps, catching stray memories in the water. Eventually the memories stilled too, all vanished to inky black, and they were just two souls sitting in the dark, eyes locked on each other's pale form.

"I don't know what happens next." Elspeth's eyes were huge, frightened against her wan sliver of a face. "I've never been this far from shore."

Alice noticed belatedly that she wasn't doing anything with the rudder. The punting pole lay still on the deck; the sails were down. The *Neurath* glided ahead on its own will, or on something greater's will.

"How do you know where you're going?"

"You don't have to know," said Elspeth. "Everywhere you sail leads to the same place. Like a bowl overflowing, like water spilling out the sides. The forces push you outward, to the end of the world, and there's nothing to do but follow."

"The pizza anus," murmured Alice.

"The *what* now?"

Alice drew a circle in the air, though she wasn't sure how much it helped. "We had disagreed over our maps of Hell. Peter and I. I liked the linear map. He liked this wonky pseudosphere thing, something that only worked in hyperbolic space. He thought you could track away from the river, access the peak of Hell through the center. Two-dimensionally, it looked like a pizza anus. And now you're telling me we're in a pizza anus."

"You're both right." Elspeth laughed. "Well, Peter was more right. We're indeed in hyperbolic space, love. Bounded by the river on the outside and infinity on the inside. When you're right next to the Lethe, it does look linear. But once you start sailing across—well, then it's out of your hands."

"What happens at the end?"

"I don't know." Elspeth said again, "I've never been this far from shore."

They were gliding faster and faster now. Alice felt cold air on her cheeks; not wind, but speed. They couldn't turn back now even if they tried; the attractive force was too great. There was an urgency to their movement; that of a boat by a waterfall, hurtling toward the edge. Archimedes sat utterly still at the prow, pupils narrowed into pinpricks.

"There," Elspeth whispered.

Alice sat up straight, peering over the prow.

Her mind could not make sense of what she saw. There was the island. But when her eyes alighted on that plane, and followed it outward, she registered a curvature that made her stomach twist. Somehow, when she followed that curve, up and up and around, she found her gaze right back on the *Neurath*, floating still in their little patch of river. It was like tracing an Escher staircase. There was no beyond.

She had to look away; the looping made her head hurt.

And yet this made perfect sense. Lewis Carroll had theorized this—how else did you conceptualize life and death, the membrane of passage, except as continuity?—but no one believed him. Take a strip of paper, twist it in the middle, and connect the ends. Very good. Now you have a ring, a three-dimensional object you can hold in your hand. But it only has one side. The inside is continuous with the outside. Now do the same thing with a four-sided handkerchief. Twist the edges, line them up, and stitch it all together so that the inside is continuous with the outside. All is external to the bag, which means all is also internal to the bag, and so the bag holds the world.

Impossible to draw, impossible to even conceive. But here Alice was looking right at it.

"The projective plane," Elspeth murmured. "Astonishing."

The black sands were so close now. All Alice could see on that shore was a single golden braid of light, stretching from the bank to the unknown beyond.

Alice's fingers curled around the True Contradiction, and she pulled it close against her chest. Now that the moment approached, she was suddenly afraid. She felt that same drop in her stomach before an interview, when she promptly forgot how to walk or breathe or talk, and feared that when she walked through the conference room's doors she might burst out singing, or slam against a wall. She had struggled mightily to get here. Yet now at the end she realized she had no clue what awaited her, and no clue what to do.

"It's all right," said Elspeth. "The Lord of Death is kind. He'll know what you want."

"What if I fudge it?"

"You won't fudge it. Just keep your wits about you, and stay the course, and—oh."

The *Neurath* struck land. They jolted in their seats.

Elspeth rose. "Time to go."

Alice stood and, with Elspeth's help, stepped gingerly off the boat.

"Alice." Elspeth's grip tightened round her fingers. "Kiss me, would you?"

"What?"

"It's been so long." Elspeth turned her cheek, so pale in the throne's reflected light. "I haven't felt—another touch, I can't even remember . . ."

"Oh," said Alice. "Of course."

Elspeth closed her eyes. Alice leaned forth and pressed her lips to Elspeth's skin. The gesture felt foreign at first. She, too, couldn't remember the last time she'd kissed anyone. She expected Elspeth to be icy cold, but though Elspeth could contain no warmth, all Alice perceived was a delicate softness. Satin skin over hard bone. Human bodies were so singular, astonishing. There was no texture in the world like this.

Elspeth sighed, and it seemed something was restored to them both.

"Thank you." Elspeth let go, and Alice took her first wobbly steps onto King Yama's domain.

"Come with me," Alice said suddenly.

Elspeth was bent down. When she straightened, she had her punting pole in hand.

"It can't only be for one," said Alice. "We can figure something out, just come with me—"

"Not my time." Elspeth pushed the pole into the sand. The *Neurath* inched backward. "Still have some things to figure out."

"Please don't leave me—"

"Go on. Be brave, love."

The *Neurath* broke free of the shore. Archimedes sat solemn on the prow, swishing his tail as the waves bore them back into the current. Alice tried to watch them go, but the light on the shore was so bright, and the water so dark. In seconds, Elspeth's face sank back into the shadow. She thought she saw Elspeth wave a hand in farewell, but she could not tell for sure.

## CHAPTER THIRTY-FOUR

Alice followed the golden braid up the bank, the Dialetheia sitting heavy in her rucksack. Behind her the Lethe lapped gently against the shore, producing a soothing, rhythmic wash. The sands were so soft beneath her feet, and her heels sank a little every time she took a step. She had the oddest sensation that rather than walking across an island, she was walking through a cloud.

She could give no reason for walking alongside the braid, except that it looked very much like a trail, and that she didn't think anything so gold and bright could lead her somewhere bad. Of course bright and shiny things made up traps all the time, but in that case they winked and glittered with purpose, enticing you with every dash of glamour they could muster. The braid didn't seem like it cared for her attention either way. Here it was minding its own business, but she could follow along if she liked. So follow she did. The braid took her up a shore, across the bank, and then up a steep hill growing steeper with every step. At last she reached the peak, and Alice saw that the braid had led her to a throne.

It was an unadorned, high-backed chair, sitting out in the open upon a raised dais. Beside the throne, three slim trees intertwined to form an arch, beyond which Alice could see nothing more than a gently turning wheel. Atop the throne sat King Yama, Hades, Thanatos, the Lord of the Underworld, the Overseer of the Yellow Springs.

Alice saw now that the golden braid was a chain of souls; mere lights bobbing one after the other, blurs stripped of all individual features, uniform in their quivering, vibrant *want*. One by one they approached the arch. One by one the Lord of Death touched them lightly with his dark fingers, and they seemed to quiver with excitement before casting forth into the wheel. The wheel shimmered each time a soul went past, and its spokes lifted them somewhere unknown, beyond.

She tiptoed as she drew closer, for she felt, as one did at christenings or baptisms, that she ought not disturb the process. She was near enough now to see every spoke of the wheel. Each was different: some were long, some were short; some glimmered bright, some were dark with rust. A little waft of air floated across the throne as it turned; a bright sweet scent, of flowers in spring, herbs in a garden, and this was so refreshing that Alice could not help but gasp.

"Alice Law," rumbled the Lord of Hell. "It is a thrill to watch new life being made, is it not?"

Alice struggled to gaze directly at him. He was brilliant; not with the harshness of the noon sun, but with the cosmic glittering of the night. He was, like the Weaver Girl, swathed in a fabric that seemed the same stuff that made the universe. Only his was infinitely darker; the color of a cloudless night when, lying flat on your back atop a hill, you might tip forward and disappear among the constellations. She could fall into that night, she thought. She could wrap his essence around her like a blanket and sleep forever, if only he would permit it.

"My—my lord." Her voice sounded so tinny to her ears. "I—erm, how should I address you?"

"However you like," said the darkness. "With whom do you wish to speak?"

Alice considered her options. The darkness took a succession of shapes before her, as if making clear her choices. Tall, bearded Hades, bearing bident and key; dark mother Kali, four-armed and beautiful; silent Anubis, his scale standing behind him.

"King Yama," Alice decided. "Yanluo Wang."

Best to keep to the familiar. Despite his bulging eyes and rage-filled grin, something about his image—scowling out at her from temples, behind incense sticks, on grocery store calendars—made her feel safe. She knew King Yama; her parents knew King Yama; all her ancestors knew, and feared, and prayed to, King Yama. She knew his long black beard, his ever-present scowl, his burning eyes and long robe. She had known him all her life.

King Yama was most fair and just. King Yama bore no grudges, and held no antipathy toward the living. Since her childhood she had understood that his scowl was only an appearance; that in truth King Yama was benevolent and compassionate, that he had indeed once been demoted to a lower rank of Hell for his leniency. He was dedicated only to fulfilling his duty, to acting as a judge—and his adherence to rules, she thought, could only count in her favor.

The Lord of the Nine Springs blurred, and then the darkness took on shapes more material. Now before her stood the great official; his skin a deep blue, his eyes glowing like twin blood moons. A tall, gold-rimmed official's cap materialized atop his head. His thick, black brows organized his face in a rictus of fury. A dreadful deity, yes; but a deity she knew.

"Good choice." He spoke to her in Chinese, and this too put her at ease. She felt she was not so much tempting the unknown as she was sinking into childhood myth. So many heroes had bartered with King Yama. She could too. "What can I do for you, Alice Law?"

She tried to remember Elspeth's script. "I seek an audience."

"You are enjoying one. What next?"

King Yama's eyes twinkled. Alice recalled then that according to some Buddhist texts, King Yama himself was not a permanent fixture of Hell, but a being who sought reincarnation himself. King Yama, like any of them, was on the path of his journey of transmigration. He had not ruled over this domain since the beginning of time, but indeed hoped to be reborn as a human, so that he might seek true awakening. And if King Yama had been human once, and might be human again, then perhaps he might have sympathy for her situation. He might know how it felt to make all the wrong decisions, and have no option but to beg the gods for mercy.

"I have something that belongs to you." Arms shaking, she reached into her rucksack and pulled out the Dialetheia. It shone even brighter now, in the shadow of the ever-turning wheel. It was heavier, too. Its leaves seemed to grow perceptibly by the minute; they were now the size of her palm.

"Where did you find that?"

"I didn't," said Alice. "It was a gift. From Elspeth Bayes. She found it—well, I don't know, exactly. Between two rocks, she said. Close to the shore."

"Where is Elspeth now?" asked King Yama.

"She's moving through the courts now, I think." Alice cleared her throat. "That is. The proper way. With her transcript."

"I am glad. I feared she never would." King Yama swept his long-robed arms forth. "I'll have that back now."

Alice clutched it to her chest. She didn't mean to—it was a possessive instinct—and she felt immediately she had committed some great affront. Who was she to defy the gods? But at least Lord Yama did not seem angered. He only waited from his throne, wearing that constant scowl.

"I—well, no." She drew a shaky breath. "I was hoping we might—make a trade. I have some demands."

He nodded, as though he had been expecting this. "What are your demands?"

"I want—" Alice halted.

She thought she knew her answer. She had been so certain, sitting on the *Neurath* with the pomegranate tree beneath her legs. She had worked out the precise wording of her request; its constraints and logic. And yet here before the throne, at the end of all things, her mind went blank.

Gently King Yama asked, "What was your purpose in Hell?"

This question was easier. She answered like a child listing months of the year. "We came to find Professor Jacob Grimes."

"Merely to find him?" King Yama raised both hands. "You need not barter for that."

Darkness flew from his fingertips and moved in a spiral over the sand between them, swirling faster and faster until the circle took on a definite shape. It was something like a pentagram, but so much more potent. Pentagrams were meticulously crafted, written in languages known to man, while this circle was wrought of ragged symbols Alice had never seen. King Yama snapped his fingers. The ground jolted. A slumped figure appeared inside the black not-pentagram, hunched and indeterminate. The darkness stilled. The figure stood.

"There," said King Yama. "You've found him."

Professor Grimes was not one of the Shades who had put much effort into preserving their appearance. The only part of him rendered in any clear detail was his head; his hawklike features somehow emphasized, both bolder and more elegant than they'd been in life. Below the neck he was a flowing, formless darkness; the same shape of ghosts hung on Halloween.

For a moment he turned in circles, taking in all that was around him. The Shade of Professor Grimes did not walk; he drifted and swooped like a bat. He observed the wheel, the golden braid, and the throne. His head tilted all the way back as he took in King Yama's form. He chuckled.

"So you are the architect of this realm? The mastermind of my suffering?" Professor Grimes stretched taller until he and Lord Yama were face-to-face. His feet did not touch the ground. His deathly form had no feet at all, only swirling gray. "Only a deity after all. It makes me wonder. What does it take to kill a god?"

"I warn you, Jacob Grimes." King Yama spoke now in English. His voice never rose above its calm rumble; not a hair in his beard ruffled out of place. And yet Alice felt the warning thick in the air; a thunderstorm about to break. "You are a guest in my realm."

"But what can you *do*?" On Professor Grimes's lips, even the vilest insults took the form of mere inquiry. "You are bound by the laws of this place, as are we all. You are a guardian, a facilitator. Nothing more." He gestured up to the sky. "No—the real big man is up top, isn't he? Go on, tell me you've never tried to pierce *his* realm." He turned to the wheel. "Fate, is that it? Suppose I choose a spoke for myself?"

"You have not passed your trials," rumbled Lord Yama. "You have no right to pass. You are here at the mercy of the girl only, and the wish I have granted."

"Of course." Professor Grimes turned to Alice. His face split into a smile and, despite herself, Alice's heart thrummed at the sight. "Dear Alice. I did wonder how long it would take you. But here you are, all in one piece—and the Dialetheia!" He reached for the little tree. Alice shrank back, but he only flew closer. There was no getting away from him. He buried his face in the petals, breathed deep, and sighed. "More glorious than I could ever have imagined." He lifted his gaze to her eyes. "Alice Law. You brilliant thing."

Such praise. She could never forget how good his praise felt, like the whole sun turned upon her. She was reminded again that she mattered. She was like a desperately convoluted proof running down two sides of the paper, lines dwindling to cramped scribbles on the margins until, magically, it came out valid. Her heart hammered very fast in her chest, and a hot heady wash passed through her mind before she could sort her thoughts out and speak.

"I don't—but you—what do you mean, *how long*?"

"I have been watching," said Professor Grimes. "Clever girl. Following all the bread crumbs. But who do you think left them there?"

Alice felt rather like a broken toy, capable only of repetition. "Bread crumbs?"

"There's quite a lot you can do from the Bridge of Sighs," said Professor Grimes. "Dreams, images, that sort of thing. I like to think I got pretty good at haunting. Tell me, did you ever dream of Ramanujan's Summation? Of journeys into the cold, dark earth? That was me. But it takes initiative, to your credit. You put the pieces together."

"But how—"

"I knew you'd come. You've too much on the line. You've always been so dogged about your degree. I never doubted once."

Alice could not make sense of this. "But then—why didn't you just wait for us?"

"Why would I do that?"

"But you could have just stayed in the fields. We would have rescued you in minutes—"

"Oh, Alice." He shook his head. "You're always in such a *rush*, that's your problem. We have talked about this. You always want to be finished, you just want the end result—results, paper, fellowship, job. Stop barreling toward the end point, start lingering in the process. There's so much that will reveal itself to you if you just pause and have a look around. Smell the roses!"

"But we've got to get back up—"

"No, we don't," said Professor Grimes.

"But what do you mean?" Alice felt so stupid then. She always felt so stupid in their advisee meetings, when her mind couldn't keep up with his racing thoughts. Always she needed clarification; always she lagged three steps behind. He had all these visions that her mind was too dull to see; she had to beg him to show her. "I mean—where else would we go?"

"Wrong question, Law. The better question is this: what are that limits of that little tree? Oh, it'll be difficult here in Hell—there's precious little chalk, and dwindling materials to write on. But we'll make do. We'll memorize as much as we can. It's a perfect research environment—no distractions, no bodily needs—"

"*You* have no bodily needs," said Alice. "I will starve to death in short order."

"Then starve to death and beg for your life back later," Professor Grimes said impatiently. "We have the *Dialetheia*, Alice, we can do anything."

"But—that's insane." She blinked dully at him. Oh, why was this so difficult—why could she never keep up? "Why would we stay?"

"The scholar does not fear death. Have you learned nothing from Socrates?" Professor Grimes laughed. "The life of a scholar is mere training for dying, don't you see? I never understood how right Socrates was until the moment of my death, when my soul was ripped free from my body, and I was cast violently from that mortal world of base appetites. The body is the enemy, is a hindrance in the soul's quest for the truth. It is as the Zhuangzi claims: life is a swelling tumor, and death the bursting of a boil. We are slaves to the body! All it provides is distractions—fantasies, desires, illnesses, fears. We are bounded, and death is the ultimate freedom. I never saw it until now." Professor Grimes's hands grasped her face, and though she felt nothing solid, the chill took her breath away. "Come on, Law. This isn't hard."

Alice had been here before.

The Lethe had not washed this memory clean. Nothing could ever wash this memory clean. It was engraved in her skull, it constituted her very being, and she was doomed to repeat it, over and over; no matter where she ran, everything brought her right back to this moment. Details of that night rose to her mind's eye, all superimposed over King Yama's throne. They stood in the same positions—he too close, hands on her cheeks; her frozen in position, head tilted up, eyes wide. Now, this was a proper seduction, whispered that evil contrarian that lived always in Alice's skull. This was how that moment in the office should have gone. Instead of offering up his body, that stinking solid thing, he should have offered to her the key to the hidden world, and an eternity to play around within it.

He seemed to recognize the resemblance, for his smile stretched, and he drew even closer. He knew what that night meant to her; he'd only ever been pretending it didn't matter. Let us play it back, let us do this properly. Here is the world, Alice Law. Here is a chance to be like me, to *be* me. You and I, spirits soaring, and rising close to meet the gods. Alice tried, but could not shake off the double vision. Suddenly she couldn't be sure where she was. If she let her concentration slip for one second then she found herself back in his office, like no time had passed, like everything that had transpired in Hell had been a dream. She was a second-year at Cambridge, her future in the balance, and all she needed to do this time was give in.

"Join me," said Professor Grimes. His cloak enveloped them

both. Made them the unit Alice had always longed for; he their champion, she his shadow. "Join me in the realm of the gods, and we will dance through the hidden world. We will live and die and live again, until these concepts hold no meaning for us. We will go where no one has ever gone. We will return, and speak to dazzled crowds of all the wonderful things we saw."

Alice could not speak so much as move her mouth into shapes and hope her breath gave them sound. "But I don't want to die."

"What do you want, then?"

"I just want to go home."

Alice had seen what the sole pursuit of knowledge had done to the Kripkes. And she would not repeat that same mistake; to remain here, whittling away until all that mattered was puzzles and abstractions. She had outshone at puzzles and abstractions her entire life, and still she had not learned a single thing about how to live. She did not want to tilt into their world anymore, she only wanted to touch something solid.

Yes, this was right. Was that right?

She tried to conjure some of Elspeth's resolve. She had been so sure of it on the *Neurath*. *I want to be alive*, she thought in Elspeth's voice. *I just want to sit on the banks of the Cam and kick my ankles over the water and eat a warm, sticky bun. I want to lick sugar off my fingers and feel the sun warm my skin. That is what I want.*

"*Focus*, Law!" Professor Grimes snapped his fingers before her. He had done this a lot in Venice. He would snap and clap or flick her on the back of her head if he thought her tired or distracted. Somehow it had never occurred to her to be offended. "Don't lose your nerve. It is frightening, I understand. But anything worth doing is frightening. The greatest mistake you will ever make is to back down now."

"But I don't want to stay down here." It was so hard to speak up; every word out of her mouth sounded childish and stupid, and with every word she uttered, she could see his disappointment spread. "Not forever."

"We won't, sweetheart. Only until we've found out all we can, and our minds are satisfied—then we'll go back to everything that's familiar."

"And then you'll pass me?"

"Pass." He laughed. "You will be richly rewarded, Alice Law. Jobs and prizes are handed out at my whim, you understand that. Everything else is water under the bridge. Let us forget about it." He extended his hand. "I guarantee no doors will ever be closed to you again."

He'd made these sorts of promises before. Professor Grimes so enjoyed making promises; he tossed them out without a thought. Of course you'll get that grant. Of course we'll coauthor that paper. And he never lied; she trusted he never meant to deceive, he was just so busy that he simply forgot.

This time, however, she thought he might be telling the truth. Sometimes he did mean it. He could be so generous when he got what he wanted.

But, Alice reminded herself, she had been through quite a lot in this past week. She had faced down the ends of time; had escaped from the Rebel Citadel; had vanquished the Kripkes; had ripped a cat open with her bare hands and eaten its heart and made its skull a shrine in the deserts of Dis. These sorts of experiences were very transformative. They gave her a bit more clarity on—well, everything.

"You know Peter's dead."

"One assumes. He came down, and here he's not."

"But don't you care?"

"It's tragic, obviously." Professor Grimes waved a hand. "But let's look forward. It's opened up possibilities."

He said something else, but Alice did not hear.

Something clicked shut in her then. It was the strangest

feeling. Indeed it made her a little giddy. She had never before exercised the ability to simply drown him out.

Coolly she looked him up and down.

She'd never looked upon Professor Grimes so frankly. She'd always felt like she was looking into the sun, somewhat; she felt that she couldn't look him directly in the face, or she'd burn away. But she had witnessed divinity now. The mundane did not compare. Now, in the afterlife, she saw him more clearly than ever; in part because she was no longer so scared of looking, and in part because she saw only what he chose to show. Just an ordinary man, puffing himself up, darting around for any way out of his predicament. Cruel, callous—and so, so full of unjustified assumptions.

Truly, he had put so little effort into keeping himself together. All fierce expression and no substance. He was less a menacing shroud than unformed brushstrokes of gray. Even the newly dead Shades she'd encountered in Asphodel had better definition than that. Professor Grimes was not good at being dead, did not have the fortitude of mind, hadn't come *close* to conquering Hell, and Alice found this deeply disappointing. It was all so unfair, she thought. You thought people were giants, and they devastated you by being so human.

This was the saddest thing. The loss of faith. If he really were a giant, she would have followed him still.

"Was that all?" she asked.

"Pardon?"

"Was that everything you wanted to say?"

He faltered. "Well, Alice—"

"May I speak, then?"

She clutched the Dialetheia tight with one arm. With the other, she reached around and dug her notebook out of her rucksack. She flipped several pages, then spun the notebook around and held it up before Professor Grimes. "You know what this does, surely."

He bent over to read. "Erichtho?" He frowned. "What is this? Did you summon spirits from below to help you?"

"No," said Alice. "It's what I would have done to you. I only mean to show you my work."

She tossed the notebook to the ground. She knew he could decipher her work at a glance. He had probably worked through something very similar already.

"I would have anchored your soul back to your body. I would have stitched your throat back to your lungs and suspended the muscles around them from electromagnetic wires. I would have tethered you as a talking head inside a wooden frame and not let you go, no matter how much you screamed, until I got everything I needed out of you."

His smile faltered. She saw it falter—only for a moment, but this gave her an absurd burst of pride, the fact that after everything, she had managed to shock him after all.

"So." She swallowed. "There."

Professor Grimes loomed over the sheets, reading in silence.

She was so familiar with this silence. She had sat so many times in his office, fingers twisting nervously in her lap while he read through pages of her work. She knew he liked to let the silence linger. It was an intimidation tactic. He'd told her as much, he did it all the time to journalists, to colleagues he disliked. Once his silence had terrified her. Now she felt a fierce, hot pleasure, knowing he was silent only because he was scrambling for a way to respond.

At last he said, "That won't possibly work."

"It does," she assured him. "It's how I vanquished Nick Kripke."

How dare he, she thought. Making impingements, implying failure, when he had no grounds to do so except for being a dick. The Erichtho spell was some of the best work she'd ever done. Cracking the portal to Hell, uncovering Erichtho's footsteps, making sense of the rotted archives, all of it. Truly this was top-notch scholarship. When Alice really thought about it, this was the worst thing that Professor Grimes had ever done to her—made her doubt she was a good scholar. He'd destroyed her faith in her own ability to think, and to judge the results of her thought, instead of turning to him at every step for confirmation. And it was just so unfortunate that it took his death for her to conceive, research, and carry out an entire project on her own.

"I can't believe you thought it wouldn't work," she said. "I mean—you absolute clown—how would you even *know*?"

He'd lost her. He knew it. "Now look, Law—"

She dropped to her knees and smoothed her fingers across the ground. The sand here felt different from the sand in the Eight Courts; different even from the islands' shores. Grittier, the grains larger, more like the grains in the world above. Not nearly so silky, dreamlike, smooth.

"Don't." A note of fear crept into Professor Grimes's voice. "Alice. Let's not be so drastic."

"I won't," said Alice. "I thought I wanted that, once. It's all I dreamed about. But now I think—I'd just like an exchange."

She drew a little stick from her pocket. It was Elspeth's chalk—Alice's last stick had turned to a useless clump in the Lethe. Shropley's Standard, alas, but Peter had also preferred Shropley's, and since this work was all his, Alice figured she stood a better chance. Magicians had theories about that. The best chalk for a spell was the chalk the originator used. A superstition, probably, but still this made her feel safe; made Peter's memory more vivid. She traced a little line against the sand and held her breath, watching, waiting.

The line remained. The sands did not eat her chalk.

Alice glanced at King Yama. She thought she saw the slightest nod of his head.

She drew a large arc then, covering as much ground as she could.

"What's that?" Professor Grimes hovered over Alice's shoulder. "What are you doing?"

"You won't have seen this work," said Alice. "He wouldn't have shown you. Not after that set theory paper—I mean really, how low can you go?"

"Stop this."

"Move a bit that way, would you? I need some more space."

"Alice Law—I command you, stop this at *once*."

She ignored him. She had to focus. She had so little chalk left; just a tiny nub, not nearly enough for redos. She had to get this right, and if she didn't—she couldn't let herself imagine what would happen if she didn't.

It was so hard to remember. She'd forgotten so much. She couldn't rely on that automatic facility anymore—what she'd gained in healing, she'd given up in skill. She'd grown reliant on picture-perfect captures appearing in her mind's eye; until this point, all her work had been mere tracing. How much harder it was to reach for memories she wasn't sure were there. Blurred now were the lines between memory and imagination. She could not trust her mind not to invent what she wished she'd seen. The best thing she could do was to try to turn off that part of her brain that thought too much. Sink into the movement of the chalk, and let the memory of Peter guide her work.

"That's not a valid pentagram," said Professor Grimes.

"Hush," she said.

"Those algorithms aren't in conversation. You're just making things up."

"Like you would know."

He slapped her across the face. He tried, anyhow. His hand

passed clean through her head, and Alice felt nothing more than the tiniest waft of air. She glanced up at him, unimpressed. "Seems bodies are good for some things."

He swiped again; a batty, pointless movement. He growled, glaring at his hand, but glare as he might he could not make the smoke materialize into a solid.

"You've got to have fantastic proprioception," Alice informed him. "That's when you know where all parts of your body are without looking. It takes years of practice, but then you can become anything. Elspeth was very good at that. She could even become butterflies."

Professor Grimes was starting to realize his defeat. He floated back, and his essence condensed around his form; a form that was not so tall as Alice had remembered. Indeed, she'd never noticed how he'd started to develop a hunch, how his shoulders were not so broad, his demeanor not so intimidating as she'd thought.

"Alice, please. Let's talk about this."

"Please, Professor. I'm working."

"*Bah*." He drifted to the circle's edge. Alice glanced up sharply. She had not considered this—she needed him inside the pentagram. But Professor Grimes seemed unable to leave. He ran up against the edge of the pentagram, but something invisible kept him from going further.

"What is this?" Professor Grimes whirled on King Yama. "Let me out."

"You were summoned for an audience," said King Yama. "Alice Law, are you finished with your audience?"

"No," said Alice.

"Then it would be impolite to leave."

"You can't do this," said Professor Grimes. "You're supposed to be impartial, you can't just—arbitrarily—it's against the rules."

"Haven't you learned, Jacob Grimes?" King Yama's smile

looked demonic beneath his furrowed brows. "Hell has no rules."

Professor Grimes wilted then. Finally, he had nothing to say.

Alice was fascinated by this. She had never seen Professor Grimes look desperate. For that matter she'd never seen him *need* anything. She wondered then if he might beg—but then, Professor Grimes didn't know how to beg. He had spent so much of his life in a position of power; he was used to granting mercies, not receiving them, and it had been so long since anyone told him no. This much was obvious, for his desperation quickly turned to indignant fury.

"I made you," he told her. "I molded you from inchoate dream. I gave shape to your clay. I lit your fire and gave you a mind. *I made you.*"

"Be that as it may." Alice did not care to contest this. "You should be kinder to your creations."

"Alice Law—"

"Shush."

Alice drew the circle closed and began to chant.

Oh, he howled then. He screamed at her all the invectives that could possibly apply, something about whores and tarts and stupid, stupid brats. She didn't make out the specifics; she let it all fade into a vicious homogenous wash. She'd heard it all before. He leaned over her, came so close that his aura was superimposed over hers, as if he could settle into her body by sheer force of will. He leaned round and screamed into her ear. He forced his ghostly head into hers and screamed into her mind. You are a child you are useless you are stupid—

Alice however was very good at incantations. Indeed, she could thank Professor Grimes for that. Concentration was so important for magicians, and he had spent much of her first year pacing around her in a circle, barking distractions while she knelt and flinched and scrawled with shaky hands. You'll never succeed unless you can draw a perfect, steady circle in a hurricane, he told her. Make your mind an iron house. Make the mundane disappear. Everything is irrelevant but the circle. Everything fades into the back, until you are standing alone on a plane with the idea—and then the work begins.

So now Alice found it astonishingly easy to just close her eyes, pretend he wasn't there, and finish what she was saying.

A wind whipped up within the pentagram. Only a mild breeze at first, but it quickly grew stronger and stronger until Alice's hair blew all around her face, and she could not hear anything but the roar. Professor Grimes jerked up as if yanked by a hook. He flipped upside down, arms flailing, and when he revolved to meet her gaze his face was slack and helpless. He might have shouted something, but the wind drowned him out.

They had been here before. This too was a repetition, this violent disintegration. She was watching now a mere replay of that first death. But this time Alice knew what she had done, and how this would end. This time she did not cower, but watched unflinching. Professor Grimes spun slowly, and with each revolution his essence spiraled away like smoke from a fire, disappearing somewhere Alice could not know. At last he was just a miserable howling head, then a bag of a face, and that too peeled away, until the pentagram was empty. The wind died. Silence fell.

The air cleaved apart, cut through by the outline of a door. A crack had opened in the world. The door swung open, and Peter Murdoch stumbled out.

## CHAPTER THIRTY-FIVE

Alice made a noise between a cry and a yelp. Peter did not seem to hear. He seemed lost in a daze. He stood stock-still, peering around at the sands, at the dais, at King Yama smiling atop his throne. His mouth hung open. He looked so heartbreakingly confused, and he kept nervously smoothing his palms across his arms.

Then his eyes fell upon her, and his face split into that bent, beautiful grin.

"Alice?"

"Peter."

He stepped cautiously across the frame. One step, then two, and then he broke into a run. Alice darted forth. They collided. Peter's arms wrapped around her, and hers around him. He was so radiantly warm, so alive and solid. She burst into tears.

Oh, how *thin* he was! This was a revelation. Alice knew Peter was a twig, but only visually. She had never grasped on a material level what a reed he was. She could wrap her arms all around his waist and still come round again to clutch his sides. Clutch she did indeed, very tightly, for if she pressed hard enough, then she could make herself his shield and protect him from everything in the universe. What a miracle a person was, she thought. They took up so little space. The difference between presence and absence was not even a square meter of matter. Yet now that Peter was here, the whole world shone brighter.

At last she pulled back, but he did not; his fingers curled into her hair, his other hand against her back, and pulled her close again; fierce, unrelenting. He held her like an anchor, like without her he would dissolve. He kissed her, and even when their lips parted his forehead stayed pressed against hers, as if any distance between them was unforgivable.

"I died," he breathed. He blinked down at his arms. Alice looked as well, and saw great arching scars. "I died, didn't I?"

"Yes."

"How—"

"Exchange." A laugh escaped her. She felt so light, giddy. She clenched his shirt in her fingers. "Your notes, your work."

"You only saw it once."

"But, Peter." She could not stop laughing. "I have a very good memory."

"Oh, Alice." His hands moved all over her, as if he had to convince himself she was real. His eyes were huge with wonder. "Alice, *Alice*—you're *brilliant*—"

"It worked," she cried. She couldn't make her fingers unclench from around his shirt. She had him now; she couldn't let him go, she would never. "I can't believe it worked."

Peter too burst into laughter, and it was the loveliest sound she had ever heard, was so much brighter than in her memory. She rocked into him; listening to his laughter in his chest, shaking even as she pressed closer and closer. So warm he was! How good he smelled. Like fresh pages. Like pencil shavings. Like reading in springtime under a weeping willow, sunlight on her face, grass between her toes. Had she always known how good he smelled? Maybe she had once—maybe she had forgotten—but now that he was alive she could learn it over and over again, now she could delight in the constant discovery of everything about him. She felt a lightness spread from her chest through her limbs. She could not breathe. She felt any moment now she might split into a million glimmering stars, that this lightness would overwhelm her. She did not know what to do with this feeling. She had never felt joy like this in her entire life.

Peter drew back. His smile dimmed. "Then—Grimes?"

"He was," she said, "the other part of the exchange."

She saw the thought passing through him, splintering into all its consequences and implications. Peter was very clever; surely, he saw the whole decision tree.

"But why—" He stopped himself, then rephrased. "But then you came for nothing."

"Not nothing." She traced her thumbs down his cheeks. *What a marvel*, she thought; *his face, his jaw, the prickly stubble where his hairline meets his temple. God carved this boy.* "Not nothing. I gained everything."

His fingers wrapped around hers. "Oh, Alice . . ."

"Listen, Peter." She hesitated. The problem wasn't a lack of what to say, it was where to begin. How dizzying was this feeling—to have someone look at you, really look, patiently trying to understand you. But there was so much she needed him to know, and it was all so tangled and thorny and full of feelings good and bad, and when she did find her tongue, the best she could get out was, "I wanted to say, I'm sorry."

"Oh." Peter tilted his head, considering. "Well. I'm sorry too."

Language failed them here; it did not come close to capturing the depth of feeling, of guilt and relief and shame and love. The abyss was still there; they had not bridged it; they had only waved at each other from across the gulf. Maybe parallel lines could meet at infinity. Maybe. There was so much else to say and miraculously, now an entire lifetime to figure out how to say it. But she felt that apologies, offered and accepted, were not a bad place to start.

Peter glanced down at the tree. "What's this?"

She beamed. "Our ticket home."

"The Dialetheia!" He reached; she passed it into his arms. The petals stretched toward his face, and the glow of him then was the loveliest sight she'd ever seen. "It's wonderful!"

"Isn't it just?" Alice turned to King Yama. "My lord, I'm ready to barter."

He gestured for them to come closer. Hand in hand, Alice and Peter approached the throne.

"What are your demands?" King Yama asked.

"Journey back up top," said Alice. "For one."

"For one?"

"For another, we want our lifespans back." Alice clutched the Dialetheia close. "We've had a very bad time, and we didn't get what we came for, and I feel we ought to get a refund."

King Yama fell silent for a moment. She could not read his face. Slowly he said, "You feel you ought to get a refund from Hell."

"Alice," Peter muttered.

"It just seems I did you a favor." Alice was still buzzing. She felt this was worth a try; she felt anything in the world was worth a try. "I rid you of some pests, I mean. And I get that, in the eternal scale of things, a few years with Grimes and the Kripkes is a mere blink to you. But so, too, should be the return of our lifespans. It's a fair bargain, don't you think?"

The Lord of Hell sat silent.

Alice could not see King Yama's mouth beneath his mustache. She could only see his thick brows furrowed, his eyes glaring intensely as he did in every image from her childhood, but she could never tell whether that expression was a laugh or a frown.

Her parents had prayed to King Yama in their youth, before they took entrance exams. But why, she'd asked; what does the Underworld have to do with your college admissions? King Yama hates corruption, they told her. He is a benevolent bureaucrat. He is harsh to cheaters, but he rewards hard work. He is nothing to fear.

At last King Yama spoke. "You know, you magicians believe the funniest things about the world. You think your spells work because you've fooled the world. You think you're simply so clever that you've talked circles around the rules, that the world is so baffled it has no choice but to obey your commands. You don't realize that nature knows you're lying. You draw your little circles, and we bend and pretend, the same way parents pretend when their toddlers lie." He scratched his chin. "But we deities are lenient, you see. We do love to be amused."

Alice dared to hope. "Have we amused you then, lord?"

"You have certainly been worth watching."

He pondered a moment further. At last he announced, "I will return half of the years you gave up in your journey. Consider the rest a payment for a lesson learned."

Alice opened her mouth to argue, but Peter tugged at her arm. "I think that's very fair, lord."

"Fine," she grumbled. "If that's the best you can do."

"Are you satisfied?"

"Yes, King Yama."

He extended his hand.

She ascended the steps to his throne, the Dialetheia clutched tight to her chest.

He reached out. She passed it over. King Yama held the Dialetheia up and, closing his eyes, pressed it against himself. The trees' petals glowed a brilliant silver then, the color of starlight, and then the tree passed into Lord Yama's chest. A bright twinkling rippled through his dark body; a million constellations winking into existence. King Yama exhaled, and the starlight dimmed. *There's more where that came from*, Alice thought. *Nothing exists without contradictions.*

"Now." King Yama gripped his staff. "Let's send you home."

A STAIRCASE MATERIALIZED BEFORE THEM, SPIRALING outward with the sound of a rushing stream. Up and up it went until they lost sight of its end, a needle through the world. Hand in hand, Alice and Peter approached its base.

"Go on," said Lord Yama. "Be careful you do not look back."

"Really?" asked Alice.

"I'm only joking," said Lord Yama. "Look however much you want. Go on."

They ascended. Alice felt lighter and lighter with every step she took. Every step brought her closer to real life; closer to fresh air trickling down from above. Air that tasted like *air*; sweet and fresh and nourishing, not the stale nothing of the deadlands. Had air always tasted so good? The lower steps disappeared as they walked, one by one until they were suspended high above the air. This did not bother her; Alice was not going to fall; indeed as the steps vanished beneath her rising heels she had the strange feeling she had never needed the steps at all; they were only a heuristic, because it was too much of a leap to fly. Never had her feet felt so sure. She had no fear she would lose her way. He must throw away the ladder once he has climbed up it, wrote Wittgenstein; and then he will see the world aright.

They climbed so fast. Soon Lord Yama and his court were tiny as a doll's house. Alice glanced over her shoulder, and the Lord of Hell waved his arm in goodbye. Minutes later they were so high above the Eight Courts she could see the entire landscape of Hell beneath her. The towers of Pride, the deserts of Greed. And the Rebel Citadel, in all its defiant fury, inhabitants trapped in the Hell of their own making. Alice could feel no animosity toward Gertrude, only a lingering pity—for Gertrude thought her refuge was so large, but from above Alice could see the citadel was only an ugly spot on an immeasurable landscape. A dollhouse, heartbreaking in its attention to detail. And here Gertrude had thought she had remade the world.

"You all right?" Peter asked.

"Oh, yes," she said. "Only remembering."

She stood a while longer, letting her gaze linger over those courts. She tried to commit them to memory as best she could. Then she turned, and continued up the stairs.

She hoped it was a long time before she returned. She hoped that when she returned, after many years of agony and excitement, these dull sands would be a comfort.

"I wonder if we'll ever get jobs now," said Peter. "Seeing as we won't graduate."

"We could write about Hell," said Alice. "Make that the dissertation."

"Would anyone even believe us? We've no proof."

"I'm your proof."

"You're biased."

"No, I'm not."

"Yes, you are. You're in love with me."

"*Hush*," said Alice, blushing. "You can't just go around telling everyone."

Oh, but it didn't matter. The academy didn't matter. Perhaps they could revise their dissertation topics in time and change their committees and scrape their way into a job, or perhaps they couldn't, but none of it mattered because the future still lay before them, delightfully open. They could fill it with whatever they wished, and Alice's only intention then was to spend it with Peter.

No more labs for a while. No more lectures. She imagined study dates with him in the future—tossing crumpled-up papers at each other, trading books, scribbling things all over each other's blackboards. But for now she thought she'd quite like to get away from campus. Perhaps a weekend away—she hadn't taken a weekend off in years, she wouldn't even know where to go. They said Ely was pleasant. Grantchester, maybe. Supposedly that was a nice place to swim. Or perhaps something more modest; a night at the cinema, a picnic under the willow by the river. She didn't know Peter's favorite foods. She didn't even know what he liked to do for fun, if he did anything for fun. She'd have to learn, she'd have to discover a million things about him. Peter Murdoch was a book with no ending and all she wanted to do with the rest of her life was to trace her finger down every page.

They reached the sky, or the part of the sky where ended this world. A rectangular sheet of metal lay horizontal above them— the bottom side of a cellar door. Light seeped through along its edges. A dozen butterflies ringed the door, brilliant glowing things. They all fluttered aside when Alice reached for the trapdoor save for one, which lingered on the cellar door's lock, its wings wafting gently. Alice stroked her finger along one wing. It was so velvety soft. The memory of a kiss.

"Thanks, Elspeth," she murmured. "I know."

The butterfly flew off into the burning orange. Alice pulled. The lock clicked easily open in her hand. She and Peter raised their hands above their heads and pushed. The door swung freely upward, and suddenly they were bathed in moonlight.

Alice recognized that night sky. She knew precisely where Lord Yama had put them. This was the courtyard in Magdalene College at the end of the Fellow's Garden by the river, the green she'd crossed so many nights with her head hunched over her chest, staring at her feet. She knew it because the stars there were uncommonly bright. Something about the effects of all the ambient magick interfering with modernity, dimming the sounds and lights of the city around. All the pollution faded back and the stars stood out with startling clarity, so you didn't have to hike miles out to trace the constellations; you could just see them overhead, clear as diagrams. Every summer you could find astronomy students lying on their backs, penciling sketches into notebooks propped above their heads.

She'd walked once with Peter through this field. The field was out of his way; he lived in St. John's, lying in precisely the other direction, but it was late and there'd been some news story about an escaped python, and ridiculous as that was, it made sense at the time that he walk her home, just in case the python ambushed from the reeds and swallowed her whole. Yes. Peter would fight the python. The stars were so bright that night and Peter had asked her, did she know about Olbers's Paradox? No she didn't; would he explain?

"The night sky shouldn't be so dark," Peter had told her. "If the universe is endless, then starlight should fill all the empty spaces. Light doesn't stop until it hits a surface—so why the dark spaces? From where we stand on Earth, all we should see is light."

"Maybe the universe isn't limitless, then," Alice had said.

"Or the universe is expanding," Peter had said. "And the stars are too young, and all that distant light is still stretching to reach us. And until it does, the night lies dark."

Looking at him then Alice was reminded of a line from *The Greek Anthology*, a text Grimes had asked her to mine for language puzzles but which Alice had lingered over much longer than she should have, astonished by its beauty. She gazed at Peter and thought, *I wish I were the night, so that I might watch your sleep with a thousand eyes.*

A breeze wafted over the cellar door, deliciously cool against their sweaty cheeks.

It all came back to her then. The sweet dark grass, the leaves rustling overhead, robins hopping to their nests. Punting poles sliding through water, bicycle wheels spinning over cobblestones. So many details she'd ignored every night as she passed, trapped in her own skull. It all seemed too vivid to be real now; an illumination, a moving picture. The world was full of so many *things*! Sunlight in college gardens; hall dinners of new potatoes in butter and herbs. Rain tapping the cottage rooftops; water pooling in the street, fat drops sending little ripples arcing about. Squishing boots, wet gloves, hot cups of tea, escaped leaves bobbing to the top. She could not believe she could have all those things back. It seemed too good a deal to be true, one little pomegranate tree for all the myriad blossoms in the world. How could she deserve life? Who *ever* deserved life?

But you could not question such gifts. Elspeth had taught

her this. There was no answer, only wondrous and inexplicable grace, and the only thing to do in return was simply to live.

She took a breath. "Ready?"

Peter squeezed her hand tight. "After you."

Alice climbed up, Peter close behind her. And together they emerged, to rebehold the stars.

# PETER'S MAP

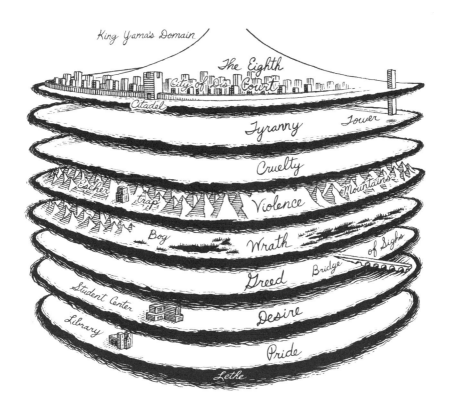

# ALICE'S MAP

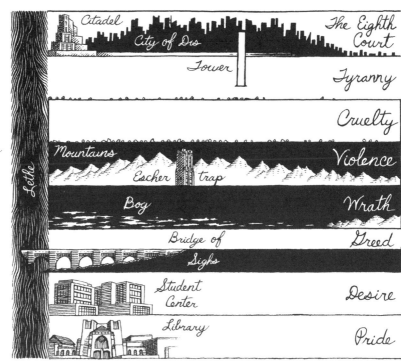

# ELSPETH'S MAP

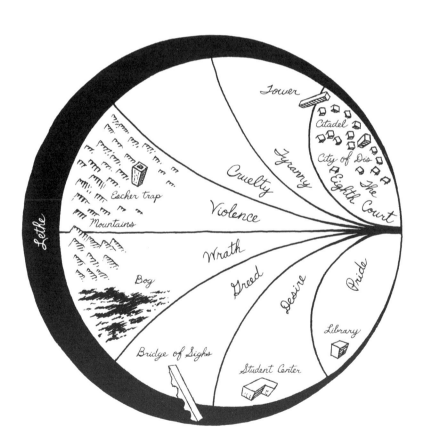